About the Cover

$\mathcal{P}$irates and privateering posed a constant threat during the late 17th and early 18th centuries when the Isles of Shoals served as a New World Port of Entry for European, North Atlantic, and West Indies trade ships. The Buccaneers by American artist Frederick Judd Waugh (1861-1940) hangs in the reading room at the Brockton Public Library in Massachusetts. By coincidence, in 1891 workmen discovered some of Captain Kidd's treasure hidden under the Jamestown, R.I., house of Seth Vose, son of a gallery owner, Joseph Vose. Eventually, Vose Galleries purchased Waugh's 1910 painting—which seems a fitting tribute to the famous Captain.

The ink drawing The Little Church by the Fort (circa 1705) depicts the early settlement of New Castle on Great Island, New Hampshire. The anonymous artist identifies the town church and Atkinson mansion to the left along the tidal mud flats of the Piscataqua River. This pre-colonial illustration is one of the oldest graphics of America. A photographic reproduction of the original (provenance, British Public Records Office) is at the Portsmouth Athenaeum.

The original portrait Mary Pepperrell Frost (1685-1766), also at the Athenaeum, is unsigned. However, the artist painted many members of the prestigious Kittery, Maine, family and is known as the "Pepperrell Limner." This portrait (painted between 1717-1720 in Portsmouth) suggests the emerging civility and social polish of the New World. Since convention (in art and society) required married women to wear bonnets or caps, it is thought the bare-headed Mary in her 30s was single. The rose she holds is symbolic of fertility and fecundity.

THIS DESIRED PLACE

THIS DESIRED PLACE

JULIA OLDER

APPLEDORE BOOKS

Published by APPLEDORE BOOKS
Hancock NH 03449-0174
www.AppledoreBooks.com

HG Graphic Design, Alstead NH
Printed in 10 pt Palatino
by BookMasters, Inc.
United States of America

Cover Art
Detail: oil painting, *The Buccaneers* (1910)
by Frederick Judd Waugh (1861-1940)
Presented to the city of Brockton, MA, for the Brockton Public Library
by Mr. and Mrs. James Stone, May 1963

Detail (tinted): *The Little Church by the Fort* (New Castle, c1705)
Original black and white ink drawing by anonymous artist,
British Public Records Office P.H.C. coll.
Facsimile reproduction of photograph, Map collection #1466.2.a
Portsmouth Athenaeum, Portsmouth, New Hamsphire.

Detail: *Mary Pepperrell Frost* (c1717-1720)
Oil portrait attributed to "Pepperrell Limner."
Portsmouth Athenaeum, Portsmouth, New Hampshire.

Illustration pp 454-455
Detail: *An Exact Mapp of NEW ENGLAND and NEW YORK* (1702)
Facsimile reproduction from Cotton Mather's *Magnalia Christi Americana*
M1995.2R. Old Sturbridge Village, Sturbridge, Massachusetts.

Library of Congress Cataloging-in-Publication Data

Older, Julia, 1941-
   This desired place : the Isles of Shoals / Julia Older. -- 1st ed.
      p. cm.
   ISBN-13: 978-0-9741488-2-3
   ISBN-10: 0-9741488-2-2
1. Isles of Shoals (Me. and N.H.)--Fiction. 2. United States--History--Colonial period, ca. 1600-1775--Fiction. I. Title.

   PS3565.L314T48 2006
   813'.54--dc22

                              2006049907

Author's Preface

When I first visited Appledore Island at the Isles of Shoals off the New Hampshire/Maine coast, it was virtually uninhabited. And yet what struck me as I poured over historical Shoals records was how many people once crowded every nook and cove. During the Victorian era literally a thousand summer guests were bedded and dined at grand resort hotels. And two centuries earlier, a thousand fishermen jammed like sardines into a score of stone hovels.

THIS DESIRED PLACE posits readers on the Isles of Shoals late in the 17th century when northern coastal fishermen and women obeyed only one law—turning a profit. Cod was King and they grew rich off the fat of the sea.

Readers often ask me if the first novel of my Shoals trilogy THE ISLAND QUEEN is fact or fiction. The distinction today often is blurred by novelists fusing the two to fit their fancy. I had a biography in mind when I researched the life and times of Celia Thaxter (1835-1894), but her grand-daughter Rosamond Thaxter already had published a detailed portrait. The novel allowed me to flesh out Celia's stormy but charming life as a wife, mother, and famous writer and literary hostess at her Shoals cottage.

THIS DESIRED PLACE also is based on documented lives and recorded New England events. The exception is the fictive orphan Thomas Taylor who narrates his tragicomic existence on the bustle and boom Isles. For although we think of Boston and Cape Cod as the epicenter of the colonies, the Shoals were an important Port of Entry to New England and a hub for tidings and trade to and from the New World.

In most history books, you won't find the northern massacre and devious round-up of 300 Abenaki natives sold to slavers in the West Indies, or William Phip's amazing expedition for gold. That the wealthy Mainer turned down British royalty to govern the colonies is emblematic of the character and devotion of the men and women bringing up our enthusiastic young nation.

What is clear to me is how removed pop cultural caricatures of Virginia and Plymouth settlers are from everyday people and life in the New World. Shoals fishermen, native squaws and warriors, maroon servants and indentured workers like Thom weren't as different as one might think from modern Americans.

They killed auks for oil and cut every tree in sight for fuel. We drill, spill, and kill wildlife for oil, and clear-cut forests. Northern settlers overfished and a moratorium was legislated. Atlantic fishermen today continue to overfish and must comply with similar limits. And then as now on a drizzly day in Portsmouth or Boston you might see men and women huddled outside public buildings because of smoking prohibitions.

Coffee houses were just as popular as ours, and though settlers first thought tea was a vegetable, they eventually learned to throw great tea parties.

—Julia Older

CONTENTS

Entry The First
In The Month of September 1670.

The Captain at his Charts has asked Me to Note in the Ship Log a Hopeful Abundance of Cormorants and Sea Gulls.

Respectfully, Thomas R. Taylor

*I*f my good uncle could have seen Henry and me, sixty-eight days at sea with still no sight of the New World, he never would have let us sign on the Charles. Granted, our seaworthy vessel had brought us through storms a lad with nightmares such as mine dare not remember.

The rats, scurvy, and brawling jack-tars in the hold with the keel creaking as if it would split didn't terrify me half as much as the memory of my own mother. I was about four years old when I lost her, and her face appeared and reappeared in the waves, a ghostly mask misshapen by the plague. In the final throes of that black and horrid death, she begged my father to transport us by livery to her sister in the country, away from the corpses and pyres of rags used to swaddle and staunch malodorous bleeding wounds. When he returned to London she was gone. Delirious with grief, he searched through the bodies heaped on the cobbles, but she had been carted away with the others.

Now, Henry's face loomed down the dark scullery hatch of the ship where I was helping the cook with some parch peas. "Thomas, fetch a dozen biscuits and some beer for the Capt'n—on the double."

The youngest aboard, I mostly was ordered to fetch and serve.

"Did you hear, Thom?" Henry's voice carried a swell of excitement. "Ambrose is at the binnacle and we're just short of land. So run along now to the Capt'n with some sustenance. We haven't much daylight left."

"Aye, Sir!" I saluted mock obedience. Henry's blond arm stretched down the hatch and ruffled my hair.

Sloshing the beer and losing hard tack along the way, I lurched to the Capt'n's quarters. A chart was spread under the oil-light and I slid the pewter plate onto the table beside it.

"See these isles here, Thomas Taylor?" he said, motioning me closer. "They call them Smith's Isles after Capt'n John Smith, and that's where we're bound."

While living in Canterbury, Henry and I had been tutored by my uncle. And although I hadn't gotten far in my lessons because of my cousins' constant badgering, I'd managed to learn enough to read the Latin on the navigation chart before me.

Capt'n Moody's chubby index finger moved over the criss-cross lines radiating from the compass rose to a small group of isles about ten leagues northeast of Cape Anna and three leagues due east. Some of the islands looked fairly large, but none had a name. An intricate coastline encircled a framed portraiture of the smiling New World explorer whose numerous discoveries were heaped on "the high and mighty Charles, King of Great Britaine."

The chart must have been several years old, because when Henry and I left England, Charles, The Second, had been defeated by Cromwell and was ruling in exile. In the shadow of Canterbury Cathedral, my brother openly ridiculed our cousins' Royalist beliefs, and Henry's seditious nature forced him to leave before he plummeted us both into serious trouble. Thankfully, the land toward which we now sailed extended far beyond the long and tyrannical arm of the Crown.

Capt'n Moody placed an affectionate arm on my shoulder. "Best fishing in New England lies right off those isles between

Scantum Basin and Jeffrey's Banke. You and Henry shall never lack for food. Last voyage we off-loaded 4,000 quintals of dunfish from the Shoals. Fetched the highest price in all of Britain. A fare of cod the likes you never laid eyes on. Ah, but I recall you were brought up a country lad, weren't you, Thom Taylor? You'll have to learn the fish trade. There's great promise in it."

"Henry and I were raised by next of kin on a country farm, but my father was indeed a Capt'n like yourself," I said with braggadocio.

"Is that a fact?"

"Yes, Sir, he—." Whenever I talked about my short bleak past my voice quavered, and I had to stop to clear my throat. "—he died in the Great Fire."

Before we boarded the Charles, Henry instructed me to be brave about our losses and keep a tight tongue. This wasn't difficult when we were together, but at night when the blurry-eyed sailors drank flip and carried on about the sweetkin they'd left behind, I made excuses to check the stays and crept away to find Ambrose.

True, my father had been a captain, but hardly of a seaworthy three-master like Capt'n Moody's. He'd owned a small wherry that ferried passengers across the Thames, and when the fire broke out, father was taking a party across the river. At my bidding Ambrose repeated the story of how he'd been anchored on the Dolphin Striker waiting to sail when he saw the flames engulf Westminster Abbey. Men and women rolled down the banks of the Thames and into the river. Some of them floundered and thrashed toward my father's boat, while those already in the wherry fought them off. My father was about seven fathoms down the side of the Striker when Ambrose threw him a lifeline. Father grabbed to catch it, but was knocked overboard and drowned. "We was good mates, yer Fa and I," Ambrose said, pulling at his wool watch cap and rubbing his hairy chest through the neck of his jerkin.

Captain Moody also had befriended me during this long lonely

sea voyage, and   now that we were so close to land I felt
indebted to the burly-bearded man leaning over the map. "If it
weren't for you, Sir, I'd still be with my Aunt Elizabeth and
Uncle John," I said. "And with due respect, Sir, I couldn't have
stayed there another moment."

But the Capt'n's thoughts were elsewhere. He continued studying the chart, then reached for the tankard of flip I'd made from
brandy, small beer and sugar. "Aye, Thomas Randolph Taylor,
you've a fine future in these parts. I tell you, Son, soon you'll have
your very own fishing fleet. I'll wager on it. And with Henry to look
after you 'till you're grown to manhood, no harm'll come to you."

"But Sir, I am grown," I asserted, standing tall and pulling my
cap down to hide the red locks that caused me no little amount of
teasing with the crew.

Capt'n Moody held out the tankard, offering me a manly
draught. I gulped the burning concoction, and turned to leave
before he could offer me more, when excited shouts rang out fore
and aft.

"Land! Land!"

The Capt'n raced behind me out the cabin and onto the top
deck. The bow of the Charles with its high fo'c'sle provided quarters before the mast for the sailors, and the higher poop deck on the
stern for the Capt'n and his mates. Between decks were stowed
chinaware, fabric, clay pipes and rations for the two month voyage.

We were an advice ship to the New World and would be
returning a cargo of prized dunfish from Smith's Isles. The vessel
wasn't bulky as a Man-of-War or even a Spanish galleon, but she
was a goodly 350 ton ship with a crew of twenty-five seafaring
men. Some of them, like us, would remain in New England to start
afresh, but most would return with salted cod for Britain and the
Canaries.

As protection, four cannon of the Crowned Rose capable of firing three-inch round shot and weighing several hundred stone each
were attached to the bulwark. On the Charles we were especially

vulnerable because we hadn't set out in a fleet. Fortunately, an argosy had accompanied us in good will, and excepting an occasional outbreak of scurvy and a few gale winds, little ill had befallen us.

A nor'easter filled the sails. At a fast clip of fourteen knots an hour we moved toward a group of lights flickering on the horizon. Night crowded down and I buttoned the monstrous great coat Capt'n Moody had thrown over my shoulders before we rushed on deck.

The Capt'n's orders scattered the sailors in all directions. "Lower those yards, men. Get down that mizzen sail. Is Ambrose at the helm? You, Thomas—." He handed me a spyglass. "Climb into the crow's nest. The only anchorage at the Shoals lies just off Hog Island at Babb's Cove, but according to my compass reading, those lights lie east of Hog. It's a mystery."

This wasn't the first time I'd been ordered to the crow's nest. I didn't mind. Tree climbing had been a pleasurable pastime back in Britain, and after all, what was a ship's mast if not a great pine with the limbs lobbed off?

Henry flashed me a queer smile as though to say: Well, Thom, what do we do now? Albeit seven years my senior and in stature a grown man, I guessed that Henry felt just as anxious as I about our future in the New World.

Letting my thin body swing with the stiff gusts, I climbed the shrouds, knowing from experience that if I didn't look down I'd be fine. When I reached the crow's nest I grabbed the halyard and lashed my waist to the mast. Even if I could steady the glass to my eye, the black sky now completely discouraged the Capt'n's intent to see what lay directly ahead as the ship lurched and pitched through the choppy waves.

One happy sight did greet me through the driving sheets of rain—those intermittent flaring lights. Surely, Capt'n Moody wasn't expected to remember every inlet of that small group of islands around which he'd navigated. The lights must be a new village that had cropped up and was welcoming the Charles safe harbor.

I waited on my perch above the sea, jostling back and forth on the tiny circular platform, buffeted like a sea gull in the sudden squall. Comforting voices from below were drowned out by the crashing waves and increasingly violent wind. It was the worst sea I'd witnessed on that entire voyage, yet foolishly I lingered for just one glimpse of solid land.

Once more I put the spyglass to a tearing eye, and my knees stiffened from sudden fear. I took a deep breath then looked again. It was land all right. The bow of the Charles surged straight toward a reef of protruding rocks. Spray and foam momentarily covered them, but they resurfaced treacherous as the tip of a giant iceberg.

"Capt'n, Capt'n!" I screamed.

Henry appeared far below, motioning for me to climb down. In vain I pointed toward the projecting rocks, but on deck they couldn't possibly see the impending danger. Henry turned away while I watched the waves break over the barely perceptible shoals, covering them with a seething maelstrom.

To climb down the shrouds would mean instant death. Quickly, I grabbed the mast, embracing it with all my might. Henry, who no doubt thought I'd been seized by a sudden attack of vertigo, started up the shrouds after me. I tried to wave him back.

The sound of the bow sprit cracking in two pierced the air with a shrill resonating screech.

"Henry!" I cried as the sea broke halfway up the quarter-deck. For a moment I let go of that proud branchless trunk, my arms out-stretched toward the only person left me on this earth and watched as Henry was catapulted mercilessly into the churning waves. Then, grasping even tighter to my own precarious hold on life, I closed my eyes.

PART ONE

Knee-deep in Cod

1

*T*he man who slapped my face had a bushy red beard and clear blue eyes that sparkled like periwinkles in the sun. "William, come look. It be a lad and alive."

Another face peered into mine, young and curious against the bright September sky. I tried to tell him about the storm but nothing came out except the stuttered beginnings of words. With strong sinewy arms the boy propped up my head. His sure fingers felt through a tear in my breeches down to my water-logged shoes. "We'll have to carry him, Origen, I fear his leg be sore lame."

The bushy one lifted me against his warm barrel chest and strode nimble as a goat over the craggy rock. The pair of them were companionable quiet and I sank into a drowse as we skirted the smelly shacks and shingled sod fishing huts along the shore.

"Pru! Pru!" the boy shouted, racing toward the dwelling they called the ordinary. Ordinary it was indeed, without so much as a sign to distinguish it from the crude stone out-buildings we'd passed. That there was a tavern at all in the squalid fishing village seemed a miracle.

But when the most comely girl I'd ever seen appeared at the cottage door, I quickly changed my first impressions and blinked the tears back into my swollen eyes so she wouldn't see them. She urged Origen up a steep ladder to a loft by the chimney. No sooner had she spread an eider quilt over my still trembling body than I fled to sleep, carrying her radiant smile like the figurehead of a ship cutting through the waves of pain.

When I woke it was nearly dark and the boy who looked to be my age lighted a rag wick hanging from the nose of a pewter boat filled with tallow.

He held the flame high and handed me a mottleware bowl of broth and a hunk of strange yellow cake. "Pru says yer to eat every bit." He smiled sheepishly. "Will Babb, and what be yer name?"

"Thomas Taylor," I croaked, my voice raspy from the cold sea. The hot liquid washed down the strange dry cake he called Indian bread. I took another gulp of mutton broth, hoping somehow to swallow the grief that overwhelmed me, and delayed the telling of my sad story.

"And did ye have kin aboard, Thom?"

I felt my cracked lips quivering and prayed I would not blubber like the orphan child I had become. I was just about to sink into a morose reverie when he unfolded a duffel cloth and to my surprise, removed a putrid lice-infested piece of cod.

"Excellent cure for open wounds," he said, pulling the quilt off my leg and pressing the fish onto the bloody gash on my thigh. "Yer a brave lad, Thom. Pru and I will have ye wobbling about in a day or two, I venture."

The food, clean bed, and even the lice swarming over the suppurating wound filled me with sudden gratitude for this newfound friend. "My brother Henry went down in the Charles." I cleared my throat and paused. "Or I think he did. It all happened so fast. We saw the lights—."

"Lights?"

"The Capt'n saw lights on the shore opposite your father's cove."

"My Father!"

William's accusatory tone did not escape me. The sound of boots clomping up the ladder unbolted him again, this time in fear.

"My Father!"

A short stocky man wearing an oil cloth apron crowded into the garret room and stared at me none too pleasantly.

"Bowels o'Mercy, Will! What 'ave ye and Origen gone and dragged in from that pitiful wreck?"

William cowered behind the trundle bed as his father squinted through a thick black lock of greasy hair. The stench of the apron covered with a thick layer of fish gory and blood suddenly made me wretch. I grabbed for the empty bowl.

"Well, if that don't rock the boat." Babb splayed brown gnarled fingers over his bulging groins. "As if we don't have enough mouths to feed a'ready, here be another."

I winced as he leaned on my bad leg with all his weight and looked me square in the eye.

"Well, boy, I doubt ye can pay yer board with pieces o' eight so I hope ye like fish." He laughed loudly.

William crossed his arms in defiance. "Father, can't ye see Thomas needs rest? He just lost his only brother, fer God's sake!"

The man's malodorous belly filled my face. He grabbed his son by the scruff of his jerkin and shook him hard. "Profane the Lord under this roof again and I'll slat yer head off, hear?"

My biliousness returned with a vengeance, and this time Babb prevented me from getting to the bowl. Yellow bread and mutton joined the fish innards already grimed on his rueful apron.

Pru entered the room, took one whiff of us and turned on her heel. Babb grabbed the girl by the waist and grinned from one gold earring to the other ear which had a big nick in it.

"Not so fast, Mistress Pru. Kindly keep in mind yer beholden to Goodman Babb 'til ye've paid yer passage, and that goes fer this shipwrecked wastrel. So come along, lass. I could use some of yer fine Barbadoes mollycoddlin' m'self."

The green-eyed servant shook her tawny tangle of ringlets, unwound herself in half a turn, and was down the ladder before Babb realized she'd given him the slip.

The next morning I hobbled down the loft ladder. A plump woman in blue homespun with a white neck scarf and cap pulled a stool up to the hearth where three toddlers gnawed noisily on apples.

"Pru fixed ye some hasty pudding afore she went off to the milkin'." She handed me a wood spoon and the mottled bowl full of yellow porridge which, though it resembled last evening's cake, was decidedly better.

The woman smiled and a dimple appeared in each cheek to match the one in her chin. "Ah, Thomas, so ye take to our Indian corn and maple syrup? Forgive me fer not introducin' myself. I be Mary Babb, the mother of this brood. I was hopin' ye'd rise early. My husband has gone to put someone in the stocks at Church Island. He also be askin' the Minister to draw up yer indenture papers. Will and I thought ye should know aforehand, being as how ye come to Hog only yesterday in such a sorrowful state."

My spoon dropped into the pudding. The purse Henry and I had given Capt'n Moody for safekeeping lay at the bottom of the sea, and I hadn't a shilling to my name. But indenture? Ah well, the Capt'n had said these were the best fishing bankes in the whole world. Would this not be an opportunity to learn the fishing trade?

The good woman laid a motherly hand on my shoulder. She seemed about to kiss me on the forehead when Pru came up sloshing milk in a redware pan. Quickly, I pushed back my stool. If I were to be in the Babbs' employ I could not loll about like a homeless waif.

Pru used a scoop to dipper milk into my bowl. When I shook my head, she poured it anyway. "Come, Thomas, ye need strength to work beside William and me," she insisted.

"You are kind, Mistress Prudence." This was the first time I'd actually spoken with the lass, and it might as well have been the last for my total lack of wit.

"Call me Pru, Thomas, since we be equal in our adversity."

Her skin was smooth and dark complected from the sun, yet she had green eyes so limpid fair I felt surely I would drown in them.

The moment Phillip Babb swung through the tavern transom, the women mysteriously disappeared. Holding an onionskin scroll to the doorway light, he waved it and shouted across the dark common room.

"Where be that puking, out-of-purse flotsam, Thomas Taylor?" He stomped over to a table in his clumsy hobnailed boots.

I walked toward the Fishing Master, relieved to see he'd left off the defiled apron of the previous evening. What I hadn't noticed from my hearth corner was that the foul apparel had been replaced by Capt'n Moody's great coat, and it fitted him remarkably well.

He thrust a grimy hand deep into the galloon-edged pocket. "What 'ave we here? A silver flask, by Gory!"

"That belonged to Capt'n Moody, Sir," I gasped. "See, there are his initials."

I rubbed my finger over the flask as if the touch of the familiar object and the damp smell of the wool coat would bring back the Capt'n's brave smile and tender disposition toward me. But up close I realized the deception of my weary senses. For the new commander in brass buttons appeared to rule Hog Island with a disposition not unlike the hog it was named for. The stench alone was good reason to keep my distance from the man. The pistol I saw tucked under the wide girth of his leathern belt was no small cause for concern either.

Master Babb unrolled the document and anchored it to the table with two beer tankards.

Vaguely, I remembered Uncle warning Henry and me to read any paper we were asked to seal with our signatures.

"Will you be reading it to me, Sir?"

"Read it yerself, blast it. I be lookin' for an ink pot that scribblin' fellow left behind." He rummaged and fumed over the ink while I tried to understand the terms of my fate:

> *This indenture witnesseth that Thomas Taylor hath put his self*
> *Apprentice to learn his Art, Trade, or Mystery and to serve*
> *from this day September 15, 1670. During a term of 6 years*
> *the Apprentice shall do no damage or mischief to the Master,*
> *waste no goods, nor lend them.*

It was slow going, and I stopped to rest my throbbing finger which I'd pushed under the words with strong pressure, as though it could help me understand how I'd gotten into such a dire situation.

Master Babb returned with the ink. "Here it be. The fellow laid over on his way from Boston to Hampton during a storm. The whole time he scribbled in his blasted Commonplace Book. Seaborn Cotton he called hisself."

I concentrated harder than ever upon the task, reading outloud to counter his interruptions:

> *The Apprentice shall not play cards, dice, commit fornication. . .*

"Ha! That be a good one." He pounded the table and snorted. "I wager the only teat this young'un's suckled was his Ma's."

I bent closer to the table, desperately trying not to let him see the color rise to my cheeks.

"Seaborn Cotton weren't good company, though come to think on it he did learn me a verse about women. If ye be stayin' on the Shoals, Puker, ye best be learnin yer way around a skirt."

Though sore tempted, I tried not to listen and continued reading:

> *And the said Master doth promise to teach the said Apprentice*
> *in his calling as Fisherman by any means—making food, drink*
> *apparel, and washing during the term .*

"Washing," now there was a word unfamiliar to Phillip Babb.

Annoyed by my doggéd determination to understand the document, Babb whipped the paper from the table, rolling the tankards onto the dirt floor.

"If ye gut cod fast as ye read, Thom, I swear I'll be tearin' up this damned indenture afore the year be out," he threatened. Validated by my startled attention, he took a wide stance, grabbed the front of the great coat in his swarthy hands, and boomed:

> *Woman's the center, lines be men.*
> *The circles of love, how do they differ then?*
> *Circles draw many lines to the center.*
> *But love gives leave for only one to enter.*

Just then Mistress Babb came and set down a juicy seared mutton chop on a shingle. Pru bent to pick up the fallen tankards and while his wife looked on, Phillip Babb patted her smooth round bum. Not to be bested, Mary Babb rushed out a door in back and, returning with a frothy mug of beer, placed it with a curtsey beside the shingle. Master Babb was in his element. He clasped the women in his broad arms and gave each a resounding smack on the cheek. "See what I means about them circles, Thom?" Babb pulled up a stool, swung the chop in the air, and savagely gnawed meat from the bone.

I averted my gaze from the grease dribbling down his black bristled chin. Self conscious with the women there, I whispered the remaining part of the indenture paper to myself:

IN TESTIMONY WHEREOF the said parties set their hands and seals in the Township of Appledore of the Isles of Shoals in the Year of Our Lord, Anno Domino, One-Thousand-Six-Hundred-Seventy,

Charles II of Great Britain, King.

I surmised Appledore must be a pretty name for Hog but didn't press the matter.

"Do you have a pen, Sir?" I asked, beginning to feel this contract was strictly between me and myself.

Phillip Babb drank a long draught of beer and swiped his greasy mouth on the coat. Before long, I conjectured, it would resemble his filthy apron.

"Do ye 'ave a pen—Sir?" he mocked in a high nasal twang. "Nah, I don't 'ave a pen, Sir."

Pru excused herself and went out the front door. Master Babb picked his teeth with a splinter from the shingle, and it was then that I noticed the top half of his second finger was missing.

In an instant the lively girl returned with a handsome sea hawk quill. "I've been saving it, but I think you ought to have it, Thom."

I thanked her, and the three of them watched engrossed as I took Henry's knife from my breeches, shaved the tip of the quill, and dipped it into the ink well. I have to admit I drew out the flourish of the letters far more than my Canterbury Uncle would have approved, but I couldn't resist. For this skill acquired by the Grace of God far away in Britain was my only defense and salvation in this strange New World. Putting down the pen that had signed away six years of my life, I wondered how I would ever manage to keep the claim these crude fishing folk held over me.

Shoving aside the shingle, Phillip Babb clapped the paper before him, stoppered the ink well with his large greasy thumb and mashed it on the paper as though he were crushing a varmint. Next to it he penned a crude letter **P**.

Once I'd seen a birthmark ugly as the cursed blotch on my name, and I worried that the vile mark could be a bad omen.

Pru must have had the same thoughts, for she covered her mouth. She should have covered her eyes for the sadness in them. Nevertheless, I pretended to smile, and held out my hand to the new Master of my fate.

Master Babb's callused paw engulfed mine. "Ye'll come in right handy, boy, even if ye don't know a Jackcod from a codpiece." It was closest he'd gotten to a compliment, and when he'd done laughing at the jibe he sent Pru to fetch two beers to seal our agreement.

"I gives ye three days to learn the ropes afore the fishermen return from their voyage on Jeffrey's Banke. My good fer nothin' son Will can set ye up at Origen's fish house near my fishing stage."

Dutiful quiet to that point, Mistress Babb stomped a thick shoe in the dirt, her dimples nowhere in evidence. "I will not 'ave ye castin' this poor lad into that den o' rowdies afore he's e'n got his legs back, Goodman Babb." Her nostrils flared. "There be no fire and the youngun'll catch his death."

Babb clenched his hands into fists and raised himself slowly from the table. "Woman, how many times 'ave I told ye not to be interferin' in my affairs. The lad be mine and I'll do as I damned please."

To my amazement, the good woman picked up the shingle, mutton bone and all, and hurled it at her husband. What is more, he snorted with sheer delight. "Ah Mary, yer a real she-devil when ye be angry. Aye, the boy can stay under our roof these three days afore he goes to the fish house. And in November when the men leaves fer the main, he'll share the loft with Will. Bowels o' Mercy, woman. Ye'd think I'd gone and kidnapped the shipwrecked puny puker."

2

*S*ea and sky conspired in pleasurably lucid days so that the Hampton Block House three leagues distant on Boar's Head seemed a handspan away. The two brass cannon mounted above Gosport near the Star Island Fort gleamed across the Appledore channel. And a red brick chapel on Church Island distinguished itself to a remarkable degree, rising from the clustered sod sheds and stone fish houses.

Will walked, waded, rowed and climbed me over every worn shore path, trap dike, and isolated inlet of the three larger islands. During the months to follow I often looked back on those brief days with the fondness of a smuggler hoarding secret glimpses at stolen jewels.

With Will's younger brother trailing along, we started our exploration behind the tavern. The pungent odor of cider wafted from Babb's brewery and followed us past the out-building. A bristly hog and her runts squealed and snuffled through apple pulp piled to the thatched roof.

We negotiated a fenced pasture and were making progress

toward the animal shed when Will's brother leapt over the fence and stumbled down the rocks to a small shack at the edge of the sea. "I be goin' to visit Aunt Sally!" he shouted with urgency.

"Does your Aunt Sally live down there?" I asked with misgiving, for the most destitute Londoner would not suffer such a hovel.

Will laughed. "He be goin' to the privy. The poor fellow's had loose bowels since I can remember. That's why we sometimes call him Skitters. Seein' how both of ye be called Thom, I fathom he'll be Skitters permanently from now on."

I ducked into the dismal cow shed and startled Pru on the milking stool. She had pushed her lovely hair beneath a cap, and to keep her indigo skirt from trailing in the muck, she'd hitched it to her knees. Her legs were smooth and tropical tan. Among other things, I wondered if she felt removed from the Barbadoes as I did from Britain.

To satisfy her curiosity about the strange cod cure, she pushed up my pant leg. I breathed fast as she probed the purple wound, thrilling with a strange mixture of pain and pleasure at her touch.

"The skin looks discolored," she worried. "You need another remedy." Before I could ask what that might be, she scooped up a handful of steaming manure and patted the malodorous slop onto my bruised skin. "Skitters, go fetch Pru one of them big mullein leaves—you know the one I mean—with the tall stalk and yellow flowers."

The obedient child ran into the sunshine and returned with a thick furry leaf. Pru deftly fashioned a manure poultice and held the cushiony leaf in place with a tall strand of marsh grass.

Espying the transaction with wide brown eyes, the cow lowed loudly. A stranger when it came to beasts of the field, I kept my eyes on the bossy with equal disdain. Uncle, a gentleman, had little to do with the everyday working of his vast estate, and the closest I'd come to an animal this size was an anxious pickpack ride with Henry on his horse.

I lingered in Pru's radiance until Will lost his patience and tugged me out the door.

A fishwife stuck her head from a Dutch transom and screamed at a ruddy cheeked urchin throwing empty clam shells at a bedraggled screeching gull. Will strode with great pride and purpose across a plank bridge toward the village well. Where was the prosperity Capt'n Moody praised? Surely the crude stone fish houses and smelly drying flakes would make neither a man of wealth nor worth out of me. Down at heart, I hung my head over the circular rim of the well and cast a cry into it.

"Nata volentem ducunt trahunt nolentem!"

Nolentem, Nolentem echoed back.

Skitters hoisted himself onto the rim and dangled his bare feet into the opening. "Listen, Will, Thom be talkin' like them Spaniards."

Will's eyes narrowed suspiciously.

I struggled to explain. "The fates lead the willing, they drag the unwilling."

But for all Will understood, my explanation could have remained in Latin. I persisted. "Word of honor, Will. I asked the Lord's will be done." As far as I could tell, the Lord wasn't in great evidence on the Isles, but thankfully his name carried clout, for Will's amicable disposition returned.

We continued over a rise and to my astonishment in a few paces came upon a wood plank bowling alley about twenty meters long and a meter wide. It was completely covered with a sturdy cedar shingle roof more substantial than on most of the island dwellings, and I guessed that rain or shine the alley was in high demand.

An ancient fisherman in a Monmouth cape and clumsy boots growled as his bowling ball fell off the alley onto the rocks. His peg-legged opponent retrieved the ball and hurled it at the ninepins, striking all but one. Only when Will introduced me to the man who so skillfully won the match did I notice his right arm also was missing.

"This be Master Stephen Ford, Thom. You both were caught in a violent storm."

The swarthy man with a gray pigtail shook my hand. "I weren't as lucky as he were. I lost my limbs."

Will placed an arm about my shoulder. "Thom lost his only kin a few days past in that wicked nor'easter."

The old salt blinked watery blue eyes. "Pardon, lad, for speaking my mind quick like. Be there anythin' Goodwife Ford and I can do?"

The man's casualties alongside my own weighed so heavily I could not speak. Will broke the silence.

"My father be takin' Thomas at his flakes. They signed the indenture."

Stephen Ford drew a rope end from his pocket and with dexterity tied one-handed knots as he talked. "Damned my infernal luck. I could've used ye myself, Thom. In a few days it'll be so busy ye won't 'have time to piss proper."

I looked around. A few sheep browsed on a grassy knoll under the empty sky. To all appearances, the entire island was deserted. Could it be Shoalers had become so used to their isolation that when fifty fishermen sailed into port they fancied themselves close as mackerel in a barrel?

As we wound around hundreds of enormous field pumpkins, Will told me more about Stephen Ford's hardships. He had set out alone to do some fishing at an island to the north when a squall blew up. He managed to hold to his capsized wherry until a fishing schooner spotted him and picked him up, but by then most of his arm and leg had gone rotten from the frigid water. Phillip Babb and another merchant collected fifty-six pounds currency from the islanders to provide the destitute man with an annual supply of food and clothing. Bolstered by their generosity, he not only recovered, but became so successful at business that eventually he was named Fishing Master.

We entered a fenced compound featuring a pond and garden of

cabbages, beans and peas. The domestic familiarity of the garden reminded me of home and I immediately relaxed in the tame comfort of the neat rows. But not for long. Always on the move, Will directed me through the swinging gate and back across the field. Skitters hit a rotting pumpkin with a stick, sending an explosion of shell and pulp into the air. Not satisfied, he molded a ball of the maggot-infested seeds and fired it at his older brother. Abandoning my side, Will vigorously returned the volley.

Certain I would be the next in line for one of the crawling live cannon balls, I stumbled toward the tavern. Ducking into the brewery, I maneuvered past the pungent fermenting tubs and in the back door. Curls from a pipe drifted lazily from one dim corner. Just my fortune to catch Master Babb having his afternoon smoke. Skitters and Will burst in the front door, arms raised to strike, when suddenly an apparition materialized in the obscure light.

Mary Babb clamped a long-stemmed clay pipe in her teeth and confronted her sons with the solidity of a Man-of-War. When Skitters neither backed away, nor lowered his arm, she grabbed him and broke the delicate pipe bowl on his skull, filling the thick-walled room with a resounding crack. Will conspiratorially motioned me out the door while the good woman caught the unabashed scapegoat covered head to foot in pulpy worms.

Being Sabbath, Will and I shoved the deep-sided Shoals ketch from its mooring at the wharf on the south shore and hopped into the rocking stern.

The women, wrapped in cloaks against the chill of the morning, were barely visible behind Master Babb's wide girth; the younger boys curled on the hull in a tangle of rope with a food basket lodged between them. Spruced up in a cambric shirt open at the neck and a leathern jerkin, Master Babb breathed heavily in and out as he rowed us across the narrow expanse to Church Island.

Will and I threw our shoes ashore and jumped into the icy

water to heft the boat above the tideline. I tagged behind,
scratching furiously at my chest. The coarse linen shirt Will had
lent me was far too bulky and itched like the devil. Slowly the
six Babbs, Pru, and I climbed single file across the ledges toward
the brick chapel.

Secure at the church threshold, Mistress Babb gathered our regiment. If she heard so much as a cough she would have the tithing
man give us a good rap on the noggin. Master Babb assumed a
pose of worshipful humility which caused Pru a mirthful smile in
the depth of her woolen hood.

Skitters and his brothers performed a duty that unfortunately
invoked no such reprimand. They hung and swung from the bell
rope, jumping joyously several cubits off the ground and creating a
clamor more in keeping with the bell on ship to keep the demons
and sea serpents away than a call to worship.

The folding chapel door stood open wide and several women
and men already had crowded past in what seemed an ungodly
hurry. Phillip Babb went in too, and in the name of preserving
what hearing was left me, I followed him. I was about to march
straight to the front when Will jerked my elbow and pulled me
aside. His father had joined Master Ford and two others. Master
John Kelly and Magistrate John Diamond, he whispered. They
were all deacons.

The one room measured a few meters less than the bowling
alley and was nearly as wide as long. Two folding doors on either
side remained closed, but sunbeams streamed through translucent diamonds of blown glass set in half-circle windows high
above the doors. Combined with the white-washed walls and
glistening pine floorboards, it had a buoyant lightness.

The interminable Shoals service dredged up recent memories of the magnificent Canterbury Cathedral stall where,
decked out in the latest furbelows, my Aunt reigned in courtly
splendor. Uncle's smallest stable stall had more room than the
rough hewn planks I now shared with mothers and children

stuck together like barnacles on a hull.

And yet, as I gazed on Mary Babb's peaceful trinity of dimples, I couldn't help thinking the Lord had a heavenly loft in reserve for generous people like her. Too young to hold my own beliefs, I'd always accepted Henry's seditious ideas without bothering to examine them. Like a hungry gull in the wake of a fishing schooner, I took what churned up. But now that I had to fish for myself, I was beginning to understand how the wealthy meted out hardship on the common folk.

Of course, this wasn't quite the revelation the Shoals minister in his white fall band and moth-eaten periwig had in mind. The barely audible sigh my revery elicited was followed by a yelp from a jab in the shoulder by a brass-tipped spear. A wave of heads bobbed from the pews in my direction.

Master Babb stood and addressed the black frocked minister, "Mister Belcher, this be Thomas Taylor, my indentured servant. Please forgive him, Sir, for not bein' used to our ways."

Pru flashed me a look of comforting sympathy and Will whispered for me to stand and be recognized. My cheeks surely resembled boiled beets and the infernal hair shirt did not ameliorate the situation.

The minister wore a hint of a smile. "Yea, Mister Babb, I've heard of the boy. Dum anima est, spes est, eh Thomas?"

Why was he addressing me in Latin? Recollecting Will's aversion to the language, I depended on the King's English. "Yes, Sir, where there is life, surely there is hope."

The minister who at first had an air of sternness seemed to be experiencing a revelation of his own. "Do you have an ear?"

I found this an odd question and did not know how to respond. Pehaps it was a Shoals version of Anglican instruction.

"Do you sing, boy? Can you pitch a hymn?" The minister leaned over the pulpit with a look of expectancy.

I mumbled and stammered, biding for time. The ornate pipe organ and boys choir at Canterbury had filled the Cathedral to brimming with glorious music unabetted by a contribution from me, though like many a sailor I could sing a sea shanty and had learned to play a lively hornpipe aboard the Charles.

Minister Belcher asked the congregation to turn to page nine of their prayer books. Relieved that my ordeal had come to an end, I held the English Book of Common Prayer with trembling hands.

"Before we recess for Godsip," the Minister announced, "Thomas Taylor will strike the tune of the Gloria Patri."

The words I sang became a heartfelt petition to the Good Lord to direct me toward the final Amen of the well-known response without my voice cracking in the chill air.

When Minister Belcher timidly repeated the plainsong, enjoining the others with uplifted arms, I recognized at once the extent of his predicament. For though he might have been a learned man and the best theologian in the Provinces, in truth, he could not carry a tune in an oaken bucket.

The worshippers cleared faster than the hold of a sailing ship in port and reassembled outside Master Kelley's tavern where the men, and not a few women, consumed an ungodly amount of Madeira while they haggled over the prices of cider by the hogshead, pork barrels, bushels of corn and quintals of cod.

Bored by the endless bartering, Will and I followed Mistresses Babb and Pru to a stone cottage set back from a small apple orchard. The woman they called Goody Rhymes was so big with child I thought for sure she might lodge in the door frame.

At the mention of herbs and remedies, I quickly persuaded Will we should go see more of Church Island.

"If you sing me a pretty tune, lad," he teased.

Secure in Will's company, I spoke my mind. "Oh, that miserable belching fellow. No wonder he finds my singing attractive. He couldn't pitch a hymn to save his soul."

"Well then, don't be lettin' the pale-faced round 'ead take advantage," Will advised. "Ask a shilling or two fer yer trouble."

"Payment for lining hymns in the Lord's house?" I found this attention Shoalers paid to business most extraordinary.

"Damn it, Thom. Do ye want to be marooned forever on these stinkin' Shoals? Buy yerself a boat and acquire some property or ye'll be smellin' of codfish the rest of yer life!"

We strolled the cliff above the shore where we'd stowed Master Babb's ketch. It was gone. Will shook his head. "That's queer. The old man must 'ave had some affairs to attend to out at Smutty-Nose."

I laughed. "Smutty-Nose?"

"Aye. Once some poor devils run aground out on the point and when one of 'em come to fetch help he yelled that his mates were yonder on that smut nose of rocks drippin' into the ocean."

We crossed behind the tavern where the haggling, if anything, had grown stronger, and headed toward a shedded ropewalk on the leeward island.

Inside the ropewalk, a vertical stream of light fell through the door and coincided with a few dozen horizontal shafts of light from square openings under the eaves. Despite the stripes of sunshine, I could scarce make out the other end of the narrow building only wide enough to accommodate the ninety meter hemp rope and an overseer. When in operation, a small tidal wheel drove the power for the ratcheted gears that twisted the yardage cord indispensable on the schooners and fishing stages.

Will closed the door with a noose of rope and surveyed the shadow cast by a post not far from the granite door step. Gauging the height of the sun falling on the noon mark grooved in the step, he suggested we hurry back. The chapel bell clanged a raucous agreement.

The Lord's Supper turned out to be a lonely table with only two celebrants allowed to participate in God's grace. I dared not lift my head for fear of being knocked to Kingdom come by the ominous tithing pole. But when we filed out nearly an hour later, I did apprehend Phillip Babb was not among us.

Minister Belcher grabbed my hand and entreated my help pitching hymns the following Sabbath. Making sure the tithing pole had been safely deposited in a corner, I mustered the courage to ask for payment. The disheveled cleric hesitated, then promised he would shell out a few shillings if I'd also help keep the chapel records. All this time Mistress Babb, bobbing her approval, rummaged in the capacious basket she was carrying. As if to sanction the transaction, she thrust the bill end of a scrawny duck into his outstretched hand. Before the startled pulpiter could ask the whereabouts of her truant husband, the good woman hurried me ahead of the others down the path whence we'd come.

Though hidden from view by the cliff outcrop, above the waves I thought I distinguished Master Babb's incomparable loud voice. "Damn ye—Rob Mase—and yer confounded—that shipwreck—and now wastin'—yer tales of—." Before the others could reach my vantage, I leapt onto the shore just in time to discover a man throw a shovel into his shallop and row away.

Privy to the fickle nature of strong drink, the younger Babbs gave their father wide berth and clambered into the boat. Laughing at their frighted faces, he shoved the ketch into the water. The youngest gazed over the side and began to whimper.

"Stop yer blubbering, ye gutless toad," he commanded, swinging the rope around his wasit and planting his feet firmly apart as if to defy access. Pru courageously stepped closer. More incongruous than ever in his mood, he smiled. "Ah, here be a winsome catch for Master Babb." He picked her up and kissed her full on the lips while she kicked and pummeled him to no avail. "Who be next?"

I stepped forward.

"Belcher and the Puker," he taunted. "Now there be a match made in Heaven." And before I could defend Pru's honor, I too was hoisted into the boat.

Not wanting any part of it, Will threw his boots near a sack in the bow and hefted himself over the side. Mistress Babb alone remained on the rocky strand.

"By Heaven A'mighty, will ye take a look at that beached

leviathan!" he boomed. His pot belly was smeared with dirt and his nose glowed like an ember from the spirits he'd drunk.

"Now, Phillip," Mary Babb said with nary a sign of provocation, "do be reasonable and let me aboard."

"Get yerself aboard, ye old thornback. I be ridin' aside Mistress Pru."

Quick as a crab, Pru darted between Will and me for protection, or so I liked to think. When one of the babes started to caterwaul, Master Babb relented and picked up his wife, dumping her into the boat for all the world like a load of fish.

The ill-steered craft zigzagged past the small island while Babb rowed first this way, then that. The three of us righted Mistress Babb on a bench and comforted the hard pressed woman.

He slammed the oars into the boat. "Damn it, Mary. Am I not Constable and Deputy of these Isles? If a Shoaler solicits my help, be it not my duty to oblige?"

Mary Babb fixed her brute husband with a stare the likes of which I hoped never would befall me. "Be it yer duty, Husband, to go off with Mister Mase whose brains be so fogged with drink and gold he don't see straight?"

Our boat drifted at the mercy of their marital squall. Suddenly, Master Babb lurched to his feet and we keeled dangerously starboard. Will implored his father to sit. A fortunate high wave accomplished the task, knocking him down, though not to his senses.

"Woman," he bellowed, "this Sabbath while ye served the Lord with the largess of yer mouth, I dutifully were helpin' my neighbor. And if ye weren't such a damned scold, I'd be showin' ye the proof."

This time Mary Babb shot to her feet. "Yer filthy shirt front and foul breath be all the proof I be needin'."

Sure we'd overturn, Will and I grabbed the poor woman. She toppled backward onto the duffel sack stowed in the bow. Skirts akimbo, the good woman was in the process of righting herself when the sack squealed in a most disconcerting manner and a terrified piglet trotted across her plump bosom, taking refuge under my outstretched legs. She screamed and Master Babb roared with laughter.

"Serves ye right, Mary Babb. I rescued Goodman Oliver's sow from them smut rocks on the point and fer my labors he offered me the runt of the litter. The proof be in the puddin', woman." Puffed up like a proud cock that has won a fight, to our great relief he gained a more solid dominion over the oars.

Only when we were back on course and everyone had lapsed into their own thoughts did I collect the sorry creature and hug it in the scratchy warmth of my shirt.

3

I sat up in my bunk, alarmed by blasts that shook the loft and sent me running to a chink in the clapboards where the daub had fallen away. In the ruddy sunrise that spread over Babb's broad harbor, four three-masted trade ships already had dropped anchor and the long boats were rowing ashore.

I couldn't see Fort Star from the tavern, but the insistent drum beat drilled me down the ladder two rungs at a time to Will who dispatched a chunk of yellow cake near the hearth.

In the common room, thirsty fishermen slapped down hard ship currency for the tankards of beer and cider Pru slid across the board. She thrust me a hunk of dry breakfast ration on her way to the brewery and Mistress Babb handed me a juicy apple. No time for milk or smiles. The busy woman shoved a pile of homespun at me and wishing me Godspeed in my new quarters, disappeared into a thick banke of tobacco fog.

From the prominence of Babb's Hill, the fishing stage now teemed with sailors and fishermen in tarred pigtails, red watch caps, and grubby boots. Will greeted several by name as they climbed toward the ordinary and we made our way down to one of the fish houses on the south shore.

My new quarters strangely resembled a stone ship in length and width, though I quickly discovered a ship was the more water-worthy of the two. The upper walls of stone chinked with shore pebbles and the thatch roof on the hovel badly wanted attention.

Unaccustomed to the dark, we groped downward into the bowels of an underground room strewn with lines, tangled hooks and other stowage. A sooty iron pot swung from a hook over a chimney fire in the corner of the rough dwelling. Someone had made an effort to sweep up whittled wood chips, codfish bones, and clay pipe stems littering the earthen floor, and we hopped over the abandoned pile to join Origen near the cheerful firelight.

"Why, welcome, mates," he greeted. "I see Master Babb's not lettin' no grass grow neath yer feet afore he has ye knee-deep in cod!"

I affectionately remembered the man's red-bearded face. "I'm indebted to you, Origen, Sir, for saving my life."

He roughed my hair and fixed me with a sincere countenance. "Now lad, don't be thankin' us for what comes natural." With a broken oar he stirred the lumpy porridge that bubbled and splat orange blobs onto the hearth. "Unfortunately, most of the men be at the ordinary or buying liquor from them floating taverns off shore. I swear, Thom, they work themselves like oxen and spend wages like asses. Never mind. Will can show ye where to dump yer quilt whilst I be tendin' to this pompion stew."

Impatient for the activity down at the port, Will pushed me up a pine trunk stuck through a manhole in the ceiling. Assuming the place deserted, I was startled by a sudden eerie moan and, falling backward, stepped on Will's fingers. To protect himself he bit hard into my ankle and I topped the ladder with him hot on my heels.

A score of hammocks hung from the rafter beams, and in the ghostly half light at the far end, one of the hammocks jerked and bulged ominously. Ducking a rafter, Will held tight to my arm, and

I hugged the protection of my quilt. The groaning recommenced louder as the hammock chains creaked and rattled faster and faster, pitching with devilish contortion.

We were about to dive below for safety when a disheveled woman bobbed to the hammock surface. Astonished, we crept closer. Her bodice hove wide open and Will gawked ever much as I did at her rounded silhouette clothed only in obscurity. Trapped by curiosity, we crouched under the sagging roof while she fastened her stormy hair and sailed a petticoat over her head. A bottle clanked to the floor, followed by regular snores which muffled the sounds we made crawling away on our hands and knees through the dust. We remained close enough to admire her calves as she hoisted her skirt, and to smell the heady fragrance of her pomander bracelet. An even better opportunity presented itself when the woman's modesty piece caught on the pine peg of the ladder and our roving eyes were allowed free navigation on the deep departing waves of her bosom.

Will and I selected a hammock not yet burdened with gear and fell upon it, whispering excitedly. Since women weren't permitted into the ordinary, he kept with his brothers, and I confessed I hadn't seen that much of a woman either. The strange nature of the groans led us to speculate wildly, and we were amidst a gale of laughter when Skitters' small head protruded through the manhole.

"Will Babb," he shouted, squinting and blinking in the gloom, "Father says if ye don't appear afore him immediate, he'll tie ye both to the whippin' post."

The fishing stage had transformed into a boggling enterprise of sailors, off-loaders, and sea merchants equal to any in London Town. Brawling fishermen so clogged the wharf that Will made a stirrup of his hands and lifted me onto a barrel to locate his father. Over the babble of drunks and shouting fish mongers, I perceived an oaken baton waving tirelessly in the smoky air to the hounding tune of Babb's curses.

After three or four wrong turns around stacks of cod, dice games, and poking cutlasses, we came upon the island constable clearing the deck with charging vigor. Two off-loaders carrying a pallet of fish were ordered to drop the cod and attend to a sailor whose arm bled profusely from a dagger wound. Rolling the man onto the pallet, they lugged him away.

Babb brandished the club in our faces. Will didn't flinch, but I jumped back, landing in a heap of fresh cod.

"There ye lazy lunk'eads be, " he menaced. "In case yer pea brains be too small to fathom it, the rest of us be workin' the fish flakes. Or do ye think I be payin' for ye to loll about like swine?"

"I be paid nothing," Will retorted in a belligerent tone.

Trying to extricate myself from the slimy mess of fins, I advised Will to hold his tongue.

"The puker's right, ye ungrateful wretch. Who put them cloths on yer miserable bones and fed ye all these years?"

"Mother," Will rebutted with fearsome nerve.

Though large for his age, Will was no match for his father, but I could see Babb conjecture whether a good wallop now might not backfire on him in the future.

"I've no time fer yer damnable insolence, ye unappreciable brat. At least the puker here shows respect fer 'em 'at feeds him. I rule this roost, and if it sore provokes ye, Will, go fend fer yerself."

He took an angry swipe at a nearby black piglet which turned out to be the same one I'd comforted in the boat. Wiggling its curly tail, the runt trotted at my side, glad as Will and me to increase the distance between its vulnerable flesh and the threatening baton.

The fish dressing process already was well underway when we arrived. Chagrined by my tardiness, I preserved every detail Will explained as though it were one of the prized dunfish we soon would be shipping to London and Madrid.

Cod large as myself were being rowed to fishing stages and wharves owned by more prominent Shoalers about the shore. Otherwise, the fish were taken from the schooners to more modest fishing rooms comprising a few dilapidated sheds and the bleached table-like drying flakes. A dozen people were busy heading, slicing, cutting, and salting the fish at Mister Babb's warehouse.

I had counted on my friendship with the son of the most propertied man on Appledore to make up for my late appearance, but not one of them noticed, so up to their necks were they in blood, guts, livers, and heads of the seemingly endless line of cod flung onto the work table.

Will shoved me between two of the dressers.

"I've orders from the High and Mighty Babb to carpenter some of the fish flakes and set up a pen in the tide water fer cleansin' the salt cod tomorrow," he told me. "Joan here can show ye how to behead a fish."

"Joan?" But he was gone.

Both persons beside me looked like good-sized men with tobacco stained teeth and coarse weathered faces. Their hair was pulled beneath hoods and they wore oil cloth bibs and boots. The one Will called Joan let the monster fish knife fall on the cod and with one blow severed the head from the body. She slid the huge fish down the table to the slitter and raised the knife again.

"If that son-of-a-horn-headed rogue Babb be gettin' rid of ye at my expense, this be what'll happen to him!"

Fish scales flew in my face as she cracked off the head and pushed it into a tub under the table. Her arm poised for the next fish.

"Ye look like ye 'ave enough strength to be'ead a minnow."

The slitter down table threw a handful of guts and fish gurry into another tub beneath the table and took up my defense.

"Shut yer mouth, Joan. Can't ye see the kid's green as an apple in spring. Come over here, kid, and stand atop this hogshead."

I stood on the barrel and watched him at his art of slitting open the cod's silver white belly. It looked effortless, but when I dug in the small sharp knife, the fish slipped and zigzagged all over the table without making a dent.

Holding the knife plumb, he gouged deeply into the flesh.

His simple example led me to instant success, but in the meanwhile Joan had beheaded half a dozen more.

"Sorry, kid, I got no time now." The kind fisherman took the knife and proceeded to make up for my loss. "See 'em salt boxes? Why don't ye go help Skitters salt 'em down."

Disheartened by such a brief education at fish dressing, I did as told. With a good deal more importance to his voice than necessary, Skitters explained that because October and November were chill, the cod required less curing salt. "And that be a boon," he lisped through a gap where a front tooth was missing, "cause the Hampton salt works ask the devil's price for sea salt."

I followed his motions—removing the dressed cod, sculpin, and haddock from a wood trough, sprinkling the filets with salt and layering them between seaweeds kept in faggots under the protective roof of the shed. Leaving me to the mindless task, he skipped off to see Aunt Sally. Starved on the meager rations I'd eaten at dawn, I was imagining a delectable cod fillet with a glass of Madeira when one of the women blew a conch shell horn and we all hurried off to the noon meal.

Origen had slopped his thick pumpkin stew into a common bowl for the shore workers and they passed it around, supping loudly. Just before my turn he refilled the bowl and, as if on purpose, left the long wood spoon in it. I thanked Providence for this small favor. However grim the thought of eating the slop, the thought of putting my mouth to that bowl filled me with even greater revulsion. Unlike the ebullient rabble of fishermen, the fish dressers talked little, so concerned were they with getting back to the fish stage.

Then, suddenly there was Pru beckoning me from the gloom. It was no place for a girl on the cusp of womanhood, and I jumped up and hustled her back into the sunlight.

From the folds of her apron she took a bundle and spread the contents on a boulder. "Look Thom," she said. "I brought some cheese and biscuit which you can keep out of sight in your quarters."

I could almost taste the rich odorous cheese she offered, but for some perverse reason I told her Mister Origen was providing for me.

Her green eyes flashed. "And you'll be runnin' to me for a cure, Thomas Taylor, when a steady diet of pompion stew gives you worms. This cheese was all I could ferret away without Mistress Babb suspect, but I'll bring more next time."

"Pru, really. I don't—."

She stamped her foot and thrust the bundle in my arms.

"Night is so cold in these heaps of stones," she said, ignoring my protests. "On the Barbadoes at this time of year it was always wondrously warm. We slept in hammocks beneath the palm trees in the lea of the island near the plantation house. French buccaneers burnt it down. My father was inside and—."

She picked up a corner of her apron and was dabbing at her beautiful watery eyes when the conch blasts called us back to our stations. In my haste, all I could think to say was that I was sorry.

It must have been enough, for she smiled and handed me an oval black sea stone bound by a white band. "Shoalers say such stones bring good luck."

On my way back I noticed a great many more just like it.

4

*E*ach evening after a supper of pumpkin stew I fell into an exhausted sleep among the snores, grunts, and jibes of the fishermen. Several days in a row I stood knee deep in water, sloshing the cod in the pen Will had constructed. Though I wore wool stockings and oilskin boots, my feet were numb and my hands chapped raw from the frigid ocean water.

Seeing me shivering from cold and fatigue, Origen cleared a place near the hearth stones for me to lie down.

Fortunately, the next few days I was ordered to the fish flakes where women and orphans my age tended the cod by covering the filets with quilts in the lowering weather. Babb's curses were mere banter beside fish-wife Joan's acid tongue. The woman berated and abused me incessantly.

"Joan Andrews or Ford?" Will asked when I complained.

As a tike he remembered his father had Joan Ford hauled to the Saco Court for her insolence whereas Joan Andrews had received lashes by the Constable Babb for her ranting. "Not that her walking tavern of a husband don't give her sore reason," he added.

One fog drenched October morning Joan appeared later than usual. I'd already unquilted the dun colored fish as the first rays of sun burned through the heavy cloud bank. Indeed, I was feeling much less the apprentice and more of an overseer now that the flakes were about to close for the winter. I'd just decided to give the abusive woman a dose of her own medicine when I saw her eye so bruised she looked like a one-eyed Jack with a patch. The purple-black socket had a mean circle of yellow around it and a pink one encircling that.

"Well, what ye be starin' at? Ain't ye n'er seen this kind of ornament on a woman afore? Damn sight better'n yer pompion round 'ead," she snapped.

I looked down at the endless rows of fish and fingered Pru's smooth keep-stone in my grimy pocket. The severity of her bruises sent a shock down my spine, and cautiously taking up her brown dried hand, I molded her wrinkled fingers around the lucky stone. Slowly as the flowering scarlet pimpernel which opened its petals after a storm, she uncurled her fingers, and surprise glinted from the rainbow sockets.

"Someone special gave it to me," I explained. "But I think you could use some Shoals luck, Mistress Joan, don't you?"

The black piglet who had become a daily resident beneath the fish flake nudged the woman's boots. Usually, she would have given him a solid heave-ho followed by a barrage of blasphemous oaths. But now both of us were too preoccupied with the peculiar torrent of tears streaming down her weathered cheeks.

I sat the sobbing woman down on a nearby hogshead.

"Come, Mistress Joan, it's only a beach pebble. I'm afraid I have nothing more of value." In light of this new aspect of her character, I was beginning to wish for her familiar old diatribe.

"Thomas, the devil tries me sore," she sobbed. "Ye 'ave been kindness, and I've been such an ungrateful soul."

"I know it isn't my business, Mistress Andrews, but can't you hide from your husband when he's in his cups?"

A fierce gleam ignited her face, then faded. "I once stayed with good neighbor Becky on Malaga, but he up and followed me in his ketch and threatened my life if I abandoned him again."

Phillip Babb strode toward the flakes at a goodly pace.

"Come now, Joan," I said, helping the broken woman back to her station. "Pray quickly that the Lord will dispatch Master Babb and your husband, so we can serve both of them wide berth."

She closed her eyes, spat on the stone I'd given her, and dropped it into those mysterious pieces of cloth women wear. Whatever Shoals magic she had in mind seemed to work—for Babb disappeared over the hill, the sun sparkled on the dark blue sea, and she smiled at me the livelong day.

"Psst, kid."

I turned, tripped, and accidentally dropped the heavy mutton carcass I was portering down the hatch of the Mermaiden. The man who accosted me had a harelip, red bulbous nose and protruding eyes that left an immediate impression of gross protuberances. He didn't carry himself like a captain, though he introduced himself as one.

"Ye look a trustworthy lad. Could ye deliver a message to Phillip Babb, Esquire, of Hog Island?"

I slipped down the hatch, hoisted the lamb haunch back over my aching shoulder, and reconciled myself to the captain's fatuous commentary.

"Aye, Sir, I am in Phillip Babb's employ," —my insinuation being that I was not in his. However, this distinction was lost on the man.

"Splendid. Then convey this important document to him at once, and relate that Doctor Greenland of Kittery and myself will meet him sennight. Is that understood?"

The captain's harelip sneered and his eyes bulged. No doubt he pictured me a New World dimwit, and to prove him right, I dropped the bloody haunch at his feet like a faithful dog, grabbed the proffered parchment, and bolted down the gangplank. Hopping onto the off-loading dock, I scrambled over a pile of provisions and mountain of dunfish still to be packed in hogsheads for their final voyage to Britain.

Though the Mermaiden called herself an advice ship, like her captain she dealt in more than that, picking up prize cargo when and where she could to profit from the booming trade from Portsmouth to Boston. Though I still was a relative newcomer to the Shoals, I'd overheard more than one idle conversation about nefarious trading ventures concerning the ships in the harbor, and I suspected the Mermaiden's captain was engaged in one of them.

I stopped to catch my breath and examine the document. The parchment was folded, sealed with wax, and stamped H. G. My only chance to discover the contents would be to offer Babb my expertise as courier and scrivener. Provoked by curiosity, I dashed around the brewery and into the back of the tavern.

Master Babb sat in an inglenook beneath the quarrel smoking with Master Ford. I stuffed the document in question into my belt alongside my brother Henry's treasured blade and approached them.

"Thom? Can't ye see Master Ford and I be droppin' anchor for the day?"

"Aye, but the Captain said I was to deliver this message with appropriate haste, since it pertains to a matter of some importance," I gasped, winded from the errand.

"The Captain? I know an hundred captains. Be specific, boy." He tapped a wad of tobacco into the bowl of his pipe and turned to his companion. "The Puker comes in handy at the fish flakes, but he's got the sense of a horse mackerel."

"Forgive me, Sir. I meant Capt'n of the Mermaiden."

"Well, why didn't ye say so in the first place?" Babb snatched the crumpled parchment and unfolded it. At once I gathered I'd remain in the dark, for to my surprise his eyes roved the parchment as though he could read, and then he stuffed it into his great coat pocket with no more attention than if it were a dirty muckinder.

I pressed him. "Will you be needing me for reply, Sir?"

"Whatever fer, ye numskull?" If I wants to reply, there be the Mermaiden in plain view."

"But Doct—."

Babb wrenched my wrist so badly I bit my tongue. He looked me straight in the eye. "Aye, Thom Taylor, docked —in plain view."

"Yes, Sir, I do see your point." I not only saw but felt it, and with a conciliatory bow I left the tavern.

Pru stood in the glow of the late afternoon sun talking to a young man I vaguely recalled was Lawrence Carpenter. But I paid them scant attention, and a few paces from the ordinary I collapsed beneath an ancient apple tree to peck at the brooding secret like an unhatched chick trying to crack through an egg shell. Master Ford soon appeared and limped on his peg leg toward the bowling alley. I was about to try my luck again while Babb was alone when a troubled cry brought me to my feet.

Pru, who never raised her voice, screamed, "No, Mister Carpenter, I beg you! Leave me—!"

The strapping blond fisherman had pinned her arms over her head and hove her against the tavern wall. Pru's wool cloak slipped off her shoulders to the ground. Pressing tightly, he buried his mouth in her tangled hair, then between her breasts.

Not stopping to think, I charged at him. Pru's screams and my pounding fists only contributed to his passion. The black pig squealed, splitting puddle ice with his sharp hooves and trampling her cloak in the water as he trotted in circles. Master Babb ran out brandishing his club, followed by Mary and the wide-eyed children hiding in the dark labyrinth of her voluminous skirt.

Carpenter swiped his mouth with a torn shirt sleeve and backed off. "Whore! Ye deserve what ye gets, leadin' me on with yer pretty talk!"

Master Babb jerked the heated fisherman aside. "Lay a hand on her again, Carpenter, and I'll 'ave ye in the stocks afore ye can petition the Lord Almighty to save yer fishing stage from the Saco Court."

Mary Babb took Pru through the doorway to the hearth and I heard her within, weeping grievously. Discouraged by my failure to protect Pru, I retrieved her tattered cloak and on the way inside, pelted the poor companionable piglet with chunks of drift kindling from the tinder barrel.

To add to my vexation, Babb dismissed the chamber chaser as if nothing had happened and beckoned me into the brewery. It was dark and he lighted an oil lamp swinging from the rafter. The parchment I thought I'd seen the last of reappeared, and this time Babb ordered me to read it.

So the grand Master Babb who owned most of Appledore, was Shoals Magistrate to the mainland, the Shoals Constable and Fishing Master, could neither read nor write. Smug with this secret, I smoothed the paper flat under the flickering light.

Doctor Henry Greenland
Kittery 2d of November

Dear Phillip Babb, Esq.

    I writ this letter and dispatched it by the Captain of the Mermaiden in reference to the serious matter of treason against his Majesty King Charles II and local subjects of New England. My petition concerns one Gentleman John Cutt residing present-ly at Strawbery Banke, who includes in his inventory the whole of Star Island. I desire you take care to secure Mister Cutt's hold-ings on that Island. It would not be braking the law, for indeed, more than once the said Cutt has writ and spoke against the King's Charter. Therefore, the Captain and I have designs to confiscate his possessions and return the treasonous Cutt to London. This may be effected with ease, and the purchase would be worth £10,000 in King's ransom. As Magistrate at the Isles of Shoals I desire you to receive £1,000 sterling for securing

Mister Cutt's Star holdings, and his safe passage thence from Appledore to Britain. I would not have any taulk about this business, but desire it be kept secret. Pleas dispatch a speedy reply to the Mermaiden Captain—for Mister Cutt shall be in the hold of that ship by Meeting Day.

Yr Most Humble Servant,
Doctor Henry Greenland

Phillip Babb spat on the ground a few times and cursed while I read.

"Treason, Sir?" I whispered, suddenly afraid without my brother there for counsel.

Babb needed no counsel. "Burn it."

"What did you say, Sir?"

He lowered the lamp by a rope, snatched the paper, and thrust a corner into the sputtering flame. In a second, the burnt offering whirled into the air and I grabbed it before it set fire to the thatched roof. Babb threw what remained of the charred writ onto the earth and ground it in with his wooden heel.

"Ash to ash, dust to dust," he announced, snitting the lamp.

Feeling like an accomplice, I groped my way behind the inscrutable man back into the tavern—only to confront another disturbing situation. During our absence a Mister Pepperrell had appeared and was asking after none other than John Cutt, Esquire, of Star Island. Master Babb and I could not help exchanging hasty glances when Mary confided this remarkable coincidence. The Pepperrell in question had seated himself at the table and Babb approached him, playing the role of taverner to the hilt.

The roughness of Pepperrell's hands belied a ruder history to his score of years than one would have suspected from his winning smile and commanding demeanor. Unaware I was staring, Babb's hobnailed boot on my shin informed me otherwise, and I repaired to the kitchen.

Will dragged in weary from the wharf and Mistress Mary bustled over the spit, carving off a mess of succulent ribs for us. My stomach flip-flopped with the first few bites, for I had not tasted meat in a month. This, coupled with the vision of the black pig that followed me around like my shadow, did no favor to my digestion.

While the Mistress went up the loft with Pru to make up the trundle for the unexpected Mister Pepperrell and fetch our bedding, Will took a deck of cards from the fire mantel and shuffled them. Remembering my indenture strictly forbade card playing, I shoved them away.

"Be ye soft in the 'ead?" Will pushed the worn deck back in front of me. "Everyone plays cards at the Isles of Shoals. Skitters will beat the britches off ye if ye don't learn a trick or two. Besides, my father and that stranger over there be deep in their own games, I'll wager."

The wind picked up and howled around the corner as methodically we slapped down the cards on the hearth brick. Mistress Mary deposited our bedding on the slawbank bed pulled down from the kitchen wall, and accompanied her husband and guest to the back rooms.

I decided to unburden myself of the treacherous plot.

Will hung onto every word. "Father be in a pickle, a'right," he agreed.

"And Mister John Cutt? Guilty or innocent?"

Will roughed my hair as though he were ages older than me. "Ah, Thom, be everythin' black or white as an auk where yer concerned?"

"An auk?"

"Auk, Auk, Auk," Will grunted and laughed.

I giggled, giddy with the events of the day.

"An auk be a cross between a shag and a duck. Sailors bludgeon 'em fer their oil. I been rollin' barrels of auk oil into the warehouse this entire afternoon."

"And what's a shag?" I asked, caught up with the sheer oddness of Shoals language.

"Blessed Jerusalem garter—must I give ye the whole New World lexicon at one sittin'? All I'm sayin' be that ye don't want to see everythin' black and white, or ye'll end up fer ever on these stinkin' Isles. That's where the Cutt brothers be smart. They could not abide the likes of my father and the lawnessless of this wretched place, so they absconded with their fortune to the main. John Cutt be one of the wealthiest men in the Provinces. He and his brothers own land grants, a prosperous lumber trade, and a shipping business. Ye don't see em dressed in a filthy apron with a club fer a rapier and a curse fer a mouth."

I crawled onto the slawbank and rolled into my blanket. "But he is your father, Will. Are you not afraid for him?"

Will rolled beside me. "Aw go to sleep, Thom. Phillip Babb can worm his way out of anything."

At dawn I opened one eye on a ghostly form in a night shift hunkered over the kitchen embers. The barefoot apparition tossed back her hair, and Pru's beautiful soft figure backlighted by the firelight stoked an immediate fire of my own. Will was straight out, and I stirred the coals she'd ignited long as I dared.

Master Babb noisily lumbered into the cold for his morning constitutional, and Mistress Mary prepared an iron kettle of gruel big enough for a garrison of soldiers. A frowzy wisp of curls peeked from her ruffled pinner cap and the young ones caterwauled, jabbering and poking their drowsy brother with pudgy fingers. Skitters crashed into the stranger on his desperate charge to visit Aunt Sally. In brief, it was an ordinary chaotic day at Babb's Ordinary.

Pru distanced herself from the mysterious guest, but I could tell she too had fallen under his spell.

Winking at Pepperrell, Babb boomed, "The serving wench be a fine lass from Barbadoes. When I tire of my Goodwife Mary, I be trimmin' and unfurlin' Pru's sails—if ye get my drift."

The Mistress grabbed a loaf of bread from the sideboard and

whacked her husband hard on the head. In mock defense, Master Babb raised his hands, and Mister Pepperrell broke into commodious laughter at the domestic farce. Even Pru was smiling and swished her skirt to fetch something in the kitchen.

Suddenly, I loathed the handsome outsider who had stolen my loft bed and won the Babbs' affection. And when I heard he'd be sailing with Master Babb to Portsmouth, I secretly hoped he'd keep on sailing until he was back in Devon where he belonged. Unctuous as a snake, he kissed Pru's hand while my Master issued orders for Will and me to get to the wharf and finish packing the dunfish.

The once crowded fishing stage messy with halyards, barrels and dunnage had taken on a listless laziness. Freed from the tyranny of Babb's watchful eyes, Will and I lolled in the sun among the barrels, fabricating verses.

"I be a far sight better at cards than ditties," Will complained. "Let's see. All right, I have one:

New England's annoyances, ye that would know 'em,
Ponder these verses which briefly do show 'em.
When the northwest wind with violence blows
Then every man pulls his Monmouth cap over his nose."

I chuckled at Will's stresses quarreling and crowding to stay in line, and chimed in where he left off:

Our clothes we brought with us are apt to be torn.
They need to be mended soon after they're worn.
Instead of puddings and custards and pies
Our pumpkins and parsnips are common supplies.
We have pumpkins at morning and pumpkins at noon.
If it wasn't for pumpkins, we'd all be—

"Psst, kid."

Startled, I jumped down from the barrel and held onto Will's arm.

"Did ye deliver the message?" The Mermaiden Captain gave Will the once over and picked at a wart to the side of his barnacled nose.

"Aye, Capt'n. Master Babb would have replied sooner, Sir, but he's laid up with terrible gout."

Will snickered into his elbow.

"Laid up, ye say?" His harelip lifted over the decayed stump of a black tooth. "Well then, I guess I should pay my respects."

Before I could repair the damage, we were gazing at his broadside on the way up the hill.

"Now ye've done it!" Will exploded.

"Try to waylay him while I take a shortcut to warn Pru," I called back over my shoulder.

My young age and hard work at the flakes gave me the advantage. As I rushed in the back door, Pru looked up from her sweeping and smiled brightly, all traces of her previous troubles with Lawrence Carpenter forgotten in the wake of Mister Pepperrell's arrival.

"Please listen, Pru." I gasped, bending over to relieve a stitch in my side.

"The Mermaiden Captain thinks that Master Babb's in bed with the gout."

Pru leaned on her corn husk broom and eyed me skeptically.

"No time to explain. I need you to substantiate my tale."

"If you please, Thomas, in plain English. To what?" Pru smiled at me the way she used to and I ebbed into her like the sea onto the shore.

"Stand by my tale," I pleaded, hearing Will's voice outside the transom. "It's a grave matter—on my honor!" I crossed my heart, faint at the thought of mixing her up in my lies.

The panting Captain entered and stood in a rectangle of light falling through the door.

Even less adept at acting than rhymes, Will shrugged his shoulders. "It seems father be truly run afoul with his damnable gout."

Pru made a pretense of sweeping while the ship captain pulled impatiently at a gold earring. "Where be yer Master, wench?"

She leaned on the broom and looked him squarely in the face. "He's laid up, Sir, with terrible gout."

The formidable captain closed his distance. "I wishes to see Master Babb now!" he ordered, wading into the pile of chop bones and broken pipe staves.

To my delight Pru thrust the broom out for him to hold. "I'll see if he's up to visitors, Capt'n."

I could have kissed her, and the way he ogled her, I'm sure he could have, too. "Well don't just stand there, wench. On yer way fetch me a beer."

Pru returned. "Why, Capt'n, I do believe Master Babb is gone!" she reported in a flustered voice.

I gripped her arm. "Are you certain?"

"Yes, Thom. Mistress Mary and me were after him to see the doctor, and I believe he shoved off and done it." From her sudden pallor I could tell the anxious situation was pushing Pru overboard.

The captain drank a tall draught of beer and heaved a settled sigh, his dark eyes popping in their sockets like knots from a pine plank. "Ah, so Babb's gone to the doctor's. That's just what I wanted to know."

Evidently, Pru had not spoiled the pot at all, but had sweetened it, and I squeezed her hand in gratitude.

"What do ye do fer sport on these finny isles, wench?" he asked as Pru refilled his tankard with beer.

"Over to the spring we have bowls, and there's the Guy Fawkes Dance come Thursday Meeting."

The captain caught her by the apron sash, hauling her in like a prize fish. "And will ye save me a dance, lass?" His hand was about to roam where it wasn't invited.

With my toe I roused the black pig under the stool and as I'd hoped, the startled runt knocked against a loose leg, toppling the rogue. Apologizing for the animal's sorry behavior, I ceremoniously brushed off his waistcoat.

Despite the upset he grinned, unfurling his harelip on the crossbones of his besmirched mouth. "I reckon this be Hog Island for certain," he jibed, and disappeared down the lane toward the bowling alley.

Guy Fawkes was a day I remembered with joy and sorrow. Master Babb kept mum about the conspiracy to kidnap John Cutt, but my stomach suffered from constant worry and expectation. Everywhere I turned I was reminded of unsettling circumstances, from the Mermaiden's silhouette in the harbor to William Pepperrell who continued to sleep in my loft bed. If that wasn't bad enough, while Will and his brothers fashioned effigies of pumpkin heads on sticks, I had to learn several new hornpipe tunes to play at the dance.

Unable to swallow a bite of food, I petitioned Pru to concoct one of her potions, or I'd never make the channel crossing to Church Island for Meeting Day Lecture. Distracted by the robust newcomer gulping down my breakfast in the next room, Pru hastily stirred some Bezoar into treacle and ambled off like a moony calf, leaving me to keep down the vile stuff best I could. It worked like a charm.

During Godsip before a blazing fire at Andrew Diamond's Tavern, everyone was in a festive mood anticipating the Guy Fawkes Dance at Babb's Ordinary.

Will, who had been drinking more than his fair share yelled, "Hear! Hear!" And sloshing the common punch bowl, he shouted: "Gun-powder, treason, and plot. I see no reason why it should be forgot."

Minister Belcher grimaced at the rhyme and sank into a corner to review the second half of his sermon under the curled recesses of his periwig. By the end of the service I was so caught up imagining

Master Babb, Doctor Greenland, and the dubious ship captain dragging Cutt gagged and blindfolded into the hold of the Mermaiden, I quite forgot where I was and nearly missed my cue to pitch the hymn.

Just before sunset, a party of villagers from Star and Church Islands disembarked at south cove and wound across Appledore singing at the top of their lungs. Will and his brothers had made pumpkin effigies that were neither Guy nor Pope, but a Puritan roundhead in a wig suspiciously similar to Minister Belcher's and a Shoals fisherman with a wool cap over his orange forehead and Master Babb's gory apron covering the pole.

Waving pitch torches and swinging lighted jack o' lanterns, the chanting assembly crested the knoll. They were such a sight to behold that I forgot the whole stupid affair.

Master Babb came up and pressed a shilling into my palm. "Make the piping lively, Puker," he ordered.

Men in great coats, gloves, and red shoes crushed through the door and surrounded the bowl of Barbadoes rum. Women in muffs and with velvet masks fastened over their ears to stave off the cold crowded around the kitchen fire. Some of the girls left on their masks to keep the lads guessing, but I easily discovered Pru's green eyes dancing like emeralds through her white satin domino.

The floor of the tavern had been cleared and couples hit the dirt with serious abandon as I launched into a Fore And Aft hornpipe reel. I was at the refrain when I imagined I heard a fiddle and screeched into my hornpipe at the sudden appearance of a dark skinned man in a fringed leather jacket, leggings, and moccasins, who had slipped beside me. His fiddle fingers raced to a quivering bow and elated with the sound, I retrieved the tune, nodding for him to take over the harmony. Heels flew, the dancers shouted, and the fiddler beamed down at me, his pleasant face framed by two dark pigtails. As the frantic reel wound to a stop, he slapped me on the back. "Good! You play good."

"And you play a merry fiddle!"

Master Babb shook the stranger's hand. "Scozz, ye devil Indian, I hoped ye'd come. Thom, this Micmac savage Scozzway be the best fiddler in New England."

As the two talked I observed the soft-spoken musician was a far sight less savage than my Master.

Impatient with the interruption, the dancers were clapping and calling for Cuckold's All Awry. Scozz and I smiled at each other. It was obvious more than one couple included 'cheats of both sexes,' —as a popular romance called it.

Pru swirled by on the arm of the dashing William Pepperrell, and Will bobbed past towing his plump proud mother. Puffing rhythmically on a clay pipe, over in a corner Master Ford beat out time on his wooden stump. The next round provoked a flurry as the couples exchanged partners and moved down the room. Lawrence Carpenter swung Pru so high her feet flew off the floor. Irritated by the glee he took throwing her around, I unraveled the jig and stopped. Panting from the exertion of breathing the smoky haze, I suggested to Scozz we get some refreshment. I'd had no appetite for supper and now ravenously chasing down two large chunks of Mistress Mary's spice cake with a frothy mug of applejack and cider.

The heavy atmosphere had set more than one reveler on edge. Lawrence Carpenter and William Pepperrell pushed their way outside, glaring at each other. Grubb, Gibbon, and Babb disappeared into the brewery to ferment a card game, and from the shouts behind the closed door, already were immersed in a brawl. The women tippled applejack, wrongly assuming it the lesser of evils. From my short experience with the stuff, I reckoned another mug would have me tongue-tied and incapable of blowing a single note.

Pru stood suitorless at the cottage door when another of her admirers listed over the sill into her arms, pickled to the gills. His blotchy face and mouth full of dry rot attempted a greeting. "Aye, ye be the servin' whore," the captain slobbered, stumbling past Pru and looking furtively from one face to another.

Ignorant of the man and his mission, Mistress Mary offered her assistance, and in return he offered her his most congenial sneer.

"I come to see Phillip Babb and this time I means it," he growled.

She sidled away, nodding at Scozz and me to pick up a tune. We obliged with a Brantle guaranteed to wear them down to their exuberant toes.

From my perch on an old sea chest, I suddenly sighted a company of militia poised at the threshold. Weaving through the milling crowd, the wily captain hastily grabbed the nearest skirt, which happened to be attached to Joan Andrews. An equal match for any rogue, she buffeted him over the head with her muff while the dancers wheeled around them.

The company of four Massachusetts Colony footmen scarcely could be identified as soldiers. One wore a gauntlet, another a lobster-tailed helmet, and the other two presented a pair of dented breast plates. The vulnerability of each in his costume caused me some speculation as to the efficiency of their profession.

I was piping furiously when the leader motioned for me to quit. Rowing his pike across the waves of dancers, he cleared the floor and announced: "We have business with Constable Phillip Babb."

Unaware of the danger her husband was in, Mistress Mary returned from the brewery, slamming the door. Astonished by the soldiers, though somewhat overconfident in her state of inebriation, she marched straight up to the front rank and fired a volley. Couldn't poor fish folk enjoy a day of rest without the law exercisin' undue influence?

Put off guard by the woman's effrontery, the chief of artillery apologized for the interruption, but a matter of grave urgency required the immediate presence of Constable Phillip Babb.

Losing her composure, Mistress Mary rushed back into the brewery. Scozz too had disappeared swift as an apparition. I nailed my gaze on the dubious captain who scanned the room in search of an outlet. He had Joan by the waist and was forcing her to look pleasant—not an easy task for either of them.

One of the younger soldiers stood near enough my high post for me to lean over and whisper in his ear while the chief with the pike stormed behind Mistress Mary into the brewery. Afraid the foxy ship captain meant to flee the coup, I convinced the soldier to way-lay him. But crafty to the core, he thrust poor Joan in front of him to deflect injurious blows, and slowly edged toward the open door.

"Not so fast," the artillery chief shouted over the hubbub. Caught off guard, the captain loosed his hold of the blaspheming woman. With a crack of her solid arm, she bashed the scurrilous bastard to the floor, dispensing him like a beheaded cod.

The Massachusetts Lieutenant was given wide berth. He jerked the captain to his feet. "Are you the Captain of the Mermaiden at anchor in Babb's harbor?"

"That I be." His harelip quivered and stretched into a pout.

"And I believe you are Phillip Babb, Magistrate of the Township of Appledore and Constable of the Isles of Shoals?"

Master Babb held cards in one hand and grasped his trusty baton with the other.

"Aye, Sir, fer nigh seventeen years," he announced, lifting his chin and striking a pose.

"I am here to inform you that to the General Court of Boston, Massachusetts, this man is a treasonous rogue who has plotted against the Honorable John Cutt of Great Island and the Isles of Shoals. The Court has ordered me to place the involved parties under arrest. Have you ever had dealings with this man before you, Phillip Babb?"

Master Babb stuffed the cards into his great coat pocket, suddenly aware he was messing with the Bay Colony Militia, albeit a shabby representation.

"First time I ever clapped eyen on the evil lookin' curmudgeon, and that be God's Holy Truth."

"Why ye cheatin' blackguard!" the captain shouted, his beady eyes all at once shifting to me on my perch. He strained at the firm bondage of the soldiers. "Boy, ye delivered the Doctor's message. Were it not addressed to this filthy scum of a taverner?"

"Message, Sir?" I'd already invested a great part of myself in the Babb family and wasn't about to lose the rewards, be they ever so small.

"Yer double-crossin' liars, the finny lot of ye!" the captain bellowed as he was removed forcibly from the premises.

With Scozz nowhere in sight and the tension playing my nerves like a fiddle string about to snap, I slipped the hornpipe in my vest and headed down to the wharf with the rest of the crowd.

Aware his station of importance was on the wane, Master Babb fell in with the leader of the militia while the unwilling prisoner was kicked, shoved and otherwise maneuvered downhill to the wharf.

"What's to become of my ship?" the captain blubbered.

"We will sail it to Boston where you will be adjudicated for piracy."

"I swear—."

"Swear all you like," the lieutenant countered. "Plotting against the Colony is ever much a treason as Guy Fawkes'."

Will fell in beside me. "He ain't the first pirate 'at graced our shores and won't be the last, Thom. Godsip has it there be enough buccaneer booty on these isles to make us all rich as John Cutt."

"But, Will, I do wonder who ratted on the captain," I whispered.

Will's eyes gleamed bright as the overhead pointer star. "Who do ye think, Thom? Only five of us was privy to the kidnapping, and but one of us left Appledore."

" I thought your father couldn't stand John Cutt."

"Aye, Thom, but the King of Britain be two months from the Shoals and the Massachusetts Bay be in our back yard."

We reached the wharf where the Militia long boat was hauled up and sloshing in the tide. One of the soldiers jumped into it and cried in alarm for a torch.

The smoky light wavered over a white masked girl in the bottom of the boat—her skirt hoisted and thighs covered in blood. As Master Babb crouched over the dock, one by one the playing cards tumbled from his breeches and fluttered down on her limp body.

"Bowels o' Mercy," he groaned. "Some devil's gone and raped our Pru!"

5

*B*eset by despondency, Pru turned pale and thin yet would not declare the perpetrator of the foul crime inflicted upon her. No matter how much we importuned, she remained stubbornly silent. Lawrence Carpenter denied having touched her, claiming the last he'd seen she'd been standing in the doorway while he and a stranger stepped out for fresh air. It's not the way I would have put it, but few had noticed the conflict between Pru's two admirers.

To my amazement, the bachelor fisherman was petitioned to pay but a small fine, and did it grudgingly. Used to Britain's stiff penalty for rape, I could not understand Babb's leniency. Shoals men abused their women with impunity while the wives of the so-called "disorderly marriages"were locked in stocks for their complaint. I promised myself that I'd never tip the scales of justice against a woman to such a precarious degree.

The Isles froze into a desolate place and human cheer sank to a parsimonious low. Christmas came and went unobserved. By January the doldrums took their toll on the tavernkeep as well and, cranky as a bear, Master Babb hibernated in his flock bed, drinking nanny plum tea and baring his broad consumptive chest to a steady stream of poultices. When the coughing abated Mary propped him up like a newborn babe, wrapped a wool sock about his thick neck, and had Will and me take turns rubbing his hairy back with goose grease and mustard. The very stench of the man made us gag.

Pru regained her color and figure, though her disposition sadly wanted and she wept like a leaky boat. When I asked if I could help, she gave me a sharp rebuke to mind my own oars. Only Phillip Babb with his rough jibes and bawdy talk seemed to return the maid to her saucy good nature.

One afternoon I carried a mug of hot mulled cider to the sick chamber when I overheard the convalescent's booming laughter mixed with Pru's giggles.Their mirth was so infectious I smiled to myself. My bedside visits usually provoked Babb's guttural curses, and bracing myself for his scurrilous tongue, I dwelt on the reassuring hope of seeing Pru.

Never in my wildest fancy had I imagined her green eyes would accost me from the intimate down of Master Babb's pillow-bear! She scrambled to extricate herself from his clutch, but it was too late. Shocked by the unexpected sight of Pru wrapped in the flaxen sheets, I ran from the room, ducking the pewter mug he threw. It sailed into the hall, striking the lantern on the great sea chest with a resounding ring. The commotion brought his wife, and though I tried to block the door she rushed in. I stood in the hall attempting to sort out the surprised screams, laughter, crashes, and clopping feet that unwound inside like the works of a Harrison clock set into perpetual motion.

Will bound down the hall without stopping to ask me for an explanation — though I probably could not have offered one—and burst past and into the bed chamber, too. He had left the door wide open and I gazed on the bed rocking like a wherry at sea with Master Babb in a mess of sheets. Pru's tangled head coyly rested under one of Babb's stinky arm pits while Mistress Mary secured the other.

The three-some pitched like a three-master in the storm of Will's fury. He punched and lashed out until Pru broke loose and cowered behind a cupboard. Undaunted, Master Babb held onto his wife, planting a lusty smack on the tight curls of her forehead.

"Why, Phillip Babb, the fish be spawnin' early this year," she teased.

"Shame, Mother!" Will shouted. "The devil has given ye four bastards a'ready!"

To my wonder, Mary Babb flounced out of bed and slapped her eldest son wicked hard across the mouth. All this time I stood outside gaping in as if I were a spectator in the gallery of the Globe Theater in London.

Avoiding my eyes, Pru brushed past, fastening the cord of her stomacher. Will, too, did not seem to see me as he stalked out. I stooped to pick up the dented lantern from the floor and when I turned back the curtain had dropped on their lively theatrical.

As the days gained an agreeable longitude, Will and I covered Origen's fish house with new thatch, repaired the cow shed, and polished the blackened equipment of Mary's kitchen artillery with shore pebbles from Malaga Island. The pots weren't the only ones to benefit from this spring renewal.

One dazzling Shoals day Mary Babb impressed us to help her make a new batch of soap according to the Shoals peculiar custom— on the incoming tide.

I was sent to collect six bushels of ashes for the oak leech barrel positioned high on a stack of bricks. We then ran water through the ashes so the lye poured out the holes in the bottom and into the cooking cauldron. Pru dropped an egg onto the surface of the mess to see if it was thick enough. Meanwhile, Will rolled a hogshead of the mysterious auk fat out of storage and added this grease in great quantity to the lye. Skitters' task was to stir the slop with a sassafras switch as Will and I fed the fire and occasionally relieved the boy so he could relieve himself.

It turned out to be an all-day affair and after the last soap had hardened in molds I overheard Mistress Mary boast that we'd had the best batch she'd ever made.

The next day, the entire family took turns in a vigorous spring scrubbing of flesh and clothes, starting with Master Babb. The previous week Minister Belcher, with his characteristic solemn sanctimony, had entrusted me with a poem appropriately titled The Day of Doom. Nicely fitting one of the two hundred stanzas to the occasion at hand, I read them my version:

Ah, dear New World, clean as this soap to me
which hitherto the Isles of Shoals hast steered clear
of and thus may stink far less than formerly
now that Mistress Babb has scrubbed my dirty ear.

Skitters enjoyed it, but Mary dampened my effort by dumping a bucket of cold spring water over my sudsy head.

When we'd done, the women barred us from the kitchen while they too washed themselves and dried their under garments by the fire. Pru momentarily appeared in her shift, and not even my innocent eyes could help but notice she was big with child. But whose?

I couldn't get it off my mind and approached my Master with a set jaw and a keen resolve I'd learned from his brute example. For good measure I threw in his favorite oath, though its puniness in my mouth elicited a derisive laugh. When my deliberations upon Pru's fate were fully spoken, Phillip Babb, smelling oddly of rose water, tapped the stump finger of his right hand against my head. "Ye be thinkin', boy, but too late."

"Why, Sir? Surely, Lawrence Carpenter is the father," I said, trying my best to dismiss Pru's recent entanglement in Babb's bed linen.

"Because Carpenter jumped into the nearest boat, and I wager he still be rowin.'"

I looked away.

Babb pulled me around. "Look here, Puker, it might ease ye to know I posted bond with the Kittery Court. That man's abuse of the lass be duly recorded and if the filthy beggar shows up, I'll whip him 'till he can't stand."

When the spring fleet left for Jeffrey's Banke and I once more bore the yoke of enforced labor, this time I sadly resented my chores. Will also grew restless. One day in early April he convinced me that instead of wasting our strength cultivating the garden as ordered, we should look to our future.

Will's future, I thought ruefully, always lay somewhere beyond the Isles and his ubiquitous father, whereas mine depended on the both of them. But strong-headed as usual, he picked up the spade meant for the corn and beans and headed toward Babb's Landing.

"Where are we bound?" I asked, following.

Will picked up a broken bird's egg from the path and held the turquoise shell to the light. "Swallick, I reckon," he said, and threw it down. "We be huntin' fer treasure."

I held as much store in treasure hunting as in the lottery. One consumed a great deal of the colonists time, and the other, their hard earned pine tree shillings. Still, had Will asked me to jump off the cliff I'd have done it out of sheer recklessness. It was just one of those days.

Adjacent the privy was a bilge pit I'd never noticed before. The mottled stone and sludge seemed a most unlikely hiding place for treasure.

"Looks like Father and Gabe Grubb done excavated the place a'ready." Will said, irritated.

I sprawled on a boulder not worried one wit.

Will planted his shovel.

"Father was sure Capt'n Harding stashed his booty here. It was just after his arrival at the Shoals in 1653. Mister Harding robbed a Spanish galleon, and the Barbadoes Governor convinced Governor Winthrop to clap the captain and sailors in gaol. But when they inventoried the cargo at Salem, the treasure wa'nt to be found."

I shrugged.

Will overflowed with the tale. "Ye see, in the meantime Spain claimed The Holy Ghost frigate theirs and reported Harding stole a six foot chest of gold dust, another chest of jewels and pearls, and seven hogsheads of pieces-of-eight. Rumor had it that Harding sailed to Pemaquid, Maine, and father swears they stopped at the Shoals."

I picked up a pebble and threw it into the pit.

"Aw, Will, if you were on the run and had treasure to dispose of in a fearsome hurry, would you be so foolish to bury it in plain sight? Bowels o' Mercy, Man, use yer damnable 'ead."

Will smiled at my mimicry of his father's speech. "Aye, Thom, but ye must mark that the Shoals had but few folk back then. Father's fish stage wa'nt nothin' but a heap of rock."

I threw another pebble into the dank pit.

"I'd say your father did a good business of fish and made an equal work of this hellhole."

I lay flat on the rocks and looked at the sky. A gull swooped over with a mussel and dropped it from on high. It bounced and cracked on the ledge.

"Say, Will, where else would you hide a treasure chest that heavy? The both of us together couldn't heft such bounty."

Will scratched his blond arm. He resembled nothing like his mother or father, although his hot-headed temperament loomed closer and closer to Master Babb's every day.

"I'd 'ave dumped it onto the south cove Shoalers calls the Devil's Dance Floor. Ye could beat a fast retreat to my thinkin'." He suddenly sprang to his feet and harvested the shovel. "Let's go."

Lollygagging in the warm sun seemed the best treasure I could hope for, and I was painfully rousing myself to Will's enthusiasm when Master Babb's querulous voice sought a victim, possibly two.

His piratical torso crested the squabble of rocks. From my angle of repose the man's demeanor bode less than well.

"Ye shiftless gambrels of horseshit. Did I not order ye to plant the cabbage? I should throw ye into this blasted empty pit and be done with the pair of ye."

Will struck a bold stance of defiance. "Well then, at least there would be somethin' of value in it."

Babb leapt forward. "Why ye miserable waster. I'll murder ye!"

Will held the spade before him, sparring his father's blows. Staggering and bleeding he half-cried, half-sobbed, and in self defense, flung the spade with all his might. It bonged and disappeared into the pit. Babb swaggered backward to dodge the flying object and cursing, disappeared in an avalanche of debris.

I turned the fight over in my mind, waiting for Master Babb's exit from the morass to take his revenge on Will who taunted him from above.

"Come out ye feckless rat. What scoundrel would murder his son?" Tears flowed down Will's sunburnt cheeks.

A song sparrow perched high on a shadbush and sang a mating call that sent a shiver through me. Glad the fight was over, I resolved to extricate my bested Master from the bilge.

Will tromped up. "Damn the wretch, Thom. Let him molder. I hope the devil broke a limb."

"But Will, he's your father," I argued. "Besides, I'm beholden to him as though he were mine." I hardly believed what I was saying. Phillip Babb and my own father were less alike than night and day. Yet something inexplicable tugged at my heart.

Will swiped his tear-stained face. "Damn it, Thom. Be ye totally blind? It be this stinkin' scoundrel what sunk yer very own brother!"

His accusation stunned me speechless.

"My father and his redoubtable mates lured the Charles to destruction with the lights ye saw in the storm. I wager my life on it!"

The sparrow hopped closer and chortled. It could have been a funeral dirge for the sudden hate that sunk my spirit like stone ballast. I walked a few paces from the loathsome pit. Will was right. Let the despicable dog grunt himself out of his villainous slough. I'd have none of it.

We set out for the Devil's Dance Floor so caught up in what had taken place that we were surprised to see the strand completely covered by the incoming tide. Thwarted in treasure, and much else besides, we headed back to our chores.

I thought of Minister Belcher spinning his moral fiber into the whole-cloth design of preparing me for a Godly vocation. If this were the case, he would be sadly disappointed. For I could not comprehend how the cruelty Phillip Babb meted on my brother and the unsuspecting sailors of the Charles could ever be forgiven. A tear blotted my vision and something I couldn't name gnawed in the hold of my stomach.

"Will, we must go back and fetch your father at once."

Will strode purposefully forward. "Ye'll never learn, Thom. My father can worm out of any muck. Mark my words, he'll be waitin' at the tavern with a strap to tan our hides."

But he too slowed and veered back toward the pit.

We ran like the wind, tumbling headlong to the bottom of the hole in a heap. Babb lay on his back in the mire and pebbles, his face twisted into a fearsome grimace.

"He's hurt!" I cried. "We've got to get him out."

Will placed his blond head on the bloody apron.

"Ain't worth the trouble. He be dead." No emotion toiled in his pronouncement, nor hint of the previous wounding anger.

I stared into Master Babb's dark eyes sinking fast into his gruesome face and closed the lids. To my amazement, they scrambled back open like a fish flipping to safety from a wherry. Will reached in his breeches and pulled out a shilling. I weighted it on one eyelid and found a Shoals lucky stone with a white band around it for the other—not that either currency would do much good where Babb was bound.

6

Mistress Mary and Pru set up such a wail that Master
Ford and Robert Mase came running all the way from the
bowling green.

Master Ford slid beside me into the sludge and toed Babb's
sinking body. "Near a month ago he told me the pit was too deep
and he was giving it up."

I bit my lip and decided to unburden. "The fact is, Sir, that Will
and I were surveying the pit when Master Babb discovered us, and
in a rage he fell backward into it."

"Looks like the horn-headed devil's gone and dug his own
grave," Joan Ford muttered from above.

Her husband reached up and grabbed a straggle of her grey
locks. "Woman, how dare ye revile Phillip Babb when his generous
nature has provided fer us all these years."

Her eyes in the hood of her cloak glowed like embers in a deep
cave. "Generous!" She bent over and spat on the body. "Dyin' ain't
good enough fer the dog what put me in the stocks and give me
nine stripes. A curse on the scurrilous rogue."

Master Ford tussled with his wife, sending her in a landslide onto the stiffened corpse.

Unable to take any more of their slings and arrows, I retreated to the ordinary where Goodwife Andrews was consoling Mary and Pru in their lamentable misery.

Everything was in a turmoil and no one in charge. After a heated discussion, the men decided Phillip Babb might as well rest where he lay and save them the hardship of "haulin' his brute body out of the infernal pit." Muffled in a monastic frock and sniffling from the grippe, Minister Belcher delivered an incomprehensible elegy carried in fierce gusts of wind to the bereaved Babb family.

One of the children stood at the edge looking down.

"Fa! Fa!" he cried as Mary pulled him to her, tears streaming down her cheeks. The morose Anglican cleric listlessly sprinkled a shovel of tidal debris over the body.

"Ash to ash, dust to dust."

The minister's words dredged up an image of Babb stomping the ashen remains of the traitorous letter and hounded by recollection, I hurried to the tavern where the promise of free drink had attracted a large gathering, including Mistress Ford, who thought nothing of swilling down her worst enemy's best brew.

Exhausted by the unwinding events, Will and I beat a hasty retreat to Origen's, tripping in the dark over hand lines stretched on the rocks. We ducked more hooked lines as we entered the fish house and circled a heap on the floor. Groping up the ladder, we clung to each other for comfort, and fell asleep in a hammock beneath the sweet smelling grass of the new roof.

At first light we entered the ordinary and stared in disbelief at a massacre of stone-drunk bodies sprawled on the floor, over the table, and across the slawbank bed. All four vats of beer brewed to sell to the returning fishermen had been consumed in Dionysian revelry within a matter of hours.

Will made a gallant effort to appease his hungry younger brothers while I lighted the fire.

"You're Master now, Will." I told him.

"I murdered him," he whispered.

I shuddered at the word. "He fell."

"It be the spade I flung," he insisted.

"On my honor, Will, I kept watch. The spade didn't touch your father." I wished I could be more positive of my account.

Pru appeared, shoving me aside to busy about her habitual duties and then some. I could not believe the expression of determination in her countenance. It bore a strength so radiant I struggled to keep my own weak resolve. She fed the children, entreated Will to visit his mother at once, and went off down the lane to milk the cow.

Feeling left out, I scooped up a handful of peels for the black pig who had grown so fat and ornery the Shoalers called her Satan.

"Here, Satan!" Samson Babb gurgled, patting the sow on her solid rump. "Ye be a good little Satan," the child prattled, unaware of the contradictions of his compliment.

A year ago I too was as naive. In despair I climbed the hill overlooking Babb's cove. What was to become of me now that my Master was gone? Though he'd been a loose canon, he also had been our anchor. Bowels o' Mercy, Bowels o' Mercy—I chanted to staunch the flow of tears.

Will crept up on me unawares. "Mother be askin' after ye."

Mary Babb was propped on a feather bolster looking none too well. "Ye must excuse me, Thom. I been sufferin' the mornin' sickness."

Did she have a hangover? Unlike the other Shoalers, I hadn't seen her drinking.

Will intercepted my confusion with anger. "Mother be with child. She'll be lyin' in come September."

The dimple that rested on Mistress Babb's chin rescued me from drowning in Will's self pity.

"Thom, I can truly say ye been like a son and I be countin' on ye. We must pull together now that Goodman Babb be—." Her lips quivered. "But of course, if ye want release from yer indenture—."

I leaned over the sickbed in a confidential manner. "No, but would you find me rude, Mistress Mary, if I inquired after something that concerns my future and has a bearing on your next of kin?"

The dimple that proved my salvation on this uncharted voyage was joined by the Nina and Pinta dimples in her cheeks, and seeing the coast clear, I sailed on. "Did your husband leave a will or testament in safe keeping?

Mary picked up my hand and held it in hers. "Mister Babb and I never married, Thom."

No longer able to control his temper, Will shouted, "I told ye the lot of us were bastards, Thom, but ye paid no heed."

"Hold your tongue, Will!" I ordered, surprised at the reliance of my voice.

"Or what?" he jeered, punching me in the chest.

Pru rushed into the chamber.

"Thom Taylor, ye should be ashamed, upsetting the Mistress when she be in mourning and ill besides."

"I be to blame," Will shouted, "fer putting up with you whores!"

He ran from the room while I helped Pru comfort Mary whose convoy of momentary joy had sunk deep in a sea of tears.

That summer everything seemed to be giving birth, including Satan who managed to increase the swine population of Hog Island by ten. The enormous sow chose to give suck to her voracious litter right at the front door. If this wasn't enough of an obstacle, the rumor of a dearth of beer sent the thirsty fishermen across the channel to our competition at Master Kelley's Tavern.

I didn't hold much faith in Mistresses Mary and Pru keeping us afloat, but soon changed my mind. The women hitched themselves to the burden like a yoke of oxen and pulled us courageously through the busy fishing season.

I did my utmost to contribute, too. The captains of the ships in the harbor brought bills of lading which only I could make sense of. Master Ford took time from his own fishing stage to kindly sit down with me and go over the sums and tallies.

One day as Will and I were at the table discussing how many hogsheads would be required from the cooperage, who should stroll in breezy as you please but William Pepperrell. Pru quickly sidled from the room, making a ludicrous effort to hide her enormous belly.

"Bring me a beer," he ordered without so much as a by your leave. When no one jumped to attention he greeted Master Ford, no doubt dismissing us as mere kids.

The man's swarthy good looks tried my patience.

"We're closed," I told him. "You'd best quench your thirst over on Church Island."

Master Ford stood to depart.

"Well, Master Thom," he said clapping me on the shoulder, "I'll be stoppin' by later in the week."

"Master Thom?" Pepperrell got a queer glimmer in his eyes, as though he'd just woken up. "Ah, I remember now. Ye be Phillip Babb's son."

"Will spoke up. "No, Sir, I be Babb's son— though there be little proof of it," he mumbled ruefully.

Pepperrell pretended not to hear. "And both ye boys be keepin' Babb's accounts while he conducts his affairs elsewhere?" He rubbed his clean shaven skin and tugged his blade buckler to assure himself it was still there.

Will warmed to him like fire.

"Father passed away several months ago. The men be comin' to inventory the estate this very day."

Pepperrell's face lit up like a candlewood torch.

I nudged Will to shut his hatch, but he seemed stricken with volubility, perhaps because Pepperrell knew wherefore he steered and Will hadn't a clue.

"I be leavin these stinkin' Shoals for good." Will boasted. "Matter of fact, I approached a sea captain bound fer the Indies this morning."

Pepperrell glanced at my bills of lading. "And Tim," he inter-vened, "do ye plan a life of adventure on the high seas, too?"

"Thom," I answered, annoyed that he'd seen me more than once and hadn't cared enough to remember my name. Popular or not, he'd find it hard to slip around the Shoals without Master Babb to grease the pole.

Pepperrell glanced at the mess of papers. "I admire yer readin' and writin' skills, Thom. I'll be spendin' some time here on the Shoals. Do ye think ye could learn me?"

While Will searched the man's face as though it were the Holy Grail, the very thought of Pepperrell rubbed me the wrong way.

"I'm busy."

"Tell ye what, lad," he prodded in a confidential persuasive tone. "Learn me to read them bills of ladin' and sign my name, and come September I'll give ye a brand new wherry."

I was so hung up on his forgetting my name, I wasn't sure I'd heard him correctly. Did he say wherry? A small vessel was the linchpin for a viable business on the Shoals and here the man was promising me one for very little in return.

The whole summer long Shoalers struck bargains with the ambi-tious man from Devon, England. He was all over the place.

Without a will and testament, Mary Babb was at the mercy of the Provincial Court. Nathaniel Fryer, the Shoals administrator, was ordered to auction off our warehouse, the fish stage, flake rooms, moorings and cables, hooks and hand lines, an old boat and a good furnished shallop, cod liver oil vats, the cow, iron pots, pot hooks, pewter plate, grinding stone, and the various sheds and fish and auk oil on hand at the time of inventory. The Seeley broth-ers from Smutty-Nose along with other prosperous Shoalers all got a piece of the pie.

Though new to the Isles, Pepperrell managed to come out with a handsome parcel which included the dwelling and brewery.

He graciously offered Mary Babb a room in her own house

since he would be moving to a new mansion farther up the hill. As for the other Babbs, he'd sign on Will as an indentured servant and Thomas Randolph Taylor, whose indenture papers he'd purchased with one of the fish flakes. He and his partners indentured Skitters and his seven year old brother to mainland families who would give them bed and board for doing chores. Mary could keep the toddler Samson and her newborn babe, but if she was counting on the milk cow, it had been sold.

Unable to listen to any more, I was nearly out the door when Pepperrell ordered me back.

"Not so fast, young Thom!"

I hated this appellation and ground my teeth. Pru sat wordlessly behind the spinning wheel, hiding her ungainly, unlaced belly from the fortune hunter.

"Will you be keeping on Pru?" I asked in a low voice.

My new owner raised a questioning eyebrow.

I nodded toward Pru.

"The servant girl can stay with Mistress Babb, but after her lyin' in, the girl must go."

"She's a hard worker," I entreated.

"I don't doubt it, young Thom, but there be no father, and we can't have that, can we?"

I desperately tried to salvage this wreck of a life we clung to. "Pru's ever so smart, Sir, and look how pretty she is. Everyone dotes on her."

"Why, Thom, I think ye be smitten with the lass." His teeth mocked me like a set of oak nine-pins I 'd like to knock out.

"Please don't make fun of me, Sir. You know I could not provide for her as you would."

"Me?" Pepperrell laughed even louder.

Pru looked up anxiously from the creaking wheel.

"I daresay I've got my sights on a marriage of good breeding calculated to line my coffers, not that penniless Barbadoes whore with a bastard in her purse. Now, young Thom, let's—."

I swallowed hard and could feel my cheeks burn crimson as Pru waddled across the room grasping her belly inflated as a pair of bellows. When she reached my chair she gasped. "Thom, fetch the Mistress, hurry. Oh please, Thom, in the name of the Blessed Virgin, hurry!"

I summoned Mistress Babb who came swift as a slug, being in the same peculiar state as Pru. The sod Pepperrell would have had his ABCs in the midst of the crises, but Mary Babb sent him packin, despite his protestations to the contrary.

And then we all got on with the arduous process of birthing.

I was dispatched to fetch a bucket of well water and sloshed much of it onto the ground, so perplexed was I at hearing the screams issuing from the house.

Meanwhile, Will rowed back from Smutty-Nose with Goody Rhymes and Goodwife Twisden. The three women ran back and forth with boiled water, torn sheets, and heated fire tongs.

Pru's howling gave me such goose bumps I could barely stand the anguish. The sun cast a shadow on the noon marker at the front window sill, yet the racket continued. Mary Babb came from the birthing chamber with beads of sweat rolling down her brow. Pru was too tired to push any more. She poured us mugs of 'groaning beer' brewed especially for the two birthings. The women drank and in hushed voices told tales of other Shoals births.

Overwrought by the strange complexity of bringing a new creature into this sorry world, I walked out.

Avoiding the path that would take me by the hobs' hole of Phillip Babb's grave, I skirted the cove in search of a smooth-banded stone like the one Pru had given me. Returning to the mysterious sisterhood, I implored Mistress Mary to press it into Pru's hand.

The screams were intermittent now, and weaker. I'd portered three more buckets of water up the lane, played Nine Man Morrice with Skitters, prepared my next lesson for Pepperrell, split some kindling, and politely sampled the succotash, roasted pig, herring in vinegar, hasty pudding with huckleberries and other dishes brought by Appledore women throughout the interminable August afternoon.

For all of Pru's great suffering, the babe still hadn't come.

Goody Rhymes collapsed in a corner with the Twisden woman, both of them potted to the gills from the groaning beer. Only my Mistress Mary prevailed, and late in the afternoon my heart jumped as she called Will and me into the hall. She held a bundle which at first I mistook for soiled sheets, so roughly did she treat it.

"William Babb, take this!" Mary's voice and hands trembled as she handed him the bundle.

"Dead," I guessed, near in a blubber at seeing the small shroud.

Fear crept into her face. "Ye needn't grieve, Thom. This be the devil's work fer certain."

Though ordered to go easy on the groaning beer, Will was nine sheets to the wind, and for all he noticed, the babe in the winding sheet might as well have been a cod. Recognizing the uselessness of his condition, Mary grabbed back the bundle and handed it to me. "Beware of pryin eyen, Master Thom. Wha' ever ye do, keep the babe swaddled!"

Will hiccoughed loudly. "Has it got one of them horrid lobster birthmarks, Mother?"

"None of yer business," she snapped, sorely tried by his dis-obedience. "Now take the boat while there's still daylight and row over to the dike on Star Island. Make sure the curséd babe be lost in the tide afore ye return. Do you comprehend?"

I nodded for both of us and made a sign of the cross over the poor aborted babe.

Mistress Babb cupped her cheeks in her hands and let out a tearless sob. "Ye can bless the child from now 'till doomsday, Thom, but it won't do no good. It be cursed by the devil!"

The breeze settled down with the setting sun, and we were just rounding the leeward side of Cedar Island when Will suddenly let go of his oar and stared straight ahead.

"Confound it, Will, pull your share or we'll lose the daylight!" I ordered in a sweat to get the task over and done with.

We passed a few fish flakes below the Star Island Fort, but the major part of the fishing operation took place on Smutty-Nose and Hog. I couldn't see hide nor hair of the island's only occupants, Robert Cutt and Mister Tucker. Yet Will wore a most peculiar expression, as if he saw someone on the ledges.

"Father!" he shouted. "Father, I didn't mean to murd—."

I lurched and clapped my hand over his mouth. "I told you never to say that, Will. It was an accident."

Taking over, I maneuvered us into the lagoon and tethered our boat to a rock. Will had pointed out the place where we were to dispose of the babe, but though we'd run aground, he made no earthly effort to move.

"Damn, Will, shove on!" I cried, shaking his inert body.

All at once he grabbed the bundle and with a contorted face he hollered "Bowels o' Mercy, if this be my bastard I'll 'ave nought to do wi' the black-faced, horn-'eaded kid."

Frightened at the sound of Phillip Babb's voice emanating from Will's body, I leapt ashore.

As if in a dream Will stood in the boat with a far off look in his eyes. Then turning, he spat in the water.

"Seek yer fortune in gold, boys," he growled. "Women be momentary pleasure. But gold! Now there be solid treasure."

When he stumbled getting out of the boat, I recaptured the bundle and dashed with it to the dike channel.

Will's disturbing oaths and sea chanties resounded from above as I groped along the narrow ledges of the leviathan rock face that made up the tidal crevice. A shaft of sunlight pierced the frothy green waves, and calculating how easily a man might drown, I hugged the wall.

Just as I was about to drop the bundle into the seething whirlpool, a niggling question caused me to hesitate. Who had fathered Pru's hapless babe? Surely, there was no harm in one quick look. I pulled off the sheet and stared in shock at the black eyes and skin. God help her, Pru had given birth to a Negro!

PART TWO

Love and Wanton Juices

7

A number of folk on the Shoals still believed the sun revolved around the earth and Astronomy conflicted with God's Grand Design. My observations through Captain Moody's navigational instruments as we sailed across the Atlantic Ocean convinced me otherwise. But seeing Will so out of orbit threw me into a wave of doubt as to what did and did not exist in this Universe.

Phillip Babb apparently had been seen circulating around our island galaxy by others than Will. Gabriel Grubb wore his jacket turned backward and inside out to keep Babb's noisome ghost away, and William Mase was discovered crazed beside the bilge pit where we'd laid Babb in what we'd presumed to be his final rest.

Mase jabbered his story to us workers at the flakes:

"Master Babb's ghost said it were diggin' fer treasure, and said it could use some help. I swear on the Bible the spade dug itself and before I knowed it, I struck a chest. 'It be mine, ye double-'eaded, two-timin' snake!' the ghost cried. But I already was on me knees openin' the lid. Sulfur thick as porridge burned me eyes and a red-hot horseshoe flew straight at me fore'ead. Struck right 'ere. See?"

Mase did have a nasty gash on his forehead, but I suspected he was drunk to the gills and clobbered himself on a rock.

The next Meeting Day Minister Belcher made a point of explaining to his frightened flock that the supernatural apparitions recently seen on the Isles were nothing but the devil in a jug. Several Shoalers interrupted his sermon with voluble protest and fed up with their rabble rousing he had me line a hymn.

If only the wrinkled face of Pru's black baby could be as easily forgotten with song. It hounded me night and day, and I longed to talk about it with Mistress Babb. But her own lying in was near and I didn't want to add to the poor woman's travail.

By the September fishing season, Pepperrell could sign his name and had learned enough under my tutelage to read the accounts. When I reminded him of the boat he'd promised, he offered me Babb's dilapidated old ketch with its torn sails and worn ropes. I had no recourse but to take the weathered tub.

Fortunately, the fifth Babb child entered this world with considerable less effort than Pru's baby. Sadly, Mistress Mary could not supply enough milk and Pru was asked to wet nurse the child. I was shocked that Mary Babb would allow her baby to suckle the milk of a Negro babe. But when Pru took the new baby, Peter, to a cottage down the lane, I was even more crest-fallen.

Then, Skitters left to live with the Green family in Hampton and though at times he riled me no end, I knew I would miss him, too.

After the last vessel in the harbor was loaded with prize dunfish and sailing for Britain, I enlisted Will to help repair the battered old boat, offering him a partner-ship. We scraped and pitched the hull, gave her a coat of paint, and invested in new oar fittings and a rudder of ironwood.

By early spring, we were hiring the boat out to floating taverners, fishermen, and an occasional sea captain with business on the other islands and Piscataqua River.

The Massachusetts Bay Colony had banned Shoal mackerel and herring fishing until July so the fish could spawn. Their numbers were being depleted and if we didn't watch out, the cod would disappear, too.

Not to be bested by Massachusetts laws or the laws of nature, Shoals fishermen turned into middlemen, trading with Newfoundland Plantation to the north, and suffering little loss in the bargain.

Robert Cutt, unlike his round-head Whig brothers on the Main, was so cunning in his Star Island fish business that he actually turned a profit by shifting with the banns according to the ebb and flow of commerce. In this respect he was a true Shoaler, hedging his bets for the least likely interference in his mercantile affairs.

Master Robert had gotten wind of our start-up boat business and offered to employ us during down times. After the spring shad run, he hired us to sail his sloop to Hampton so he could pick up a load of salt from the marsh works. Pru went along to collect medicinal herbs she couldn't find on the Isles, and when I saw her all decked out in a gay pink bodice, I thanked Providence for the crossing.

While Mister Cutt tended to business, the three of us walked from Hampton River Landing to a flotilla of prominent dwellings on the cow common. A scowling cowherd pointed his crook up a muddy cart path to Little Boar's Head where Skitters was working for room and board.

Goody Green told us her "dear little boy" was out back, and we barged in on the boy as he pounded wood pins into shoe leather. At the sight of us he spewed half a dozen pins from his lips into the air.

Mister Green turned from his cobbler's bench long enough for us to ask if Skitters might come out for the day. The elderly man intimated the goings on had them in such a muddle he'd thought of giving his apprentice a holiday like everyone else in the village. No doubt he would tell us all about it—though he and his wife refused to talk about the wretchéd affair.

The bent cobbler offered us rooms for the night, but Will and I assured him we'd be comfortable on the deck of Cutt's sloop, and that Pru would find lodging with the Godfreys who were friends of her deceased Master, Phillip Babb.

Green knew the Godfreys and Skitters was no stranger to their household. He'd nearly worn a path to their door visiting Ann Smith. Of course that was before the horrid goings on.

The longer we lingered, the more I desired to know every scandlemongerous detail of the so-called "goings on." And although Mistress Mary had made us promise to ask a pester of questions concerning her son's well being, once we had Skitters in broad day-light, we tossed them to the wind.

What goings on was Mister Green referring to? Who was Ann Smith? Why wouldn't he talk to us?

Skitters looked like he was about to bawl.

Pru placed a comforting arm around his thin shoulders. "We missed you," she said, squeezing him affectionately.

Happy at last to be the center of attention, Skitters regained his volubility and endearing over-confidence.

"Well, I admit I was at the thick of the muddle for awhile myself," he boasted. "Sarah Clifford and her mother Goody Bridget sent me to Goody Cole one day fer—well, fer my problem and—promise not to breathe a word of this to anyone—to spy on the ol' witch."

Pru's eyes narrowed and darkened.

"Whoa, Skitters," I told him."Slow down and pull on the bit."

"When Goody Cole first come here in 1645 she were accused of bein' in covenant with the Devil. My friend Ann told me that Eunice Cole called Mistress Hussey a whore and her husband a whore-master." Skitters' delivery swelled with pride at his store-house of tattle. "Well, Hulda Hussey took Goody Cole to court fer the slander. And when the thornback were stripped fer whippin', the constable saw an unnatural long blue teat hangin' off her. Then, at Sunday Meeting, Preacher Dalton saw a mouse creature fall from

Goody Cole's bosom yelpin' like a pup, and that be God's truth."

"You backed up way too far, Skitters," I objected.

Will reddened with impatience. "So who be Ann Smith?"

Skitters flush of importance disappeared at the mention of her name and he cast a downward glance at a calf nuzzling his breeches through the fence. "I'm not suppose to talk about it. She be my friend, but—."

"And what did Goody Cole do?" I prodded.

"Well she—Goody Cole, I mean—she cured my—well my problem, and now I visit Aunt Sally only once a day!"

"Goody Cole practices herbal medicine?" Pru asked.

"Aye. She give me a potion what cured me and I'm ever beholdin' to her but—."

Skitters scratched the calf's nubby horns through the fence and the cowherd strode over swinging his crook. "Get off that fence and on with yer business."

Will pulled Skitters down and we scrambled away.

"But now Ann won't talk to me," Skitters continued in a teary voice. "She says I'm in covenant with the Devil, too, and it be a real vexation fer I adore Ann Smith. She be an orphan like me." He stopped short, nearly toppling us in a heap. "I mean—an orphan like all of us. Ann and her brother Nathaniel were fostered in the Godfrey family, but she couldn't stand it so the Cliffords, who have a dozen children, took her but—."

Skitters' tongue was wandering hopelessly far from its destination as we reached ours.

Pru could not stay with Mistress Godfrey after all. She had a houseful of inlaws for the widely publicized inquest. Henry Rob's Ordinary was full, too. If we hurried to Tuck's Ordinary she knew the new owner, Mister Deering, and we could mention her name.

Skitters rushed our pilgrimage up Rand's Hill where we secured a small spare room for Pru at a conversely large price.

Pru followed us outside. "Take me to Goody Cole," she ordered.

"You can't—Pru—Prudence," I stammered, suddenly aware I had

never known the surname of this head-strong girl who cut such a fine figure against the tidal marsh.

"Oh can't I, Thom Taylor? Just you wait. I'm going to learn Goody Cole's herbal secrets before she takes them to her grave!"

Ranting on about his connections with the alleged witch, Skitters led us onto the Hampton River path. Will and I were tuckered out with the wending and winding, and paused to reflect on the convenience of Appledore Island in relation to Hampton's scattered properties.

Boar's Head was above a sandy cove surrounded by tidal flat far as one could see, but here there were scattered stone ledges more suitable for dwellings. On an inlet beyond Hampton Harbor we came to a hovel of clapboard and thatch half hidden by marsh grass.

The sky glimmered with herring clouds and thunder rumbled close. Startled by the glowering firmament, Skitters hugged Pru's waist in a less than dignified manner. Will trod on, oblivious of the resonant sounds which at first I thought were overhead, but I soon realized came from the hovel.

Reason often held me in good stead, and with all my might I summoned up that faculty to arrive at Goody Cole's threshold.

We paused on the path a few meters from the door sill.

Pru straightened her wind-blown hair. "Barbadoes féfé women who practice herbal magic would never have lodged in such a frightful place as this," she said. "I remember one féfé at Mardi Gras—how she would call on the Holy Mother to watch over us. When someone got the evil eye, she'd make a poppet of cloth to place under their pillow and ward off the spell."

Through a clump of river reeds I watched Pru's green eyes gleaming like a wild cat's as she talked about her native island. A shiver spiraled down my spine at the memory of her black babe. Did Pru know, or must I harbor that lonely dark secret forever?

As if in answer, the sky filled with fast moving clouds and a breeze caught at the torn corner of Goody Cole's thatched roof, sending a wisp of grass heavenward. A water rat stuck his snout through a tangle of rushes and made away with some grains of corn that had been scattered for a scrawny chicken outside the cottage door.

Loud grunts and snorts from inside joined deafening blasts of thunder. Skitters clung to Pru for dear life.

"Goody Cole has turned herself into a hog. Let's go!"

Pru bravely stepped over the threshold.

"Goody Cole, you've got visitors," she called.

The snorting stopped. I sighed relief seeing an ancient woman fast asleep and snoring on the disheveled bed.

A mouse rustled through a crack carrying a crumb from the half-eaten loaf of bread moldering on the table. Bunches and garlands of herbs, berries, twigs, and leaves hung from the rafters in such profusion we had to hunker and dodge not to disturb them.

Skitters had a sneezing fit and the reposing woman blinked. "Wha? Who the? S'at yew, Thom?"

I was astounded. How did she know my name?

Emboldened by our presence, Skitters trotted over to the bed. "Aye, Goody, I brung company. This be my brother Will, and Pru our servant maid."

Pru's pretty mouth turned down at Skitters careless allusion to her menial status.

"And this here be Master Thom Taylor."

The woman unwound her flesh from the soiled drapery. "Youngun t' be a Mastr—," she grunted, huffing as she tried to right herself.

Shrugging off Skitters absurd title, I urged Will to heft her other arm, and we managed to lug the wobbling widow onto the edge of the creaky bed.

She weighed many stone and her puffy ankles and face added to her corpulence. The voice that resonated with thunderous fortitude while she slept turned so frail we had to strain to catch the meaning of what the agéd woman was saying. This incomprehensibility was compounded by a lack of teeth, so that the crone's speech came out a gummy glossalia no one could decipher but Pru—and she did so with consummate skill.

In fact, the one so fetching and the other sadly worse for her earthly trials, at once fell in as if they'd known each other a lifetime. On and on they whittie-whattied about purslane, hyssop, tobacco, and pennyroyal. All the while, I let my gaze rove the cobwebby corners, looking for voodoo poppets with hog bristles stuck in them, nails, slivered glass and other charms that might convince me she was a witch.

But much as I tried to transform the square face framed by greying hair into a witch, all I really discovered in Goody Cole's rheumy eyes was a look of confusion and loss. Once more I searched her bare arms and what bosom was showing for a devil's teat or mouse creature. She was surely three-quarters of a century, yet her skin was remarkably soft and luminous. I gave up in shame and not a little self disgust.

As Goody Cole shuffled outdoors with Pru close behind her, a clap of thunder sent Skitters down the path at a run.

"I'm late," he yelled from a distance. "Meet you— morning— at the inquest."

The old woman peered after Skitters' flying heels and pulled a black shawl over her head, bowing in abject misery.

Pru led her back inside and Will and I followed.

"I'm staying," she announced, helping the ancient woman back onto the bed. "You and Will take my room at Tuck's Ordinary. It's way too far to return to the boat landing in this storm. Besides, Mistress Cole is afraid. She needs me to look after her."

"Are you not afraid, too?" I whispered.

Pru stepped back outside with her hands on her hips.

"Whatever of? Tansy and balm of Gilead? Goldenseal and swamp root? Why, Thom, can't you see the elders of this town are sadly wanting in Christian charity? Shoalers wouldn't treat a hog the way Goody Cole's being treated and you know it. Run to Tuck's Inn before you lose your way in this God-forsaken place!"

Mister Deering at once noticed we had returned without Pru and tried his best to add a surcharge for another bed. When Will and I agreed to share the cramped accommodations he griped, "Well, you won't be sharing vittles now, will you?" and thrust his hand out for an extra shilling. We were so annoyed that when he'd gone we ordered drink.

Hail the size of grapeshot pelted the sides of the house and flashes of lightning limned the black rolling clouds. It was a wicked evening and the harder it poured the more ale we poured down our gullets. A handful of garrulous guests were finishing up at the board. Will tugged me forward so I nearly fell off my stool and slapped my back, striking his tankard so hard against mine that an earthenware chip flew off and nearly hit me in the eye.

> *Bring us no eggs for there be too many shells,*
> *but bring us good ale, and give us nothing else.*

Familiar with his drinking song, I bellowed back at the top of my inebriate lungs.

> *Bring us no mutton for that is often lean.*
> *Nor bring us no tripe for here they're seldom clean.*

Mister Deering hurried over.

"Sit to table or clear out," he ordered. "I won't have you rowdy Shoalers disturbing my paying guests, understand?" His eyebrows emphasized 'paying' in explicit parenthesis.

Elated that our disturbance unwittingly led to a dinner invitation, we immediately pulled our stools up to the table.

Will pinched my leg. I looked straight from the gnarled hands serving us into the bold eyes of a full-blood Indian squaw and started at the encounter. She also flinched, then smiled and dished us inordinate large portions of salsify pudding, fresh chunks of tender salmon, salad greens, and a peculiar pile of unidentifiable leaves. This was the first time since I'd left England that I'd eaten respectable food off proper porcelain, and I savored each bite with great relish, that is until I came to the leaves.

The squaw who was brushing crumbs from the table carpet pointed at the leaves that had the look of chopped tobacco with spittle, and I suspected tasted a deal worse.

"Tea," she said.

I swallowed a spoonful, washing it down with ale. Will spat the stuff unceremoniously onto the floor.

Mister Deering appeared and looked down at us with arch disapproval. "Waumausu is the best cook in all of Hampton. In case you lads aren't aware, that is highly prized green tea from China sold to me by a Dutch trader. He plans to market it in Boston and you are fortunate to be among the first New Englanders to eat this tea. I daresay you'll be bragging about it when the herb catches on in Massachusetts Bay."

He went on and on, which gave Will and me time to stow away the pudding, salmon, and several slices of ginger cake. Every once in awhile I pretended to eat the disagreeable substance, spitting mouthfuls of it into my empty tankard. Will made no pretense of his dislike for the stuff, continuing to spit it onto the plank floor. If Mister Deering weren't such an odious person I'd have been embarrassed. But by then I was too drunk to care, and took amusement in the thought that Will was the spitting image of his father.

Mister Deering ordered the Indian woman to sweep the soggy leaves from the floor and banished us to our quarters.

Apprehension from leaving Pru with an accused witch caused me to toss and turn from one nightmare to another. Goody Cole's kind face turned into that of Satan my black hog. Pru was tied up to a whipping post, and Mister Deering spat his vile tea leaves onto her bare back. Through this ridiculous battery of dreams, a voice

inside my head recited over and over some lines that had lodged in
my memory from when I was young.

> *Go and catch a falling star,*
> *Get with child a mandrake root,*
> *Tell me where all past years are,*
> *Or who cleft the Devil's foot.*

At dawn I extricated my tired body, used the chamber pot, and
stood at the gable window. From Rand's Hill I watched the sun
pierce the horizon and shoot over the fields and the sparkling ribbon
of river winding from the ocean.

The rhyme in my head took on new meaning as I looked down
at the Meeting House on the cow common. Today was Goody Cole's
inquest. Even now Pru would be helping the ancient woman prepare
for the ordeal. This realization mysteriously produced the final lines
of the verse, jolting me wide awake.

> *And find*
> *What wind*
> *Serves to advance an honest mind.*

8

People were converging on Hampton from every direction. Boats choked Mooring Turn on the river, and at the Meeting House saddled horses with women's pillion cushions were tethered to fence and hitching posts.

Just as we arrived, a Selectman ushered Pru and Goody Cole onto the granite step at the entrance. A rabble of children crowded around her jeering "Witchy Cole, Witchy Cole!" A bold boy ventured up and hit her lame flesh with his open palms yelling:

> *Old Goody Cole*
> *of Little Boar's Head*
> *sickens newborn infants*
> *until they lie dead.*

Pru shielded the ancient woman from the threats and blows of the taunting crowd. Will and I grappled forward and were confronted by a constable who officiously secured the entrance. "Yer not from these parts," he stated, crossing mammoth arms over his barrel chest.

"We be Shoalers," Will declared, fight in his voice.

"Well, this hearing be fer dignitaries and Hampton folk only."

Skitters crawled through an opening and bounced up like a jack-in-the-box near his brother.

"They be wi' me, Sir." He smiled winsomely at the constable.

"And when 'ave I ever set eyen on ye?"

"I be wi' Mister Green, Sir."

"Then where be the Green folk?"

During this dull discussion the restless crowd pressed forward by increments, pinning us against the stocks. Will fell onto the ducking stool which fortunately was fast secured by a rope.

Master Cutt materialized and quickly vouchsafed for us.

The constable stood Colossus large in his path. "And pray who be ye? The King of England?"

"Surely ye've heard tell of John Cutt, Esquire, of Great Island. I be his brother Robert."

The constable mopped his dripping brow, letting the prestige of the name sink in.

"The boy boards with the Greens of Hampton," Master Cutt placed a hand on his rapier for emphasis, "and these older lads be in my employ."

The constable waved him through with Skitters, but dismissed Will and me with a perfunctory grunt.

Hampton notables and wives dressed in Sunday best flowed through the entry like a bright rivulet of ants while we milled despondently with a score of women and children beneath a horse chestnut. All of a sudden Skitters burst through the ebbing tide and called across to us.

Beset with duties, the red-faced constable barked, "I thought I told ye to go in."

"I be wantin' a word wi' my brother, Sir."

Skitters' pluck worked on the security officer. "Well hurry up, boy, or I'll give ye a solid kick in the ass."

Skitters took us aside with a hurried scheme. "Back of the

Meetin' House there be a hole. Crawl through and behind the chimbley be a stair. In the garret ye'll find plenty of cracks to observe the hearing. But hurry, Will." he whispered, "the Selectmen be seated."

The constable stepped inside and let the iron bar fall with a resounding clunk.

Will and I ducked behind the long building, startling a hedge-hog as we clambered through the dank cellar hole and hurried up a flight of rotting stairs. At the top we met a handful of other curiosity mongers already sprawled belly down at openings in the plank flooring.

Contrary to expectations, the testimony was delayed while a Selectman read a list of assize statutes and regulations recently issued by the Massachusetts Court.

Bored to tears I sauntered over to the sooty gable window where torn wedding banns, old postings, and advisements cluttered a dusty table top. At random I picked one from the pile and took the ripped parchment over to Will who, exhausted from my twisting and turnings the previous night, was fast asleep.

"Heyday, Will." I shook him. "Listen to this warrant dated over ten years past. It says:

> TO THE CONSTABLES OF DOVER,
> HAMPTON, SALISBURY, NEWBURY, ROXBURY, DEDHAM.
> You are required in the King's name to take vagabond Quakers, Anne Colman, Mary Tomkins, and Alice Ambrose and make them fast to the cart's tail, and driving the cart through your several towns, to whip them upon their naked backs not exceeding ten stripes apiece in each town; and so to convey them from Constable to Constable till they are out of this jurisdiction or you will answer at your peril.
>
> THIS BE YOUR WARRANT
> Richard Walderne
> Dover Dec 22 1662

Will yawned and rubbed his eyes. "Yea, they got far as Salisbury where Major Pike told the round 'eads to whistle for the rest. He told em it would be a blot on em for all futurity."

"And this took place here in Hampton?"

Will nodded and yawned again.

"Then Goody Cole is doomed to a similar fate."

Before Will could answer, three loud thumps sounded on the floor below and we dove for the crack like sand crabs into their holes.

I scrutinized the Magistrate in his fine apparel, imagining I was on a scaffold at a theatrical. And I might well have been, for the man conducted himself in a booming baritone which inflected insinuations and whittled accusations to a bare whisper. Never had I heard speech with such insidious intent. If anyone had charmed the devil, it was this court-appointed advocate.

Goody Cole sat in an obscure corner with Pru while the fop in tight curls and French laces held center stage with his liquid litigation:

"Before the Court sits Eunice Cole, an aged ward of Hampton who took up residence in 1644 and has been the gapeseed of this God-fearing town ever since. Consider the charges against this Witch of Endor who on no less than five separate occasions has been presented to court. I request that the jury entertain no doubt as to her guilt."

Will and I looked up and down our crack hoping to catch a glimpse of the Selectmen. But our line of vision was sorely limited, and we immediately returned to the upper-cruster in his embroidered doublet and stifling trunk hose who dished out his sophistry as though he were Boston's own Cotton Mather.

"In 1645 Eunice Cole was charged by the Salisbury Court for slanderous speech. In 1647 Mister and Mistress Cole were sued in a matter of swine appropriated from the Hampton constable. In 1660 the devious woman was prosecuted for unseemly speech with her neighbor Hulda Hussey. Should I go on?"

Though the question warranted no response, to my surprise several voices from below chimed their approval.

"In 1662 Abraham Godfry testified that a hollow unearthly voice issued from Goody Cole's hut as if from an earthen jar and witnessed he saw a shimmering red apparition in her chimney corner. Mark me well," the Magistrate declaimed, "the Court ruled: 'Widow Cole, not having the fear of God before her did on the 24th of November in that year enter into covenant with the Devil' "

A mutiny of gasps pierced by a child's shriek at the back of the hall were silenced by the hoisting of the Magistrate's doily-fringed sleeve:

"I've reviewed the testimony of these past occasions and found the Hampton Selectmen lenient to a fault. While Eunice Cole was lodged at the Boston Gaol, her invalid husband William transferred his wife's half of their estate to Goodman Webster in return for the neighbor's care during the remainder of his natural life. His will appropriated Goody Cole the clothes on her back. Now, Gentlemen of the Assize, be apprised that the Hampton Court in its charitable mercy decided to allot Goody Cole half of the estate totaling £ 59 pounds sterling."

"Ur od ur saen pian!" Goody Cole's head shook and wavered. "Ur od ur saen Pi-an," she repeated dolefully.

The Magistrate raised an eyebrow. "I beg your pardon?"

Pru's auburn ringlets cascaded down her proud straight back as she stood and faced the Magistrate.

"If you please, Sir, Widow Cole says 'it were a God-forsaken pittance.'"

This time the ruffled sleeve had no effect whatsoever silencing the hubbub. Choosing to ignore the outburst, he raised his voice and continued:

"The remaining £ 8 pounds was put in trust by Hampton Select-men to provide this ungrateful woman with shelter, firewood, and food. Time and again the record proves this town magnanimously has tolerated Goody Cole's complaints, insults, and outrageous enchantments. In particular, I would like to remind the jury of the mysterious and sudden death of a year old infant whose mother refused to let Mistress Cole act as midwife at her lying in."

Goody's black brimmed bonnet shook and circled in the air like a cormorant drying its sodden wings in a sea breeze. "Unt aye alt. Or ass ad all ox," she moaned.

The coxcomb impatiently gestured for Pru to stand and translate.

"Sir, Goody Cole says 'It wasn't my fault. The poor lass had small pox.'"

"And who might I be addressing to sort out this wretched woman's incomprehensible gibberish?"

Pru raised her chin and I saw the tip of her pert nose. "I am Prudence Monforte of the Isles of Shoals, Your Honor."

Put off by her speech which showed breeding equal his own, the Magistrate sniggered.

"Ah, the glorious Isles of Shoals where one man in fifty owns a cow, and the Almighty cod reigns at Sunday Meeting."

Pru did not rise to the bait. She sat back down.

The ancient woman, exhausted by the strain of the hearing, slipped into a bowed sleep. Will rolled over and sighed. It was abominably hot in the garret and I too was growing torpid and listless.

The Salisbury Magistrate took out a pouch of snuff, pinched it into his flared nostrils and waited for a sneeze while the clerk of writs scribbled into a record book. When he had finished he stood and announced:

"Goodwife Bridget Clifford, please bring the child Ann Smith before the bench."

My eyes traveled the crack like a halibut skimming the shoreline for dinner.

A grammy woman accompanied a young girl before the Magistrate. I could see how Skitters had been smitten by the lass. Her face was round and fair as a porcelain doll's with ruby lips and long dark eyelashes. Her straight chestnut hair was simply tucked beneath a white lace pinner cap which matched a summer shift drifting above her ankles.

Looking up and pointing directly at the plank through which we peered down, she cried, "Oh Lucifer, how thou art fallen from heaven!"

Will clapped his hand over his mouth to stifle an exclamation.

Fear crept into my being, too. The girl was much too distant to discover us, and yet I felt as if she had poked my eyes out. The more I stared at the pale moon face, the more skeletal it became. This odd sentiment of starvation so unnerved me that I had to turn away. For although the child by all appearances was well fed, her brown eyes seemed to hide an insatiable hunger.

The grammy woman held tightly to the small girl's hand and glared at Goody Cole.

"Tell the jury your name and the reason you have lodged a disposition against Eunice Cole," the clerk ordered.

"I am Bridget Clifford, mother to Sarah Clifford and wife of William Clifford. We took Ann Smith in when her stepmother remarried, and she be like my very own daughter." The woman made a show of hugging the silent child.

A thin smile visited Ann's lips and disappeared fast as the aroma of a fatty soup on a passing schooner.

The Magistrate curled his blond mustache with his ring finger, raised an eyebrow, cleared his throat of phlegm.

"Goodwife Clifford, your complaint?"

"Aye. Well I sent Ann Smith to the cabbage yard to select one fer supper and I heard her cry out in the orchard."

"And this would be?" The Magistrate twiddled a curl on his gold wig.

"This would be the orchard back 't house, Your Judgeship."

The Magistrate swatted at a mosquito with his muckinder and loomed at the grammy woman as if he'd enjoy giving her a swat, too.

"This is not a trial, Woman. I am an advocate sent by Justice Jonas Clark of Salisbury to hear depositions against this alleged witch, and I wish to know the year, Goodwife Clifford. The year!"

"Ahh—! Well your Avo—, Sir, that would be sixteen and seventy-three."

"Proceed."

"Ann was cryin' so pitiful that my daughter Sarah put her in the cradle and rocked her."

The Magistrate hoisted a lace sleeve and she obediently halted.

"Tell me, Goodwife Clifford, how old is this child?"

"Nine, Your Estimable Advocacy."

His mouth simpered at her ridiculous title.

"Isn't she rather old for a cradle, Woman?"

The Hampton grammy sighed and looked affectionately down on Ann Smith.

"Well, she be the babe of the family."

He slapped the noisome mosquito, leaving a dot of blood that resembled a beauty mark on his white powdered cheek.

"Proceed."

"Well, when we finally calmed the poor infant down with a nip of Barbadoes and the rockin', she told us what happened."

"Pray, tell." The Magistrate's initial vigor waned into the impatient tone of ennui.

"Well, Your Estimable Advoship, Ann related that whilsts she were collectin' the cabbage this old woman come in a blue cap, apron, and white neck clout, and carried her under the persimmon tree. The woman insisted Ann must come live with her."

"And is this kidnapper you describe present in this Meeting House?"

"Aye, Sir. There!"

Goodwife Clifford pointed out Goody Cole who listed her slumbering head on Pru's shoulder.

Meanwhile, the Magistrate thoughtfully studied Ann Smith who had not moved or shown the slightest expression since her initial outburst.

"Proceed."

"Well, Sir, my daughter Sarah and I saw a bump on Ann's fore'ead so we asked where she'd got it and Ann told us: 'The old woman struck me on the 'ead with a stone, turned into a little dog, and ran into the tree. When I looked up she flew away like an eagle.' "

Recollecting Goody Cole maneuvering her decrepit body over the edge of her bed like a lumbering Man-of-War, it was hard to envision her flying, much less climbing a tree. The Magistrate must have had the same trouble conceiving it, for he dismissed Goodwife Clifford with a flick of his ring studded fingers.

Crushed by his preemptory manner, she argued, "But don't you want to hear Ann Smith's testimony? She been practicin' a week altogether."

He leaned over and petitioned, "Do you have ought to add, Ann Smith?"

The girl smiled sweetly. Her dark gaze sucked him in like a ravenous diner tonguing a marrow bone, and the accusatory finger that had raised heavenward now shot from her arm and pointed at Goody Cole. But the effect she desired was lost. For the ancient defendant dozed peacefully unaware of the girl's voracious appetite to destroy her.

When the complainants resumed their places at the back with the other women, the same beefy constable who had denied us access to the proceedings was called to stand testimony.

The entire time, Will had been fidgeting with a knot in the pine plank and it was so damned annoying I growled for him to quit. He promised he would if I'd loan him my blade. He'd left his at the inn and wanted to pry the knot loose so we could see the jury. To keep him quiet, I unsheathed my brother's dagger and thrust it into his outstretched hand.

The Hampton constable already was midway through his speech: "And it were me that took Goody Cole's food to her. She complained it was inferior to what had been brought afore, and oncet she threw it at me. Another occasion, she crabbed the ground with her stick and picked her way around the cow common to badger my wife and me in person. After that, we ne'r could make decent bread at home but it would stink rotten and proved terrible loathsome."

The old woman roused herself. Her black hat circled and shook and she gurgled a gummy retort.

"W'nt fit ea."

Pru stood.

"Your Honor, Goody Cole says: 'It wasn't fit to eat.'"

The constable's thick neck reddened and he planted his boot heels firmly apart.

"The cursed witch enchanted our oven wi' her putrid stench. And that ain't all. After she quarreled with Hampton's night watchman, he fell dreadful sick."

The knot Will had been working with the sharp knife point bounced on the floor below so that now we could see the jury. Unfortunately, my prized knife hurtled through the crack as well, grazing the constable's sleeve and sticking in the soft pine floor with a resonant twang.

Horrified, I stared through the knothole at the astonished jurors and the constable's broad-beam shoulders.

"That be Eunice Cole's doin!" he ranted, running his hand over the tear in his shirt sleeve. "If makin' objects appear from nowhere ain't witchin', I don't know what be!"

Without bidding, Pru rushed over and examined the wound in an attempt to appease the riled constable. We all stared as she pulled off her bodice piece and tied it round his arm.

"It's only a scratch, Your Honor," she said, looking up at the Magistrate with her clear green eyes.

The Magistrate nodded distractedly, scrutinizing overhead where our eyes were fixed fast as nails in a coffin. Delegating two sizable louts seated toward the back, he ordered them to the garret for search and seizure.

Will made a dash for the stairs and I barreled pell mell after, with half a dozen others not far behind. But our escape hatch had been plugged by the brute men, who marched us single file around to the front entrance and straight up the aisle to the Court Magistrate.

Barefooted and with his shirt tail hanging, Will looked a miserable sight, and I cut no fine figure either, so worn was I from lack of sleep. I worried that we could be indicted for attempted murder and no one would believe us, for Hampton folk were none too fond of Shoalers.

Glad for the diversion from the tedious Provincial Assize, the Magistrate commanded, "Constable, pull out that blade and hand it to me."

The constable stepped back and stared as though the dagger were a two-headed rattlesnake. Sucking in a large breath, he grabbed the hilt of the knife and yanked it from the worn board. When this feat had been accomplished with no smoke, flying horseshoes or other appurtenances attributed to the devil, he held the dagger aloft proud as Arthur extricating the sword from the stone. Holding it like a lady displaying her finest silver plate, he presented the dagger to the Magistrate.

The sight was so comical I smiled, though my heart ached at the loss of my brother's knife. My spirits sunk even deeper when the fop held it up for all to see.

"A right handsome dagger, finely wrought with hand-chasing and an elegant tooled leather hilt," he declaimed. "None of you wasters seems worthy of such a blade. Still, I suspect the owner would hate to part with such a treasure. I'll ask only once before confiscating it. Will the rightful proprietor of this blade step forward?"

Will gave my hand a hard squeeze to keep mum. I reciprocated, though cursing him under my breath for his carelessness. As for the others, they beheld the dagger in a daze, no doubt believing like the constable that it had materialized from thin air.

"So be it. Constable, you may keep the dagger in your possession since it obviously was intended for you." The Magistrate sniggered at his wit and stepped down from the high bench. He approached the Hampton Selectmen, returning to his former oily declamatory of the morning. They absorbed it smooth as mutton fat on chapped hands, each vying for a glance or nod from the powdered dandy.

"And therefore, bringing this inquest to a close, do any Selectmen have any particular to add concerning the indictment against Good Widow Eunice Cole of Hampton?"

A yeoman oddly dressed in soiled leather leggings and a fancy brand new cravat stood up. Dewy drops glistened on his brow and his sunburnt lips quivered with the bold delivery his wife had urged him to make before he had left hearth and home. He'd rehearsed it over and over, yet when finally he had the chance to deposit it in the port of call, he reefed on his own importance.

"I 'ave one. Er—Ahhh—Just" He started over. "I 'ave somethin' to add, yer Honor."

The Magistrate sighed.

"Proceed."

"It be just this, that ummm. Let us see."

He fumbled with a parchment which in all likelihood he could not read, for from where I was standing I could see he held it upside down.

"Huh, she—Goody Cole set upon the Selectmen whilst they were in meetin' to demand help with wood and other comforts we already provided her with. She vexed us no end with her complaint. Ah—now let me see. Ah, where were I?"

The Magistrate's tether had run out.

"Her complaint," he snapped.

"Ah!" With the facility of a parrot promised a sweetmeat he recited: "She complained that we could help Goodman Robie, he being a lusty man, but she, a weary old woman, could have none."

Another Selectman shoved his fellow townsman onto the bench and took his place.

"Your Honor."

A quizzical eyebrow.

"I would further like to interject and amend that the following day Goodman Robie's three cattle strangely died."

The clerk, who already had closed his record book with a loud crack, meekly reopened it and penned this final statement. The Magistrate adjourned the assembly and hastened out.

By the time we reached the entry with Widow Cole, they'd decamped, leaving Pru, Will, and me to barge her voluminous body back along the river path.

The oppressed old woman who allegedly enchanted ovens and flew like an eagle collapsed in a heap on her soiled trundle and fell into a commonplace snore. Pru set her out a bowl of curd and loaf of bread a farm woman had given us, and we departed.

Glad to be out of doors for awhile, Pru took off her bonnet and let her curls dance over her shoulders in the sunlight. Will skulked in the shade.

I was in no mood to let him off the hook without an apology.

He barred his teeth and spat on the ground. "That shittabed Hampton constable. If he had let us into the Meetin' House in the first place I'd never have dropped your knife."

It wasn't the apology I wanted, but figured it was close as any Babb could get to remorse.

Pru insinuated herself between us.

"I just remembered! The constable invited me to sup at Rob's Ordinary in the village, and I don't plan squandering the opportunity."

I gripped her arm. "Pru, surely that oaf entertains crude ideas. Let him be."

She tossed her head insolently. "That fellow? Why he couldn't catch a minnow in a basket. Bowels o' Mercy, Puker—!"

I relented, realizing it was useless to squelch the lass's designs.

"Do be careful," I entreated.

"And you two eat something at the inn." She searched in her satchel full to the brim with herbs, twigs and roots. "I have a shilling here somewhere."

I touched her gently, letting my fingers slip down to rest on her hand. "We men have our ways, too. Don't we, Will?"

His stomach growled.

Pru laughed. "Well, You'd better hurry before you turn into dogs and fly into a tree!"

The Indian woman, Waumasu, saw us climbing up Rand's Hill and motioned us to the back of the inn. Mister Deering had told her of the scene at the Meeting House and instructed her to throw us out on our ear.

Will quickly collected his belongings and we were about to hightail it when the squaw gestured us over to a bare patch of sand. Lowering gracefully to her knees, she scooped away the sand and removed an old piece of canvas to reveal a layer of steaming seaweed. Having tried Mister Deering's tea, I wasn't about to eat seaweed no matter how good a cook she was and, refusing with a wave of my hand, I politely stepped back. But remaining on her knees, Waumasu continued to draw aside the cooking damp seaweed.

To our delight, beneath the steamy layer of sea wrack and kelp were a bushel of the largest most redolent smelling quahogs I'd ever set eyes on. Will and I gulped down a few dozen on the spot, accompanied by a moist piece of Indian bread and tankard of well water. Regretting I had nothing in return for the feast, I offered to hoe her corn patch. She beamed her thanks, running into the inn for a pot of herring heads which we dug into the base of each corn sprout.

It was nightfall before we stumbled up the ladder to the deck of Cutt's schooner. Will went off and slept by himself, leaving me to a nightmare in which Pru pressed the cold steel of my brother's knife firmly against my gut. "I did it, Thom. I did it!" she rejoiced, rubbing my stomach in provocative circles with the flat blade as though I were an oiled grindstone.

The sooner we were back on the Shoals the better, I thought, waking long enough to discharge my cocked pistol over the deck.

9

Something jabbed into my thigh. I reached down, and as if by divine miracle discovered my brother's knife. Pru sat beside me laboring at a snarl of hair with a broken-toothed comb. She smiled at the glint of the knife which I held close to my heart. But somehow the perversity of stubborn pride would not let me show how glad I was.

"The constable had his way with you, then!" I croaked, hoarse from the morning air on the river.

She pinched color into her cheeks. "My hair is in such a tangle. I must look a fright."

"Oh no, Pru," I whispered, locking her in my memory, "I've never seen you so lovely."

She pinched her cheeks again and without the least modesty, began lacing her bodice which she had loosed for the night. The thought of that ruddy ox of a constable handling her smooth olive skin sent me into the doldrums.

Pru moved closer. "Here, Thom, cut this snarl out with your knife, will you?"

I took a lock of her auburn hair between my fingers and sliced at the burnished knot, stuffing the little nest of hair into my breech pouch when her back was turned.

She whirled around.

"Oh Thom, how could you possibly think the Hampton constable had his way with me? The truth is, I had my way with him—though for awhile I thought myself in dire straits, for he's a giant and it took much longer than I'd reckoned to get him drunk as a sailor."

Her gaze darted to the wharf where Master Cutt engaged in deep converse with the Salisbury Magistrate.

Taking refuge behind a barrel, I thrust the knife into my belt before they could see it.

"Nay, that will not do!" she whispered. Digging beneath my belt with her soft fingers she swiped the knife and buried it in her satchel, arranging bunches of twigs and blossoms around it as they boarded.

Decked out even more flamboyantly than the preceding day, the Magistrate winked at Pru whose blush and breathlessness he attributed to his own irresistible charm.

"Good day, Mistress Monforte, an exceptional day for sailing to Salisbury."

She curtseyed. "Good Morn, Sir. Then you are on your way to Salisbury by sea?"

Robert Cutt scowled and answered her, tapping an official ribbon-bound scroll against his leg. "I have orders to deliver Goody Cole to Salisbury by water," he announced.

The Magistrate bowed close as he dared to ogle Pru's fine complexion. "Mistress Monforte, if ever you are in need of counsel—for whatever reason—please consider me your humble servant."

At this particular moment a country cart rattled up to the piling with the ponderous hulk of Goody Cole fastened by a chain to its tail.

Pru's green glance seethed. "Dear Sir, I'd rather be confined in a leglock like this miserable woman than be on the receiving end of your counsel!"

Master Cutt stepped forward to apologize for Pru's temper.

The Magistrate chuckled. "I've partaken of strong Barbadoes drink, and now that I've had a taste of their women, I find both quite intoxicating."

Goody Cole was bodily hoisted into a wheel barrow and teetered up the gangplank by a pair of stevedores. The old woman's abundant girth would not fit the cabin opening and Skitters, who had come to see us off, went with Will to fetch a captain's chair to secure her aboveboard.

Pru implored Robert Cutt to loosen the leg shackle. He promised he'd attend to it after we'd safely cast off and were past the Block House on Great Boar's Head.

As I untethered the shore rope from the piling, the fop flourished his plumed hat, ecstatic to be rid of the annoying prisoner.

Pru turned her back on him. "They might as well drive a stake through her miserable heart," she objected over the scraping and churning of our departure.

The salt air and sight of the Isles of Shoals once again filled me with joy. Bottlenoses dove in and out the blue wake, and on the port side, Boar's Head reared into the cloudless sky. Such days are God-created for the gratefulness of mankind, and I hummed a tune hoisting the foresail.

Captain Cutt gave Will the key to unlock the leg iron from Goody Cole's swollen ankle. One could not help feel sorry for the old woman cast hither and thither at the merciless whim of the Massachusetts Court. Her eyes were puffed with disease, and a clump of grimy grey hair escaped the brimmed hat that rode upon her large head like an ominous black nimbus. She burped and retched in the bobbing billows—her skin a sickly verdigris.

I thought of the Quaker women who had been so courageous in their belief while I, fickle to the core, took part in the delivery of this sunken old dame helpless as a leviathan on the beach.

Cutt's two-masted hermaphrodite with the foremast of a brig and the main mast of a schooner allowed the three of us to man the vessel, provided we kept hopping about. But the heavy load of salt in the hold decidedly was slowing our progress. Even with a stiff tail-wind, we wouldn't reach the Merrimack River until sundown, which meant another stopover in Salisbury before our return to the Shoals.

In passing, I offered a few words of assurance.

"We have fair weather, Mistress Cole."

She cast her bleary eyes heavenward. "Wa air weth."

Pru shook her head disconsolately. "Goody says: 'It was fair weather.'"

Preoccupied by securing one of the rig yards, I paid the odd comment little heed—until a shadow fell on me fast as burlap on the head of a condemned man. A black cloud blotted the sun and large drops pelted my uplifted face. Never had I witnessed such a rapid sea change.

Goody Cole pulled the ungainly black bonnet brim down so only her smiling lips were showing. Alarmed by the inexplicable weather and her peculiar levity, I dashed aft. The rising wind buffeted my course and I gripped lanyards and yards for support, beating a hasty path to Captain Cutt. He peered into the sheet of rain blowing horizontal midship; hail glittered and rolled like brimstone over the tar swabbed deck.

With scant time to deliberate on his orders, I hauled down the main sail. A bolt of lightning struck so close it singed the hairs of my nostrils and lit up the square rigged worn face of the water-logged woman.

Pru hovered near her ward, an ornate Spanish cross pressed to her lips. Strangely, not a hint of fear appeared on the face of our drenched prisoner, and a shipwrecked smile lingered at the corners of her sallow lips.

Captain Cutt blew clear across the deck and crashed into me.

"We must set to whilst the gale abates!" he yelled, crawling on his hands and knees toward the hatch. "I'll not jeopardize my boat for that pompous round-'ead Magistrate. He'll have to find one of them feckless Hampton toads to do his bidding."

No sooner had he spoken than a comforting bight splendid as New Jerusalem presented itself on the coast. Captain Cutt brought us around and into a strangely becalmed cove.

I paid out the rope to the bottom of the lagoon, dropping the killick anchor of spruce crotch weighted down with hefty stones.

I was thinking how Divine Providence had brought us to safety when a swarm of mosquitoes thirsty as leeches attacked every bare patch of my flesh. Shoalers had little experience with stinging insects, protected as we were by the sea breeze and our distance from spawning shore marshes.

The women covered their exposed faces from the aggravating hoard while Will and I danced, swatted, and finally ducked under a canvas sheet with the mosquito legion hot in pursuit. Captain Cutt disappeared into his cabin and returned a few moments later portering a large bottle of Canary. He poured a cup for Goody Cole and Pru, and we took turns at the golden spirits from the bottle.

Goody Cole raised her cup. "Oo ooturity," she crooned, happier than I'd seen her.

Pru pointed to a rainbow encompassing the Isles in an arch of azure, emerald, and ruby light.

"Goody says, 'To futurity.'" She added, "On the Barbadoes, Féfé women divine futures in the rainbow."

Delirious with release from the tension of the storm, I brandished the bottle.

"To Prudence Monforte, a seafaring maiden of noble beauty, and to her native home of Barbadoes."

Goody Cole grinned, her pink gums shiny as the inside of a whelk. "Wool eans rue arm. Ut om ee consan i's laa."

Pru shivered. I offered to fetch her a covering from the cabin, but she shook her head.

"Well, we be waiting," Will urged, nodding impatiently at the old crone.

Pru wrung out the hem of her skirt, pretending not to hear.

"What did Goody Cole say?" Will insisted.

The old woman picked up Pru's soft young hand and engulfed it in her wrinkled liver-splotched grasp. Unable to grab it away, the girl relented.

"She says: 'Will means Pru harm. But Thom be constant in his love.'"

I ducked back under the canvas, mortified by the embarrassment of her revelation.

Will seized the empty flask, wound up his arm, and flung it into the sea. "Poppycock! The old woman's crazy as a louse."

"Otch out or I'll urse yer othe."

Pru fixed Will with an insolent look. "Goody says: 'Watch out or I'll curse your mother.'"

"You wouldn't dare, you old witch. I'll set my father's ghost on ye, and ye both can stew in hell!" he yelled, frenzied by the incessant buzz of mosquitoes and arrogant with drink.

Robert Cutt picked up the chain and dangled it before the ancient's rheumy eyes.

"Watch yer tongue, woman. I'll 'ave no curses aboard my ship."

Goody Cole grinned. "Wown ee er shh er lon. Ul ee om's."

Cutt crossed his arms. "Confound the thornback! What in the devil does she say, Pru?"

Pru again pretended not to hear.

"Well, lass, out with it!" he ordered.

"She says—Oh, Mister Cutt, please, Sir, don't make me repeat what she says, for the poor woman has lost her reason."

Robert Cutt started to fasten the leg iron back on Widow Cole's ankle.

"All right, Sir. I'll tell if I must. She says: 'It won't be your ship for long. It'll be Thom's.'"

10

Several old-timers moved lock, stock and barrel to the Main rather than endure another cruel winter on the barren Isles. Babb's ordinary sagged and buckled in sad need of repair. Will and I shored up the stones best we could, but no sooner had we chinked one troubled wall than another showed daylight.

To add to these worries, after we returned from Hampton, Mary Babb dragged about scarcely able to keep up with the chores. Most of the time Pru minded three-year-old Peter, leaving him to entertain the old salts while she fetched them their beer. Mister Pepperrell forbade kids in the tavern, but since the roustabout hadn't made an appearance for months, we figured he'd be none the wiser.

A premature sleet storm blew down from Newfoundland early in November swelling our cares, for we'd scarce enough firewood and food to last through January thaw. Trade from my little boat purchased us a bushel each of peas and parch corn, but severe drought drastically diminished the field pumpkins and cabbages.

The day after the icy blast, Will and I shoved off, hoping to take a seal or porpoise. Armed with Phillip Babb's ancient musket, a club, and harpoon points for jigging a handline, we rowed north to Duck Island through the choppy black sea. Waves crashed and sprayed over us and we were relieved to scramble onto the solid, albeit slippery ledge of the island—which had scant to recommend it but a fresh water pond.

I spotted a crested cormorant stuck in the ice like a ship's hull encrusted by ballycater and pulled my dagger from beneath Captain Moody's moth-eaten great coat. The starved bird looked half dead already, but somehow I could not bring myself to plunge the blade into its soft breast. The cook at my uncle's estate had dispatched the barnyard fowl with one twist of their necks. Closing my eyes, I grasped the oily feathered appendage, and pretending the shag was a corked bottle, removed the vacant-eyed head from the ice-imprisoned body. There was one slight impediment to this method, the eyes on the decapitated head continued to blink.

"Will, Will!" I cried.

But Will had problems of his own, having harpooned a gull still very much alive. The herring gull shrieked and hopped up and down, tangling his captor in a mess of jig line. Will resorted to the club, intending to do the garrulous bird in once and for all, but slipped, and seeing its advantage, the gull struck at Will's face with its sharp yellow beak.

"Thom!" he cried.

I raised the musket and put it back down, realizing the ball might hit Will. Quickly I cut the line and watched the raucous gull float away towing the harpoon rigging behind it.

Will stood and brushed the snow off his wool cape, cursing the gull for the loss of our rigging.

"But look, Will," I said, swinging the shag now stiff as a poker by its headless neck. "We've got dinner!!"

By Christmas the snow was piled nearly to the thatch roof. Our peas were almost gone and it took too much precious firewood to boil the parched Indian corn into samp.

Will and I carried Mary Babb to a hinged bed near the kitchen hearth where she could be more comfortable. The toddler sprawled next to her, resting on a plumped eider pillow. He stuck his tiny finger into the dimple on his mother's chin and two other dimples appeared in her pale cheeks.

"Hole," he chortled.

She took his little finger in hers. "That be a dimple, Peter. Can ye say dimple?"

"Dim-pull. Dim-pull," he sang joyously.

Pru stirred a pot of porridge while beneath the bed Satan the pig groaned and snorted in a lethargic stupor. He hadn't had a pail of slops for weeks. I visited and revisited the happiness of Mister Deering's salmon dinner and the succulent quahog clam feast of the summer, wondering how we possibly could survive much longer in such dire straits.

As if reading my mind like a book, Mary gestured me closer. "Don't despair, Thomas. The Lord provides fer 'em that serves him. Yerself and Will dress warmly now and get down to the fish flakes. And don't come back 'til ye 'ave a sledge of wood."

I feared she'd taken a turn and was delirious. Long ago Shoalers had cut down every tree on Appledore to fuel their hearths.

Mary's voice quivered through her son's babble. "The flakes be rotten, Thom. Tear 'em down fer firewood. Ye can rebuild in spring if Mister Pepperrell be so inclined. Pru and I'll tend to the rest."

Taxed by this speech, she sighed and collapsed back onto her pillow. The swift disappearance of his mother's dimples prompted Peter to tumble off the bed and run to Pru's comforting embrace.

Depressed by the inactivity from the string of snow storms and his mother's illness, Will had retired to the tavern with a deck of cards and a bottle. He brightened like a button on an Admiral's coat when I told him what Mary proposed.

Jolly as sea captains setting off across the Atlantic Ocean, we muffled ourselves in jerseys, cloaks and mitts. Shoving the sledge from the shed, we hopped on and flew through the ice-sheeted snow to the shore.

It took the greater part of the morning just to clear the snow off the flakes. The invigoration of the activity bolstered our lagging spirits, and we whooped and shouted as we ripped, stomped, and cracked the rotted boards. Load after load of the bleached wood was hauled to the cold brewery which, for wont of customers, had fallen into disuse.

During the afternoon I looked up to see Pru hurry out the front and down the snow-covered lane toward the well. It had started snowing again. My fingers itched from frostbite, and Will's nose matched the red of his Monmouth cap. We went inside the warm tavern, slapping our numbed hands in an effort to circulate the blood enough to uncork a bottle of rum from the sideboard. It was dark before we finally quit stacking the wood without and within the door.

At the hearth steam escaped from an iron kettle and in amazement I noticed the barrel of peas once more full to the brim. A sack bulging with corn meal kept company beside it. I thrust my hand in and sifted the gold through my tingling fingers. Pru beamed, and I decided not to spoil her delight by pointing out the inconspicuous worms curled within the grains.

She shoveled an ash cake from the hearth and handed me a bowl of porridge to share with Will. The food tasted like manna after forty days in the wilderness.

Mary's good sense had brought us to the other side of adversity and I went over to tell her this, but she seemed far worse. Pru motioned us to let her sleep, banked the fire, and took the children into the back bed chamber for the night.

I ladled leftover porridge into the bowl and shoved it under the bed for Satan. Then, drowsy from the warmth of our sustenance, I dragged my aching body up the ladder to the loft.

Pru often appeared in my dreams, so when I saw her glorious hair tumbling over a white gown and her face glowing in light like the Mother of Christ, I did not wake up.

"Thom, please. Come quickly," the apparition whispered.

Will kicked me in the shin and I sat up with a jolt, annoyed that he'd rouse me from such a compelling vision.

But it was no vision. Pru stood framed in candle light, her face pleading with an urgency that had me on my feet before I fully realized I was naked. Too distraught to notice, she hurried away.

Fumbling with my breeches, I found her at the kitchen hearth wildly throwing wood onto flames reflecting traces of tears on her glowing cheeks.

"What's wrong, Pru?"

She crossed herself and pointed toward the shadowy bed. "Mistress Mary has died."

The pair of pinetree shillings Pru had placed on Mary's eyelids glinted eerily in the firelight. .

Mary Babb gone? She had treated me like her very own son. What would we do without her? The ache of grief lodged in my throat, but seeing the Barbadoes lass warm her trembling hands over the fire, I steeled myself.

"I thought we could move her out to the brewery."

I turned toward the loft to get Will.

"I didn't want to wake the poor fellow," she said with a look in her eyes I hadn't noticed before.

"I can't possibly lift the body myself. Besides, Mary was Will's mother, not mine. You'll have to wake him."

Pru left without a word at my insolence, My pent up grief spilled onto Mary's brow furrowed by the five sons she had borne in a dozen years. Yet to me, her worn face was a landfall of light and understanding.

The sight of broad-chested Will beside his dead mother sent a wave of compassion through me. How manly we thought we were, when in fact we were motherless children. Will swiped his face with a sleeve, took a corner of it and honked his swollen red nose.

Pru stoked the fire thoughtfully. "Don't let the children see her this way, Will."

His eyes rested on her gown which had slipped wantonly off one shoulder. "Why not?"

"They're too young. They won't understand."

"What's to understand?" he asked in a tremulous voice. "That by law she weren't even their mother? That she left 'em destitute?"

"Will, don't start," I pleaded. "Your mother and father were a sight more married than any creatures on God's earth."

"She didn't deserve this," he sobbed. "The scoundrel left her scroungin' like a rat on this stinkin' island!"

I dug my fingers into his shaking shoulders. "Brace up, Will Babb. You aren't the only one in pain. We all loved her."

But he wasn't listening. "Now I'm expected to care for his pukin' bastards!"

I lowered my voice to steady my nerves. "Pru and I are going to wrap your mother in a clean muslin sheet and transport her to the brewery. You can stand there whining or be a man and help."

I stared down at Mary's sallow face. Pru fiddled with a carved cross around her neck and looked at me expectantly. "Would you say some words in Latin, Thom?"

Sorely worn by our misfortune, I wracked my brain while Pru and Will waited in mournful silence. Finally, in a lugubrious voice like Minister Belcher's I entoned:

> *"Et maiores vestros et posteros cogitate.*
> *Mors ultima ratio. Acta es fabula.*
> *Mary Babb, requiescat in pace. Amen."*

What a travesty. The only Shoaler who had treated me with respect and I'd sent her to her grave mumbling: *Think of your ancestors and posterity. Death is the last accounting. The play is over.*

"That was beautiful, Thom," Pru whispered.

Will cleared his throat. "Aye, Thom. Ye be far too gifted to waste yer talent on this—."

Before he could resume his pathetic complaints, I begged him to

help me lug the sledge in from the brewery and roll the body onto
it. As we scraped the sledge runners over the sawdust floor to the
back I sang:

> *Let the world slide, let the world go.*
> *A fig for care and a fig for woe.*
> *If we can't pay, why we can't owe.*
> *And death makes equal the high and low.*

We dumped Mary Babb on the brewery table beneath the hanging lantern where years before Phillip Babb set fire to the traitorous
letter. Pru drew a shawl about her thinly clad flesh and Will's teeth
chattered so, he couldn't stop. Snuffing out the flame, we hurried
back to the comfort of the hearth.

I awoke to the insistent din of knocking. Still in her night shift, Pru
let in a woman swaddled in so much fur she resembled a bear.
Behind her was an equally furry cub.

"Well, I thought ye'd up and gone," the woman exhaled in the
frosty air.

The icy blast of wind cleared my spinning head enough for me
to recall bits and snatches from the preceding evening.

After disposing of the body, Pru had produced a jug Mary kept
for special occasions. The idea that the special occasion was her
very own death struck me as hilarious in a most peculiar way, and
once I started laughing I couldn't stop. Pru and Will fell into a similar disposition, and succumbing to the devil in the jug, as Belcher
would have it, we were merry as a room of drunken sailors.

I 'd lifted my beaker to toast Mistress Babb when Pru cried,
"God have mercy on us. Goody Cole has bewitched and murdered
Mary with her curse!" Her eyes widened with unbridled fear.
"Don't you remember, Thom? Eunice Cole said she'd curse Will's
mother!"

I caressed her smooth, very bare shoulder.

"Goody Cole told Will to watch out or she'd curse his mother, Pru," I said, hoping to calm her. "It was a threat, not a curse."

But my explanation did little to convince her. All of a sudden she started shaking and her eyes jangled in their sockets as if she were terrified out of her wits. I had never witnessed such a strange seizure. Her limbs flew at angles and she shuttled over the hearth like a popinjay. Will and I worried out loud that Pru herself might be under Goody's spell. She knocked over the stool and would have fallen into the fire if I hadn't caught her. Desperate to control the hysterical woman, we tied her arms close to her body with a shawl and gagged her mouth. It was a most sorry way to treat Pru and, seeing her in broad daylight, I blushed with shame at the memory.

Our unexpected guests crawled out of their hirsute cloaks and stared with more than a little contempt on their faces. They eyed Pru's disheveled appearance and Will sprawled on the slawbank with the empty jug still in his hand.

"Well, this be a fine kettle of fish," the woman I knew as Goodwife Hannah remarked.

I managed to stand and tuck my shirt into my breeches, suddenly aware of the prickle of a three day growth on my chin.

"Debora and I come to see how poor Mary be doin'. But I guess ye've shuffled her out back so ye can be at yer fun and games." The woman stepped forward to shield the girl of about thirteen, who until then had been ogling Will's bare torso with an unabashed smile.

From my viewpoint, the most prominent feature of the cub was a mature bosom whose mammothness seemed to dwarf everything, including a prim pair of tiny narrow fur-lined boots peeking from beneath her linsey-woolsey.

"Where be Mary, then?" asked Ursa Major. "It be nearly noon and I brought her some vittles. Deb and I spent all yesterday puttin' up that black pig ye brung us."

Black pig? Black—Oh God—I couldn't—Not—But of course! What else did we have of any value save Satan? Tears coursed down my cheeks. Pru moaned and broke into sobs.

"Well fer the life of me, yer a sorry lot. Show me to Mary at once, ye drunken wretches." Goodwife Hannah steered her daughter past us bosom first like a proudly wrought ship's maidenhead.

Will, who I could tell still was feeling the liquor, jumped up. "Ye'd better put them furs back on if ye plan visiting her in the brewery."

Goodwife Hannah rested her hands on her hips. "The brewery? Sakes, what be Mary doin' out there?"

"She be dead," Will said, smiling playfully at Debora who continued to fix him with her small pale eyes.

Goodwife Hannah dropped the basket she was carrying, opened her considerable mouth wide, and emitted a piercing wail that echoed down the hallway.

Peter and Samson came running from the back with terrified cries for their mother.

Encouraged by Debora's attention, Will swung Peter into the air and caught the child with one powerful arm. With his free hand he opened the basket, removed a trotter, handed the round greasy morsel to five-year-old Samson and took one for himself, gnawing it ravenous as a wolf. Peter drooled and teethed on the other side of the pickled pig's foot.

Reminded of Mary's belief that 'The Lord provides fer 'em that serves themselves,' I went over and offered my hand to Pru in forgiveness.

Goodwife Hannah commandeered Debora toward the door. "Let us know when ye plan the wake," she growled.

Will rubbed oily dribbles from Satan into his chapped hands. "There won't be none."

The ruff of ursine fur nodded. "Aye. This winter has been a particular hardship fer Shoalers what with the death of Mister Baker of Star Island last year, and Robert Cutt's passin' just last week, and now Mary."

Pru dropped onto a stool and held her head in her hands.

"Robert Cutt?" I cried in disbelief. "But he was perfectly vital last we saw him."

Huge in her hides, the woman swayed to the door.

"Aye, all the more reason fer yew young folk to tarry and marry. We Shoalers be depletin'."

At the mention of marriage, the cub, who was putting on her cloak, thrust forward her bosom one last time and licked Will with her eyes. Pru also was looking at Will, but for all he noticed she might as well have been a tree stump.

I excused myself and climbed the ladder to the loft. I would get over the pig. And eventually I'd get over Mary Babb, though her presence would infiltrate the first line of my defenses for some time to come. But I would never get over Pru.

11

*P*epperrell was back. One more year of my indenture and I'd be rid of him. Soon after his reappearance, Robert Cutt's brother Richard summoned Will and me to Star Island; his brother had died and he wanted to know if we'd be interested in a quarter share of the hermaphrodite brig.

Remembering Goody Cole's prediction that I would own Master Robert's ship, I marveled at the offer. Granted, it wasn't an entire ship. But even if I was offered the stern, it was a great boon for an orphan like me.

"Of course we be interested," Will shot off his mouth swift as an unaimed arrow. As it was, he consistently squandered what profit we made from our boat, but I was linked to him like a ball and chain.

Unlike his brother Robert, Richard Cutt calculated ahead of himself, plotting and conniving.

"Ye'll be paid wages for sailing the vessel to Salem, Hampton, and down the Piscataqua River. Yer combined wages'll comprise one share and the two of ye will take a quarter of the trade in credit, barter, or cash."

"Who will be the other partners?" I asked over the drum roll of my excitement.

"Mister Nicholas Shapleigh of Kittery, myself, and possibly Mister Pepperrell."

"But Sir, would our working the ship not comprise at least a third of the trade?" I conjectured.

We were seated on a settle at his brother's stone dwelling on Star Island, and like Babb's ordinary, it could have used some shoring up. A shaft of white spring sunlight pierced a large chink, illuminating Richard Cutt's sagging dewlaps and double chin.

He blinked back his surprise. "Now don't that beat all? Before we know it, Thom Taylor'll be Admiral of the fleet. No, Thom. It be a good try, but two wet-behind-the-ears fifteen year olds be equal to one thirty-year devil like myself."

With the paper signed and in hand, we set a course straight for Pepperrell's house on the south shore. I berthed the boat along a new staging area in the sheltered cove. For half a decade I'd struggled on the Shoals and had only Babb's small shallop and the fourth of a trade schooner to show for it while Pepperrell owned Babb's property, a fishing stage, a recently built manor, a third of a schooner, and no doubt soon he'd make a bid for Cutt's Star property as well.

We knocked on the freshly hewn door and peered through a folio size window of bullet glass, but could see nothing. We were departing when Pepperrell hallooed and trotted robust as a Narraganset stud from the hillcrest. Suddenly, I rejoiced that Pru was saddled with Babb's brats, remembering how women reacted to this energetic man.

"Good day, Mister Pepperrell," I greeted him. "Will and I have signed a partnership for Cutt's brig and were asked to deliver it to you so the schooner could be registered with the proper authorities."

He winked, took the paper, and made a cocky show of his newly acquired reading skills.

As we proceeded down to the cove, he followed. "By the way," he preambled, "I understand ye both be responsible for the disappearance of the fish flakes down at Babb's Cove. Word has it ye burnt 'em fer firewood this winter."

Will yanked angrily at a yard and unhitched the mooring. "The stinkin' flakes was rotten. My mother caught her death from yer neglect and the property fallin' to ruin."

His speech elicited not one cockle of sympathy from the up-and-coming Mister Pepperrell. "I expect both of ye to replace the flakes before the fleet arrives in April or I'll take more than this paper to the proper authorities. Do ye catch my drift?"

I spat at a spring violet harbored in the grass and pretended it was his pretty face. Why did he vex me so? Any fool could see he harnessed the misfortune of others to turn his own wheel of fortune, and where was the reward in that?

A fish flake is a simple construction requiring countless staves of wood hammered in endless straight rows. We were charged with the purchase, payment, transport, unloading, and carpentry of a mountain of staves in two short weeks. My only pleasure came at day's end when Pru beckoned us from the hillcrest.

No sooner had we driven in the last nail than we were ordered to the sheds to clean cod. Pru and six-year-old Samson took over the newly built flakes with a ragtag bunch of orphans that had arrived on a London ship. Will and I suffered the ignominy of working for a loafer who refused to lift a finger while he spun tales of treacherous sea monsters, sinking brigs, grisly plagues and any other yarns tainted with his sinister preference for blood and gore.

I'd just about put up with all I could stand when I learned the fleet was sailing out to Jeffrey's Banke the following morning.

Will and I dashed over to tell Pru. Poor Samson sat on a rock holding his head in his hands, looking more like an old man than a carefree little boy. I hunkered down to his size and smiled. "You know the story of how Samson lost his strength because Delilah sheared his locks?"

He nodded glumly.

"Well, you look just like that, Samson. Won't you give Thom a smile? Tomorrow is a day of rest."

A grin perched on his rosebud mouth. "Truly?"

"Truly. So why don't you go see Peter. He's waiting for you at Grammy Andrews." I gave the kid a push and he skipped away.

Pru smiled. " Thom, you have a wonderful way with children." The late afternoon sun danced over the water, sending a shower of diamond reflections across her bronze face.

Oblivious as usual, Will shielded his eyes with one hand and peered to the north. "Thom, take a look."

I blotted out the western sun with one arm and looked where he pointed. Flames leapt into the blue. "Fire!"

"Aye, and somethin' more."

I looked again. A dark pole loomed from behind the flames and pierced the sky northeast of the island.

"A Maypole!" Will whooped. "They be makin' merry on Devil's Dance Floor."

Pru frowned. "But Will, it goes against Massachusetts law to hoist a Maypole."

"Pru has reason to worry, Will," I said in her defense. "A man was exiled from the provinces for erecting a Maypole out on that spit of land. I read it in the court record when I was helping Minister Belcher over on Church Island."

Will switched his gaze from the bonfire to me. "Aye, my fa told me all about it. A poor devil called Morton was banished from the Shoals fer dancin' around the Maypole. Bowels o' Mercy, Thom, that were half a century ago!" He raced away.

"Don't blame me if you land in gaol!" I shouted after him.

I wanted no part of the pagan pole and the mindless drunken orgy it stood for. But unable to resist Pru's entreating eyes, I relented and went after him. Hearing her panting and stumbling behind me, I stopped short. Didn't she know this wasn't any place for a woman? The revelers might be traitorous free booters and murdering pirates.

"Like the Mermaiden's captain?" she said with a saucy swish of her skirt.

Remembering her pluck in that particular situation, I relented and offered my hand to haul her onto the ledge.

From the headland above the strand we surveyed the enormity of the fire sighted from Babb's Cove. Flames spewed up the cliff-face from the wrecked hull of a ship torched by the merry-makers. Her timbers crashed and exploded fireworks above the secluded pebble beach.

The Dutch pennant aflutter on the mast of the anchored ship didn't bode well. For though the Prince of Orange flag was a familiar sight that year, it was by no means a welcome one. The frigate *Flying Horse* made a villainous habit of plying the Maine coast, storming French forts and looting trading posts of peltry in the name of New Holland. With a dearth of French vessels, Dutch privateers settled for Shoals fishing shallops and coastal traders. Thankfully, our hermaphrodite brig was on the mainland, safely careened at Hampton Harbor for repair and caulking.

Flushed from the heat of the conflagration, Pru and I left the billowing smoke so we might keep Will, who had fallen in with a threesome of carousing brigands, in our sight.

Near the long boat a pair of sailors in leather breeches and bloody shirts turned a live sea turtle over with a grapple hook while a shirtless Blackamoor prepared a bed of coals on which to roast the enormous creature. I winced as they impaled the flippered beast with a pike in order to swing it between them onto the coals.

Indian squaws portered baskets on their heads laden with bunches of short green plantains and bushy crowned pineapples such as I'd once savored on Babb's wharf. My growling vacant stomach advised me it was way past the supping hour.

In the absence of a green sward, the buccaneers had fastened budding shad and huckleberry branches to the top of a cast-off mast and managed to lodge it in a rock crevice.

"Drink and be merry, mates!" shouted a stalwart Cornish man who seemed in charge of the score of revelers.

A swarthy man wearing a fringed crimson sash and wide cuffed boots pushed Will into the clearing near the Maypole. From his dress and what speech I could make out at such a distance, I decided he must be a roving Shoaler come home to raise a rumpus. Will took off his fishing boots and pulled his father's soiled apron over his head. I worried that this might not be a voluntary gesture and he was being coerced by the stocky Shoaler.

Pru gripped my shoulder apprehensively as Will hopped and hobbled in his tender bare feet over the sharp cobbles.

A strapping Flanderkin wearing a wide-brimmed black hat strolled up to the pole. His arm firmly clasped the waist of a bare-breasted Indian squaw. Letting go of the woman, he unlooped a whip from his belt and with extraordinary skill snaked the lariat about Will's ankles, sending him crashing to the ground.

Until now I'd been reluctant to interfere with the cutthroat scoundrels. Their nefarious business obviously included kidnapping, and we very well could end up at Port Royal as Jamaican plantation slaves.

A westerly breeze shifted, wafting the billowing smoke seaward and exposing us to plain view. Afraid one of them might look up and see us, I sequestered Pru behind a shad bush and with a ready hand on my blade crept down the steep embankment. Divine Providence cast the shadows in my favor and I reached the strand unnoticed.

Unfortunately, Pru wasn't as lucky, for while she moved to keep me in her sight she slipped, and an avalanche of pebbles from above brought an immediate bellow from the Cornish captain. Swift as a deer, the Blackamoor slave raced to intercept Pru. I stepped forward into the firelight cursing Will's penchant for trouble.

He gave me a once over. "Look what we have here, men. Boomer the Red!"

I was too preoccupied with Pru's loud protestations to take offense at his likening my hair to a red squirrel's. The black buck shoved Pru past the heckling men to where I braved their jibes. The turtle, whose flesh had been cut from its valuable shell, dripped and sizzled from a roasting platform and onto the coals. The stench of seared meat combined with the creature's ghostly eye sockets produced the queasy sensation that I was the one on the spit.

"Boomer the Red has turned green!" a wag shouted from the dark.

The Flanderkin boatswain came forward and doffed his wide black chapeau. "We be wantin' a Jack o' the Green for our Maypole, Capt'n Williams. Do ye thinks this lad fills the bill?"

"Aye!" the Cornish man agreed. "And the green-eyed wench can be your Queen o' May."

Squaw slaves scattered to gather chokeberry, shad and other dewy flowers on the headland to festoon us.

Meantime, the Blackamoor produced a leather pouch containing a goodly amount of dry leaves which diverted their attention to a peculiar extent. This interruption gave me a chance to devise a plan of escape before the rogues made us the scapegoats of their wanton revels. Will picked himself off the ground and limped over to join us. His arms were scraped, but relieved, I saw the only injury he had suffered was to his considerable pride.

"I'll stand on my head if they want me to, Will," I whispered, "but you've got to get Pru away. Act like you're drunk and drag her into the dark at the first opportunity."

"I'll be needin' yer knife," he whispered.

Not on your life, I was about to tell him, but seeing Pru wide-eyed beside me, I handed it over in the nick of time.

Looking our way, Captain Williams told the Flanderkin to pass the lighted smoking pipe to us. Surprised by his generosity, I accepted the hand-carved elaborate pipe bowl. But I was inexperienced in the draught of the wretched implement, and sputtered and coughed.

The Blackamoor chuckled. "Ai hombre, che chiste." He grabbed the pipe and inhaled deeply. "Si fuma así."

He demonstrated a deep draught.

Pru leaned over with serious countenance. "That man's an escaped Maroon slave from Port Royal. Give these wretches no quarter, Thom!"

I heard what she was saying yet it made little impression on me. Insouciant and relaxed, I reclined on the ledge and watched Will smoke.

A long-tailed animal with a face like the devil howled and performed absurdly comical antics from his perch on the Blackamoor's shiny shoulder. Before I knew it I was laughing so hard I wept. Will shouted for a drink to quench his thirst. The dark man obliged him with a skin filled with Madeira which Will proceeded to squirt about, aiming every direction but his mouth.

"You are smokin' hops or a more potent hemp we called *bangue* on my island, Thom," Pru beseeched.

I sobered somewhat and took her hand. "Dearest Pru, you worry far too much. Look! Yonder come the squaws to deck thee with May flowers and boughs," I poeticized in my uncommon airy dalliance.

The squaws placed a woven wreath of blue flags on Pru's glorious wavy hair and slipped a garland of woodbine over her neck. I completely forgot myself for what seemed hours, luxuriating in the adornment ritual until I realized they had similar designs on me.

The boisterous sailors faded into a dizzy blur as they pushed and spun me around the Maypole. They'd attached so many branches and leaves to my body that I felt like an Abenaki Indian ambushed in greenery. Only a small peek hole around my eyes prohibited me from crashing into the Maypole.

The gang took great pleasure swinging me around their erect

phallic shaft. And the brew in the pipe, embellished with bottles of kill-devil rum and molasses, only added to the gusto of their lascivious chant:

> *Let your delight be in Hymen's joys.*
> *Dance to Hymen now day is come,*
> *about the merry Maypole make room.*
> *Deck green garlands, bring bottles out.*
> *And dispense sweet nectar freely about!*

The strong boatswain sent me careening toward Pru. We collided. "There's nothing but to go along with them," I shouted through a meshy tangle of trailing arbutus.

She whirled gracefully near me, the smile on her lips fixed as in a portrait. "What, Thom?"

"I said—."

But the rogues once more shoved me into orbit around the worm-eaten mast. While I spun endlessly around I recalled the new fishing overseer's tales of atrocity and mutilation. Once he'd seen a Dutch buccaneer tie a string so tight around the captive's neck, the man's eyes popped out. Each pass of the green turtle spread-eagle on the platform vividly brought to mind another tale in which an Hispanic grilled his captive alive over a slow fire.

To evade the buccaneers' outstretched hands and the honed points of their jabbing cutlasses, I moved ever inward toward the towering pole. Chanting and carousing, they too narrowed the circle.

> *Lasses in beaver coats come away,*
> *ye shall be welcome night and day.*

I staggered in stench and sweat, overcome by the danger of their inebriate frenzy. The renegade Shoaler called Edward Uren grabbed Pru and held her so close I heard the breath go out of her. He planted a kiss of spittle and rum-molasses on her lips and tore at the neck of her frock.

I cast an apprehensive glance at one of the gentler squaw slaves seated beside the black man Pru called a Maroon, but she nodded against my interference. Tears of anguish flowed onto the trailing arbutus flowers covering my face. The mockery of their fragrance and of the free loaders suddenly filled me with such indignity that I collapsed at the base of the pole.

From the time Will had stuck the pipe with the odd brew of dry leaves into his mouth, his spirits had altered to the point that now he kept company with the rowdiest of mariners. Swaggering to one side, he swigged and chanted, often thrusting at me with the point of my very own knife. I tried to convince myself his despicable conduct was but a pretense to make a run for it.

Pru fought with dwindled reserves. The wreath drooped over one of her eyes and nothing was left of her outer clothing but a tatter of muslin over a torn camisole. Blackstrap and rum smeared her mouth and her hair was matted with leaves and grime from her fierce struggle with the horny men.

The Flanderkin cleared a path to her. Spitting on a bandolier from around his thick ruddy neck, he rubbed a smudge off her cheek. If ever the opportune moment had arrived it was now. I prayed for Will to come to his senses before the blackguard partook of "Hymen's joys" in earnest.

To my relief Will boldly stepped up to him.

"She be mine."

The Dutch bastard sneered. "Prove it."

Will brazenly walked up to Pru, grabbed her hair with one hand, and forced her head back with the other. She relinquished herself to him like a gunny sack to a stevedore. When I saw her effortless submission I almost wished the Flanderkin had gotten her.

Captain Williams strolled up.

"Best go back to yer squaw," he advised. "This lad obviously has won the affection of the May flower.

"But has he paid for her?" growled the Flanderkin.

"Aye, with a kiss." the Cornish captain said, grinning.

At this, the salts broke into hardy laughter and lewd jests, prodding Will with their cutlasses. "Take her, lad. Take her!" they shouted.

Emboldened by the devil knows what, Will tarried instead of making off with Pru as planned.

"Let them alone!" Captain Williams commanded his ribald crew before returning to his pipe.

Shoaler Edward Uren seized the captain's words, if not their intent. "Aye, let's put 'em adrift in the jolly boat so's they can 'ave a bit of privacy."

The boatswain motioned the Blackamoor and aroused a group of able-bodied men to shove the long boat into the pounding surf. He took the oars from the towed dingy and forced Pru and Will into it.

"Anchor 'em off shore, men," the Flanderkin yelled. "We'll fetch the jolly at dawn."

Depleted of victims, he turned his malicious countenance on the sad heap of wilted branches at his feet—me!

Mister Uren, who never seemed to tire of ideas, sidled up to the bored boatswain. "At Twelve Penny Cove we oncet awarded he 'at could climb the Maypole fer his freedom. Course it were greased," he added.

Hooting and roaring, the Flanderkin snatched a hunk of greasy turtle meat from one of his feasting mates, and kicking me aside, he coated the mast with oil as far as he could reach, which was a good two ell. Reduced to the status of a dog, I gobbled the fallen pieces of meat from the ledge. This abominable scavenging renewed some of my dwindling strength, though not near enough for the ordeal that seemed to lie ahead.

"See that crown of greenery atop the Maypole?" the Shoaler said. "Ye'll be attendin' Sunday Meetin' before ye know it if ye hand me that green wreath up there."

I cowered at the base of the pole asking the Lord's forgiveness for the grievous sins that had brought me to such a pass. The devil Flanderkin flicked his whip. I jumped high as I could, digging with my fingernails into the rotted wood to outsmart him, but the whip cracked and I fell back onto the rock ledge. Brambles poked my chest and scratched my face—for in addition to leaves, the branches had barbs.

Once more the whip struck a resounding twang, and this time I leapt even higher, driving splinters under my nails. The small animal leapt on top of my head and a boisterous cheer arose from below. The creature's wide lugubrious eyes peered into mine through the mask of leaves. I lost my grip, crashing to the ground a second time.

Most of the men were placing bets with the boatswain who swore their currency was safe with him, for he'd never seen anyone climb a greased pole, though once he'd greased his Indian squaw and climbed her to the very top. He guffawed loudly and ran his hands through the shiny pieces-of-eight glinting in the firelight. The Shoaler Mister Uren and a few other lost souls squandered a bag of gold dust on my ascent.

There was slim possibility that greasy phallus of Beelzebub was mountable by man or beast. Man or beast—that was it! I would send the little creature up the Maypole to capture the crown in my place. Gently, I touched the furry animal with my fingers and in a low singsong voice I explained my predicament, feeling certain that he'd been in captivity long enough to obey an order, provided I could hit upon the right one.

Seeing a morsel of the turtle meat under a pebble, I pulled it out and was about to eat it when the creature howled in such anguish I offered it to him. Reserving the next scrap for myself caused the creature such annoyance that he wrenched a branch from my head and chattering angrily, hopped onto the Maypole. I hunted at the base of the mast for another scrap, and throwing down the branch, he took the proffered food in exchange. Regretting I had no time to repeat this trial, I scratched the creature's fuzzy black head and hoped my plan would turn out better than the one to save Pru.

Having placed their bets, the sailors gathered in a circle around the Maypole, cursing and pelting me with pebbles. So terrified was I at the sound of the Flandekin's whip that I nearly jumped beyond the oiled section. The animal sat on my head, wrapping his tail around my neck. My legs hugged the slippery pole so tightly the friction from the barbed branches held me long enough to produce a tidbit of the turtle meat with my free hand. Then, making sure the creature was watching, I ate it.

Infuriated, the animal again leapt onto the pole. Before it could tear a branch from my head, I clamped my teeth firmly on the middle of its furry long tail. Howling in dismay, the wee beast clambered to the tiptop of the mast. Chattering and barring his teeth, he flung the greenery down at me. I lunged and caught the May wreath which, though I had not climbed to the top, I held in my hand. As I slid down with it the Shoaler came to my rescue. Whooping with glee he tore the Jack o' the Green nonsense off and set the May crown on my bleeding noggin.

Blaspheming and reviling both of us, the Flanderkin flung the pieces-of- eight at our feet and stomped off. I made to leave, but the short Shoaler and tall Blackamoor hoisted me onto their lopsided shoulders, loudly proclaiming their victory and parading me about.

A planter's moon swabbed the water with silvery light, and from their shoulders I looked for the anchored boat with Will and Pru. Amidst their rowdy cheers I cried in rage. The dingy was gone!

Mister Uren set me down. "And right ye are to rejoice, lad, fer ye outwitted the lot of 'em. The Shoals may be barren but they breeds bravery, by Jove. Who be ye called?"

"Thom Taylor, Mister Uren."

"Well then, Thom, come along and I'll quench yer thirst."

He picked up a broad sword and whacked off the top of a brown hairy object. Pulling a flask from his pocket, he poured a stream in the opening and grinned. "It be fermented coconut Arrack, boy, and sweet as mother's milk. Try it."

I quaffed every blesséd drop of the tasteful ferment from the hairy shell. The Shoaler further opened the nut and pried loose some milky meat with his jack knife.

The furry animal climbed up my breeches and sat on my newly crowned head, then sailed over onto the Blackamoor's arm. The liquor was taking effect and I covered my tired eyes with my hands. The little imp also covered his eyes.

The Blackamoor chuckled at the animal's mimicry, and sitting on a log, he pulled a bamboo flute out of a jute sack. The tune was mellow, and I succumbed to his drowsy music, lounging on a pillow of seaweeds near the embers of the burning ship's hull.

The Shoaler eyed me curiously.

"I oncet were a hard-workin' slave like yerse'f, Thom." He dropped the coins I'd won him into a draw-string pouch. "One day I be crossin' the Thames mindin' my Ps and Qs, and the next thing I knew I'd been clapped on a Man o' War up to my neck in bilge water.

"After the crossing, I managed to bribe the captain to drop me off here at the Shoals where I were a captive of cod more years 'an I care to remember. I were converted by a cat o' nine tails, and the Brethern of the Coast forced me to sign their Articles."

He pulled up his striped jersey, displaying an archipelago of white welts.

"I fell in with Captain Cornelius Andreson who be in Boston gaol this very moment awaitin' trial fer the plunder of Nicholas Shapleigh's shallops—among others."

The mention of Shapleigh roused me from my exhaustion, for though I'd never met the man, his name was knocked about in the northern provinces like a shuttlecock.

"As luck 'ad it, I come ashore with Captain Williams and not Captain Andreson—since Andreson's vessel was seized and towed into Boston Harbor. And now Dame Fortune has smiled on me oncet more." Uren patted the pouch of coins he'd won strung around his weathered neck; his long-winded yarn drove me nearly to the shores of sleep.

The Blackamoor offered me his bamboo flute to try, and though it wasn't a hornpipe, I quickly got the hang of it.

"Bueno. Muy bueno, hombre," the Maroon encouraged, tapping a lively accompaniment on the turtle shell with his long black fingers.

Ignoring our desertion, Mister Uren pissed on: "Captain Aernouts were a queer one, though. He 'ad the quartermaster order me to bury a bottle with a copy of his commission at every port we took for New Holland. Imagine me, a gunner—."

The men drifted in and started to jig. Their rat tails flopped merrily up and down, and one of them danced so vehemently, he split his breeches.

"Let us see," his mate shouted. "Did ye split 'em i' the crotch?"

"Nay, in the cock," he jibed to gales of laughter.

The garrulous Mister Uren stopped talking long enough to retrieve another coconut, whack it open, add more Arrack. . . and we were back where we started.

12

*T*he sun blazed over the wide empty ocean. A pair of yellow spindly legs strutted boldly up to my nose and a curious gull pecked at something on my head. I reached up and divested myself of the wreath of branches. My body ached all over and I could scarcely move without resistance in every sinew.

The gull flapped its wings and swooped over to its mates which were tearing at something on the ground. Vivid scenes of burning ships and rowdy sailors wrestled my thoughts. I was gazing around for a sign that I hadn't totally lost my mind, when I noticed a hemp sack bulging and flipping at my feet.

I brought a hand to my pounding brow, and to make sure I wasn't dreaming. gave the sack a solid kick. A furry black head poked from the mouth of the satchel with screams that immediately restored my memory.

The jabbering creature fisted the sudden light with his tiny hands, and with a deafening howl landed on my sore shoulder. I retrieved the sack, thinking it the more useful of the two, and a second surprise tumbled out—the Blackamoor's flute!

Bolstered by the tropical wood responding to my parched lips, I rejoiced that I'd been spared to see the sun rise once more over the sea. And to the accompaniment of pebbles shifting and jingling on the incoming tide, I fell to my knees in gratitude.

A black hooded gull swooped down the strand carrying a clawed turtle foot in its yellow beak. The tortoise shell had been loaded in the long boat and rowed back to the Dutch ship for its highly prized translucent buttons, periwig combs and snuff boxes. The cooking platform also had disappeared and remnants of the burnt hull were swept away by the tide.

I hobbled over to the ledge where the men had inflicted their tortures. The abhorrent Maypole was dislodged and one end of it bobbed in the frothy surf of the rock channel.

Returning from a survey of his own, the furry animal handed me a broken piece of driftwood. I was about to pitch it when I sensed a familiarity in the shape and feel of the wood and looked down to discover Pru's Barbadoes cross! While I squandered precious time, she might be kidnapped by the rogues, and stowing the animal and flute in the sack, I climbed the headland above Devil's Dance Floor.

At the ordinary I came upon Samson with traces of tears and porridge on his thin face. The kettle had toppled in the cinders and spilled onto the ashen hearth. New World children often entered Heaven sooner than they ought from hellish scalding, and quickly I swiped away the soot to ascertain if he'd been burnt.

Meanwhile, the loose animal chattered and clucked, gobbling up the mess on the bricks. Sam had acquired one of his mother's dimples and it made a brief appearance. "What be that varmint, Thom?"

"It's a long tale," I told him between mouthfuls of cold porridge scooped from the over-turned kettle. "Have you seen your brother?"

Tears slipped through the palisade of his long lashes. "When Will didn't come home, Peter and me shoved off to stay with Gwammy Andrews."

I reasoned their surrogate grammy had returned them to the ordinary confident that Will would look after them.

Leaving Samson with the Indies creature, I wandered down the dark hall to Babb's old bed chamber and barged in. Absorbed by visions of Pru and William dashed against a shoal or imprisoned in the hold of the Dutch ship, I glanced hurriedly around the room and was turning to leave the dark quarters when a moan sent me to the bedstead.

Affectionate as a rose vine climbing an arbor, there were Pru and Will entwined in each others arms. Their naked bodies, one olive, the other fair and ruddy, took me by such surprise I stared long before wading back through a heap of clothes on the floor. The light from the cracked door blinded me with a steely glint, and I stooped to retrieve my knife thrown carelessly atop Will's britches. I was so distraught I could have stabbed him in his wanton juices!

At the hearth, Samson fed his new playmate a handful of dried crane berries one by one. I climbed the loft ladder for what I concluded would be the last time.

My possessions were few enough to hide in the lining of Captain Moody's great coat. I took my Shoals indenture paper and Wiggleworth's *Day of Doom* book—which ruefully summed up the present situation. I thought of leaving behind the red Monmouth cap Pru knitted my first winter on the Shoals and, though it had grown way too small, shoved it into the coat.

From a loose chimney brick I secured a pound note parsimonied from my considerable Shoals labor—along with my share in the hermaphrodite brig. Stabling the dagger in my belt, I threw the weighty coat over my shoulders and hastened to Babb's Mooring. Samson tagged along, unaware of my sudden sea change.

On the stage, a few shoremen hooked their lines, holding them between their bare toes and skillfully jigging the twisted hemp. It had turned fair and warm with blossomy spring clouds. A group of orphans, released from work while the fleet was out, had started a game of pawpaw with four seashells. One pence, two—what did it matter if they gambled away their paltry wages?

I flung the great coat into the bottom of my ketch and was about to follow when I spotted the buccaneer's jolly hove to on the muck near Miles Pyles' old fishing stage. Perplexed by my brusque mood, Samson stepped aside to let me pass.

Too bad. I'd had it with the lot of Babbs. For five years they'd dominated my life and from now on I was on my own.

The pirate's dingy was jolly all right.. In broad daylight I admired a pair of red eyebrows and blue eyes watching me from a hull of prize lignum vitae. It would serve Will right if I took the jolly for myself and left him his father's leaky tub. But when I jumped in and discovered a piece of Pru's under garment fluttering like a victory flag from the rudder-post, I quickly leapt ashore, sick as though I'd been shipwrecked.

Samson and the West Indies animal took it all in from their height on the dock.

"Confound it! What are you staring at?" I yelled, clomping back onto the loading platform. The indefatigable animal scolded me and my lack of temper while Samson, who sat cross-legged where I'd left him, covered his face with small chapped fingers.

How could I possibly blame the child for his brother's selfish neglect? Pru not only happened to be convenient and willing, but she was his surrogate mother. I dared not speculate further about their arrangement and, crouching, pulled Samson's hands away from his face. "Samson, please forgive me," I apologized. The animal stuck its sad little face into our intimate circle, curling its tail around my wrist.

The boy with lustrous eyes looked into mine. "Please, Thom, don't leave us."

I sat on the wharf and bent toward him. "Sam, I have to live alone for awhile. I promise Will'll look after you. Besides, I'm still bound to Master Pepperrell; you'll be seein' me every day."

He petted the furry creature with determined concentration.

I tried another tack. "Last night someone confided a secret I'm urgently wanting to share. If you promise not to tell anyone, I'll let you in on it."

"Ye can count on me, Thom," he said, perking up.

"Well, Sam, it seems that Captain Aernouts of the *Flying Dutchman*—do you recall the commotion his ship caused when we sighted it off the Shoals?"

"Aye, we feared it'd storm Star Island Fort."

"That's the one, lad. Well, it seems that Jurriaen Aernouts buried a bottle with his commission and ordinance at every fort he took from Port Royal to—"

"Port Royal, Jamaica?"

"No, Sam, Port Royal, Newfoundland, and Pentagoet Fort on the Bagaduce in Maine, and possibly at the Portsmouth Fort—and Star." According to Uren they never reached the Shoals, but I said it to raise the boy's spirits.

Samson's face flushed with excitement. "He buried a bottle here on the Isles?"

"Could be."

I congratulated myself for swabbing his grief and my own, though I figured mine would be back once I crossed the channel.

Just as I was about to shove off, John Odiorne's wife crested the hill in her finest silks. She had prospered from her husband's Hog Island brewhouse and fish business. No longer content with their dinky Shoals cottage, they'd purchased the Great House at Pannaway Plantation on the main.

I tossed the mooring cable onto the wharf and jammed the oars into their grooves.

"Good Day, Master Thom. A lovely May Day, is it not?" she called, fast approaching the stage.

I recoiled from her pleasantries, pretending I was too involved coiling rope into the boat bottom, and sighting the top-heavy girl Debora with her, I could scarcely hide my anxiety.

"Look at that adorable little monkey!" Mistress Odiorne gushed, patting the beast with an affectionate bejeweled hand.

Monkey? So that's what it was called. Well, farewell and good riddance to the howling little devil. "I must be shoving off," I told her, staring into Debora's bodice as she bent to chuck the creature under its furry chin. To make sure I got an eyeful, the little tart-thrust her protruding powder pigeons from their lacing.

"We be a'Mayin', Thomas," Mistress Odiorne announced. She looked down at the forlorn Samson. "How would you like to accompany us, Sam? We be strollin' over to the headland above Devil's Dance Floor."

The very mention of it made me shudder.

"Ye can gather some May flowers fer Pru. Wouldn't she like that?" The woman cooed in a motherly voice.

"No!" I answered even as the lad whooped with joy. He fastened me with such an expression of injury that I quickly fabricated an excuse for my response. "What I meant was—I *KNOW* Pru would love some flowers, Sam."

I stirred my ketch over to the wharf to make amends. "And be sure to tell her I wish her every happiness," I whispered.

Samson leaned over the wharf and patted my shoulder in that grown-up manner of his. "Don't worry, Thom. I'll look after her."

I was rowing away when he shouted an afterthought—"I'll say the flowers be from you."

"No!" I shouted back. But he had run over the grassy knoll and disappeared.

13

Will and I ordinarily crossed the channel together and as the stiff current picked up, I missed another pair of arms. I rowed past the village at Gosport Harbor to the Malaga end of Star.

The Cutt dwelling appeared as I'd last seen it—worse for wear but still standing. Master Richard had been ill and I doubted he'd be on the Shoals anytime soon. But to make my presence known, I stopped at Mary Twisden's. Her brother Peter was out with the fleet, but she invited me in for some chowder.

Mary's late husband Joseph Baker died in debt to about everyone on Star, and since her husband hadn't left a will, Mary's house was given to Edward Beele. John Tucker and Philip Hatch made sure the rest of the property was divvied between them, forcing Mary to move in with her brother.

I thought of Pru on her own with nothing but a promise and a song from Will. But I hadn't come to idle my first day of independence on regrets. Had the woman any provisions she could spare? I plunked down a pine tree shilling.

Mary Twisden stared as if it were too good to be true. "Tell ye what, Thom, Peter and I'd be glad to set a place fer ye at table fer another shillin' and ye wouldn't be worryin' about the cookin'."

I didn't have to think twice. I wanted no more ties or obligations and assured her I'd best put away my own provisions since my work with Master Pepperrell required long uneven hours. Disappointed by the lost opportunity, she hustled out to fetch gunnies of corn meal and navy beans. Her brother Peter would cart me a hogshead of beer when the fleet came back. Until then, of course, there was always the alehouse.

I thanked the plain woman who, like many elderly females on the Shoals, looked and acted strangely like a man. Balancing a heavy gunny in each arm, I took the narrow path to my new home over-looking Gosport Harbor.

If Richard Cutt showed up and accused me of squatting, I'd tell him I was keeping an eye on the hermaphrodite brig. This was closer to the truth than I'd realized, for with Cutt ill and Cornelius Williams skulking about the Isles, securing the brig and keeping it under fast surveillance was not only prudent but long overdue.

Fortified by a sudden burst of resolve, I dumped the vittles on the dusty table and went back outside to climb a rickety ladder onto the thatch roof. Tying a frayed rope to a stone, I cleared the chimney of a huge heron nest and considerable soot. Next, I swept the hearth and toted a good bushel of dirt, broken delftware and fish bones into the sunlight. The cottage had no window glass, but the weather was warm enough so I could remove the scraped oil skin at the door and windows. Someday, I might even get around to re-chinking the walls.

A mouse fell from the mattress. For a shilling Mistress Twisden would jump at a chance to stuff and sew me a new one. In the interim, I lambasted the moldy mattress with a batten until the clouds of dust got so thick they incited a skirmish of sneezes. Leaving the bedding to air on its own, I shoved off and rowed over to Belcher's on Smutty-nose.

I found the Minister in the brick church house pouring over

some Latinate text or other. He scraped aside his chair and stood. "Thomas Taylor, where have you got to, lad? You look like you've been to the devil!"

He was one to call the kettle black. Without his Sunday periwig, the opprobrious Minister cut a very different figure. On his receding hairline loomed a mark which either was sepia ink or an extraordinarily large birth strawberry. White wig powder encrusted the deep furrows of his temple and, dulled by reading, his eyes peered through puffy slits in his wintry face.

"In a manner of speaking, Sir, I've been through hell."

He nodded knowingly, though he knew fair little, and crushed a miller moth eating the lapel of his wool frock coat. Leaving the silvery smudge intact, he smiled amiably. "And are you catechizing regularly, Thom?"

The man might as well have asked when I'd last answered the call of nature. "I uh—."

He sighed and fixed me like I was blazing in eternal combustion. "*Nemo repente fuit turpissimus,*" he reproached.

"No one becomes depraved overnight," I ventured.

"In a moment," he corrected.

But overnight was good enough for me. I wondered how long the priggish fellow would have lasted under the Flanderkin's whip. In short order he would have stored up a thing or two about depravity.

Belcher rummaged in a drawer and held a shilling to the light as if he were about to administer the holy sacrament. "Here, Thom, I've been meaning to pay wages for your assistance last season. My soul, look to thy appearance, man. Get to Mister Glanfield the tailor and have him make up a homespun, and while you're at it, a linen shirt for Sundays. That one will not pass muster."

I looked down at my shirt for the first time in several days. Twigs and turtle fat adorned the front, and one sleeve had been ripped clear away at the elbow.

He closed my fingers over the shilling and sighed. "I suspect it's a woman. As the Simple Cobbler of Aggawan says, 'He that makes shirts for the moon need take measure every noon, and he that makes shifts for women, as often keep them from lunacy.' I won't pry, Thomas, but she's best forgotten."

He expected me to hang my head in remorse and spill the beans. But that was the old Thom. I took the proffered shilling, notified him of my change of residence, and left.

As I rowed back to Star Island I thought how each of the islands fostered salient traits much like people whose dispositions resemble their physical features. The way Church Island stuck into the Atlantic Ocean somehow made it more of a third party; whereas Star and Appledore, facing each other, shared pleasantries across the channel. Star had the practical advantage with its forts, though the garrison had but two rusty cannon.

I sheltered my ketch in the lee of the hermaphrodite brig marooned by the low tide and walked the wobbly wharf to Cutt's stage and up the ledges to my humble dwelling. In the lingering light I darted about collecting enough driftwood to cook a kettle of mush for supper. In my haste to leave Mistress Twisden I'd forgotten to ask for bayberry tallow to fill the cruisey on the mantel.

Never mind. I was too tired to do anything but fall onto the musty mattress and swaddle myself in the warm comfort of Captain Moody's venerable old coat. The dislodged mouse scuttled back and forth in the gathering darkness wondering where its home had gone. It wasn't alone.

Pepperrell's stage crawled with fishermen dumping cod and brawling vendors selling freeboot liquor. I scrambled up the sail loft where the overseer extemporized to a nodding assemblage of sea urchins. With feigned attention they listened to his gory earbenders.

"Excuse me, Sir," I interrupted.

He fixed me cross-eyed and peevish.

"Where do I work, Sir?"

His neck jerked forward like a chicken's and he shot a hideous green stream of saliva at my feet. "Em 'at don't 'preciate me yarns can empty casks of blood and water. Ye'll be workin' wi' at shit-tabed Will Babb at the cod liver press tryin' the oil. The devil knows ye've tried me patience—Arhh Harr."

I laughed louder than any of them. So what if the overseer thought he was the life of the party. I had my own company and it was a damn site better than his. But it was just my luck to be paired with Will Babb.

When Will saw me coming he waved and smiled innocent as a newborn babe.

Wordlessly, I donned my oil boots and tied on an apron.

He picked up the long gaff used to spear the fish. "What be eatin' ye, Thom? I hope yer not frettin' about yer knife."

"I found my knife where you left it."

"That be a boon. I feared I'd lost it." He rolled a full cask on its rim to the sea water. The blood seeping from the barrel into the limpid waves could have been my heart-blood watery with regret. How could I ever have counted on his friendship?

I crawled upon the high vat and unlocked the lever to the press. Two small boys dumped a sweetgrass basket of the slippery empur-pled cod livers into the vat and I turned the screw on the oozy mass. My head swirled and I leapt back onto solid ground.

Will grabbed my shoulder. "Thom, I don't reckon why ye be so bent out o' shape. I promised Pru wages fer lookin' after Peter, Sam and me. She be family."

I set my jaw and adjusted a hogshead beneath the cod liver oil sluice. The stench was appalling, but I was so livid with anger that I held my breath until I felt like my legs would buckle.

Will grabbed his codpiece. "I did offer her som'n more'n wages and she offered me a bit o' tart. It were reciprocal."

The mastery of my fist took me by surprise. I'd never practiced using it, yet it knew exactly where to go. Will sprawled backward in the muck. I picked up the hogshead of cod liver oil and dumped it over his arrogant head. Not waiting for the overseer to catch wind of the affair, I threw down my apron.

At the hillcrest I slowed stride and paused to look down on the exuberant stage below. The salters and coopers, cutters and splitters worked busy as bees at a hive. Trouble was, pitiful few of us ever tasted the honey. I knew only too well that Master Pepperrell might prolong my indenture, but I went to see him anyway.

Robust as ever, he threw open the door. "Thom Taylor, yer just the man I wanted to see."

His welcome tone of voice took me by surprise.

"Come in, come in." He ushered me into the parlor bright with window light. "Aye, Thom. I've a score of letters to answer and though my readin' be quicker than lightnin' my penmanship be slower than a Man-o' War comin' about." He picked up a sheaf of papers from an escritoire near the casement and waved them at me. "What say ye leave off fer awhile and help me swab the decks of this mess?"

I thought I'd better own up to the truth. "Well, Sir, I'm in a bit of a mess myself."

Pepperrell pushed me into the desk chair and sharpened a few quills with his pen knife. "Ye don't say."

"Aye, Sir. Will Babb and I had an altercation."

"A fight, more'n likely. Who won?"

"In a matter of speakin', he did, Sir. Because I'm obliged to pay the overseer for the keg of cod liver oil I poured upon him."

Pepperrell pounded the escritoire so hard it vibrated on its spindly legs. "If that don't beat all."

I looked at him in disbelief. "Then you aren't angry, Sir?"

"That Babb brat had it comin'. Now, Thom, rid me of this horrid letter-labor while I sup, and then I'll convince the overseer to write off yer debt."

Doing my best to ignore the pleasant clink of dishes, I set to work. On his way out, Pepperrell offered me a bite in the kitchen.

The servant girl stood on a stool to return a bowl to a corner cupboard. With the surprise of my greeting she lost her foothold, and as the stool toppled I caught her. Without daring to think how, I held Pru in my arms.

" Thomas Taylor, what are you doing at Master Pepperrell's?" she asked, smiling up at me—for I'd grown a head taller.

"Putting my learning to good use," I confided. "No more stinkin' fish for me."

She placed her hands on her hips the way women do when they think they know a thing or two. "You look different Thom—changed somehow."

It had scarce been two weeks since we'd seen each other, but she too looked somehow different.

"Oh Thom, can you keep a secret?"

"Better than most," I said, trying my utmost to keep my new-found wellspring of reserve and cool-headedness.

She eyed me doubtfully. "You do care for me, don't you, Thom—and will be happy if I'm happy?"

I sat down at the table and pulled a trencher toward me. "Master Pepperrell invited me for some vittles," I explained, though suddenly I had no appetite.

While Pru stirred a pot of beans over the fire I broke off a piece of the trencher and fixed her with a devil-may-care look. "I had a fight with Will this morning."

"Will?" Her voice wavered.

"I left the weasel-face down in the mud."

Pru leaned on her knuckles and brought her face close to mine. "You did what?"

I shoveled the beans into my mouth with a piece of the trencher. "You heard me."

Pru turned on her heel. Her shoulders shook and I stood to comfort her, only to discover she was shaking with laughter. "Ah, Thomas, you jealous dog!"

I grabbed her hand. "Will Babb has used and abused you, Pru. Why would I be jealous of that? And when you're carrying his child, what then?" I blabbered, letting the mercurial lass breech my best intentions.

She smiled sweetly as a sea rose in full bloom. "We'll marry, of course, Thom. He told me as much. We're in love."

I dropped her hand and shouted with abandon. "Love! So that's what they call bottoms up in a boat."

"Ah, Thom. You seem different."

She stood by, anxious for a kind word. I had paltry few. In all fairness, once I too had been charmed by Will. And now that we both were under the same roof maybe I could alter her feelings toward the slippery rogue. I made as if to sweep past but halted. "Since we're both indentured by Master Pepperrell, I think it best to lay aside our differences, Mistress Monforte, and at least be civil."

PART THREE

Rude Awakenings

14

*F*og thick as pea soup drifted over Great Island. I threw a rope around a piling at the landing and hopped ashore glad to be alive. A ship on the Piscataqua River had nearly swamped me as I rode the incoming tide. In the nick of time I shoved myself off one of the enormous masts sticking out her stern and made for shore at New Castle.

How the bulky vessels reached Britain integral was a mystery to me, for only a thick coat of resinous pitch around the pine trunks kept the sea from sloshing into the ship's hold on the long ocean voyage. Nevertheless, the barges delivered their timber cargoes to his Majesty's Navy—as well as pressing New World communications.

I trudged uphill past the deserted fish flakes to George Jeffrey's house, hoping to learn the whereabouts of Mister John Cutt.

I'd seen less of Pru and to ease my disappointed heart as the summer wore on, I took out the hermaphrodite brig for weeks at a time. Will Babb was so busy drinking, brawling. and generally running amuck that he never noticed the brig was gone. Between the

wages from Master Pepperrell, Minister Belcher, and cod merchandising, I'd made a profit and aimed to secure a piece of New
World prosperity—if not my own peace of mind.

Mister Jeffrey apprised me that several prosperous Shoalers,
including John Cutt, had moved to Strawbery Banke and I ferried
over to Portsmouth to see him.

An Indian servant boy dressed in a red and white candy-striped
sateen vest and velvet knee breeches refused to let me in, eyeing my
muddy Shoals boots with contempt.

Exasperated by the waif's insolence, I pulled off my boots and
entered the wide-planked room. The boy returned with Mister Cutt
who didn't seem any more pleased to see me than his servant. "Sorry
to bother you, Sir," I said, holding out my hand. "Thomas Taylor
from the Isles of Shoals."

A grin surfaced on the Welsh man's weathered face. "Of course.
Both my brothers held you in high regard. What brings you here,
lad?"

"Well, Sir, I heard about the death of your brother, Master Richard,
and I came to pay my respects."

He went over to a table on which stood a pewter tankard,
fished in it, and handed me a handsome gold funeral ring. The man
was on his way up and pleased to show it. "And?" he said.

"Uh, Sir?"

He laughed. "Now don't go beatin' about the bush, lad. I heard
you been squattin' in Richard's vacant cottage more'n a fortnight."

"Aye, Sir. And I wish to make an offer."

He stroked his chin. "Well, Thom, it has to be inventoried. Then
we'll see what we can do. And?"

His expedient nature seemed hopelessly unlike my present
confusion. "Well, it's about the brig, Sir."

"Aye, the brig. I suppose that will be inventoried too, along
with my brother's estate. But until that time, I see no reason for you
not to continue as part owner. Keep strict accounts of the quintals
of cod and bills of lading. And?"

I was flabbergasted by his dispatch. "And—thank you, Sir."

The Indian boy bowed with quiet reserve and was ushering me toward the door when Mister Cutt barred the way. "Go and summon the Major. I believe he'd like to meet Mister Taylor.

The young servant looked confused.

"Major Richard Walderne," Cutt repeated slowly. When the boy was out of the room, he sighed. "You know, Thom, that Nipmuck boy was dropped from the deck of a ship at anchor in the river and near died from the dunking. Not one of the squaws on board claimed him, probably hoping he'd escape. They're in slave chains at Portsmouth until the squall blows over and they sail for the Barbadoes."

Preceded by the clack of jackboots, a gentleman of commanding stature entered the room and gave me such a thorough once over I feared he'd open my mouth and examine my teeth.

Cutt clapped me amiably on the back while introducing the man in British uniform.

"Thom here's a fine lad, Major. Wet behind the ears, but he knows his letters and, if I'm not mistaken, he helped Minister Belcher keep the records on the Shoals. The lad probably can't fire a musket, but you might give him a pot o' ink and have him fire a few missiles off to the big Whigs in Boston."

I didn't like the past tense of his conversation and hastily sank in both oars. "Master Pepperrell's expectin' me to clear up some business on Appledore Island, Sir."

Cutt offered the Major his snuff box while keeping me in his sights. "Hang that Devon pisspot, Thom. You be sadly behind the times on the Shoals, lad. The Major and I have news of Indian savagery that would curdle yer blood. Six houses burned at Oyster River and worse in Hampton on the same day."

Major Walderne pushed snuff up one effete nostril which he looked down on me.

"The soldiers be bedded at Jeffrey's barracks and I expect you to be among them, Goodman Taylor. We be marchin' at dawn from Newichewannock up the Piscataqua River and then to Wells and Saco, Maine."

His salvo of high-pitched sneezes gave me time to think. "My lack of soldierin' could prove costly, Sir."

The Major marched over my objection. "At Salmon Falls one brave woman piled the furniture against the door while the others fled to the garrison. A three year old boy didn't make it—they bashed his head against a tree." Walderne's face was strangely unmoved by the horror coming from his lips. "That night the settlers come upon five of the savages around a fire and smashed in their feathery skulls with their muskets."

John Cutt thumbed the snuff box back into a slot in his sateen waistcoat. "Now, Richard, about the supplies you be needin'. I've talked with Mister Jeffrey. These be lean times and it weren't easy, but I've fitted up a cart with hogsheads of saleratus, beans, and salt cod, and I expect the General Court to reciprocate in beaver skins from your trading post up river at Cocheco."

Summarily dismissed, I grabbed my boots from the Indian child, pulled them on, and left reeling from the sudden black turn of events.

In the drisk I hugged my warm great coat close and thanked Divine Providence I'd worn fishing boots. It was more than a fortnight's march up river from Salmon Falls above Cocheco where Walderne had charge of the Militia, and then north to the Maine coast. I considered getting in my ketch and high-tailing it to the Shoals, but Cutt had me over a barrel. If I wanted the Shoals property, come hell or high water, I must stay in the Major's good graces.

So many Shoalers had moved from the Shoals to Portsmouth: There were Phillip and Elizabeth Tucker, Captain Snell and Hannah Alcock, Thomas and Jane Turpin, Richard and Hannah Yeaton. For convenience sake, I went to the Hilton brothers in New Castle where I'd beached my ketch.

The brothers had been fishing all day, and hunkered near the fire in their britches but welcomed me with warm smiles and bowls of porridge, agreeing to keep an eye on my boat while I was gone.

Afterward, I found my way to Mister Jeffrey's barn for a few winks before we marched. Raucous shouts from the soldiers reached me as I passed the sentry at the palisade gate.

Lanterns swinging from the posts and beams shone off the eyes of cows, horses, and men. I gagged from the stench of wet wool, animal manure, and the vomit of drunken soldiers, and backed into a corner I thought unoccupied—only to discover a score of Indian women and children huddled in a somber circle.

An abject squaw stood inside the drafty door looking downcast at her bruised chained ankles. My remorse for the poor woman increased with the accost of a rum-sodden soldier hoving her against the wall.

Major Walderne's grand entrance brought several soldiers to their unsteady feet, and I boldly leapt to his side.

"Begging your pardon, Major, but that soldier's conduct is inexcusable." I said, pointing at the man who had knocked the shackled woman into the hay and rolled atop her.

Walderne absent-mindedly stroked the shiny silver pommel of his sword as he watched. "And how would you conduct yourself with her, pray tell, Goodman Taylor?"

In response, I jumped into the fray, giving the scoundrel a judicious kick where it hurt the most. The brute howled and cradled his privates.

The squaw seemed strangely familiar and while I surveyed her Walderne walked up with crossed arms. "Not a good start, Goodman Taylor," he commented.

"But Major, couldn't you please unshackle the poor woman so she can at least defend herself?"

A hint of curiosity crept into his eyes. "And if I give her to you, Mister Taylor?"

I cursed the rosy flush that was a dead give-away to my

considerable humiliation. "What do you mean, Major?"

"You've never had a woman and that's why you denied this fellow's cod a little swim up stream, eh Taylor?"

My scalp prickled. "Certainly not, Major.

Walderne snapped his fingers and the guard came at a trot. "Unshackle this squaw and entrust her to this lad for the night." He palmed the sword pommel and smiled faintly. "First's always best. Mind you, bring her back at dawn or you'll have the devil to pay."

I seized the freed woman's hand before he could change his mind and pulled her into the driving rain.

Though it was pitch dark, the night watchman hadn't made his rounds.

Time was on my side, and I shoved the drenched woman behind some gorse so the lantern would not light on her. Surprised at my voice, the eldest Hilton unbarred the door.

I explained how depressed I was with the barracks and that I'd let a drunken soldier take me to an ordinary on Strawbery Banke. In short, I wished to sample a marmalade madame and was desperately in need of the shed he'd offered earlier.

My request seemed to tickle his imagination, and the simple Shoaler trundled out back to unlatch the shed door. "I keep a cock and some hens in that shed, Thom, and ye'll be in perfect company," he jibed, hitching up his under britches. "Let the rooster come in here afore ye depart in the morning. I don't trust 'em prowlin' redskin savages."

The room had an earthen floor and embers still glowed on the shallow hearth. In the corner was a trundle bed covered with a wondrous woolly bear pelt. The woman shivered something terrible and I built the fire to a roaring blaze.

Our communication was less than encouraging. Thinking she'd be more comfortable if she removed the wet blanket, I made the mistake of gently tugging it away. Terrified, she grabbed the damp homespun tighter. Abandoning words for gestures, I pulled my rain-soaked jerkin over my head and holding my arms to the flames, breathed an exaggerated "Ahhh" of satisfaction.

Slowly, the squaw unwrapped the blanket and let it drop. "Ahhh," she sighed, turning to me for approval. And I wasted no time giving it, for the woman was most beautiful in the firelight. The fullness of her bronze breasts peeked through a mat of thick black hair. I watched in awe as she unraveled the two wet plaits, spreading the confusion of dark waves over her bare shoulders to dry.

When she had finished, I led her to the bed and, spreading out the great coat near the fire, pretended to sleep. Unable to ignore her disconsolate sobs, I sat on the edge of the narrow trundle and looked down at her pooling eyes.

At last she calmed and, placing her hand on her chest, she whispered, "Metacomet—squaw."

If she had told me she was a witch I couldn't have been more startled. Had God in his Firmament delivered the squaw of King Philip into my protection? The brazen Indian warrior who had declared war on the British had long been forced by the Massachusetts Regiment from Mount Hood into Nipmuck wilderness. With every settler from Boston to Hadley after his scalp, by now Metacomet surely was dead.

She covered her face with her hands and I pulled them away, suddenly remembering who she reminded me of—John Cutt's servant. She must be the boy's mother!

Not knowing what to do, I took the sobbing woman in my arms. The plan I hatched while holding her unleashed such passion that I landed a kiss on her lips. Misinterpreting my sudden affection, she shoved me away.

I'd always prided myself on knowing Latin and French, but was hopelessly inadequate in her native tongue. Trying to ignore what she might think of me, I bound her hands and feet to the bed. She didn't struggle, but let out a heart-rending sob that followed me into the rain.

When Cutt's servant boy answered my hesitant knock, I

clamped my hand over his mouth and dragged him through the mud. He was only four or five years old, and small enough to hide under my coat until we got past the night watchman. We slipped through the stormy night to Hiltons' shed. The idea that the boy was Metacomet's son filled me with apprehension, but I was in far too deep to retreat.

The squaw took one look at the child and I couldn't get the rope off fast enough. After the excitement of their reunion, the exhausted boy fell asleep. She came over to where I was standing near the fire and embraced me. I had never known such an embrace, or to put it mildly, what came after. The tongue of King Philip's woman held a treasure of caesuras, ellipses, and ligatures that left me speechless.

Startled as much by the warm caresses of the Indian squaw as by the persistent crowing of the cock on the rafter, I awoke before dawn.

The boy awoke and playfully waved a huge bear paw at his drowsy mother. She padded over to him, whispered in his ear, and they tussled in the deep furry pelt. Victorious, she held up the object they'd been fighting over, which I couldn't make it out in the dying firelight.

She came over and placed a shell necklace over my head. I'd heard stories of Indian wampum from traders who remembered when shell belts and necklaces were common currency. One Mainer told me he'd exchanged a hundred beaver pelts for a belt of quahog wampum shells offered by a man at Plimoth Plantation.

The squaw solemnly straightened a silvery star hanging from the necklace. "Metacomet Pokanoket squaw," she said, gesturing toward her son, herself, and patting the wampum on my chest. "Metacomet wampum."

If the Major were to get wind I was wearing King Philip's Indian beads, I'd be a goner for sure. But as luck would have it, I could resist neither the gift nor her beauty.

At dawn the child and I caught the wretched cock. It crowed

thrice according to Biblical proverb, and then some, before we shoved it into the Hiltons' house as promised. I wrapped the squaw in a dry blanket, donned my great coat, and the three of us left in the half light, sneaking around the backs of houses to Puddle Dock.

Once safe in my boat, I stuck my hand in the lining of my coat and, discovering Cutt's funeral ring, gave it to the squaw. The boy giggled and produced two exactly like it. Laughing at the abundance of rings, we sped with the tide across the Piscataqua River to Shapleigh's Landing at Kittery.

As a befriender of Indians, Nicholas Shapleigh was used to visitors at his door. Still, we must have presented a strange sight—the squaw so silent, me weary to exhaustion, and the boy lively as they come.

Without hesitation, the congenial man invited us into his ancestral home. When he said he'd heard my name, I confessed that the squaw and boy were wanted by Major Walderne and Mister Cutt and admitted I hoped he could take them, because I'd been ordered to march with the Militia at dawn.

Shapleigh took aside his wife and she disappeared with the squaw and child.

"I'm journeying up river this week," Shapleigh said. "I'll take them to a friendly Penacook scout. Does that suit thee, Thomas Taylor?"

I apologized for the risk he was taking—though I felt it best to keep him in the dark about Metacomet.

He placed a finger on his lips. "Not another word, Thomas. Our debts be reckoned on the ledger of a Higher Magistrate."

The Mistress beckoned us into a great chamber where the squaw stood self-conscious and uncertain in a grey homespun dress. Her transformation in these clothes was dismal, but I affected delight for her sake. While she was preoccupied by a honied almond, Mistress Shapleigh gave me a pair of scissors and ordered me to cut off her braids. Recalling the night before, it was a challenge to shear off the lustrous plaits.

Without so much as a look backward, I grabbed her blanket and ran to the boat landing. Fortunately, the tide had turned and carried me swiftly again to Puddle Dock.

The sentinel waved me through the stockade to the barracks; I pushed open the barn door and a wide shaft of sunlight fell on a scene entirely different from the night before.

A soldier and roan mare pissed golden arcs of urine steaming in the chill. Glass flasks and broken flagons littered the straw. "Shad-up," a drowsy voice grumbled at a soldier who broke several notes on a trumpet and unsuccessfully tried to repair them.

The Indian women, who had not left their huddle, were chanting as they solemnly passed around a pouch of cornmeal. Their peculiar chant sounded for all the world like distant thunder on the horizon.

I guessed Major Walderne soon would be there and rushed into their midst. "Do any of you speak English?" I whispered, crouching so as not to be seen.

A young squaw nodded, fixing on the blanket of Metacomet's Squaw with a grieved look.

"Please tell the others I have helped the Squaw of Metacomet flee, and now I need their help."

Her countenance brightened as she conveyed my message through a confusion of questions.

Time was running out.

"Gather them around to hide me," I pleaded.

Some remained obstinately where they were while others shielded me as I fashioned a mound of straw and hurriedly threw the blanket over it. I took the squaw's braids of hair from my coat and was accosted by a high pitched wail.

"Tell them Metacomet's wife and son are alive and hush the old woman, or we are done for!" I pleaded with the young squaw.

She chattered with them while I laid the braids at the top of the blanket. Hearing the telltale click of Walderne's jackboots behind me, I jumped to my feet.

"Hurry!" I whispered.

Major Walderne approached in sudden silence.

"Good Morrow, conscript Taylor."

He looked down at the inert mound and toed it thoughtfully with a glistening boot. One of the loose braids rolled off a fold of the blanket and into the straw.

I held my breath as the Major, scarcely able to contain himself, pulled me aside.

"I see you have wearied the squaw beyond arousal with your flying shuttle-cock, Thom. Was she a fighter? I favors 'em 'at puts up a row and leave scratches."

Mistaking my blush for innocence, he escorted me into the light while continuing to toy with his insipid innuendo.

"If we be needing any drilling, Goodman Taylor, I'll keep you in mind. In the mean-while, round up these motley soldiers. This be the poorest excuse for a militia I've set eye on."

Broad daylight sorely defined the shadowy scene of the night before. The conscripts tottered and loitered near a huge charred iron kettle full of tawny colored porridge with an unfathomable odor. A youngster of twelve years or so proudly strutted in his bare feet, displaying a dented metal gorget he'd taken from a heap of armor. I estimated there was enough armor for less than half the company. The gorget could deflect an arrow from the chest, but I decided against it for fear someone would spy the wampum under my great coat.

"The Major wants us to rally," I told the stragglers slopping porridge from cupped hands for want of any other vessel. I was about to stick in my hands and test fate with the mean gruel when once more the young squaw tugged on my sleeve. How was it that she'd lost her shackles, I asked in surprise.

She smiled. "I be Piscataqua—porte provision to my sisters for journey on great water." She peered into the porridge, made a face and handed me her deer hide pouch. "And to my brother—for his journey."

Inside the pouch was enough corncake for several days. I handed it back and shrugged. "No shillings," I told her. Thinking I might have something of value in trade, I motioned her around the corner of the barn and started to take off my great coat.

She recoiled.

"Wait, don't go. I have wampum," I said with my hand over the prize necklace.

The young squaw froze like a frightened rabbit as I took off my shirt. The Hilton shed had been too dark to really see the wampum and I was dazzled by the dancing black beads awash in a wave of pearl shells. Carefully, I lifted the precious object over my neck and handed it to the young squaw—filled with misgivings for bartering such a treasure.

"Metacomet Squaw give you, and I give you journey cake," she said, handing it back.

"But—."

Scozzway the fiddler was the first Indian to disappear before my very eyes and she was the second. I pulled the wampum and shirt back over my head. Chewing off a bite of the cake, I stuffed the pouch into my coat and slung it over my shoulders.

Back around the corner, I came on the porridgey conscripts pointing, exclaiming and gazing skyward at a pair of sundogs. The Anglican Portsmouth minister who had come to wish us Godspeed had dropped to his knees. Startled by the gifts and signs of that day, I did likewise.

"Bless these soldiers, Dear Lord," he bellowed from his bowed position. Thank thee for thy divine sundogs that guide them in their fight with heathen savages."

Major Walderne rode up. His horse skittered into a considerable puddle, spattering mud into our uplifted eyes.

"And bless and protect Major Richard Walderne, thy servant, leading him and this company again to safety."

Major Walderne reigned in his fidgeting horse. "Safety," he scoffed. "Portsmouth won't be safe until we kill every last Indian savage."

With a vehement thrust he dug his boot heel into the horse's flank, and freeing his sword from the scabbard, brandished it dangerously close to our bowed heads.

"Now march!"

15

*U*nlike the Thames in London, the Piscataqua River had no bridge, and we were forced to march up river west to Cocheco, crossing the narrows beneath the monster-bulk of Salmon Falls before heading eastward to Wells and Scarborough.

Two ox carts creaked with provisions of food, dry powder kegs, and musketry at the rear of the militia while Major Walderne pranced ahead on horseback.

The porridge eaten by the men stepped up our pace considerably at the outset. "Falling out, Major," a soldier cried, flying by on the run. "Begging permission, Sir, " another grunted from the nearest bush, reappearing wan and pallid.

I thanked Providence for delivering me from the poison gruel. I was exhausted, not having slept more than a few hours, but walking in the brisk revived my spirits. The maple leaves wore rouge, and Metacomet's squaw glowed in my loins like the September sun.

As we followed the cart path along the river, I thought I saw Mister Shapleigh's vessel adrift on the incoming tide. He stood with the squaw and child on the deck and I abandoned my place in the ranks to halloo and wave, but they sailed on without any indication that they'd seen me.

An elder Kittey conscript gummed a steady stream of complaint. To avoid listening, I returned to my reverie of Metacomet's squaw. The subject provided endless satisfaction and strangely, the squaw moving in my arms often was replaced by Pru. These vagaries kept me well occupied until the trumpeter grunted into his infernal horn.

Past noon, we refreshed ourselves at a fisherman's well. Major Walderne watered his horse at the trough and soaked his large white feet alongside the horse's muzzle. Gazing at the assembled troops sprawled on the grass, I asked myself how we ever would reach Scarborough, let alone fight enemy Indians. Nearby, a lad sucked a belly of water and threw up the contents of his distended stomach. He was by no means solitary.

Veteran soldiers from the Portsmouth Garrison played cards for firearms under the shade of a horse chestnut, oblivious of the discomforts of the conscripts Walderne had rounded up.

The Major hobbled over in his stocking feet. "Taylor."

"Aye, Capt'n."

"We be infantry, not sailors," he complained.

In truth, I had little idea how to conduct myself and resolved to stay detached as far as possible.

He took a parchment from his saddle and thrust it into my hand. "Here, read this."

The document seemed to be ordinances passed by the General Court of Massachusetts in regards to soldiers at camp.

"I did not give it to you to read to yerself, Conscript Taylor, but to this assembled company of dim wits."

If my reading skills were flaunted I'd surely be ridiculed for the duration of the march. I stalled. "Major, Sir, wouldn't the company respect your parlance to mine?"

"See that stump by the well, Taylor. Hop onto it and read!"

The sun beat down furious as summer and I could feel trickles of sweat under the weight of my coat. Cupping my hands into the bucket, I splashed water on my burning face and obediently climbed upon the tree stump. Not one soldier paid the least notice.

The Major cracked his riding whip against his thigh, strode over to one of the card players, and picked up the musket by his side. "If ye don't want this musket confiscated and the Provost Marshall to have ye off to gaol, get to yer stinkin' feet and call 'em to attention."

The man he roused was the trumpeter and it was all I could do to keep from holding my hands over my ears while the infernal herald blatted and screeched them to their tired, and for the most part bare, feet.

Stone faced as ever, Major Walderne pointed his finger at the paper I held.

"Read!"

The twenty long ordinances reminded me of a French witticism my uncle once quoted: "I have made this letter longer than usual because I lack the time to make it short."

"All of them, Sir?"

At the stub end of patience, he growled. "Those 'at ye see fit for this poor excuse of soldiery."

The first ordinance mentioned God, and I decided God might be a welcome relief at this juncture. "One." I announced. "Let no man presume to blaspheme the holy and blessed Trinity—God the Father, God the Son, and. . . "

"Damn ye, Taylor, this ain't no church. We be on the war path. Apprise these rogues of the punishment due 'em for mutiny, drunkenness, card playing and the likes."

While Major Walderne chewed me out, I perused the regulations unevenly impressed on the parchment and smudged with red sealing wax.

"Ten." I announced loudly. "No man shall utter words of sedition or mutiny upon pain of death. Twelve. Drunkenness in an officer shall be punished with loss of place." I looked askance at the Major who at that moment quaffed a flagon of whiskey. Obviously, in the provinces this was a moot regulation and, swigging his brew, the Major ambled away. "Thirteen. Rapes, ravishments, unnatural abuses. . ."

One of the Portsmouth Militia shouted, "'Us 'at mean doin' it wi' a cow?"

Embarrassed by his bawdry, I bridled in the aggravation shaking my voice. "And adultery shall be punished with death. Fourteen. Fornication and other dissolute lasciviousness. . ."

"What the devil!" Another militiaman assumed an innocent tone. "'Us 'at mean doin' it wi' a lass?"

Major Walderne returned from the fisherman's cottage sucking noisily on a chop.

With haste I read another ordinance. "Eighteen. If any negligently lose or sinfully play away their fire arms at dice or cards or other ways, they shall be kept as prisoners until they furnish themselves with as good arms."

He shoved me off the stump and brandished the chop in the air. "And if I find arms or ammunition stole from the cart ye'll hang by the heels. Also, Conscript Taylor, did ye apprise 'em of the grievous punishment that will befall 'em 'at refuses to abide by the rules?"

"Nay, Sir." I handed back the paper, anxious to be done with it before I was strung from the nearest tree.

The Major pitched the gnawed chop and hit the elder conscript from Kittery on the forehead. The dazed man lifted his hand and brought it back bloody.

Though Walderne raised his voice he was contained as a cod in a barrel. "Ye'll be cachiering the strapadoe, and if that don't do it, I'll have ye ride the wood horse to fetch blood, understand? And another thing—once we cross Salmon Falls, if ye sight an Indian—whether he be praying or heathen—report the savage to me. Dismissed."

Feeling sorry for the Kittery graybeard, Pardon Cook, who caught the chop in the noggin, I bound some healing leaves to his forehead with one of my shirt tails. He was in a bit of a fog at first, but soon companioned me around the marshy inlets that doubled the length and effort of our expedition.

As a boy, Pardon had worked at the flakes on the Shoals and recollected some memorable dealings with Phillip Babb. We laughed heartily at the thought of Babb's schemes and remembered the blaspheming Shoalers with something akin to affection.

By camp we had reached no farther than a split in the Piscataqua River, one tributary of which led to Major Walderne's garrison at Cocheco and the other, north to Berwick. In the morning we were to take the Hilton brothers' ferry over to the peninsula between them.

A young lad and his father built a great bonfire and with a hunk of salt pork, beans, and greens bartered along the way, they cooked us a fine supper. Most conscripts carried bowls from home. Pardon handed me his when he'd done eating. In return I cleaned his wound with tide water and bound fresh evergreen leaves onto it. The good man seemed genuinely pleased, for though he and Major Walderne were of an age, sixty years of pioneer life had worn Goodman Cook's face to creases and sags.

A chorus of snores and groans crowded the hemlock glen. I couldn't sleep thinking about Bloody Point and the Indian ambush responsible for its name. I pulled my coat over the old man, turning so he wouldn't discover the wampum against my chest. Long after he fell asleep, I was listening to the eerie hoot of a large white bird in the tree above. How odd life was. I'd rarely slept next to anyone, and now for two nights running a warm body curled close beside me in the dark.

The broken sobs of the bugle for reveille brought me to a rude awakening. The smell of smoke and barley porridge wafted into the clearing and the Major marched through, slashing his rapier at the rising sun and calling us to muster. Hoar frost coated the leaves and the chill of the river sank even to my fingers buried deep inside my coat sleeves.

It took our company forever to ferry across. But once we were at Hiltons' Point on the opposite side, Goodman Cook took out a blade and whittled on a hunk of pine as we walked. "I'm carvin' ye a bowl of yer own, Thomas," he told me. Shavings dropped in his tracks as he talked. "I admire yer learnin', Mister Taylor," he confided. "I'm too old fer book learnin' but I 'preciate the praticalness of it."

The man sounded so genuine that I promised to teach him the alphabet. And so, during our march to Wells, with a stick I formed letters on the ground. When we stopped to rest, Pardon practiced carving new letters into sapling bark. The strong will with which he worked at this woodland sampler sparked me with a sense of pride, and the more Goodman Cook learned, the less I minded the burning blisters on my heels and toes.

Not one Wabenaki Indian had been reported by the threescore men and I doubted there would be, since the woods constantly were alive with whoops and hollers, cursing, bugling, and an occasional musket shot. Several of the soldiers took great delight hunting down anything edible, and as often, not.

Swamp hog was abundant and we were forced to high-step around the wigwams and dammed ponds of the toothy creatures. At Londoners Trade Post on the Shoals, beaver pelts fetched a handsome price, but eating the varmints was a different matter. And while the soldiers exulted over their swamp hog tail simmered in bear grease, I ran into the woods to eat my journey cake.

At Salmon Falls, Lieutenant Plaisted and Major Walderne disappeared into the log garrison while we dragged hemlock boughs to the palisade—it was our last safe refuge before we reached Storer Garrison at Wells.

Men of the northern provinces called the Piscataqua basin Drowned River Valley, and I could see why. Goodman Cook gave up practicing his letters because we were up to our knees in marsh grass. Both supply carts disappeared in a bog and the oxherd had to secure as much of the burden as he could on the oxen.

Musketry was distributed among us. The newer snap-haunce revolving flintlocks were reserved for the regular Portsmouth Militia, and we were given ancient firearms. It took two men to fire these older rifles and dependence on their accuracy could leave one mortal.

That evening, Pardon and I lugged our nine kilo musket beneath a tree to figure out its cumbersome workings. A chest-high staff with a fork on one end cradled the musket while a pike on the other end secured the portable rest in the ground—provided there was any. I secured the musket cord to my wrist and dragged it into position. Supposedly, with our hands free, we could aim the charged rifle and not spill the priming powder. But a sudden rain storm ruined the powder and sent us scurrying for shelter before we had time to fire one blasted ball.

We were following paths blazed by the Saco Sokokis, Kennebecs, Androscoggins, Piscataquas and other tribes named for the rivers of their provenance. Word of the Oyster River massacre had reached the coastal people and they'd gone into hiding. Only we were dumb enough to march in plain view, and I breathed a lot easier when we crested a knoll above the Atlantic shore at Wells.

Pardon picked up a sharp shard to scratch his name on the smooth rock ledge beneath our weary feet. Not thinking, I took off my soggy, burr-studded great coat and spread it in the sun to dry. The salt air and safety of the Storer Garrison at Wells filled me with such relief I sank to my knees in prayer.

Goodman Cook shook me out of sanctity, excited by the large letter P he'd written, if not for Perpetuity at least for the next Precipitation threatening to the north.

Major Walderne clopped up on his filly, which had sadly lost its prance.

"Attenshin!" he ordered.

Pardon groaned his aching joints to a facsimile of order. To make up for his lack of expedience, I stood alert, saluting as I'd seen the regulars do.

Sheer terror distorted Goodman Cook's gummy mouth and before I could figure out what was happening, he flung the shard in his hand at the rump of Major Walderne's horse. While the filly shied, the old man flung my coat at me and wheezed, "Whatever ye be wearin' 'neath yer shirt, Thom, hide it!"

I looked down to see King Philip's star dancing a silvery jig through a gape in my shirt linen.

The Major leapt off his filly. His stiff composure belied the seething anger behind his precise speech. "I 've a mind to put ye in the stocks, man. What be this graffito in plain sight?"

He stared at the P in outrage. Pardon hadn't got the letter right the first time and had made a few false starts. Walderne examined the letter more closely, yelling for his aide de camp, who came running. "What does this look like to you, Jones?"

The aide knelt and traced the P with his finger. "Why Major, Sir, this be the mark of King Philip—the letter P with two dots aside it."

I quickly stepped forward. "Major, may God strike me dead if that is anything but the letter P for this good man, Pardon Cook." I shouldered Pardon, who at this point looked near to fainting. "I 'm teaching him his letters, Sir."

Walderne did not speak but turned to Pardon who had half his beard in his mouth from sheer fright. "Pardon Cook!" he shouted.

Pardon nodded like a puppet with palsy.

"And pray tell, what do ye know of King Philip, Goodman Cook?"

Pardon spat out his beard, pulling stray hair from his gums with trembling fingers. "He be the devil incarn and a traitor to the Good Lor' at made 'im. I hates the scoundrel to perfidy, Major."

Walderne crossed his arms and scowled at me. "Keep it up, Mister Cook, and the men'll be so full of arrows they'll look like porcupines." He scuffed out the P with the toe of his jackboot which incredibly remained polished and shiny as the day we'd started out.

I stood at attention while Major Walderne swatted at a large orange and brown butterfly. It fell onto the stone and fanned its lovely wings like bellows in the radiant noonday sun. At the Shoals we welcomed the industrious migration of these wondrous butterflies southward, often wishing we could as easily fly away from the rimey north. I watched the Major intentionally stomp on the fragile creature.

"Taylor, run ahead and inform the Wells Garrison sentry we intend to stop," he ordered. "I'll be wantin' supplies and a cart. Ye've wrought enough mischief for one day. Now move!"

I sped away to do his bidding—for whatever punishment the ordinances offered, I felt certain he would delight in. And I ran ever faster, imagining the strapado apparatus by which the wrist-bound victim was lifted off the face of God's beautiful earth and dropped with a jerk halfway to hell.

The Storer Garrison palisade was unguarded and the dwelling completely deserted. An iron pot on the swinging hook above the hearth hung empty and not a kernel of corn or a powder horn was to be seen.

Many of the men, including myself, blamed our present dire predicament on a British know-it-all named John Josselyn who arrived in the New World a few years before fate had cast me onto the Shoals. During Josselyn's stay, he concluded Indians were animals and said as much in a book written several years later, giving as evidence that he'd seen them paddling like dogs.

When I first heard this, I laughed. But it was no laughing matter, because within a fortnight a couple of betting seamen swamped a canoe with a squaw and her papoose to test Josselyn's authorship. Though the Indian squaw fought the deep to retrieve her babe, ultimately the poor soul died of immersion in the icy water. Within days, every Sokokis village from Saco to Portsmouth knew of the incident.

Led by Squando their Sachem Chief, they now were on the warpath. Furious that Josselyn had put our lives on the line, I determined that if I could, I'd use my own gift of letters to undo his ink slinging calumny.

Major Walderne was none too pleased to hear of the deserted Wells Garrison. It meant we must march on to Scarborough where the Blackpoint Garrison might already have fallen to the enemy.

My cheerful countenance in the face of adversity rubbed the Major the wrong way, and I quickly sought Pardon who, bolstered by the salt air, sang a sea chanty at the top of his lungs. I watched the moon rise over the waves and drifted in the revery of their lilting refrain. I'd recently memorized a broadside by a London poet ambivalent about a book he'd authored. "Some said, 'John print it.' Others said, 'Not so.' Some said, 'It might do good.' Others said, 'No.'" If only John Josselyn had as much conscience, we all might be safely asleep and not praying God to preserve us from an arrow through the heart!

At Kennebunk we were treated to a chowder of quahogs, cod, saleratus, and milk from a freshened bossy that had been deserted. Alas, our respite was brief, and once more we slogged through a maddening tangle of gorse, juniper, and sumac. A proliferation of hares hopped in and out the humanly impenetrable thickets, and by nightfall we'd snared enough to roast on hickory sticks.

Pardon and I kept apace, he being worn and I, overly anxious for his safety. But it wasn't until Saco that I was struck by the real danger of our involvement.

Stark against the north river edge stood the charred remains of the sawyer mill and several houses burnt to their stone foundations. While we were brooding on the scene, all at once across the river a lone Indian appeared on a pinto pony. Conscripts scrambled and scattered while the Major silently backed his mare into the pines.

Seized by a sudden awareness, I plummeted forward.

"Stop!" I shouted, "I know this man. He's Scozzway."

The sound of musket balls rolling down the flintlock barrels drove me into the Saco River waving my arms above my head. "Scozz, take cover!" I screamed.

Major Walderne cantered into the Saco, sending a cascade into my face. I thrashed against the undertow and grabbed the horse's tail in desperation. The filly lost her footing and treaded for the opposite shore with me in tow. The volley exploded in my ears and when I surfaced, both riders had disappeared. Soaked to the bone, I crawled onto a sandy spit.

The Major trotted into the open waving his sword overhead. "Hold your fire, men," he shouted.

A dozen wary soldiers appeared in full view.

Scozzway led his pinto from behind a sycamore and helped me onto a huge polished river log. My heart danced at the sight of the fiddler I'd met on the Shoals.

Water sloshed in the Major's pretty boots as he walked toward us. "Conscript Taylor, do I understand you two know each other?"

I tried my best to answer but my lungs were so waterlogged I could scarcely talk. Hoisting me up by the armpits, the friendly Micmac placed me face down over the log and thumped me on the back until my gurgles returned to common parlance. Only then did he recount to Officer Walderne the events of the past two days.

With knowledge that a party of enemy Indians was advancing on Saco, Scozz warned the villagers. They fled to Major Phillip's house and hurriedly prepared for the immanent attack. This was on September 15—the very same day Oyster River settlers were killed by enemy Indians to the south.

In Saco they set fire to Phillips' sawyer and corn mills and made for his house. The Indians were armed with muskets and as the Saco yeomen fired from an upper window, Major Phillips and two others were wounded. Disguised in ferns and leaves, the enemy Indians loaded a rotted field cart with flammable birch bark, pitch pine and gun powder. Fortunately, before they could crash the combustible cart into the house, it stuck in the mud. But though it had to be scuttled, they fired all night and into the dawn on Sabbathday.

Visibly upset by the Micmac's tale, the Major turned nasty.

"Why be ye hanging around, and precisely where has Major Phillips got to?"

Scozz answered only what he had to and no more, and I gazed on him with admiration, for it was no small feat to talk to Major Walderne and come out unaffected.

"He was wounded," Scozz explained. "I transported him by litter to Major Pendleton's at Winter Harbor, then I turned around and came back at his request."

He remounted his pony natural as I boarded a boat. His muscular legs sheathed in deerskin hung from the animal's groomed belly and sunlight glinted off the colored porcupine quills adorning his handsome fringed coat.

Walderne fixed on the soggy tip of his jackboot. "We owe ye our gratitude. I apologize for having my soldiers fire on a praying Indian."

Failing to look the Micmac in the eye, Walderne had missed the comical face Scozz made at the inference that he was a praying Indian. I stroked the pony's spotted cheek. It bobbed its head and snorted a dewy cloud in the crisp air.

Scozz leaned with the grace of a doe bending over a stream. "Gluskab, our God, honors Thom Taylor who would risk his life to save a friend." He placed his ruddy hand over the hidden wampum I wore beneath my shirt. "You have much power, Meeko," he whispered. "Make peace and I will walk with you. Kolele Mooke."

The Micmac's reassuring words filled me with joy. Still, Walderne could have had us both by the heels had he been paying attention, and I shivered with relief when they both rode away.

Down river the soldiers dislodged a raft hidden in the reeds and ferried across. I sought Pardon among them, but though his face gladdened at the sight of me, the excitement of the encounter had addled him to such a degree that he could not remember my name.

The dwelling of Mister Bonighten remained unharmed and Major Walderne disappeared inside to partake of hot cider, a cozy eiderdown and other amenities afforded an officer. Nearby, I found a crevice between a pair of boulders. It smelled of animal scat, but I freshened it up with a bed of fir boughs and laid a plank overhead to protect Pardon and me from the elements.

The following morning Walderne took a score of soldiers with him to Winter Harbor, leaving the trumpeter in charge. Within the time it takes sand to fall in an hourglass, the windy-cheeked man blatted a series of petards. He had calculated a musical code, he told us, demonstrating on his horn—one blast to assemble, two to reassemble, three to dissemble, and so on. While conscripts beat the bushes and listened for the intricate farts, he and his Portsmouth cohorts played at cards.

I was forced to surrender Pardon to his dim-witted chase after nonexistent Indians, for prior to his departure Major Walderne had instructed me to draft a letter to Major General Denison wherein I was to set down Mister Bonighten's tale of the Saco skirmish.

When I asked if Scozzway's account shouldn't also be included, he near had a seizure. "By God, Taylor, how dare ye utter the name of Goodman Bonighten and that musician savage in the same breath? I wonder why ye come so highly recommended?"

The man Bonighten and his busy-body wife not only furnished the facts of the skirmish, but recounted the Genesis, Exodus, Leviticus, and Numbers of Saco and its residents in such detail that I actually welcomed the noon trumpet blast.

Not one of us saw hide nor hair of an Indian, friend or foe, though many villagers stayed barricaded at Major Denison's. A few of the men ventured into the fields to gather corn and other crops the Indians hadn't plundered. I truly felt sorry, for the mill had burnt to the quick and they would be forced to grind meal like the Wabenaki on stone troughs with stone pins.

Pardon equally worried me. He had not returned to his right mind, and though he welcomed me with smiles, it seemed the ancient man had no idea who I was. To worsen matters, the wear and cold of the forced march caused such rheumatism in his limbs that he could no longer walk without the aid of a tree limb crutch.

"Do you recall the letters I taught you, Goodman Cook?" I asked on the fifth day after Walerne's departure. He did not answer and collapsed at the base of a yellowing willow that dripped fronds into the burbling green river current.

He blinked watery blue eyes. "I want to go home," he said with a tremor.

I pillowed my coat under his greying head. "I do too, but we must stay and fight."

"Why?" His childish innocence broke my heart. Why, indeed?

The prow of a sailing vessel rounded the bend of the river and Mister Shapleigh of Kittery stood on its deck. "Good Day, Thom Taylor," he hailed. "I am most happy to see thee alive and safe. Could you meet me at Major Phillip's Landing?"

I pulled Pardon to his feet and dragged the poor soul along. Before I could stow my sorry charge at our boulder den, Shapleigh had docked his vessel and entered Bonighten's dwelling.

"Sit down, Thom. Do sit down." he greeted me as if we were lifelong friends.

There were but two chairs in the room and both were occupied. "Goodman Bonighten, would you mind retiring?" he solicited. "I have a private matter to discuss with Mister Taylor."

I was so astonished by the good will with which Bonighten fulfilled this request that Shapleigh literally had to shove me into the vacated seat.

"To business, Thom, before Mistress B. burdens us with Saco Godsip. The Narraganset squaw has been afforded safe conduct to the Penacook winter camp where Wannalancet looks after her. The boy, too, of course."

I flushed with gratitude.

"The scuppernong be strong these parts," he said, kindly passing off the humility of my indebtedness to the wine.

Silence passed between us.

"We do good when and how we can, Thomas. The friends we take into our hearts come of Divine Providence. Me and thee—."

Goody Bonighten bustled into the room with her best plate piled high with a stew of pork which she amiably informed us came from two hogs that had wandered into Major Phillip's privy the Sabbath of the skirmish and ended up slow-cooked by the enemy.

"As I was saying—." Mister Shapleigh glanced at the woman hanging onto his every word, "Let us pray." His soft-spoken, long-winded thanksgiving over the food had its desired effect and the impatient woman bustled out.

The provenance of the vittles did little to commend them, and harpooning pumpkin and apple with our fingers, we steered clear of the charred hog chunks.

Gaining confidence in the man before me and in myself, I told him of my endeavor to save Scozzway from the perils of war and asked, by the way, what Meeko might mean. Discovering the word was Wabenaki for a red squirrel I could not hide my disappointment.

"Vigilance and industry are qualities Scozzway saw in thee, Thom," Shapleigh palliated, "not thy red hair."

He then offered me dry accommodation at Bonighten's. I asked if I could fetch the ancient Mister Cook as well and with his consent ran into the frosty night.

Near the boulders I nearly dropped my pitch torch when the light shone on a green-eyed creature with notched ears rimmed in black and bared white teeth. I backed up and reached for a stone but the bob-tailed animal gave no quarter, snarling and hissing. It was her den and she was out for revenge.

Fixing the flickering torch on her, I scrambled atop the boulder and took aim. Before the beast could spring, I fired the stone at her head. Yowling pitifully, the cat slunk into the darkness. Not one soldier stirred as I walked my ancient companion through the bushes.

To my surprise, Mister Shapleigh embraced Pardon like a long lost brother. "Mister Cook, you old coot. Don't you recognize me? We worked fish flakes together on the Isles of Shoals."

Pardon blinked. "I want to go home."

I didn't know what to say to account for the poor man's lapse of memory. "If it's any consolation, Mister Shapleigh," I said with a pang of sorrow, "Mister Cook and I have been in each other's company more than a sennight, and he doesn't recognize me either."

The next morning Shapleigh told me that Goodman Cook would be returning to Kittery by boat and he wished me to accompany him. Much as I longed to leave, Major Walderne had commissioned me to write a letter to General Denison recounting the events at Scarborough, and it required Walderne's signature.

Shapleigh smiled faintly. "Duty calls, eh, Thomas?"

"Major Walderne could have me on the strapadoe," I said, embarrassed by the fear in my voice.

He patted me on the shoulder. "The Major and I make strange bed fellows, but we both are in command in the northern province, Thom, and I'll vouch for thee. We Shoalers must stick together in time of need— and Pardon doth seem in dire need. "

Brimming with thoughts of Christian charity and Shoals brotherhood, while Mister Shapleigh loaded his vessel with supplies, I hastened to inform the trumpeter of my departure.

He threw down his dice and grumbled to his feet. "Yew whot?"

"I said, I'm departing with Capt'n Shapleigh on his vessel bound for Kittery. Goodman Cook is too worn to continue the march and I must care for him."

He curtseyed and mocked in a falsetto voice, "Goodman Cook be too worn and I must care for him—and I be a simperin' pansy."

The soldiers roared, affecting womanish poses, blinking, and pursing their lips.

Thankfully, Mister Shapleigh appeared and they clamped shut like a bed of clams. He stared solemnly at the trumpeter.

"Who is in charge of these troops?"

The Portsmouth herald puffed his chest like a powder pigeon.

"I be, Sir."

"Well then, I spoke with Major Walderne at Winter Harbor yesterday morning and I have his authority to remove any wounded in the Saco skirmish. Pardon Cook has been thus afflicted, and I plan to transport him by boat to Kittery. Mister Taylor here has agreed to look after him while the bo'sun and I navigate. Am I to understand that you object to Mister Taylor's leave of absence to assist me in this matter?"

"Why—I—uh—. No, Sir."

Shapleigh seized the man's hand and pumped it. "Then I'll let thee get back to thyr soldiering. Major Walderne will be pleased to hear I found his men dutiful and ever vigilant."

16

I stood at the stern and stared at the Isles of Shoals until they floated out of sight at the mouth of the Piscataqua River. Shortly after, we docked at Gunnison's Ordinary on Kittery Point, Maine. The tavern had been Shapleigh's house before he moved up river to his estate on Sturgeon Creek. Nicholas Shapleigh inherited his father's vast timber holdings from Kittery to York and it caught my attention how he acquired land and titles with the same ease as John Cutt and Richard Walderne.

With due respect to ambition, it seemed those who came during the Great Migration had an easier time, although I was surprised to learn the Courts hadn't always treated Mister Shapleigh fairly. During our voyage, I pieced together the flotsam and jetsam of his life from his arrival on the same ship as Phillip Babb in 1641.

While an officer with the Maine Militia, Boston round heads accused Shapleigh of not following their considerable rules and regulations and booted him out.. So he became a Selectman. But Kittery accused him of holding illicit Quaker meetings. Not only did they force him to resign but bodily dragged him from his

manor. The Boston Puritans, with nothing against him but tolerance for his fellow man and intolerance for British law, threw him
into gaol. But finding he knew a great deal more about the north
country Indians than they did, they released him, and with Major
Walderne, he was ordered "to meet and treat savages of the northern Province."

Shapleigh left me with his son John at Kittery while he delivered
Pardon Cook to his family.

Crossing the river to Portsmouth, John sprang a leak that he
was adopted, which led me to confess he was talking to an orphan.
With the same kindness his father had shown, he said that if ever
I needed help I could count on him—it was a crying shame how the
King tore families apart to line his coffers. This wasn't the kind of
help I needed. Worried that his forthright remarks may have been
heard across the water, I pulled harder on the oars. Once at Puddle
Dock, I lost myself in the crowd.

The first tidings that reached me in Portsmouth were that the
Boston gentry had raised a call-to-arms escalating their war on
enemy Indians. Having dispensed with my letter writing, I rushed
to Major Walderne's billet at Mister Jeffrey's to ask if I could return
to the Shoals in my ketch—if only for a few days.

I stood at attention while the Major spat on a muckinder and
polished the toe of his jackboot. The upshot of my big mouth was
the impoundment of my ketch by the newly assembled Provincial
Militia and an order to ride his lame filly to Mister Cutt's and give
him the letter.

As the skittish filly trotted contrary to my posting and jerked at
the reins, I was beginning to feel my ordeal would never end. I'd
just gotten my stride when I happened on a brawl of soldiers outside the Puddle Dock Tavern.

Suddenly, out of nowhere, a woman dashed into the path with
the suckling infantry in hot pursuit. I pulled on the farthingale, but
instead of halting as I'd expected, the filly broke into a canter.

Swerving to see if I'd knocked anyone down, I recognized Will Babb on top of the heap.

"Will!" I shouted.

The filly reared and raced away with me. It was just as well. Obviously, Will hadn't changed, and I felt wonderfully superior riding off.

Mister Cutt was in the same room I'd left him an eternity ago. Curiosity getting the better of me, I asked about the servant boy I'd kidnapped from under his snuff-stuffed nose.

The lad had disappeared, Cutt told me, and good riddance. The devil Indians were spoiling everything he'd worked for, and if he had his way, by God Almighty, they'd pay for it in land and lives.

"Have you heard of John Abbot?" he queried.

"I know he comes from the Shoals."

"Not any more!" Cutt cried, pacing back and forth with his story. Abbot had been fishing near Richman's Island when enemy Indians kidnapped and carried him north to the St. Francis River. Once Cutt presided over the New Hampshire Council, by God Almighty, he'd rout out every last one of them.

Hearing Cutt's story, I worried about Pru and the young Babbs out at the Shoals. Whether Will had been conscripted or deserted them for greener pastures didn't matter. They were on their own and I had to find out if they were all right.

Mister Cutt didn't offer me a seat, but himself took a high-backed bench near the fire.

"Major Walderne rode by on his way to Cocheco," he said. "Ye'll be stationed at his garrison up north."

The thought of being holed up all winter under Walderne's surveillance stoked my courage into a blaze.

"Mister Cutt, if I may be so bold? In light of Mister Abbot's disappearance, wouldn't I be more useful on the Shoals? We could outfit the hermaphrodite brig with canons. And you may recall I 'm lodged within a short distance of the Star Island Fort."

"Not any more." Mister Cutt tapped the lighted pipe bowl on his forehead.

This seemed an odd gesture, for it glowed red hot. Perhaps the worry of war had loosed the man's senses like those of Pardon Cook.

"What do you mean, Sir? Have the Indians taken Fort Star, too?"

He stared at me, taking more time than my question warranted.

"What do I mean?" he repeated.

"Yes, Sir." I waited.

"I mean you're no longer lodged within a short distance of the Fort, Goodman—ah, Thom. I do apologize, but I forgot you'd asked for my brother's Star Island cottage and I transferred the deed."

I prayed the Lord would stop me from strangling John Cutt then and there. The influential man's holdings amounted to greater than Major Walderne's and Nicholas Shapleigh's put together. Yet, careless as taking off his nightcap, he'd taken the roof off my head.

"And the brig?" I asked, prepared for the worse.

"What brig would that be?"

His forgetfulness increased my exasperation. "Your deceased brother's hermaphrodite brig."

"Ah yes, the brig. Mister Pepperrell required it for a mercantile affair commissioned by Mister Bray of Kittery." He set the clay curling iron to his forelock and drawled absentmindedly, "I do believe that young man has designs on Bray's daughter Margery."

Eclipsed by Pepperrell again. And where was the Grand Acquisitor now? No doubt conveniently sailing for London or the Barbadoes or the Good Lord knew where, while we risked life and limb defending his damn acquisitions.

Defeated to silence, I bade Mister Cutt a stony good day and returned to Great Island on foot.

The Massachusetts Bay called for a Day of Humiliation to fast and pray for our sins and afflictions. Added to their grievances were

my own humiliations which would take more than a day to overcome. Major Walderne's son Richard had charge of the Provincial
Militia and drilled us ceaselessly. The flintlock muskets issued on the
first day of our drilling required the patience of a clock maker, dexterity of a musician, and strength of a blacksmith to load and fire.

Days shortened and my patience with them. When the sun
dropped so did I—into the fetid straw at Mister Jeffrey's barn. The
long awaited October Humiliation Day lured only a handful of
men from their dwellings,so great was the fear they would lose
their scalps.

Not knowing how I fit into the the Creator's Grand Scheme, I
concentrated on the musket problem. Early failures were visible in
powder burns on my hands and face. A conceited fop who danced
his way through the about-facings and doublings held up a mirror
after drilling one day and advised me to give up. I'd taken to raz-
ing with a blade and in addition to nicks from barbering, the blue-
black powder burns made my face look like moldy cheese. Tired of
it all, I went out and shot pumpkins full of musket balls.

The last drill after Thanksgiving, the Portsmouth and New Castle
Artillery Companies held a firearms contest. In the final round, a
pair of hot shots from Hampton faced off with Will Babb and
myself.

I bit the cartridge paper with my teeth and stared at Will whom
I'd successfully avoided since our encounter on the bridle path.
"Did you leave Pru on purpose or were you conscripted?"

Will spat some powder that had gotten into his mouth and
poured the rest from a twisted cartridge into the priming pan of his
musket. The spring on the pan closed with a snap.

"Yer stupid anger be costin' ye, Puker," he taunted, standing
his musket on the butt stock to load it.

Furious, I wrenched loose the iron rod. "You think you're a
man because you've had a Strawbery tart."

Will wordlessly tamped the remaining powder down his
gun barrel.

I jammed the rod down my musket barrel and slid a ball on top of the powder, aware too late that I'd forgotten the oiled patch to facilitate the speed and direction of the projectile.

Will sighted his musket and chuckled. "Better grease yer balls, Thom—if ye plan to fire the Barbadoes slut someday."

I was so disturbed by what Will said that I didn't prime the charge well either, and the fire flash in the barrel caused such an explosion it knocked us both into the dirt. Once on the ground, we abandoned musketry for kicks, punches, and curses wherever we could get them in.

Captain Walderne Jr. disengaged us with difficulty and summarily dismissed us for our conduct, leaving the glory prize to the Hampton muzzle-loaders.

I could not believe how easily Will got to me. Why should I care what he did? Losing the contest hurt my pride, but to lose the respect of the soldiers who counted on me sent me into a gloom glowering as the sky.

With the prolonged autumn, Portsmouth settlers ventured out of their houses, knowing the Piscataqua abenaki had gone up-river to their winter camps on northern lakes. Wonnalancet moved the Pawtucket tribes on the Merrimack River up to Penacook, and the Pequokets migrated north to Lake Ossipee.

At Christmastide, shops on the lanes at Strawbery Banke sold English cravats, snuff boxes and laces—though peas and beans were scarce. The Boston round heads were waiting for a shipload of food from England to stave off hunger, Indian skirmishes having left them in narrow straits.

As for us, we hoarded provisions like squirrels cached acorns, tightening out belts and living off what we always lived on—fish, pumpkins, and rum. Enterprising mast merchants expanded their ports-of-call to include the Barbadoes, and while the King's men in Boston were preoccupied, we smuggled as much as we dared, kept our traps shut, and did what we pleased.

One day I patrolled the coast and discovered a doe lying on the ground. She'd been caught in a snare and her leg was badly ruptured. The soft creature's neck twitched in pitiful contortion. My musket trigger was half-cocked and I pulled it. The sound of the hammer on flint and striking the steel plate alerted the doe to danger. Her supplication was helpless as Christ on the cross as sparks in the saltpeter exploded the ball into her snow-white bib. Seeing the creature's wide eyes frozen in fright, I prayed for her soul as I'd never petitioned for mine.

To avoid thinking how I'd feel had I fired on a man, I fabricated a makeshift sledge with willow poles and a hurried weave of the sinuous deer gut. The doe weighed little and I dragged her across the field to the garrison where the cook gladly took her flesh in return for the scraped hide.

Next, I commissioned the cobbler at Strawbery Banke for a pair of deerskin boots such as those Scozz had worn, my oilskin boots now being far too small. Promising the cobbler the used boots and the tailor a kilo of musket balls, the day before Christmas I pulled on my new doeskin breeches and wool-lined muckluks. Happy as a child with a string of rock candy, I decided to treat myself at the ordinary near Puddle Dock Landing.

I passed the entrance to the waiting room for ferry passengers bound for wilderness destinations and was entering the tavern when a gentle woman in a cloak with a silk tiffany hood brisked out of the waiting room. She was in a great hurry.

I seized her arm. The red silk hood slipped back and Pru's green eyes blinked in the flakes of snow sifting through the sunlight.

"Do I know you?" she asked with typical Shoals candor.

"Surely you must remember me, Prudence Monforte!"

At once she removed a small gloved hand from her sealskin muff and smiled mischievously. "Bowels o' Mercy, if it isn't Puker."

Her allusion to by-gone days filled me with delight and I ushered her into the waiting room. We settled into an inglenook away from the fog of tavern smoke. Finger by finger she pulled off her gloves. I reached across the table and caressed her hand. The hot toddy was strong and my desire so aroused that it put the snug fit of my breeches to the test. She was shamelessly pretty with her curls piled lady-like on her head and secured with a tortoise comb. She wore a homespun winter dress that off-set the gentle rise of her breasts beneath a plain white linen collar.

She pulled her hand away. "Thom, I hardly recognized you."

I ran my fingers over my barbed face.

She blew on the toddy over-heated by the fire poke. "Nay, it's not your beard." Sadness crept into her voice. "You've grown up."

"Better than to grow down." A quick smile passed over her lips, but these days few were in a mood for rejoicing. "Are you and the children all right, Pru? Have you enough to eat?"

She tossed her head and squared her shoulders. "It's not your place, Thom. Will Babb must provide for us. It's his duty."

"Will wouldn't know duty if it hit him from on high and knocked him unconscious." I tried to make light of this observation, but my rancor ate through. Pru and Will's entanglements were like the installments of Mademoiselle de Scudery's concupiscible romances.

"And where is Will?" she asked, unsuccessful at keeping her voice steady.

I couldn't bear her longing for the two-timing devil, and the drink in me took a turn for the worse. "He's at the Portsmouth Garrison. I'm billeted with Richard Walderne Junior, and the Provincial Militia. I'm his Courier." As if this weren't enough self-congratulation, I fired another volley. "Mister Shapleigh has employed me as Associate to treat with the Indians in the North, and I'm also Emissary to the Honorable John Cutt."

Pru clasped my hands. "I'm not at all surprised, Thom Taylor. Anything you do surely will bring the favor of God and men."

I'd become bigger than my britches in more ways than she imagined and was indeed glad she couldn't see beneath the table.

I held her hands. "Pru, only ask and you'll have my assistance."

More empty words. My ketch was impounded. My cottage was gone, and the hermaphrodite brig but a dream on high seas. I'd traded everything I owned for my dashing wilderness apparel. All I had left to my name was a moth-eaten, straw-covered great coat and the dangerous Indian wampum beneath my shirt which could land us both in gaol.

"If you care to help me, Thom, direct me to Will." Her importuning eyes reminded me of the doe I'd shot.

"More than likely he's in the loft above us with a Strawbery tart," I said. At once I regretted it, for she brushed away a tear, picked up her muff, and without another word hastened out.

During January thaw, Major Walderne sent for me from his Cocheco outpost. The flyboat I boarded at Puddle Dock Landing swiftly sailed past the snow-covered pines lining the shores like white-shawled penitents. In three hours we had covered the same distance to Bloody Point which had required a day on foot. Given how swift river travel could be, I wondered why the Major had worn out our boots and dispositions marching overland to Saco River.

The pilot, Thomas Laighton, lived in Cocheco and pointed out various landmarks on the way.

"It be a hand of rivers," he explained as we rounded Bloody Point. Grabbing my right hand, he held it knuckles up.

"The little finger be Newichawannuck—which be a mouthful—so we call it Fore River—and it leads north to Salmon Falls on the upper Piscataqua River." He pointed to the bottom of the V made by my little and fourth fingers. "That be Dover Point which we passed, and yer fourth finger be our destination, Back River. The space between Fore and Back Rivers be Dover Neck." He gazed on my hand chart with growing excitement. "Now ye see, Thom, yer middle finger be Oyster River and Royalls Cove. The landfall between Back and Oyster Rivers at the V between them be Fox Point. Little Bay be that skin between yer first and second knuckles. Yer very first finger be the Sqamscott River which leads to the Puritans at Exeter." Captain Laighton spread back the thumb of my right hand. "All this space between the tip of yer thumb and first knuckle be Lubberland surrounding the Great Bay."

The more he explained, the less I knew of the complication of creeks, coves, and points. What I did retain was that the fore and aft rivers conveniently stretched along either side of Dover Neck, and that Major Walderne owned and operated several mills on each.

Chunks of ice heaped the banks, leaving a navigable salt channel up the middle. Through bare trees on Dover Neck I made out a stark meeting house and fort. Not a single smoke curl wound from the chimneys of the few scattered cabins. Portsmouth had bustled with the activity of merchants and mast-men a thousand strong, and I wondered how long I could stand the dreary place.

Captain Laighton tied his boat at the mouth of Nute's Creek on the west side of Back River. Watching him secure the knot formed a knot in my own throat. The Major had sent for me and little more. Where was I to lay my head in this God-forsaken wilderness? The ferry captain lived in a rude log shelter hardly large enough for himself, and since "night was falling faster than the hood on a condemned pirate," he suggested that I seek refuge at Mister Dam's Garrison the next lot over.

I was trudging through the rotten snow when a figure in the distance crossed the twilighted path. Heart pounding I raised my musket.

"Who goes?"

In response, a creature the size of a horse with a wide rack of antlers lumbered off into the pines. I had no idea what it was and didn't waste time to find out.

About forty rods up Back River and eighty rods inland I came to the pole stockade. No sooner had I entered the make-shift enclosure than I stared directly down Mister Dam's musket barrel. He had no orders from Major Walderne. What proof did I have that I was soldier Thomas Taylor? For all he knew I could be a vagabond Quaker.

True, I wore no uniform and had nothing but powder burns and a musket to show for my wondrous appointment in the Portsmouth Provincial Militia. The redolent odor of cooked venison wafted through the cracked door, and the inviting firelight and howl of a lonely creature in the dark forest prompted me to step closer.

Mister Dam cocked his ancient rifle.

"Wolves, stranger Taylor. Take one step more and ye'll be their guest for supper, not mine."

Emboldened by hunger and the damp cold, I held out my musket and ammunition. "I have a pound of musket balls, Sir, nineteen to the pound, and this flintlock. With due respect, Goodman Dam, this snaphaunce was provided by the Portsmouth Company and Major Walderne's son trained me."

The grim settler was still none too friendly, but he lowered his musket and, confiscating my snaphaunce, waved me inside. A woman plain as sin was about to hand me a charred hunk of venison on a trencher when her husband yanked it out of my hands and forced me to my knees on the wide brick hearth. Ravenous as I was, I mumbled my way through half the prayerbook, ending with the The Lord's Prayer. By the time we had finished, the venison was stone cold.

Whispering to themselves, the couple retired to a dark corner of the garrison. Though I practiced invisibility, I could not refrain from stealing a glance at them. They moved back to a small trundle bed in the corner and again fell to their knees. A whimper filled the room, then a sob.

The wind moaned across the chimney and the wolves joined their lament. No wonder Mister Dam had been so upset. His child was sick and I was yet another burden. A sudden solemnity took such hold of me that I failed to hear the pounding on the door.

Before anyone could open it, an Indian brave bound across the threshold. He slid his moccasins out of a peculiar pair of wood circles strung with gut and heaved the heavy door shut with astonishing broad shoulders. His fur bonnet grazed the low rafter.

John Dam moved into the firelight and held out his hand. "Wahowah, what brings you to this neck of the woods? I haven't set eyes on ye since the long-night-moon."

"What you would call Divine Providence, Deacon," he retorted.

Deacon! So that's why he wore out the floor boards on his knees.

The handsome brave neared the child's bed. "Your son William appeared to me in a dream, John. I strapped on my snow paws and followed the Great Bear to carry a medicine song to my little brother."

They were a tight stopper of friends and I was about to withdraw to the loft when the brave came up.

"I be Wahowah, Sachem of Squamscott, son of Robinhood, Sagamore of Kennebec."

"Thomas Taylor of the Isles of Shoals, son of Thomas Randolph Taylor of London," I reciprocated. Seeing a tubular strand of wampum on his chest, my hand darted to the shell necklace beneath my shirt.

His hand went to his chest as well. "Meeko, you too appeared in my dream."

Before I could wonder at this mysterious encounter, he handed me a doeskin pouch. "Remove the herbs, Thomas, and have Goody Dam brew them. I must make a Dance of the Spirit to bring little William Dam back to life."

Glad to have something to do, I fetched snow so the woman could brew the herbal concoction. Meanwhile, the Sachem had removed his shirt and leggings. Standing half naked in the firelight, he puffed long draughts of tobacco from a red stone calumet pipe. From the medicine bundle he took a finely wrought carving of a snow hare leaping as if in mid-air. Beside it to the right he placed his quiver, arrows, and hunting bow.

For his part, Deacon Dam produced a flagon of rum and sang the English version of Wahowah's medicine song.

> *These are the songs of the Friend*
> *made by the Medicine Man*
> *at the hour when balm-giving herbs*
> *lie under the snow..*

Their combined shuffling loosed a steady trickle of dirt from the rafters above. The smoke and steam from the boiling herbs blurred my vision, producing a double haze in my head. The Sqamscott Indian had daubed his face with colored clay, held the calumet aloft in supplication, and whirled in the trickles of rafter dust.

> *The eyes of the Medicine Man*
> *were pale as dawn. The Manitou*
> *of the hare leapt to earth.*

His bare back glistened in the firelight and sweat dripped from his chest on which he wore the sacred shell wampum of his tribe. Deacon Dam also threw off his shirt in the frenzy of their hopping and stomping. They appeared to me as night and day with the brave's dark skin smooth as golden birch and the Cocheco yeoman sprouting bristly hair like a swamp tamarack tree.

> *The shadow of his songs*
> *scattered hollows into the cheeks*
> *like ash in the pits of the hearthstone.*
> *The Manitou of the hare leapt to earth.*

The Deacon downed his spirits. The Sachem smoked his calumet, and I succumbed to the rattle of deer hoofs fastened to their dancing calves.

Bitter and thick was his voice
with the dust stirred by his dancing.

The repeated chant carried me like a soaring frigate bird over the waves. No longer a spectator, I swooped and swayed to the unrelenting rhythm. The brave's gyrations grew too intense even for John Dam's muscled body, and he expired in a heap on the floor. Distressed by her husband's collapse, Goodwoman Dam ran over and poured a tot of the herbal brew down his liquor-parched throat.

His eyes shot open. "Wahowah, ye red-skinned devil!" he shouted from the floor. "Do ye mean to kill or save our son with yer infernal herbs?"

The chanting Indian took the cup and bent over the bed to administer it to the child. From where he'd fallen, Deacon Dam no longer translated the English. But something exceeding strange entered my own head, and without a break in the rhythm I sang the words to the song. To this day I don't know how I did it, for though I'd picked up a few words of Micmac and Piscataqua, this was the first time I'd heard Squamscott. Yet, I stood and in wondrous voice I sang:

> *What is this that stirs beside me?*
> *What sweet troubling?*
> *It is my thought that quickens to my friend, William.*
> *The Manitou of the hare has leapt to earth.*

The nature of the ceremony affected me so profoundly that I quaked with their combined power. As different as the two men seemed, they obviously were amicable and trusted each other.

> *Now is my walk changed*
> *and my strength braced with laughter.*
> *I am so much more than myself*
> *as the friend of my friend.*

I momentarily drifted into darkness.

"Please don't sleep!" Goodwoman Dam pleaded, shaking her husband's sagging shoulders.

A falcon swooped over my head from the rafters and I catapulted forward straight into the arms of the Squamscott Sachem. Despite herself, the woman sank into a swoon, joining her husband who slept peaceful as a babe.

Were the Sachem and I the only ones awake?

Wahowah held me in his strong hands while the words of the song poured from my mouth fully formed.

> *All night we sing,*
> *until the wolf hour of the morning.*
> *My heart is a lair hidden under my songs*
> *and my dancing a screen before its ways.*
> *When illness pursues my friend*
> *he shall lie safe there like the hare in its nest.*

The feverish child sighed and tossed restlessly under the quilt. I tried to back away but the Sachem held the cup to my mouth.

"Drink. We men must partake the blood of the hare."

He was by far the stronger in body and spirit, and without protest, I swallowed the bitter brew.

I awoke in a warm bed with a coverlet over me in the pitch dark. I assumed it was still night and had just convinced myself I must have been dreaming when a trap door brought to light the tousled curls of a child.

"Mother says fer ye to rouse yerselves," he pronounced in a small voice. Climbing the ladder into the garret, the boy padded over to a mound beside me on the plank floor.

"Sachem Hopehood!" he whispered loudly, picking up the corner of the fur robe. "Mother has fixed yer breakfast."

The Indian brave bound to his feet lively as though he'd slept the night through. While he was rolling up his fur robe, the boy stared at him in disbelief.

"Mother says that yer Squamscott medicine cured me."

He smiled. "Thom and your father helped me to obtain a good outcome."

The boy's mouth hung open. "You mean the stranger cured me, too?"

The brave acknowledged me with smiling eyes. "Aye, William! All of us be infused with the Spirit of our Fathers and the peace of the calumet."

A flood of gratitude crept into my aching body and eased my backward descent down the ladder and into the kitchen. Mister Dam and I companionably razed our faces from the same bowl of water. Then, we all made short order of Goody Dam's hot porridge and fresh corn cake.

My first step out the door landed me in a snow drift up to my knees.

"Try these, Meeko," the Sachem said, handing me the odd bear paw shoes.

Knowing he must return to Point Hood, I gave them back.

"I canoe the Big Squamscott Water," he said, picking up my musket and caressing the smooth stock with obvious pleasure.

.I'd have given it to him—were it mine to give.

"Tell you what, Thom. I'll come when the salmon leap. Maybe you'll bring me a moose."

"I'd gladly shoot one if I knew what it was," I told him.

"Have you no moose on the Isles of Shoals?"

"Not unless it's a fish," I said.

He laughed. "Moose be king here. He stands tall with antlers far as you can stretch and nose of great measure."

"I saw one yesternight on my way here!"

He bent to help me strap on the unwieldy paw shoes.

"Moose hide be warm and strong. We string moose gut for snow paws and smoke moose meat for journey pouch. Take, take."

I chewed off a bite of the smoky strip, depositing the rest in my coat lining.

He laughed again. "Just like Meeko to cache food for winter."

Feeling foolishly like a babe learning to walk, I took a step on the round woven shoes.

"You look like Mister bear after a long sleep," he said, kneeling to tighten the rawhide ties, "but by full moon Meeko will sail through the forest."

Deacon Dam came to the door to wave good-bye and I slid away in the direction of Spruce Lane. The land had disappeared under snowfall, leaving a doubled-file gauntlet of whipping branches and plopping snow.

17

On the fleet shoes I sped like Mercury along the snowy path, crossing a bridge at Sawyer's Mill and entering a hamlet not far from the crash of the upper Cocheco falls.

Major Walderne's house was protected by a stockade inside of which stood a new brick and clapboard mansion. The windows of five gables sparkled in the sun and several chimneys vented smoke into the bare branches of a giant oak.

I shivered on the granite step, unaccustomed to the sudden bitter cold. On the Shoals we had brown winters, but here the snow seemed endless. My shoulders were white with it and my breath steamed as I listened to the chime of voices aroused by my impatient knocking.

The Major himself appeared in his usual bellicose attire, which I suspect accompanied the military man even to his wife's bed chamber.

"Taylor," he said lackluster as ever, "I trust you had a safe journey."

I was too dumbstruck by the grandeur of the dwelling to do anything but nod and gawk. Above my head floated a shiny silver candelabra attached to a pulley for lighting a score of beeswax candles. A wondrous staircase with a graceful smooth wood banister replaced the usual ladder to the upper story. A domed sea chest gleaming brass hasps and eyebrow hinges sat beneath a magnificent gilt-framed looking-glass.

I stared into it with complete shock. Gone was the clean-faced scrawny boy who had been cast on the Shoals and in his place stood a stranger. Surveying him, I could not wholly discredit my twin. His eyes were clear blue, and a red-gold beard offset his broad shiny forehead. He looked stalwart enough—though very perplexed. Behind this apparition I noticed a pair of tiny slippered feet and the hem of a skirt. Quickly, I turned to the stairs, but she had vanished.

Major Walderne bore my self-appraisal with cross-armed impatience and I hurried after him into a side chamber.

Red Turkey tapestries draped a drawing table and satin-upholstered day couch. Lined up at the table were a set of high-backed basswood chairs with carved eagle feet and ornate scrolled arm rests. The sideboard overflowed with silver plate, and British soldier andirons stood at attention on the hearth. A silk fire screen had been shoved aside, allowing heat to suffuse the room, and fireglow glinted from the showy chasing of a silvery saber dangling from a beam. The wide granite mantel was strewn with a battery of muskets, admitting a striking disorder to the otherwise commodious room.

Major Walderne barked orders. He'd be in Boston during the March town meeting at Cocheco. I was to go so that I could apprise him of the proceedings, learn the assessment on his holdings, and vote in his absence. As soon as the snow melted, I'd be drilling at Mister Tuttle's Field. His son Richard had informed him I was a hot-shot. Unfortunately, he'd also told him I was a hot-head. I could be Ensign in the Provincial Militia on one condition—that I stick to my guns.

Having left me with more commands than Moses, the Major said I could stay at Deacon Dam's for the duration.

His clammy hand left mine for the safe refuge of his sword pommel. "The Deacon was kind to put you up, or I should say to put up with you."

I laughed to hide my exasperation. "What I'm trying to say, Major, is that John Dam has sent me to you."

Walderne groped the pommel with such abandon his knuckles turned pink. "Well then, I guess we'll have to billet you at the Dover gaol."

"Oh, Father!" The interjection of a feminine voice caught us both off guard. Assuming she belonged to the tiny feet I'd seen on the stairs, I craned around. She was from the Walderne mold all right, but where the poker countenance of father and son paid them little compliment, in her it passed for graceful composure. The whalebone stomacher under her bodice made nothing of her breasts and even less of her waist. In her hand she carried a broad brim hat with a white curved plume and over her arm, a purple capuchin cloak—though the Good Lord knows where she was going in such apparel leagues from nowhere.

One by one she closed the distance to the last stair upon which her height equaled that of her father's.

"I see no reason why this young man could not occupy John Reyner's dwelling. After all, his house remains vacant and well provisioned from mill rents and the town does own it." She sighed. "Alas, Mister Reyner's Christian charity requires him to be with the brave soldiers fighting Narraganset savage Indians in Massachusetts."

Her contagious smile broke through the stoic family reserve and Walderne glowed like a candle. She glanced my way with curious hazel eyes and then back at her father.

"So, it is settled."

"If you ever have daughters, Thom, mind you don't spoil them as I have," Walderne reproached. "I swear Esther should have enrolled at Harvard College with my sons! She be in advance of the lot of 'em."

The enigmatic Esther passed between us to the looking glass

where she put on her hat. "I'm taking the pung to visit Mistress Otis on Dover Neck and by your leave, Father, I'll deposit Thomas Taylor at his temporary dwelling." Whether or not "father" liked this proposition, he acquiesced.

The stable boy had brought a two-horse sleigh to the front gate. I tossed in my bear paws and made a production of tucking the intriguing Esther and myself beneath the fur lap robe. She flicked the whip ever so lightly and the horse trotted through the blinding snow toward still another wilderness destination.

A few leagues down the cart path we stopped at an unimposing log dwelling on Dover Neck and, contrary to my better judgement, I let her follow me inside.

But after stepping into the wilderness dwelling I forgot propriety and thanked her for suggesting I stay there. Ministers live with their books and Reyner's library was a far sight better than her father's musketry. I marveled to myself how the girl had divined my true nature when I hadn't begun to fathom hers.

Little wood and logs already were laid on the hearth and I struck a flint to splinters of kindling. When the fire was pulling a draught I turned back to find Walderne's daughter gravely altered.

Her lips quivered with emotion. "John—uh, Mister Reyner took it upon himself to teach me Latin and I was catechized by him. I love the man more than my own father but I fear he could be dead."

She collapsed in disarray on the day bed. Thinking I'd comfort her I drew closer.

"I'm the cause of his hasty departure," she confided, looking up from the quilt. "We were consumed by desire. Oh—of course I'm not implying John was impious. But during his parting sermon as we gazed at each other I saw how worried he was that our feelings for each other might be discovered."

She clutched her throat. "If John dies I'm to blame."

Flustered by her grief I took her soft hands in mine and we prayed aloud for the minister's safe return—or rather, she prayed while my head spun with the proximity of her.

A week later when I stopped at the Major's, I came upon the family busy with preparations for their departure to Boston.

As a pretext for seeing more of the manor house I offered to fetch down a trunk and bound up the stairs. The stable boy had dragged the trunk into the narrow hallway just as Esther Walderne peeked out of her bed chamber. To tell the truth, I'd thought of her long supine body more than I ought that week. Waving the lad to lift the far end of the trunk, I took the other.

"Set it down, Thom," Esther whispered from the doorway.

I released my hold and the lad, who seemed not to have heard me, let go all at once. The trunk crashed to the floor.

"What in the name of the Portsmouth Militia is going on up there?" Major Walderne yelled up the stairs.

Esther placed her fingers on my lips.

"Nothing, Father," she called. "Don't fret."

The stable boy looked ready to bolt.

She squeezed close beside me in the narrow corridor. "I shall miss you, Thom."

Before I could say the same she planted a kiss on my mouth. The flounces of her brocade travel dress against my legs smelled deliciously of rose pomander. In desperation I gestured toward the gawking boy. When she kissed me again the wide-eyed lad and proximity of her father added deliciously to our excitement.

"Not until the sap stops running do the frogs chirp," she whispered in my ear. "I bet you another kiss the boy won't say a word. And what will you give me?"

"I—ahhh—." Never had I met a girl so comely and daring rolled into one, and at that moment I would have given her anything.

"No matter, Thom," she said, stepping backward into her room.

"I'll collect my kiss when we return. You can depend on it."

The stable boy and I wordlessly hauled the trunk down the stairs and set it before the Major.

"Confound it, Mister Taylor, what took you so long?" Walderne griped. "Good thing that lad is dumb as an ox or I'd give him a tongue lashing, too."

I smiled at Esther's ruse to collect another kiss.

Unfortunately, the Major misinterpreted my levity for derision.

"Laugh if you like, but expediency is of the utmost importance when dealing with Richard Walderne." He fixed me with a pointed stare. "I'm entrusting you with this sheaf of papers with the understanding that you execute my business in a manly fashion."

I promised I'd do everything in my power to carry out his wishes, bowed, and departed with my head spinning from his doughty dictums and the lingering damp of his daughter's lust.

I arrived early at the March town meeting thinking I'd find the barn-like building vacant, but a bon fire warmed the drafty hall and a gathering of Selectmen stood around engaged in discussion as heated as the crackling flames flowing from the massive logs.

One of the Selectmen spat out the name Mason like it was snot. Although I'd never met Mason, I knew that during the early settlement, he and Mister Gorges claimed land on both sides of the Piscataqua River. Half a century later, the pilgrim leases on improved land with river landings, mills, mast roads and dwellings mattered little to Mason who imposed such high rents on the provincials they were being evicted—even though they held the deeds.

I sidled in and eavesdropped on the fine points of a petition to be voted on at meeting. When Richard Walderne's name was called by the secretary taking the roll, I shouted my name and over the din let him know I'd be standing in for the Major.

Men continued to stomp snow into the Dover Meeting House—those from Bloody Point and Oyster River sitting apart from the

Dover Neck and Cocheco men.

Deacon Dam waved me over and I took a place at his side. The Cocheco constable stood up with a pike. He pounded it on the floor three times. Someone near us suggested Deacon Dam moderate the meeting. I sighed in relief when he declined because I was sorely beyond my depth and needed his counsel.

The hubbub died down and John Woodman was chosen as Moderator. He made no bones about fining Mister Clements and Ensign Dawes six pence each for smoking tobacco in the Dover Public Tavern.

Selectman Clements made a grand show of reaching in his vest and counting out every single pence he placed on Moderator Woodman's pulpit. This done, he asked our leave to read a petition.

"Aye, Aye," everyone shouted.

Clements held the paper at arm's length:

Certain petitioners pray his Majesty know that ye inhabitants of the northmost point of Massachusetts have made an order giving liberty of buying and selling land to have and to hold, with heirs and assigns for. . .

He stopped reading and conferred with a man in the front row. "What be that word, Ensign Dawes?"

"Forever!" Dawes shouted from behind a post.

Selectman Clements held the parchment up to his face, squinted, and looked up at the wintery light from the high windows.

"Does anyone own a candle wick or creuset of oil for me to read this petition?"

The man who had read the roll call produced the desired light and holding it in one hand and the paper in the other, Mister Clements continued:

Furthermore, considering the present Indian war princi-pally be in these parts, we have by the assistance of the

Bay Colony and of God Almighty defended our Land and
Estates with expense of our money and blood.

A chorus of yeas, ayes, and hurrahs hurtled to the rafters. The
constable's pike resounded, and the men again fell silent.

Therefore it is unanimously agreed, voted, and ordered that our
trusty and well beloved Richard Walderne, Sergeant Major, does
in the name of our Town petition his Majesty that he interpose
his royal authority and afford us his favor that we not be dis-
turbed by Mister Mason or any other, but continue in our pres-
ent rights under his Majesty's Massachusetts Bay Government.

Moderator Woodman held his taper high and peered into the
dimly lit hall.

"I say, Goodman Taylor, before I take the vote, be there any
objections?"

I had read Walderne's papers backward and forward. No mention was made of this petition. And though I could have written a
most eloquent answer to this effect, speaking to the assembled
landed gentry gave me a sudden attack not unlike pleurisy and
ague rolled into one. Where only a fortnight ago Deacon Dam had
seemed my worst enemy, I now turned to him for salvation.

"Use yer judgment, Thomas," he whispered. "The Major has
vast holdings in these parts, and though he undoubtedly knows
Mister Mason, I suspect he does not relish losing his dwelling to
that shittabed any more than we do."

I stood. My knees nearly buckled with the weight of addressing my elders.

"Moderator Woodman, Sir. Major Walderne hath left me no
instruction in regard to this petition. Let it be recorded along with
your vote. But let it be so worded to allow the Major ample leeway
if he be otherwise disposed." I resumed my place on the crudely
hewn bench.

Deacon Dam patted my shoulder. "Well done, lad. Well done."

My heart had just slowed to its normal pace and the queasiness left my stomach when Walderne's venerated name resurfaced. The assembly was to vote on the Selectmen for the coming year. Each had taken a handful of corn and beans at the door and was required to deposit a corn kernel in the tithe box for yea and a bean for nay. Major Walderne was one of the chosen and once again I had to stand.

Unable to sustain my bravery under the fire of their glances, this time I accepted the Major's appointment with as many ahs and uhs as words.

Though more than a hundred men crowded the benches, the same names kept popping up on the roster of the governing body, and most of the Selectmen were in the Provincial Militia as well. Major Walderne, Lieutenant Nutter, Ensign Dawes and Sergeant Roberts added to their influence by signing up for jury duty.

The town meeting plodded on with the question of land grants. Most Dover yeomen had ten acre parcels adjoining their original lots. Peter Coffin was the exception, having sold Major Walderne his land between Lamprey River and Goddard's Creek.

No wonder Shoalers never attended town meetings. We could ill afford losing a day's profit. Besides, the less landlubbers knew about our business, the better.

In late afternoon I sneaked through the yard and out the stockade gate. The melting snow left puddles in the high way, and I cut through the woods to Mister Reyner's dwelling.

Pausing to look down at a sparkling patch of lazy water on Back River, I saw a sudden movement in the river brambles and a moose creature like the one I'd seen on my arrival crashed onto the shore. He stood taller than a Narraganset pony and wore a great spiked rack. If I didn't fell the beast on my first ball, he'd surely charge and gore me.

Toting the musket I crept closer.

Quickly, I poured powder into my musket pan, rolled a ball down the barrel, rammed, aimed, and pulled the trigger. The mammoth beast lifted his head heavenward and bellowed a frightful appeal. I grabbed twigs and branches sliding to the place where the moose toppled and stared in awe at a creature surely large as the Behemoth of Job.

Primed as a pump, a passage I'd learned from Minister Belcher gushed into my head: *Like an ox with strength in his loins and belly he lies hidden in the marsh surrounded by brook willows. And though the river is turbulent he is unfrighted.*

I sank beside the awesome animal wondering how I'd haul the giant carcass when Dame Fortune in the guise of Sachem Wahowah paddled his birch barque along the shore.

"Good day, Thomas Taylor," he greeted leaping over silvery salmon strung through the mouths from a willow branch. "I see thou hath shot the moose you promised."

My eyes must have gaped wide as my mouth.

"Did I not say I would cross the great water when the salmon were spawning?"

"You did, but—."

He smiled at my surprise. "Mister Moose walked through my dream and you were with him, Meeko, chattering away."

He unsheathed a knife and hacked at a piece of flesh from the bloody mess where the musket ball had lodged. Cutting it free, he held up the gob.

"Great Spirit, we give thanks for this moose that giveth his life for ours."

His words were so similar to Christ's Holy Sacrament they bordered on blasphemy, but I was silent as I watched him ceremoniously place the bloody hunk of flesh and fur on the tidal muck.

"I was returning from town meeting," I said. The uselessness of this news echoed lamely in my ears.

He nodded as he deftly separated the moose flesh from its

thick gray hide.

"They took their time with a petition to the Massachusetts Bay in regards to Mister Mason's taxes and his assertion that he owns this land."

The Sachem looked up. His eyes narrowed.

Mr. Dam had told me Sachem Wahowah owned all the land from Oyster River to Hood's Point, yet the imposing Kennebec brave hadn't even been mentioned at the meeting. I gripped the sharp skinning tool in my hand as Wahowah stuck a piece of the raw moose heart into his mouth. His blood-smeared face filled me with sudden foreboding.

"Did you wish your name affixed to the petition?" I asked, though I had no authority whatsoever in the matter.

He stooped, took a pinch of earth between his fingers and dropped it into my hand.

"Mister Mason does not own this land. White men who wish us to sign their talking leaves do not own it. I who have hunted and fished here with my father Robin Hood and his father before him do not own it. Mister moose who overcrosses its boundaries does not own it. As long as salmon spawn the rivers and moose roam the forest, I have no quarrel with my white brothers."

I was relieved and not a little grateful for his company.

The sun was dropping behind Huckleberry Hill by the time we'd finished butchering the moose. Wahowah gave me a slimy ball of gut-flesh wound with sinew strands.

"You need not eat again for three days after eating moose." He smiled. "Do you have a squaw, Meeko?"

I faltered.

"Eat Mister Moose and you will have two or three squaws. I tell thee, Meeko, moose be a creature of great power." With this strange advice he crouched in his canoe and paddled away.

Moderator Woodman announced my regiment would be drilling but the next morning when I went to open the cabin door I could barely budge it. Snow blew horizontal and the first fragile blades of April grass in the yard were buried in a fathom of the stuff.

I speared a few chunks of moose meat on the fire spit and already was dreaming about the women I'd attract. After consuming a few chunks of the rutty magic moose, I gave in to my lusty cravings to snoop through the man's private possessions.

Hoping to find out more about Esther and Mister Reyner, I pilfered through his library. Ignoring the DAY OF DOOM, which seemed to follow me everywhere, I was removing a gilt-edged book when a sheaf of parchment paper dropped out. Tempted by the handwritten script, I held it to the firelight.

From what I could tell, Minister Reyner had copied passages from a transcript of the First Boston Synod held on November 7, 1637.

Anne Hutchinson's trial and banishment from Wollaston Massachusetts to Rhode Island were no secret. Like Mister Shapleigh she had been accused of holding illicit meetings at her house and the Boston Synod had hanged Mary Dyer who was one of Anne's followers.

Minister Reyner must have come across the Hutchinson transcript when he was a student at Harvard. He showed more than a casual interest. Several passages were underscored, and he'd squibbed and scrawled in the margins. I squinted to read a line at the top of a page:

The damned soul is one which refuses to accept its own divinity.

Hail beat against the roof and a stiff wind whistled across the chimney, sweeping a gust of snow onto the fire. I threw on another log and read more of the trial:

Governor Winthrop:
By what authority do you hold private meetings?

Mrs Hutchinson:
By Titus 2 where elder women are to teach the younger.

Governor Winthrop:
*So we allow. However, you teach many an elder. Nor do you teach
what the Apostle commands, to keep at home.*

Mrs. Hutchinson:
Then why do you call me here to teach the court?"

I imagined the forty men in their somber cloaks and Geneva
caps plying her with their Puritan theology. She had been with child
at the time and I couldn't help admiring her courage.

Mrs. Hutchinson:
*Take heed what ye do unto me, for you have no power over my
body, neither can you do me harm, for I am in the hands of the
eternal Jehovah. God will ruin you and your posterity and the
whole state.*

Mister Endicott:
*I hope the court takes notice of the vanity of her speech and heat
of her spirit.*

I turned the parchment in the light to decipher a minute
word in the margin near this last entry. The writing was so small I
retrieved a candlestick from the table and held it to the miniscule
word.
Esther!
My concentration broke with that one name. Every detail of
Esther's dress, stature and countenance flickered in my mind. I
couldn't dismiss her as readily as the Massachusetts Governor had
banished Anne Hutchinson. Drowsy from the fire and lack of exertion, I fell into such a stupor I crawled back to bed.

On the first of April the storm had abated and the warm sun shone through the cracks.

I scooped buckets of snow away from the door, delighting in the energetic blue sky and singing birds ready for spring. A spray of pussy willows stuck out of a high drift and snow plopped from the eaves in the rutilant sun.

I threw off my great coat and rolled a barrel from the door to clear a path through the snow. Heated by the effort, I packed a handful of icy slush on the back of my neck, paused, and closed my eyes on the memory of Esther as I'd last seen her. No sooner had I opened them when Walderne's pung careened over the horizon with Esther at the helm. She wore dainty red boots and a scarlet feather in her broad brimmed hat. But her face was ashen, and I could tell she was pushing containment to the limit.

I tethered the horse to the low branch of an apple tree and we stood in broad daylight together. "I'm glad to see you Esther," I said. What a lie! I was ecstatic.

"Could we go inside?"

My heart drilled in my chest like the beak of a red-headed bird I'd seen rat-a-tatting for insects in a fallen maple. A drift still blocked the doorway and I lifted Esther in my arms. The intensity of my desire mounted as I circumnavigated that drift slowly as Captain Columbus on his maiden voyage to the New World.

Remembering she was Major Walderne's daughter, I set her down inside the door and stood my distance.

She gazed about the room without seeming to notice the mess. Indeed, she was so pale I went over to the dry sack and poured her a tot.

"I'm to be married."

Unprepared for this revelation, I gulped sherry straight from the bottle.

"I'm sure you'll make Minister Reyner a fine wife."

A discomfiting cold laugh escaped her.

"It's because of Mister Reyner's shilly-shally that I'm to be married to my father's associate, Henry Elkins. They pronounced the arrangement in Boston a fortnight ago." Esther fell onto the day bed and buried her face in the eider pillow.

I closed my eyes momentarily to hope for Divine Intervention. For as much as Sarah Walderne loved the absent minister, I was in love with her.

She sat up. "You could make my father an offer."

I let the thought float in my mind. Blood coursed in my neck and arms, pumping through my body like the unblocked rivers and spring sap-flow in the trees. What children we'd have with her hazel eyes and high cheek bones—well bred and indomitable.

She smoothed the long waist of her tight bodice, shook out her hair and stood beside me. "Mr. Elkins is a sickly elder gentleman, and—. Oh Thom, I could grow to love you as much as John Reyner."

Her use of the conditional could not be ignored, but before I could say a word, Esther flung her arms around my neck and pressed her mouth to mine.

Had Reyner taught Esther to kiss like that? And if he loved her so much why hadn't the Dover divinity agreed to marry her before leaving on his soldiering duties? Our embrace awakened that hidden side to her nature that pleasured me so. Nevertheless, the thought of us marrying bordered on madness. I barely owned a pot to piss in and Major Walderne was the wealthiest man in the provinces. It was some solace to think he wasn't giving his daughter to the Puritan minister, despite his Harvard degree and Dover subsidy.

"I think I've fallen in love with you, Esther, but—."

"You think!" She fixed me with terrible insistence.

"The Major would never consent."

"We could elope, then," she pleaded.

"And break your father's heart Esther? I have nothing to bring such a marriage. Hope alone won't feed us."

Her lips trembled. "Then I must be going."

I caught her arm before she could flee. "Do we part friends?"

She managed a faint smile and slipped beyond my grasp.

Too heavy-hearted to watch her leave, I removed the impeding drift from the path and anxious to be alone, shut the door—only to be summoned back by insistent pounding.

Expecting Esther might have returned for a parting kiss, I closed my eyes. But when my embrace went unanswered, I opened them on a totally strange woman not in the least embarrassed, though like Esther she seemed overwrought. I began to suspect Wahowa might be right about the moose meat. Since eating it, I'd been visited by two women in as many hours!

"May I come in?" the blue-eyed stranger asked with more than a thimble of impertinence.

'Faint heart n'er won fair lady,' as Don Quixote might say, and I swept my arm low over the threshold to welcome her.

"Wilt thou not take my cloak?" she scolded.

Worried she might be Quaker, I moved quickly behind the door to stow the heavy cloak while bidding her make herself comfortable—which she certainly did. For as God is my witness she wore nothing but a sackcloth and his Almighty Grace! Her blond hair was sprinkled with Lenten ashes and straggled about her shoulders. She could have been twenty or forty. The apparition of her unclothed figure frighted me so much that then and there I vowed to give up moose meat forever.

"Thou dost not approve of my appearance," she said. "Wait until Sabbath when I walk naked into thy meeting house. Dover hath passed judgment long enough and I will bare my spiritual nakedness in this town, Minister Reyner, as Christ be my Holy Covenant."

No one had told me of the lunatic that lived on Dover Neck, but here she was. I could only hope that like Esther she had a temporal disturbance that would pass with the waning moon.

Once I'd gained my composure I addressed her. "Goodwoman—ahh—?"

"Deborah Wilson."

"Then Mistress Wilson, it is my bound duty to report this remarkable occurrence to Deacon John Dam who is in charge of Sabbath meeting until Reverend Reyner returns."

I'd left the door open and a crooked little man entered behind the wretched woman. Hoping he might be her ward I waited for him to speak, but he seemed transfixed at the sight of me.

At last he held out his hand in greeting. "I be Edward Wharton, a Quaker and proud of it, and who art thou?"

I thought for sure he wanted to say 'who in the hell,' and smiled at his better-thought omission.

"Thomas Taylor, late of the Isles of Shoals. I've been posted here by Major Walderne until Reverend Reyner returns."

Wharton hobbled full circle around the woman critically eyeing her attire—what there was of it.

"This will not do, Goodwoman Wilson. Have I not told thee more than once to visit only the private homes of them that will receive thee?"

"But I must," she cried defiantly. "I must witness my belief!"

The stooped man made up for his deformity with a spirited order to cover herself at once.

"I apologize for this inconvenience, Mister Taylor. Since that horrid day Major Walderne beat and banished three of our women, we Quakers have kept to ourselves here on Dover Neck far from other dwellings. But Sister Wilson be new to the Friends and unused to our ways. I'll send her by boat across Fore River to seek refuge with Mister Shapleigh until this blows over. Please accept my apology."

The woman wrapped her cloak so vehemently about her that I felt the draft from the hem as it sailed past my face. The fury of her determination held me in its sway.

Though Wharton was soft spoken he talked fast—and soon had me on his side. I didn't know whether to trust him or not, but with a second mention of Shapleigh, I agreed to have the querulous woman delivered to Maine.

After they departed I gathered the leftover cooked moose chunks into a packet and took a walk to clear my head. Trees budded chartreuse and a red-breasted bird sat on a limb chortling. At the convergence of Styx Creek with the mill pond, I drew back my arm and pitched the magical moose far as I could. Bubbles ascended through the green slush and suddenly I felt much better. Squaws or no squaws, from now on I'd eat salad greens and beans.

18

As an officer I was relieved from the tedium of drilling, but had a constant frog in my throat from yelling at the Dover settlers who could not tell their left foot from their right. Nearly out of vocal cordage, I invented a code with the drummer and his miraculous beat did for their feet what my voice had not.

After the drill, Major Walderne looked down on me from a seventeen hand chestnut stud, no doubt purchased for the addition to his stature.

"Ensign Taylor, run over to the gaol at the fort where I have locked up Andrew, Simon and Peter. I've assigned Bickford and Bray to guard them for the Massachusetts Militia. Acquaint yourself with their duty."

The guards he mentioned were so busy gaming they didn't bother to conceal the leather dice cups. Hearing my orders, the man Bray handed me a lantern and led me back to the gaol. Unbarring and kicking the door, he thrust his musket inside and aroused a trio of Indians seated on the earth floor. My stomach flip-flopped with the stench of sweat and urine in the small room.

Yeoman Bray raised the barrel of his musket and gestured toward the cold hearth. "Who put the fire out?"

One of them stood forward. "I did. It be hot as British soldiers in this hell-hole."

"Look what ye say, Simon, or I'll blast ye to a place considerable hotter. From the smell of this chamber I reckon exactly how that fire came to be extinguished. Yer nothin' but savages, the lot of ye. Didn't I leave a piss pot in the corner?"

Simon walked a thoughtful circle. "And the Lord said, 'Simon, Behold, Satan hath desired to sift ye like meal. But I have prayed thy faith faileth not and when thou art converted thou wilt strengthen thy brethren.'"

Bray thrust forward his musket, poking the naked Indian above his skimpy loincloth. "Spout yer damned Biblical verses till doomsday, Simon, but ye still be a red-faced heathen far as I be concerned."

I eyed the preaching red man with curiosity.

Bolstered by my wonder, Simon continued. "Lord, I am ready to go with thee to prison and to death."

Bray poked him again. "Hogwash!"

I inhaled the stale air and gagged. "Can't you clear this room for these men to breathe?"

Gaoler Bickford appeared and casting us aside with the long barrel of his muzzle-loader, in a sudden fit of coughing he jerked it in our faces. Knowing it would rankle them if I pulled rank, I offered to go climb on the roof and clear the flue.

Once there, I peered down the chimney at Simon.

"The Lord be wi' ye, lad," he hollered up the sooty flue.

"Thom Taylor's my name," I shouted back. "And tomorrow I'll bring you a Bible if you like—to pass the time." But he had moved away.

The following morning with Bible in hand I entered the gaol only to find another man on duty. "Whatever happened to Yeomen Bickford and Bray?" I asked, perplexed by the sudden changing of the guard.

The mustached replacement spat on the packed earth. "Take this lantern and step this way if ye please." His la-de-da tone set none too well and I wondered what was afoot. He lifted the gaol bar and stuck his musket into the drafty dark.

"Bickford! Bray!" he shouted.

To my surprise the lantern light landed on the hangdog faces of the guards in iron collars fastened to the wall by chain. Unaccustomed to the sudden light, they squinted and blinked.

"Have ye come to pay our fine?" Bray demanded.

"What happened to Simon, Andrew and Peter?" I asked, tucking the Bible out of sight.

"Did I not tell ye they were heathen?" Bickford shouted in his gravelly voice. "Better trust the devil h'sself than that Simon Betokom and Peter Robin—because only Indian devils could escape from this stinkin' rat 'ole."

Bray hung his head. "Be a good un, Ensign Taylor, and spring us out un here. T'were yew whot oped that blasted chimbley flue in the first place. We reason that be how they 'scaped."

I secretly sympathized with the Indians and hoped for their deliverance, but couldn't imagine how they'd escaped from a guarded room. A naked toddler stuffed down the chimney pot to sweep it, as I'd seen in London, couldn't have fit down that narrow flue, let alone a full-grown Indian.

Fearing the two guards would say almost anything to get out of gaol, I forced the issue. "Escape by that chimney? What a story. More than likely they gave you the slip while you wiled away your time gambling. My word takes precedence in this affair. You rogues can bet on that!"

Walderne must have been furious with their negligence, because he'd fined them ten pounds each. Despite their weaknesses I felt sorry for them and promised to ask the Major to cut them some slack by annexing the fine to their annual tax rate. Having little recourse, the abject men thanked me and I hastened away to hole up in my cabin.

A few days later, I was summoned to Major Walderne who asked if I knew about the praying Indians.

I stroked my beard with an anxious hand, wondering if my dealings with Bickford and Bray had reached him.

"I heard they escaped, Major."

Walderne sat stiff as a poker.

"Hearsay has it I'm not good as my word, Ensign Taylor. I urged that Apostolic trio to release their settler hostage, but could not promise them clemency. I told them only Massachusetts held such authority. You've met Simon, Thom. Don't you find he speaks our language uncommonly, perhaps even deceptively, well?"

As a newly appointed junior officer my experience was sparse concerning Indian affairs. If the high-seated man was determined to confide in me, who was I to rock the boat? I nodded.

"I am fed up with nay sayers against my authority. Praying Indians got two sides to their mouth like the rest of us." The vulnerability of this confidence caused him to retrieve his Majorly voice.

"Those skunks have murdered a settler in Greenland, New Hampshire, and my courier tells of fresh atrocities in Newbury and Amesbury, Massachusetts. To make matters worse, they've joined the warring Ammoscoggins. At this very moment peaceful Hampshire Penacooks are gathering on my Dover doorstep for protection against enemy Indians."

As what he was saying sunk in I wondered how I could have been so naive. When Simon had talked about 'converting brethren' his real meaning was to convert Indians to join him.

Though I may have relieved the Major's conscience, he had summoned me to scribe copies of a peace treaty between the Provincial Committee and Penacook Indians. He cooped me up with parchment the entire sweltering afternoon.

I had finished and was out the door when Walderne waylaid me. "My courier informs me that Minister Reyner will be arriving within a few hours, Thom," he said. "You're welcome to stay under my roof, though the chambers above stairs will be occupied for the signing of the treaty."

If this was an invitation it didn't sound like one, and to avoid a run-in with his daughter, I declined. I would miss the Dover minister's well-provisioned cabin, but the weather recently had turned warm enough to camp in one of the abandoned wigwams along Back River.

The treaty was on everyone's tongue. Indians trotted in on their ponies from all four directions and boats of every make and size clogged the river and landings. The Minister's return added to the excitement because at Thursday lecture Reyner would be reading the treaty to the public. Afterward, Committee leaders and Penacook chiefs, known in those parts as *sagamores*, would retire to Walderne's manor for the signing.

At the last moment the Major ordered me to stay behind. For months I'd longed to meet the respected Minister Reyner and now I was to miss Dover's prodigal son at his finest hour.

To keep my mind off my disappointment I opened windows, fetched chairs, reread the parchments to see that they were in order and laid them out on the great table.

When the Indian sagamores filed in the open door dressed in their breech cloths, wampum and feather headdresses I thought Mistress Walderne would have an apoplectic fit. Fortunately, Mister Shapleigh was there and, observing her distress, praised the sacrifice she was making in the name of peace—which won her over completely.

I knew none of the Penacooks, and once again Mister Shapleigh stepped in, introducing Sagamore Wonnalancet, Sagamore Squando who lived near him on the Kittery side of Fore River, and four or five others. The red men dragged the chairs I'd so diligently placed at the table into the center of the room and sat in a circle. Their customs were so different from ours that they didn't even bother to rise as Major Walderne entered the room.

Nicholas Shapleigh displayed an astonishing command of the Indian language, not only reading the treaty I'd scribed but translating it as he went along. I'd changed a word here and there to ease the Committee members' provincial grasp of grammar, and took considerable pride in my contribution to the momentous occasion.

We with ye mutual consent of ye Sagamores underwritten in behalf of themselves—being about 300 in number. . .

It was I who added the word "about" since Mister Walderne did not know the exact number of Indians.

Firstly: That hence forward none of ye said Indians shall offer any violence to ye persons of English.

I wished I'd changed the word "offer." Violence isn't a gift, and for the sake of diplomacy "commit" would have been a lot better.

Secondly: That none of said Indians shall entertain at any time our enemies, but shall give notice to ye Comte . . . Comte

I'd been in such a rush I had abbreviated some of the words, causing Mister Shapleigh at the center of the Indian circle to falter.

"It's Committee, Sir," I said, wishing for his sake that I'd paid more attention.

. . . notice to ye committee. If they go forth against our enemies with the English—and if they bring in the enemy they will be paid 3 £.

A hubbub arose from the sagamores as a one-eyed Indian scout called Blind Will interpreted this item to the chiefs.

Thirdly: The Indians performing on their part, we ye committee

do ingage in behalf of ye English not to offer any violence to any
of their persons or estates. If any injury be offered to any Indians
by the English that they complain to the authority—.

This time Mister Shapleigh extemporized:

That is, if the Indians complain to the authorities, the offender shall
be prosecuted by English Laws according to ye nature of ye offense.

Signed and Sealed at Cocheco, July 3rd, 1676

Having terminated the document, Shapleigh sat down.

With somber dignity Sagamore Wonnalancet lighted the ritual
calumet and each Indian and settler in the circle solemnly took a
long draught. Mister Daniel hesitated before putting the stained
object into his mouth. A reproving glance from Shapleigh forced
him to swallow his pride in addition to a considerable amount of
spittle.

Then, standing from their chairs, they all shook hands and at
the Major's request they gathered at the great table where I'd
placed scribed copies of the document—one each for the Cocheco
Records and Court of Massachusetts, another for Major Walderne
and the Committee dealing with Indians of Eastern Parts, and a
fourth for Sagamore Wonnalancet. None of the Penacook chiefs
could sign their names so I'd left a spot for their X marks.

After the signing, Mistress Walderne carried a commodious
punch bowl in from the kitchen and ladled us cool cans of brandy-
wine.

Mister Shapleigh moseyed over to congratulate me on my new
post as Ensign of the Cocheco Regiment. He mentioned a celebra-
tion supper for the treaty signing and wondered if he could count
on my company.

This was the first I'd heard of it and I barely could hide my disappointment. All week I'd worked like an ox arranging everything

to Walderne's satisfaction. I was hot and let down after all the excitement.

Mister Shapleigh came up and placed a fatherly arm about my shoulder and drew me aside. Had I met his son John? He loved him dearly but he wished the boy had the gift for language like I had. While reading the treaty he was pleased to find I'd smoothed out some of Mister Cutt's rude syntax.

I smiled at his kindness, blinking back a tear that had formed in the corner of my eye.

He shook my hand and in front of everyone said that he'd be delighted if I'd be his guest that evening, otherwise he'd miss my company.

What remained of the afternoon I slept off in the cool of my wigwam in the glade. After I woke I plunged into the shallows of Little John's Creek for a long overdue scrub. A cloud of blackflies followed me onto the grassy river bank and before they swallowed me whole I grabbed my shirt from a nearby shadbush.

Major Walderne's guests were being treated to "tie and ride" on Dover Neck after they got off the Bloody Point ferry. The distance was short and most of the men walked Dover Point, leaving the women and elders to mount horses borrowed from our regiment.

Through the shad blossoms I could see the main cart path and I was just pulling up my breeches when a Boston gentlewoman side-saddled by on a prancing hackney. She wore a stylish broad hat with a scarlet plume and—devil strike me dead if it wasn't Esther! No less conspicuous were a pair of satin-breeched footmen bearing an elaborate lacquered sedan chair trotting beside her. Much as I peered through the underbrush at the conveyance, its occupant remained a mystery—though I guessed it must be Esther's new husband Henry Elkins.

Thinking how outlandishly straight-laced they looked, I put on my regimental jacket, which along with my musket were the only visible rewards of my junior post.

The sentinel pried my musket from me at the stockade gate, and though I hated giving it up, I well understood the need for security with hundreds of Indians camped outside the compound.

Inside the manor candle flames danced in the foyer chandelier and reflected in the looking-glass. The mute servant boy had been stationed at the door to greet guests, and remembering our previous hallway encounter, I hurried past him to the large airy kitchen.

A long pine groaning board was set with porcelain plate. A gentle breeze stirred sheer curtains at the open windows and a cacophony of courting frogs blended with the murmur of guests milling around until their host arrived.

Mistress Walderne took her place at one end of the table and the Major at the other. I sat between Shapleigh and a handsome devil with a head of natural hair that surely was the envy of guests wearing whigs. To the sound of it, the Indians also were celebrating, and their loud rattles, constant chanting, and rhythmic drumming reduced our converse to smiles and handshakes.

There was famine in Boston—but not here. Bowls of pickles, fresh garden peas and boiled salsify root flanked two huge smoked and planked salmon. The cook had griddled corn cakes in rendered pork fat and the odor drifted pleasantly over a round woven griddle-size Indian basket. An elaborate English porcelain platter held a dozen spit-roasted pigeons.

The fellow beside me reached for a corn cake. Seeing he wore a Harvard ring, one circumspect glance at his color and disposition convinced me he probably was the prodigal Reyner none the worse for his adventures. Wiping grease from my hand onto my breeches, I introduced myself.

Reyner's eyes lighted up. "You don't say. At last I meet Thomas Taylor who has kept my dwelling ship-shape while I was away."

When I told him it had been Esther Walderne who suggested I use his cabin, his smile momentarily was replaced by a fleeting look of apprehension. He glanced down at his plate. "Dear Esther, always thinking of others."

She sat to the right of her father and catty-corner from the elder man I assumed was her new husband. Reyner and I and her spouse made no secret of staring at her, for though she wasn't a beauty like Pru, she attracted a paradox of attention in her indigo summer frock with a nosegay of rosebuds anchored at her buoyed up breasts.

Esther bent forward, her eyes and lips smiling—the same lips that had kissed mine.

"Good evening, Mistress Elkins," I greeted over the din.

Too late I realized she looked beyond me to John Reyner. Their smiles met and fled, yet they gazed, locking themselves in and me and her husband out.

In retaliation I decided to engage the powdery whigged Mister Elkins. But here too I met with great difficulty because the elderly gentleman could not scrape his eyes off his new wife. My attempt at salvaging the situation fell to Major Walderne, who thought nothing of bedding his favorite daughter with a man twice his own age.

The Major grabbed a pigeon and waved it in the air at Elkins. "Say, Henry, I was just telling Mister Daniel here about an incident that happened in Newbury within the fortnight. It seems one of them confounded vagabond Quakers paraded into Meeting House fully unclothed. Thank God the despicable woman was carted off to Ipswich and tied to a fence post outside the Public Tavern."

Elkins fidgeted with a button on his sateen vest and placed a trembling hand inside. Not diverting his gaze from Esther, he pounded his other hand on the table.

"Serves the shameful hussy right!"

We stopped eating. But Walderne was so rapt sucking the parson's nose of the pigeon that he failed to notice his elderly son-in-law's outburst.

"As if that weren't enough punishment for our coastal brothers, a few days later another vagabond Quaker woman walked naked through the streets of Salem."

He threw the carcass down and licked his fingers one by one. "For more than a decade I've been chastised for whipping them three Dover Quakers at the cart's tail. But I'd do it again if one of 'em dared walk naked into Dover Meeting!" He pointed a green skewer branch with the charred pigeon head still on it down the table at Mister Shapleigh.

"Do you know about these women, Goodman Shapleigh? My sources say they stopped over in Maine."

The Kittery officer leaned comfortably back in his great chair, to all appearances unruffled by Walderne's inquisition.

The Major persisted."One of them was called Deborah Wilson."

At his mention of the Quaker woman who had knocked on my door, a morsel of corn cake lodged in my windpipe, causing a perilous coughing fit. Shapleigh clapped me several times on the back and Mistress Walderne rushed to my rescue with a tumbler of dandelion wine. Not to be diverted, Major Walderne glared and waited for a response.

"To my knowledge I have not met the women you speak of, Richard," Shapleigh said, interlacing his fingers over a full belly. "But I daresay that in Maine we find it within our hearts to be more forgiving of the religious persuasions of others."

The Major assumed an expressionless mask which I well knew meant he was about to explode.

A spot of color on Mister Elkins nose spread to his cheeks and I could see little threads of red in the whites of his eyes.

"By my faith, if my wife ever removed her clothing and stood naked before meeting I'd thrash the living daylight out of her."

Fortunately, the Indian drums drowned out his disparaging remark. Flushed by the heat of the discussion and panting like a bitch, Henry Elkins rose from the table.

"Would you kindly excuse me? I'm not feeling up to snuff. The voyage was taxing. I hope you understand," he told Mistress Walderne.

Esther made no effort to accompany him. But when Minister Reyner excused himself to finish his Sunday sermon, he was scarcely out of the room when Esther announced that she must attend to her ailing spouse.

With such sudden depletion of the ranks, I too paid my respects and hurried to retrieve my musket from the gate house.

The Penacook Indians were camped in a field not far from Major Walderne's manor and I stood a moment near a shadbush watching some red-skin boys scuffle in the dirt. The eldest boy usurped a sling shot that had fallen to the ground and with his victory they dispersed.

John Reyner and Esther Walderne stood a few paces ahead of me. The melding of their silhouettes in the moonlight threw me into confused despair. I looked back at the fire circle for the boy, but his mother must have called him away.

Startled by a pair of hands clapped over my eyes, I swung my adversary to the ground only to find the boy I'd been spying on sprawled face down in the dirt. Thinking I'd been too rough, I offered him a hand. To my wonder the boy wore Cutt's funeral ring, and apprehension fast turned to excitement as I recognized Metacomet's son and realized his mother must be camped there with him.

Before I could ask, the boy dashed to one of the Penacook wigwams and his mother stuck her head out the blanket opening. I stepped from behind the shadbush and she ran toward me with the twin plaits of her luxuriant hair cascading over her painted breasts. Yelping with joy she cupped my beard in both hands and stroked it.

I was about to embrace her when she turned like a startled deer toward Esther who held up her voluminous skirt with both hands and was so precipitous we jumped off the path. I reached out to catch her but she ignored the squaw and flashed me a look of contempt.

As weary of Esther's moods as my own, I assumed an air of

indifference and turned my attention back on the Indian squaw. But now she too seemed distracted by Esther, who had stumbled and was yelping in pain.

"I must help," I told her, waving at Esther's silvery blue skirt billowing from a ditch. The boy and his mother nodded as if they understood, and I rushed down the cart path.

By the time I reached Esther she sat up brushing a badly scraped elbow. I sopped my muckinder in the mill stream, wrung it out and knelt to swab the dirt and blood off her hands. She winced in pain when I tried to lift her to her feet.

"Reef in your skirts," I ordered.

"Whatever for?" she retorted with a flash of Walderne temper.

"God help me," I beseeched. "To get you up—what do you think?"

I bent and placed my hands on her tiny wasp waist. She stung like one too, I thought, pulling the unpredictable wench to her feet and against my chest.

Her rose corsage had fallen off—or perhaps been plucked by the Dover divinity. Though sorely tempted to embrace her, I refrained for fear the squaw and her son were watching.

"What in Divine Providence did Mister Reyner do to provoke you so?" I asked, backing her into the shadowy trunk of an ancient maple.

"He does not want me."

"I should hope not. You're married to Mister Elkins who looks quite unwell."

Esther flushed with indignation.

"And what about you, Thom? My father's ensign consorting with a savage! That Indian squaw might as well be one of those wicked Quaker women for all the cloth she's wearing. Why I could see her bare breasts!"

I pressed Esther's arms against the rough bark of the tree trunk. Her gown had ripped and slipped off one shoulder and I made a point of looking down.

"I can see your breasts too, Esther, though I daresay there 's less to see."

The shame in her eyes extinguished my passion and I let her go, leaving the sorry wench to put her déshabille in order.

"I'm going to tell you something I've told no one else," she whispered in a confidential tone difficult to ignore. "Promise you won't tell a soul."

The weight of secrets festering inside me was already considerable. There had been the plot of the sea captain to kidnap Mister Cutt. Then there was Will Babb's death duel with his father. Shortly after, I buried the mention and body of Pru's stillborn Negro babe. Tallying these with my conspiracy to save King Philip's squaw and abetting the naked Quaker woman, I asked myself what harm one more secret might do, and promised to keep mum.

Esther looked at the ground with unfamiliar modesty.

"The night of our marriage, the Honorable Mister Elkins informed me he was too ill to have children. I was heartbroken. I didn't love the man but I wanted a babe."

Uncomfortable with the intimacy of her disclosure, it was my turn to look at the ground.

She went on. "There's more. By chance one day in his private chamber I saw his underbody covered with scabs and pustules. I've been loath to confide this to anyone, Thom, but I'm greatly troubled."

Spirited Shoals women didn't even talk of such things and her confession drew me in like cod on a line.

"Perhaps Mister Elkins had the small pox."

"More than likely he has the French pox!"

"Esther, surely you're jumping to conclusions."

"Am I? The man has fought in the Indian war. He could have consorted with a squaw like you have!" She hesitated to see if this hit home, and it did—though I tried not to let on.

"The point is," she continued, "my own husband will not

touch me and is furious if I so much as look at another man. If Father had known beforehand, I'm certain he would have called off the marriage. Now, all I can do is hope and pray that I'm a widow soon."

I placed my fingers on her lips to keep her from saying more and felt them quiver like a small trapped animal, trembling and alive. Her tears fell onto my fingers and when I removed them she whispered. "Oh Thomas, kiss me. Please—."

Moved to compassion by her situation, I held her soft fair body against mine. Her skirt flounced between my legs, marooning me on the small island of her breasts. I succumbed to the listless swoon of her, buckling to the foot of the tree with her in my arms. In the moonlight I fingered the fine blue stuff of her sleeve, slipping it off her shoulder and kissing the curve verging toward full disclosure.

"John, Oh John," she moaned.

I rolled off and sat up. "What did you say?"

Esther opened her eyes.

"You still love John Reyner!" I croaked, strangulated by a wave of jealousy. "Bugger the devil! Either you come to me free and clear or I'll have none of you."

"Thom, it's not like that at all. I vow—."

"Avow 'til doomsday for all I care, Esther. I'll not be cuckolded by your wanton desire for another." This outbreak surprised me as much as it did her, and we didn't speak another word as I helped her up and walked her back to the stockade.

The guard in the lookout slumped in a drunken stupor. I was going to report him but realized the Major wouldn't appreciate my walking in the moonlight with his daughter. The crickets and cicadas had drowsed off with the evening chill and the candles in the chandelier were burnt to the wick.

"Good evening, Mistress Elkins." I bowed stiffly in case her father might be in one of the upper windows. Better soon than sorry, I thought, turning on my heel; the lass could only bring trouble. I was halfway to the sentinel post at the stockade gate when I made an about-face for a brief last look, but the step was empty.

The Indian squaw sat beside the cart path where I'd left her. Too weary to object, I let her lead me to her wigwam.

She drew back the blanket in the moonlight. The soft fir branches smelled fragrant and fresh; she must have been to the river and cut them while I was with Esther. I'd heard about the French pox from other officers and the stories weren't pretty. Yet making love was the only language the squaw and I had in common— and, well, I reasoned I hadn't gotten the pox before.

She unbuttoned the shiny brass buttons on my jacket. I threw it off while her hands reached under my shirt. When she saw that I still wore the wampum she'd given me, she removed it and flung her arms around my neck. The nipples of her breasts rubbed my chest and I buried my face in her hair.

Rocking back on her knees, she touched my chest. "Thom Taylor," she said.

I pointed back. "Squaw of Metacomet."

She shook her head and pointed at herself. "Wonnalancet."

What did she mean?

Exasperated, she continued to stab herself with a finger while repeating Wonnalancet's name. Finally. she stopped. Holding up three fingers she said, "Tree. Tree squaw."

Wonnalancet three squaw? Oh, what a fool I'd been. The powerful Penacook Sagamore who had given King Philip's squaw his protection had taken her as his wife!

In haste I drew my shirt back over my head and rebuttoned it. To linger one more moment could place us in grave danger. Who knew where Sagamore Wonnalancet might be lurking?

She followed me into the clearing imploring "Tree, tree!" in a singsong voice. I headed for the shadbush to give us cover before resuming our heated debate, if you could call the handful of words we shared a dialogue. When we were far enough from her wigwam,

I halted to make her understand she mustn't follow.

"Nay!" I ordered.

She covered her face with red stained fingers.

In the conventional sense of the word I did not love her. But when I was with her I could be myself, something I could hardly say of Esther.

She held up one finger.

"Wonnalancet one squaw," she said, pointing at a cluster of wigwams across the grassy meadow. She raised three fingers and placed them on her breast, "Wonnalancet tree squaw." She spat on the ground to show how unimportant she was in the Penacook Chief's domestic priorities. I was glad to learn she wasn't his favorite, but felt no safer.

Then, suddenly Providence provided a plan.

"Come!" I ordered, dashing across the open path and heading through the dense forest along the river. At times she was so quiet I thought I had lost her.

When we were within a safe distance of my wigwam and stood in the lacey moonlight beneath a large hemlock, I embraced her. Then, tired as an ancient husband and wife, we slept the night through in each other's arms, coupling only with the first light of dawn.

To my pleasure and the settlers' unrest, the Penacooks camped outside Major Walderne's compound all summer.

One sticky day when desire festered under my skin like a hill of ants, I lounged beneath the shadbush watching the squaw grind corn with a stone pin. The sight of her filled me with such longing that I was about to chance a foolhardy encounter in broad daylight. Thank the Lord Almighty I decided against it, for a moment later Sagamore Wonnalancet appeared.

She pretended not to see the famous chief, but when his shadow fell across her squatting figure, she stood. Despite the insistence of his voice, she took her time storing the corn she'd been grinding and looked furtively at the shadbush where I was hiding.

"Don't go. Don't go," I pleaded softly. But of course she had no choice and they disappeared behind the blanket.

Mindful that I must bridle my feelings for her, from then on I spent as much time as possible drilling the men—preparing them for God knows what.

PART FOUR

War

19

*T*he day I turned sixteen I was ordered to settle an outbreak between a handful of young Penacook braves and a settler who caught them hunting on his lot. Game was scarce, and though the braves had been told to get Major Walderne's signature before straying from their camp, they roamed freely across the settlers' plots.

The following day, a bad situation turned worse. The Major was dictating a letter when a ruckus outside drowned out what he was saying. At his bidding I ran outside just as a regiment of soldiers marched four abreast through the stockade gate. The mounted officers jumped off their horses and before I could fore-warn the Major they stood inside his keeping-chamber.

"We've sailed from the Shoals upriver to Dover at the behest of the Colony Council," one of them said. "I be Captain Hathorne and this be Captain Syll of the British Massachusetts Militia. The Council does not take kindly to your harborin' several hundred Narragansets from King Philip's traitorous tribe."

The Major and I stared in disbelief at the travel-worn

regimental officers who had barged in unannounced.

Walderne stood his ground.

"I harbor only peaceful Penacook Indians led by Wonnalancet, son of the great Chief Passaconaway. I've given them my word of honor signed and sealed the third of July of this year to protect them."

The one called Hathorne was a mean cuss and ugly to boot.

"Be that as it may, we've reason to believe a hundred strange savages have defected from Metacomet—the same who has the audacity to call hisself King Philip. And we aim to round up the lot of the scoundrels."

The Major gripped my shoulder in anger. "Bilgewater! The Penacooks be friendly Indians and I won't have the likes of you meddling in Provincial Committee affairs."

Captain Hathorne turned blue at the gills. "Our orders be to capture every last one of 'em and ship those what ain't shot or hanged to Barbadoes' plantations."

The Major moved from behind the great table. "Now men," he soothed, "I'm sure we can work out something to our mutual satisfaction. In the meantime, billet your regiment at Tuttle's barn. Ensign Taylor here will show the way. Tuttle will provide vittles at his farm until we can get this straightened out."

He turned to me. "Thom, fetch these officers some refreshment." Walderne's servant brought in shams of beer, and as they drank I went outside to lead the Massachusetts regiment to Huckleberry Hill. No sooner had I gotten to the door than I was accosted by Wonnalancet who was seething with anger at the sight of the British troops.

Choosing a few Penacook words I'd learned from the squaw, I attempted to divert him.

"Masqua wakewan," I coaxed.

But the Chief wasn't about to be turned back to the camp.

"Nay masqua wakewan. Parley Walderne. "

Grasping the enormity of the situation, I placed Deacon John

Dam in charge of billeting the British soldiers, and accompanied the riled Penacook Sagamore into Walderne's garrison house. Within a shorter span than anticipated, the Major called me into his keeping chamber.

"We need an interpreter, Thom. Fetch Blind Will."

Again, I sailed out the door.

I'd never actually entered the Penacook camp, which in many respects was a village onto itself. A longhouse had been built near the sweat lodge to accommodate the overflow of Indians from the northern lakes of New Hampshire. Fish seines and baskets hung from tree limbs and smoke wafted from stone-lined fire pits. The scraped skins of beaver swamp hog and deer were stretched between poles and drying in the afternoon sun.

The village looked uncomfortably deserted, and I felt like an intruder as a few women and children stared at me from their rounded bark dwellings. Blind Will perceived my haste with his one good eye and we trotted back to the garrison.

After off-loading him, I returned to my wigwam by the river, Metacomet's squaw and son were waiting and I called out "Winni!" which meant smile. But she was not smiling now. Her son who had grown tall as a pike wore the same look of condemnation.

"We trust treaty," he said, spreading his stolid young legs in a stance of defiance.

Though his voice sounded peculiarly like my wood flute in the transitional seasons, I was determined to treat him like a man.

"You're right to trust the treaty, Chipmunk." Out of habit I used the nickname his mother called him, hoping he wouldn't hold it against me. "The Major's talking leaves promise the Penacooks protection. You'll be safe with them."

The boy swatted a white moth fluttering at his lips. "Metacomet and Chipmunk be Pokanoket braves, not Penacook."

I glanced at Winni for support and tried again.

"You are Pokanoket, Chipmunk. But if Major Walderne or the

British Chief asks, promise me you will say you are the son of Sagamore Wonnalancet." I conjoined his hands with his mother's. "Son and wife of Wonnalancet."

The boy whispered with his mother in vexed tones and she pleaded with him. "Wonnalancet," she said sternly. "

Having lost my own father at a young age, I was tempted to let them stay with me. But the woods were crawling with Militia and I hurried them back to the Penacook camp.

The following morning Major Walderne sent me to ask Wonnalancet to gather his braves in the yard for a mock battle. When I questioned Walderne point blank about the meaning of this exercise, he nodded at Captain Hathorne with a complicitous smile. "Must I remind you, Ensign Taylor, that you are in my command and not vice versa?"

I figured they must a have been drinking shams of beer all night to come up with the ridiculous idea of a sham battle.

"And the women and children, Sir?" I asked, thinking of Winni and her son.

"What about them?" The Major absent-mindedly studied a set of toy soldiers circled by a pile of parched corn kernels. He knocked over a lead soldier and picked it up. "Blast it, Thom. Fasten a guard on and confine 'em to their camp."

"And if the braves suspect foul play and refuse to come, Sir?"

Captain Hathorne who had straw in his beard and stunk of rum put in his oar. "Oh, they'll come all right. You and your men'll be handing out firearms."

Within the hour I sat atop an ox cart distributing hundreds of muskets to several hundred over-excited warriors. In my heart of hearts I'd had enough of the Massachusetts Militia and prayed Divine Providence rid us of the rogues. The only good thing about the mock battle was that the powder would be fired without balls.

The whooping warriors followed my cart to the Major's garrison house where the soldiers milled and drilled in the cleared yard outside the stockade. To my great apprehension,

Captain Frost of Kittery had joined them overnight, increasing our ranks considerably.

"What cheer, friends?" the Major called out to the Penacooks from his side-stepping stallion.

I do not exaggerate when I say the Indians looked to Major Walderne as the settlers looked to Jesus Christ. They hefted their clumsy ancient muskets with excited zeal and watched in awe as Walderne circled his high horse among them.

The gist of the Major's speech translated to the Indians by Blind Will was this: The drill sergeants—that included me—would instruct them on the proper usage of the muskets. Both sides would fire blank so no one would get hurt. The object of the battle was to ambush the enemy without firing. But just to help them out, he was giving them a cannon and two British gunners.

With considerable pomp, Mister Tuttle led an ox team with the promised cannon on a sledge. At once the Penacooks surrounded the cannon, touching and caressing it with delight. The ruckus caused by the mammoth machine was so loud, the Major trotted off to a nearby chestnut tree. I was secretly praising this act of good will, thinking he wanted to give the braves leeway to examine the weapon. But in reality he wanted a running start to jump his horse over the cannon.

The startled Indians parted like the Red Sea and froze in rapt attention as Walderne spewed out orders.

"You take this drag rope!" he yelled, herding a dozen Indians as if they were sheep. "And Thom, get on the other side so as to point the cannon at the enemy." I fastened some braves on the drag rope like dead bait on a fishing line and was waiting for the wretched ordeal to be over when I heard a familiar whoop and Winni's son came running up.

"You there!" Walderne shouted at the British gunners. They cringed from the Major's foamy stallion and pulled the wool stoppers from their ears. "Load the cannon, but hold your fire until we're ready, men."

No sooner had the two-tongued interpreter, Blind Will, mouthed the Major's speech than the restless warriors swarmed like hornets around the cannon.

On the pretext of showing one of the braves how to fire his musket, I caught Chipmunk by his hair and dragged him to a settlers' door and pounded.

A board was removed from above and a woman in a pinner cap leaned out. It wasn't uncommon for Dover folk to pour boiling water through these upper portholes onto unwanted visitors, and I smiled winsome as I could.

"Begging your pardon. Could you come down?"

A moment later the woman with a babe under each arm like a brooding hen unlatched the door.

"Goodwoman ah—?"

"Goody Heard."

"I'm Ensign Taylor of the Dover and Cocheco Regiment. I'd appreciate your taking this Indian lad for awhile. There's no time to explain because I have to get back to Major Walderne."

At the mention of the Major her face lighted up and I pushed Chipmunk into the safety of her domicile.

Back at the yard, a great many braves who had never fired a musket were covered with powder burns. I elbowed my way through the fray, warning as many as I could that they must rely on ambush and not the muskets or they'd surely lose. I might as well have given them candy and told them not to eat it. Desperate for help, I looked around to see if Sagamore Wonnalancet might lead a surprise attack and save the day. But just as I reached him, Walderne pranced his stallion into the sunlit clearing.

"Now, when I hold the white flag aloft, the battle begins," he shouted. "And when I wave it again, the battle will be over. Penacooks, are you ready?"

Blind Will was repeating the Major's speech when one of the Penacook braves accidentally lit the powder box and blasted himself to the ground in a puff of smoke.

"Whew, them heathens make savage farts," shouted a British soldier.

Blind Will spat on the ground and cursed like a white settler. "Listen up, ye scoundrels," he yelled in English. Midway through he switched to the Penacook language and pointed at the white banner the Major held at rest on the pommel of his saddle.

A dozen Indians lined up on one side of the cannon and the same on the other. Wonnalancet and I were stationed at the far ends of each drag rope so that I could not convey my plan for ambush. Having lodged a cannonball the size of a cabbage within its depth, Captain Hathorne and two gunners stood at ready near the fuse. The British had the disadvantage, being cannonless.

A crow cawed in the mounting silence and the white flag poked into the blue sky. We tugged the rope to position the cumbersome cannon and point it at the sudden foursquare flank of British soldiers who were closing in with nary a shot.

Alarmed by the facility and speed of the trained soldiers, the Penacooks aimed their muskets in a confusion of directions and fired. Losing sight of Wonnalancet, I ordered my men to slacken so the braves on the other rope could turn the cannon on the British flank. But before they could budge the behemoth, a cannonball exploded in their midst.

Cursing the British gunner who was feeding a second ball into the cannon's mouth, I ran into the cloud of smoke.

"Put that down!" I ordered.

He eyed me with disdain. "Since when do I take orders from an ensign, or a savage for that matter?"

I trained my musket on him. "Since now. A dozen men have been struck because of your carelessness."

He dropped the cannonball to the ground, his mouth agape in disbelief.

"But I—. Uh Capt'n Hathorne told me—uh that—."

I stumbled through the smoke toward half a dozen Indians sprawled in the dirt. One of them grabbed my ankle and moaned.

In the distance, Walderne and the soldiers were shouting. Several Indians had been blasted past recognition by the explosion and I couldn't reach the others without stepping on pieces of torn flesh, bits of fingers, shreds of skull and hanks of hair. The stench of gun powder and mess of bowels pitched me retching onto a tussock of singed grass. A brave cried out. I crept close. A piece of rope was imbedded in his scorched chest, but thankfully he swooned before I tore it out. I near joined him at the sight of the bloody gash.

To add to this sorry state of affairs, Minister Reyner appeared intent on saving his soul. "Oh Lord, give unto this sinner savage thy forgiveness," he beseeched.

I looked him straight in the eye. "And forgive the murderous rogues that have sent him prematurely to his death."

Reyner put an arm about my shoulder. "Now, Ensign Taylor, take heart. I've seen battles that make this mock skirmish look like a Harvard graduation party."

I shrugged him off and went to help Sagamore Wonnalancet carry a pallet to a bleeding warrior with his leg blown off and oozing blood.

Major Walderne looked down his stirrup at the warrior and cool as a clam called Mister Tuttle to reclaim the curséd cannon. I was ordered to collect the firearms and whatever else I found strewn about the yard.

To my relief, Tuttle's sledge and log skids slid over the worst of the bloody mess. Pulling rank, I ordered a zealous settler to pick up the muskets and ran off to fetch Chipmunk from Goody Heard. After we'd palavered far more than I wanted, I got us away.

Once on the path, I grabbed the boy by both shoulders and pressured him to listen. "Danger. Get your mother! Hide her at Thom's wakewan."

His eyes opened wide. "Mother cache cache?" he asked, to make sure he had it right.

I nodded and shoved him down the path toward the camp. A few hundred Penacooks sat cross-leggéd on the ground in the yard.

They had been divided into two distinct groups with Major Walderne towering over one and Captains Hathorne and Syll presiding over another. The wounded warriors had been carried inside, but I could see squaws and children already being rounded up. I prayed that Chipmunk would realize what had happened and not come looking for us.

The braves in Major Walderne's group were ordered to call forth their wives and children. Sagamore Wonnalancet collected two squaws and a dozen children. Where was Winni? How could he forget her at such a crucial moment?

Shaken by the ordeal, I followed Major Walderne and Captain Hathorne as they strolled among the Penacook squaws and children, culling and collecting them.

"Look at this one's forehead!" Hathorne exclaimed, pulling the woman's hair and forcing her head back. At the center of her brow she wore a distinct insignia and it did not belong to the Penacooks. When Indian children reached a certain age, the insignia of their clan was stippled in ochre pigment under their skin with bone hooks. The marks were a dead giveaway and I trembled with apprehension as one of the examining party culled Winni from the women.

"Who does this squaw belong to?" Captain Hathorne demanded.

Sagamore Wonnalancet grabbed Winni and shoved her beside him with his other wives.

"I do."

"Think I'm a fool?" Hathorne spat on the ground and yanked Winni's hair back. Finding no insignia, he forced her to lift her feet. "This squaw wears the mark of King Philip on the sole of her foot."

"She be my wife and a Penacook," Wonnalancet retorted, his brave body quivering in rage.

The Captain waved at the other two squaws. "I thought you said these were yer wives."

Wonnalancet held up three fingers.

Hathorne spat again. "You damn savages and yer wives! Where be the bastards from this Narraganset whore?"

Blind Will, who had been translating, clammed shut at the insult.

I jumped in without considering the consequences. "She hath none, isn't that right, Chief Wonnalancet? Nay papoose?"

He looked at me long and hard. "Nay Papoose. "

I turned to the Captain. "You see, Sir, their son died at birth."

I don't know what prompted me to tell this lie, perhaps to put one over on the scoundrel.

The Captain pressed a grimy thumb to his bulbous nostrils and snorted snot into the dust. "Take her," he ordered, moving on down the line.

I could not just give Winni up like that and approached the Major. "Please Sir, please release the squaw. I don't deem it in our best interest to cross Sagamore Wonnalancet. "

Major Walderne looked Winni up and down, methodically caressing the pommel of his sword as he did so. "She be a beauty for certain, Thom, but—."

Captain Hathorne stalked back. "What the devil be holding us up, Major?"

Walderne took Captain Hathorne aside and spoke low. The Massachusetts officer flung his arms into the air.

"Let me perform my duty here, Major. The whore be Pokanoket, and I have orders from the Colony to take any and all eastern savages what have fled to Wonnalancet's camp."

Winni stepped forward of her own accord. "Wonnalancet wife," she said, forcing a smile. "Wonnalancet wife."

"Ye be a base Pokanoket whore," the Captain scoffed.

Whether she understood or not, I could take no more. "This woman is not a whore."

Hathorne snorted like the pig he was and gave the Major a high sign. "I vow she wa'nt no virgin wilderness when ye plowed her, lad."

I torqued his jaw with a right jab, and was about to smash his ugly face beyond recognition when Walderne ordered my arrest.

"Ensign Taylor, this is the last straw!" he shouted loud enough to please Hathorne. "I'm putting you in irons on the flankart until I can deal proper."

A guard shoved me up the ladder to the sentinel post raised like a poop deck on the stockade and fastened me in leg irons.

Down the path hundreds of Penacook captives were being toggled to a rope stretched all the way to the river. Winni looked up as she shuffled through the gate and our eyes met an instant. But soon she was a mere dot on a human line anchored to a pair of gundalows at Walderne's Landing. More than likely, the plan was to transport the betrayed Indians to Port's Mouth and load them into the hold of Deane and Whitcomb's slave ship bound for the Barbadoes.

My legs grew numb and my heart even number as I watched billows of smoke pour over the deserted camp. At first I thought the British had torched the village, but then I saw the charred frame of a pyre. They were burning the dead.

20

*I*n February I walked up the gang plank of a ship of expeditionary forces comprising several score of Christian Indians from Natick, Massachusetts, along with Kittery and Portsmouth men—about 120 Indian fighters in all. The Isles of Shoals might as well have been the Barbadoes as close as I'd gotten, and I looked longingly at them as the Boston vessel sailed north from the Piscataqua River.

I bumped into a soldier, and when he turned around I was staring smack into the blue eyes of Will Babb. The tail of his fur cap flew like a banner in the stiff breeze, and to hear each other we ducked behind a heap of provisions and cooperage.

"Why Thomas, yew Puker. Where've yew been holed up all this time?"

For some unfathomable reason his conceited mug was a welcome sight. Over the roaring wind I told him how most of '76 I'd been posted to Walderne at Dover Point and Cocheco.

"Yew lucky cuss!"

"You wouldn't say that had you been there last fall," I shouted through cupped hands.

Will struck his thigh in surprise. "What the devil, Thom, I was at Cocheco with Capt'n Frost's regiment. That was some battle, weren't it? We whipped them savages good. What a victory! I were in the squadron what closed ranks on them squinty-eyed traitors. They never knew what hit em!"

I held my tongue, having learned it was a blunt instrument on deaf ears. If the battle Will and I fought at Cocheco was a mock one, I shuddered to think what awaited us in northern Maine.

While Will went on about buskins and bodices, muskets and massacres, I huddled into a pile of gunny sacks and let my mind drift back to that September day when Winni looked up at me for the last time. Just as I was gesturing that her son had gotten away, the Cocheco sentinel yanked my leg irons, and by the time I turned back she was gone. That evening, after I watched the setting sun gilding the oaks and glinting off the oxbow of the river, sleep had become a stranger.

And now, once again I'd been dragged into another wretched expedition. With bitter tears I wondered why men could not see God in each other—why they treated each other like dung. Fearing I would go mad with this perplexity, I hummed the chant Winni had taught me.

> *Come my love, let us go up the shining mountain.*
> *There we will watch the beautiful sun go down.*
> *There we will sit till the evening star*
> *arises from behind the shining mountain.*
> *There we will hear the great spirit owl sing*
> *GO TO SLEEP ALL.*

Will and I hunkered on deck as our ship rounded the mouth of the Saco River which long ago I'd sailed with Mister Shapleigh, and we headed north toward Falmouth Point in Casco Bay. We'd been told the coast was clear, but I awoke to the commotion of an Indian party in half a dozen birch canoes.

Will made a spyglass of his fingers to see the scout who had been sent to parley with Major Walderne in the frigid dawn fog.

"Damn, I wish I knew what they be sayin'."

I scrunched into his abandoned grain gunny pillow. "They're saying: Could you spare some hot coffee, and how about a pinch of snuff?" Though I jested, my heart sank with the knowledge that the Major's word was about as reliable as horse plums.

The scout clambered from the longboat and reappeared on top of the Jacob's ladder at the side of our vessel where the Major awaited news.

Walderne cast a look about the fog-shrouded deck.

"Ensign Taylor, step forward!" he ordered.

Grabbing my musket, I shoved through the crowded soldiers and without the foggiest notion what it was all about, followed the Major down the ship's ladder and into the boat.

Once we were on the strand, Mister Pain, the scout, walked lonely as a condemned man over to talk to the braves.

Somewhat agitated he ran back to tell us Simon, the praying Indian who had escaped Dover goal, agreed to talk to Walderne on the condition that our scout remain in the Indians' custody during their parley.

I was surprised Walderne would agree to stand within a muzzle-length of the notorious Simon, but they both were devious devils and no doubt wanted to see who could out-fox the other. The upshot was that Walderne would meet Simon the following dawn to retrieve settlers being held captive by Chief Squando. Mister Pain, who resembled his name, ran on at the mouth. If Squando was so close why hadn't he come? What was going on? Did Simon have something up his sleeve? He smelled fish and didn't like it.

The following dawn it wasn't fish we smelled, but smoke. I barely had a chance to listen to my stomach growl when Walderne growled for me to take the longboat ashore and talk to Simon in his stead.

Dense as the morning fog, I queried, "Why me?"

Walderne crossed his arms and glared.

"Ensign Taylor, must I constantly remind you that I give orders and you obey them? Now get that shittabed Will Babb from Frost's New Hampshire Regiment and a few others to row you ashore. If anyone knows what a double-crosser that Simon can be, it 's you. Keep yer blasted eyes open. That smoke could be an ambush. Now move!"

As on the previous day, Scout Pain was held hostage by the braves while Simon came toward me.

"Good woban, Simon," I greeted, taking off my fur cap to make certain he recognized me.

"Good morning, Meeko. I know thee from Dover." Crows' feet spread from Simon Betokom's eyelids, but his lips remained in a straight line.

I cut our palaver short and waved my arm at smoke billowing from the forest. "Mag smoke!"

He frowned. "Wakewan catcheth fire."

I hoped that telling the truth might illicit the truth. "Major Walderne thinks it's an ambush."

Simon didn't blink. "My brethren be cold. They make fire in white man's ancient dwelling and the Lord spake with firey tongues, Brother Meeko."

The braves huddled behind Simon in the rimey mist. Behind them in the trees I spotted the charred remains of a log dwelling. One of the men at the longboat shouted and I turned to glimpse the sails on our vessel being untied from the spars. God have mercy, were they leaving without me? I no longer beat about the bush. "You promised Chief Squando would be here!"

"Chief Squando cometh, Meeko. Trust in the Lord. Wait patiently for him. He will give thee thy heart desire."

The Psalm-quoting Indian had me eating from the palm of his hand and knew it. "On the morrow, then?" I asked, in a desperate hurry to hightail it to our ship.

Simon nodded and raised his hand in peace.

"Shake a leg, Thom," Will cried as they shoved the longboat off the reef. The scout pushed me into the boat and we thrashed away from the shore.

Walderne had seen the whole business through his spyglass and when he ascertained Squando wasn't with Simon, decided to set sail.

A compassionate sailor on board threw Will a line and we were dragged on the choppy ocean clinging for dear life to the sides of the open longboat.

Fortunately, Arrowsick Island lay near Casco Bay, and with a stiff wind in the sails, we soon sat in tidal mud gazing at the charred remains of the Clark and Lake Trading House. If the burnt cabin at Falmouth had been an accident, this was not. Only the foundation and two walls of the log garrison house remained standing.

Arrowsick Island had no real place to hide and looked deserted, but to be on the safe side, Walderne ordered a dozen men to check the rime-edged slippery nooks and crannies. Four-score friendly Natick Indians were abandoned on the island to shore up the garrison best they could while we sailed for Pemaquid Point on the noon tide.

Wearing nippers and my great coat, I strove to keep warm. Will had discovered a supply of rum and it staved off the cold somewhat. When we reached Pemaquid Point at sundown the majority of us were in our cups.

On Arrowsick the resourceful Naticks had harpooned two large seal for our voyage and kept the other. The fatty blubber aswim in beans required a stomach of iron, but it staved off hunger, and after reefing in the sails we stowed ourselves below deck with the dunnage and ballast.

The next day Major Walderne, myself, Scout Pain, and three others went ashore to parley with Mattahando, the Pemaquid Chief. After an interminable discussion with snow blowing horizontal outside his wigwam and many puffs on his calumet, the ancient Sagamore promised to release captive settlers for twelve animal pelts each. Until the ransom was delivered, his tribe would hold one of us hostage. Pain said he'd had enough, and the dubious duty fell to me.

Trembling from cold and fear, reluctantly I watched the soldiers' backsides disappear into the woods, then followed a squaw escort into the Pemaquid camp. Her papoose, which was tied to a cradleboard, stared at me with wide dark eyes as I bowed through the opening of the wigwam. She built a fire and spread animal furs over a raised pallet of woven wattle. The babe gurgled in the warmth, and I admired the colorful porcupine quill turtle above its fuzzy head.

Having come unarmed, I ventured outside hoping to find a stone or child's sling shot—anything to protect myself. But the ground was covered with a thick sheet of ice, and inhospitable.

To my relief, the Pemaquid were not. The squaw cooked me a meal far better than my previous one on shipboard, and Chief Mattahando ducked in, asking, I presumed, if I needed anything.

These were not Maine Micmacs and I hadn't a clue what they were saying. I kneeled and bowed my gratitude. Seemingly pleased by this respect, Sagamore Mattahando dismissed the squaw. A few moments later she returned with a girl of about twelve years with a face like a cherub. Mattahando shoved her into my arms. When I let her go and stepped away, she turned on him and they exchanged hostile-sounding words. Faking a yawn I stepped between them, yawned again, and nodded the Chief and girl to the entrance.

Once they were gone I pulled an animal pelt over the opening and reclined near the burning embers. Unable to sleep, I thought of Winni frightened and alone as I was. To blot out the atrocities that might have befallen her on the Barbadoes plantation, I sang what I remembered of her song.

The evening comes closer to warn all that are dreaming,
but we and the little stars and their chief
are coursing along—and our minds with them.
Then the owl sleeps, his song, heard no more.
And though we're sleepy. . .

At dawn I roused my stiff gambs and went into the cold forest to relieve myself. A cadaverous dog slunk at my heels as I walked through the camp. A decrepit Pemaquid Indian at the entrance to a wigwam cradled a papoose in his wrinkled brown hands, and I stopped to pry some knowledge from him. The infant proved the more vociferous of the two, though equally unintelligible.

Fearing Major Walderne's negotiations might already be taking place, I hurried through the woods toward Pemaquid Point, but made a wrong turn somewhere along the way and ended up on the opposite side of the peninsula.

At last the Major and other officers came into view near our longboat laden with the promised animal furs. The squaws and several dozen Pemaquid braves looked on from the rubble of a cellar hole while Sagamore Mattahando dealt with our officers. As he reached out to take the pelts, to my horror Major Walderne seized the ancient Chief, and swinging him about to shield his own flesh, he made a high sign to Captain Frost.

All at once a flank of our soldiers appeared running pell mell and shooting at the fleeing Indians. With the fear of God coursing through my veins, I took cover behind a boulder at the edge of the woods.

One of the officers ran past in hot pursuit. "I'll show ye Mogg, ye filthy savage!" he cried. Overtaking a Pemaquid brave, he cudgeled him senseless with his rifle butt. When the Indian surely was dead, the officer unsheathed his knife and before my very eyes, carved off his head. Pleased by the alacrity of this dispatch, he scuttled away bearing his hideous trophy aloft as if it were a merry lantern.

Addled by the sight of the headless body sprawled before me, I ran aimlessly into the woods, and at the sound of voices flopped belly first and slithered like a snake along the ice. I was shimmying away fast as I could when to my surprise Simon grabbed me by the seat of my breeches and stood me upright. He already had Will and was tying him to a tree. In short order he bound both of us and trotted off in the direction of the wailing Pemaquid squaws.

I fumbled for Will's hand and, discovering he wore no nippers, begged him to snuggle it under my great coat or he'd have frostbite. If we were to get away before Simon returned, I must get at the truth and fast!

"Weren't we exchanging furs for captives?" I whispered.

"Ther re re wer er er no captives. We reck reck oned twer er ambush."

Will's shivering slowed my comprehension. "Their ambush or ours?"

Puffs of frosty air issued from Will's mouth. "Walder er erne said they was smooth as oil and had drawn swor ords in their hearrrts."

Having gotten nowhere near the truth, I figured we had but two chances to stay alive—escape or Simon Betokom's lenience, and seeing the praying Indian coming toward us with his musket raised, I didn't hold out for the latter.

Simon poked his musket barrel into Will's groin and he yelped in pain. "A dozen Pemaquid lie murdered by thy soldiers on the Point."

Will's voice quivered and jerked. "Ye re re red de de devils wer er aiming fer ambush!"

Simon took hold of Will's chattering chin and leered into his face. "All ye British be alike—ye've got musket balls between yer legs and worship Mammon."

He unbound me and, poking at my chest with the musket, ordered me to disrobe.

"Thou shalt not kill," I whispered, dropping my great coat onto the icy ground and taking off my shirt.

The wampum I wore had become so familiar I forgot it was there until the angry Indian jabbed the star ornament hanging from the center.

"Whence cometh this wampum?"

I clenched my teeth to brace my freezing flesh.

"Give me!" he ordered.

I hesitated.

Simon leaned his musket against a tree and unsheathed his knife. Before he could slash off my ear or a far dearer appendage, I lifted the wampum over my head.

He examined the necklace carefully. "This be the wampum of Metacomet. How dost thee come by it?"

"I am friend of a Narraganset squaw."

Simon put the coveted wampum around his neck. When I cried out, the crow's feet appeared at his eyes. "I like thee, Meeko," he said. "But I do not like thy company. In fair barter for this wampum thou art released. "

I pulled my deerskin shirt back on and grabbed for my great coat. Simon beat me to it. "I am good Samaritan. I take coat in return for thy friend." Simon waved his musket at our boots. We collapsed to the ground and tugged them off, then he marched us in our stocking feet to the fringe of a marsh.

"For thee, I turn my cheek, Meeko. But the sins of thy fathers will know God's wrath!"

His curse rang in my ears as numbed with cold we slid through slush, grabbing saplings and gorse for support. When the wailing Pemaquid women saw us, they ran away screeching and whimpering. The squaw who the night before could do nothing too much for me now anxiously pushed the girl I'd met into a wigwam. Their keening followed us through the winter-spent cattails as we stumbled around the tidal marsh on what I hoped was a trail.

My feet burned as though I'd stuck them into a bon fire, and I halted at a cleared cooking pit near an open expanse of marsh, waiting for Will to catch up.

The sun glittered on the iced tree branches and glinted in such great splendor that for a moment I forgot the enormity of our predicament. Will fell in a befuddled daze onto a punky log.

I stared at the abandoned fire circle, imagining a blazing fire with a kettle of soup bubbling over it. If only wishful thinking could keep us alive. I looked into the vernal pool that filled the pit and absentmindedly picked up a shiny stone glinting in the noon sun. It was shaped like an arrowhead but we had no bow, and I was about to throw it back when I realized it was flint!

Leaving Will with orders to gather dry grasses and bind them into a bundle, I collected brittle tree branches pruned by the heavy ice storm. From the Pemaquid camp across the marsh I could see billows of smoke and assumed either soldiers had torched the village or the surviving braves were sending a signal to a neighboring tribe. In any case, our small fire probably would go unnoticed.

After several attempts with the flint, I finally sparked the dry grass and ignited the branches. Only then did I turn my attention to Will's frozen hands. When I tried to rub warmth into his fingers he winced with pain. I'd seen many a fisherman in such straits and feared his fingers might drop off unless I thawed them exceedingly slow. I ordered him put his hands under my arm pits, and with the warmth of the blaze my spirits rallied.

"There's a fishing village and harbor on the Pemaquid peninsula," I whispered, "but I suspect they've fled. We must find a boat and get back to Arrowsick Island before the Major picks up the Natick Indians and sails for Portsmouth. Do you hear me, Will?"

As usual Will concentrated on his own desires. "I be mighty hungry, Thom," he complained.

I was at my limit. "Good God, man! You must be in a state of grace not to have run aground before this. I won't be at your beck and call forever. Use your blasted head and figure out our provisions."

Suddenly, Will resurrected. "Blimey, Puker, look at that Indian midden of clamshells. There must be quahogs in this tidal swamp and the water can't be any colder than my feet."

Before I could stop him, he had his socks off and was in the frigid salt marsh. Within a few minutes we sucked the succulent steamed flesh of those delectable tidal creatures.

"Wait 'til I get my hands on that praying Indian," Will brooded. "I'll string him up and butcher and quarter the rogue."

"Save your breath," I whispered, "and help me figure out how we're going to get to Arrowsick Island. It would help if we had shoes."

So consumed were we with this problem that neither of us heard the girl approach. Before I could jump up, she stood near the fire hiding something behind her back.

"The Pemaquid have us surrounded!" Will shouted. "We be dead meat." He knew nothing about the girl I'd met the previous evening and hung his head in despair. Remembering how the squaw had accused me with her eyes, I dared not move for fear of a tomahawk in my skull.

The girl walked up to me like a curious animal and before vanishing quick as a deer into the trees, she dropped a sealskin satchel at my feet.

"Don't open it!" Will cried, grabbing me by the shoulder. A grimace of pain and fear flashed across his pale face. "It could be snakes or evil herbs."

"Or a Medusa's head or Poseidon's bag of wind."

"Wha—huh?"

I smiled at his reaction to my literate allusions. "You can go off half cocked if you want, Will, but there's no reason not to open it— seeing as how the girl was alone."

"It be a ruse, Thom." Will's teeth started chattering again.

"Look—I'll open it. And if it's journey cake I'll eat every last smidgen."

Will hobbled into the woods while I untied the drawstring on the satchel and turned it onto the ground. Out dropped four won-drously wrought moose hide boots. I couldn't believe our luck and shouted for joy.

Hearing my shouts and mistaking them for help, Will came crashing back, falling in a heap in front of me. "What were it? What were it?"

I looked down at his sprawled body and held up the boots. "Divine Providence, Will. Divine Providence."

Though happy to be shod, I still worried over the journey that lay ahead. I thought of hailing our ship—if it was still there—but the reprisal from Simon kept me from venturing anywhere near the Point. On our voyage from Arrowsick Island to Pemaquid I'd counted five coastal channels we'd have to cross to return to the Garrison, and without navigation charts we might wander to death through the drowned valleys of Maine.

Will seemed to have recovered from the shock of captivity and resumed his familiar headstrong, albeit undirected zeal. Once more he waded back into the reeds. "Damn it to hell," he hollered, clutching one foot and hopping up and down.

"If you insist on hollerin' again, we'll part ways," I warned, "or the Pemaquid braves'll part you from your head—whichever comes first."

"But Thom, my poor feet struck a sunken object. I be in pain."

Though used to his lame excuses, I waded out. "Where?"

He pointed. "It be a cedar log."

A dark object several rods long loomed large in the limpid water. I bent down beside Will to have a look. "It could be a log or it could be—."

Distracted by another bed of clams, Will wandered off, leaving me to talk to myself.

"Will!" I whispered loud as I dared, waving. "You can savor all the clams in God's Kingdom if you help me tow this ashore."

Will waded back. "Have you totally vacated yer senses? What do ye want with a wretched waterlog?"

Exasperated, I tugged at the behemoth with all my might. He crouched down and pushed, but the infernal object wouldn't budge, and my toes were turning blue with cold. "We'll have to wait 'till the tide goes out."

"Fer more quahogs?" he asked, squishing his toes deep in the muck.

I slogged back to dry ground. "I wager a bushel of clams that's a dugout the Pemaquids scuttled before we arrived."

"Aw Puker, ye must be battle weary. It ain't nothing but a rotted log."

"Tide will tell," I answered, pulling on the Indian boots. There was a dark stain and I prayed to God it wasn't from one of the dead Pemaquids lying on the Point. As I watched Will gulp down raw clams like there was no tomorrow, it flashed on me like Ezekiel's wheels how difficult he 'd be on the voyage before us.

"Confound it, Will, get a move on," I ordered. "Don't you ever think ahead? We've only got a few hours to get away from here. Pru once told me cattails have edible spring tubers and I need your help."

Will smirked and tugged off his socks. "No wonder you never got in spittin' distance of the girl. There be a difference between talkin' tubers and plantin' 'em!"

I forced a smile and headed into the dense cattail brake. We pulled up what seemed like hundreds of splintered stalks for a piddling amount of tubers, scorched them in the embers, and ate a few. The rest I wrapped in ferns and stuffed in the satchel for our journey. I was stuffing the downy cattail fluff into our boots when Will yammered again.

"So help me, Will!" I fumed, "if you don't quit crowin' like a rooster, you'll end up in a Pemaquid pot."

When he didn't answer, I looked up to find him hefting rocks from the bottom of a dugout canoe.

"God be praised!" I whooped, mindless of my own injunctions to keep quiet.

We lugged the sodden barque from the tidal flat and managed to roll her over and drain the water out. Worried the Indians would come back to retrieve the barque, Will went searching for the paddles and found them in a clump of bushes not far from where they'd scuttled the canoe. Fearing our good fortune couldn't last, we threw in our provisions, what there were of them, and hurriedly heaved the behemoth dugout through the muck and into the water.

From the angle of the sun, I had a fair surmise how to reach beyond Pemaquid Point and across the first channel. The canoe hung low in the water with the damp from its dunking and moved with the grace of a man o' war struck broadside. Will jerked his paddle through the waves crashing over the bow and steered us across. Both of us were drenched but too intent on reaching the far side to dwell on much else.

At last we hauled the barque onto the opposite shore. Only when we stood atop a hill did we discover we were on an island amid the channel and must row the same distance before reaching the other side. Soaked and disappointed, we shoved off again, anxious to find a safe haven before nightfall. Meanwhile, the tide had turned and we fairly sped to the next point, where we drifted ashore.

I removed the precious flint from its hiding place inside my stocking and soon had a fire, over which we roasted the last of our tubers. Will already had climbed beneath our stack of soft cedar branches when I went over and shook him. "Will, I think we should keep watch," I whispered, overcome by fright.

He yawned and closed his crystals.

"Confound it, Will. Do you have any idea of the calamity at Pemaquid? Every Indian on the coast must be smeared with war paint."

"Keep yer damn watch if ye like, but I'm—." Will's towhead umbered by the coals sank onto the branches.

I threw a great log on the fire, determined to keep my windows open. But the direst nightmare paled beside the torments of that day, and I nodded off.

I awoke in the gloam wondering where I was and stiff as a poker. A tiny black-capped bird twittered cheerfully on one of my fir-branched coverlets. I threw some driftwood on the smoldering embers and hobbled down the rocky point to relieve myself.

The frigid air quickly brought me to my senses. Never in the wide world would we reach Arrowsick Island before Walderne and his men sailed back to Boston Harbor. My arms were sore from rowing, and we had at least four more channels to navigate.

Pulling off my stockings and leaving the flint ashore, I waded onto the slippery ledge, dislodged a few bearded blue mussels and crushing their shells with a stone swallowed them whole.

Suddenly something caught my eye—a gold band which at first I mistook for the path of sun on the water, except that it was moving with the incoming tide. I pulled on my moose boots and ran for a better look. The most marvelous sight greeted me. A stream of fish wide as a frigate ran boundless as God's bounty along the rivage of the point.

Aroused by my shouts, Will graced me with his drowsy presence.

"Fish, Will, fish! Hurry or they'll be gone!" I yelled, running toward the canoe.

He snatched me. "Thomas, Thom. Ye just can't put yer arm in and pull 'em out."

His procrastination angered me no end. "And why not?" I scraped the dugout a pittance over the seawrack.

He grabbed me again. "Yer always tellin' me to think. Well, I be thinkin' and I tell yew—ye need a seine or a line of hooks to catch fish."

The glint of them was enough to fire my appetite, and Will too seemed intent on the gold flashing on the sea. He walked thoughtfully along the tideline of the rocky cove looking for something.

Somewhere in him dwelt the same tenacity as Phillip Babb, and I reckoned if his lineage didn't hold him in thrall, the gnawing of his hunger would.

He returned with the carcass of a dead sea mell bleached as underclothes at spring whiting time.

"Fetch as many mussels as ye can." Will shouted.

I did as ordered. The bird skelette had an extraordinary number of sharp protuberances which Will baited with the mussel flesh. Together, we wound a long twist of eel grass, tied it to the makeshift rig, and shoved the dugout into the river of fish. Never had I seen so many, having spent most of my apprenticeship at the Shoals cutting cod heads.

I paid out the line. "Od's Pittikins!" I cried at a windy blast that rocked me into the moist hull of the dugout.

Will fixed me with a questioning look.

"'God have pity on mankind,' —an oath of my Fa's." I explained.

"Pull it in," Will ordered.

I was entranced by the steady stream of white gold shimmering deep and far as I could see.

"Damn it, Puker, do as I say or we'll lose the line."

The rig did not rupture, though a dozen silvery fish large as my hand hung from it like bees on a locust blossom. We skirred ashore with the bounty. I was putting my stockings back on when my stomach flipped like the fish we'd caught. Hadn't I tossed the flint safe on top of my stockings at the point—or was it near the boat?

Impatient with the delay, Will swung the rig in my face. "Hang it, Thom, these smelts weep to be eaten."

I unbolted the truth about the misplaced flint stone.

"I'll clean the fish while ye search for it. Pray the embers still be alive." Will said, walking away. I'd have felt better had he gloated.

Retracing my tracks on that rocky shore was impossible. The flint could be anywhere. Overwhelmed by visions of a fireless journey, I dropped to my knees and with closed eyes, I petitioned

Divine Providence to deliver me from my carelessness.
When I opened them, the morning sun glowed full in my face.
I reached down to push myself up and there, near my hand,
was the flint.

We lost count of the channels and land points, though the lowest
point of our journey was a fog so thick I couldn't see Will in the
bow of the dugout.

I knew by the glub glub of the killick stone into the water he'd
dropped anchor. Mindful that we had little room for error in the
wide ocean about us, we'd agreed not to row unless we could
sight land, however distant. One of my rowing arms throbbed for
recognition.

"Thom?"

"Aye, Will."

"Seems but yesterday we sat on the sunny wharf at the Shoals
concocting verse."

"The only verse fit for this occasion is *The Day of Doom*," I
said to the barely perceptible shape in the stern of the drifting
canoe.

"*Day of Gloom* ye mean," Will quipped.

I smiled despite myself. Like it or not, our destination was
bound together surely as wax and wick, thole and gunwale, jam
and—confound it! Why did an assemblage of words constantly run
the gauntlet in my brain? A verse reared its ugly head, hounding
my thoughts with still more useless twaddle.

> *I struck the board and cried, NO MORE!*
> *I will abroad.*
> *What? Shall I ever sigh and pine?*
> *My lines and life are free—*
>   *free as the road.*

Poets lied their way to the truth, no doubt about it. The English rhymester most probably never set foot abroad in his life.

> *Leave thy cold dispute*
> *of what is fit and not. Forsake thy cage,*
> *thy rope of sands.*

What I wouldn't give for a rope of sands, a spit of sand, anything but the murk engulfing us. Damned if the versifying blighter ever found himself anchored to a killick stone off the New World coast.

> *Tie up thy fears.*
> *He that forbears to serve his need*
> *deserves his load.*

High and mighty the lot of them, choked by their Anglican collar, a starched necklace of moral turpitude. Tears rolled down my cheeks from the pain in my arm and the hopelessness of my soul. The dank fog at least had the attribute of masking my emotion from Will who practiced a sea chantey in his butt of the boat. To drown out his cheerful voice, I kept up my private recital:

> *As I raved and grew fierce and wild*
> *at every word*
> *I thought I heard someone calling, CHILD!*
> *and I replied, OH. . .*

"Lord o Mercy, Thom, I sight land!"

A heavenly shaft dropped momentarily on the shore, and in its swift glimmering stood the Arrowsick Garrison.

21

We were hailed by an ancient shepherd who was using the regiment's new-built stockade for his flock.

"They all be departing!" a wool-clad man shouted over the creature-bedlam. A dam round as a barrel twitched her ears as he approached us. "At dawn a courier come to warn me the Woolwich folk be gatherin' at Master Phips' shipyard to depart fer Boston on the next tide. Yer soldiers have turned the Indians 'gainst us. Hope they get away afore savages scalp 'em."

The bleating sheep joined Will's whoops of relief.

"Won't you come with us?" I yelled from the canoe.

The ancient man's knotty hand fondled the woolly head of a sheep. "Thank ye, lads, but this be lambing season and five dams be needin' my help at their labor."

We paddled to the Town Landing on the Sheepscot River and were nearly at the town landing and we were nearly there when the sloop of Woolwich settlers headed out on the tide. A lad on her rigging waved us to steer clear, but the fleet schooner irredeemably drew us in her undertow. Just a moment and the dugout surely would be sucked under by the racing ship.

The wreck that took my brother passed before my eyes and I prayed for salvation before we capsized. Mistakenly thinking Will had jumped into the sea, I was about to follow when he shouted to me from above.

Somehow he had managed to leap from our canoe onto the Jacob's ladder on the speeding sloop, and stretching out an arm, he yelled for me to grab on.Unable to reach him. I lunged. My moose boot slipped and I grabbed the rung. My hands were so raw from rowing I nearly plunged into the waves. Someone on deck swung a grapple hook dangerously close to my head. I heard my great coat rip as the hook caught my collar. Dangling like a hanged man, I managed a toehold on the ladder and pulled myself on the deck in a painful heap.

Woolwich natives were packed stem to stern like a barrel of dunfish, and for awhile Will and I stayed exactly where we'd boarded, pressed against the rail. The crowd of caterwauling, fearful settlers filled every possible nook between us and the captain's forecastle.

A Woolwich settler with a peculiar green face blanched at my request to see Captain Phips and shoved me aside so he could retch over the railing.

Will straddled the rail and yelled to some boys squatting on a spar of the main sail. "Throw us a yard, lads," he shouted over the bobbing heads.

The boys tossed him a line and Will sailed over the gawking Woolwichers to mi- ship. He threw the line back, I took a deep breath and swung beside Will at the forecastle hatch.

"Where in the devil did you soldiers come from?"

The man I assumed was Captain Phips apprised us with piercing black pupils. I sank onto a chair with a telescopic leg while Will launched into a long tale of our Pemaquid adventures.

I was thankful for the stability of the chair because, despite Will's tale of daring-do, our last ditch effort coupled with hunger had my head spinning like a top.

I was so out of it that when the Captain shoved a plate of salt biscuits and a bottle of Madeira before us I thought it must be the Last Supper.

But the young Captain seemed to be facing incongruities of his own. "Damn it anyway," Phips mumbled. "Well, there's nothing for it. I guess I'll just have to start over. This be a brave sloop. I can always sell it to my creditors and build another ship in Boston."

Unaware the man was engaged in a monologue, Will cut in. "Thomas Taylor and I be masters of a hermaphrodite brig, Capt'n, if ye be in need of a trade vessel."

I could have clobbered him. Fortunately, Phips had his own plans. "Many thanks, lad. I carpentered this sloop to haul wood to Boston and, by Divine Grace, I be haulin' the folk of Woolwich. I couldn't leave them to the enemy Indians. With God at the helm, the next schooner I build will sail to England full of gold."

I'd thought no one could match Will when it came to the con-fabulation of heroic exploits, but I swear Phips was a veritable Homer. I was noisily chomping hardtack to blot out his far-fetched tales when a Woolwich man entered the cabin and surprisingly confirmed everything Phips was saying.

Yes, it was true. Everyone in the Sheepscots believed that Willie Phips was destined to meet three Kings in his lifetime. The midwife who handed Mistress Phips' twenty-first son over to his father told him as much. Everyone knew the seventh was a lucky child, and three sevens were astrological.

"How many Kings have you met so far, Capt'n Phips?" Will mouthed, onery as ever.

The Woolwich man grew red in the face and intercepted Will's query. "This very day he has rescued our entire village. And by God, you owe your very life to this man!"

Undisturbed by their quarrel, Phips mumbled to himself about a recent trade voyage to the Carolinas on which he'd heard of sunken Spanish galleons heavy with treasure. All he had to do was dredge them up and he'd be the richest man in the New World.

Will shot to his feet. "My Fa dug treasure chests all his life. Know what happened to him?" He laughed like he was out of his skull.

I grabbed his arm to silence him but to no avail.

"Fa ended up with a chest all right—full of his own stinkin' flesh and bones. Only rogues fathom the deep fer more 'an cod, Capt'n Phips." Will sneered and stomped off leaving me to apologize for his crude lack of respect.

Phips assured me it took more than an ill-tempered lad to set him off course, and a few hours later, the kindly Mainer dropped us off at the Isles of Shoals.

I made my way across Babb's Rock and down the busy wharf so full of Phips' dreams that I forgot my own—until I saw Pru.

Will took his usual unabashed advantage of her welcome, and when at last she did hug me, my arms were in such pain I yelped.

She cradled my shoulder. "Why, Thom, are you wounded?"

I wanted to tell her, Yes, I've been struck by Cupid's arrow, but it was lame as my limbs, and I sat while she removed my coat and shirt, which was nearly as healing as the berry salve she rubbed on.

Jealous of her attentions, with a feigned limp Will hobbled off to fetch a bucket of spring water.

While he was gone, I told Pru how Simon had bound us to a tree and we near froze to death. Rowing a boat great distances was hardly anything to brag about on the Shoals and I skipped that part and asked after little Peter Babb who like Skitters had been indentured to a family in Hampton.

Pru answered my questions but kept looking up for Will. The cold spring water and a strong potion of hemlock resin anodyned the pain in my arm and I smiled my gratitude.

"What about me?" Will complained.

Pru laughed at his childish insistence. "What about you?"

"Don't I get nothing fer my troubles?"

I watched while she drew Will to her and planted a long kiss on his wind-parched lips.

Will beamed. "That be a damned sight better."

When Pru offered a room in her cottage for payment in trade, Will clucked. "What a conniving wench. Fine, I trade my britches fer a piece of skirt." He lifted her dress, exposing her calves.

Embarrassed by their flirtation, I put on my shirt and made to leave.

"Thomas Taylor, come back here," Pru patted the sling she'd fashioned out of a piece of her petticoat. "You can't leave until you're properly healed."

I had no means to pay for lodging and told her as much.

Her voice took on an edge Shoalers assumed when talking business. "You and Will have your soldiering commissions, don't you?"

Like many northern soldiers, we'd arrived home with scarcely the clothes on our backs and I was forced to tell her the Provincial Regiment had abandoned us.

Pru patted my arm. "Don't worry, Thom. We'll think of something. Meanwhile, I have a handsome cod for supper."

I strolled with Pru in the sunlight where hens pecked among the cobbles.

"How about a roasted fowl, Pru?"

"Or a juicy mutton chop?" Will prodded, close behind.

"Or a wondrous porterhouse steak?" I bellowed.

Astonished by our vociferous appetites, Pru disappeared with her sack of cod. I don't know what spell that extraordinary Barbadoes woman cast, but before the sun set we were feasting merrily on chops and loins chased with freshly-brewed Smutty-Nose beer.

We boarded at Pru's until the summer solstice. Will lorded over the place, but soon fell into his old habits and wandered off. I didn't miss him, because it left Pru and me playing at the fringes of domestic bliss.

But at the wick-end of June our arrangement flickered out

when curiosity and cannon shot propelled Will and me across the channel to Go's Port.

Captain Swett of Hampton had attracted a crowd of Star Islanders in the tavern yard. "I have a commission to assail and annoy the Indians much as I like," he shouted, "and I aim to do it with your help."

I buried myself in a shoal of fishermen as two boys not more than twelve years old stepped forward to enlist.

Stephen Ford waved his cane in the air. "Ain't yew ta'en enough of us? We be short-handed a'ready, and quintals o' cod are waitin' to be off-loaded before they stink. This be no time fer bother-in' us with yer troubles."

Will pushed from behind John Tucker to join the lads.

"They'll be yer troubles soon enough if ye allow 'em savage redskins to do as they please!" Will shouted, slamming his gun butt on a rock. This gesture brought forward a handful of malcontents.

Captain Swett looked them over with a calculous eye. "I admit I could use some experienced men on this expedition."

Will spat on the ground. "I were the best shot in the Portsmouth Company and I dare say the second-best be within ear-shot."

Everyone to a man gawked at his neighbor. I'd shave off my beard, and the blush that crept into my cheeks was a dead give-away to Peter Twisden who stood beside me.

"Thom Taylor! It be Thom!"

The Shoals grapevine trailed over every crack and cranny. Bearded or not, they knew I was back. They knew where I'd been. They knew I was living with Pru, what I ate for supper, and the make and year of my musket.

"Aye, it be Thom Taylor," Will said, full of himself.

At Pru's I'd pretended to wear the sling she made me. I didn't really need it, but now, fast as I could, I secured my arm in its cra-dle. Neither Will nor anyone else would get me to fight any more Indians—praying or savage.

Captain Swett took one look at my arm and hollered.

"I need able bodied soldiers, damn it!"

Smarting from his remark, I sank back into the band of fisher-men who'd counted on me to bolster the troops while they salted away their dunfish. Why should I feel guilty? If Will wanted to for-feit his life to the whims of the Massachusetts Militia, let him.

A fortnight later, news reached us from Black Point that Captain Swett with most of the New Hampshire Company had been shot full of arrows in a swamp ambush. One of the young lads returned wounded and died in his mother's arms.

We'd been told forty were dead at Black Point, yet Pru held the odd belief that Will would return.

"He's a survivor," she'd say looking up from her spinning. "I know it in my heart."

Plagued by stories of widespread uprisings and fearful for their safety, Appledore Islanders gathered at the well to talk about moving to Go's Port where it was safer because of the fort. I had to laugh. The fort they set so much store by consisted of a rotted pal-isade around a hovel fitted with two rusty cannons. It was inade-quate to protect the twenty families at Go's Port, let alone forty more families.

Will's unexplained absence swelled his stature to that of hero and island oracle. "If Will Babb were here, he'd want us to protect ourselves," I overheard a woman at the well say to her husband.

"Aye, his father were a fighter a'right, and he be the spitfire kin of Phillip Babb, God rest his soul."

Pru encouraged their idolatry to the point I could barely stand it. Seeing the hermaphrodite brig anchored at Pepperrell's fishing stage, I quickened my pace, hoping to catch the Devon man at home. Recollecting my first impressions of Pepperrell, I was amazed how they'd altered in his favor. During the Indian Wars he'd gone off and plied his trade in Spain, returning only when the coast was clear. Whereas once I might have thought him a turncoat, now I admired his foresight.

Over a foamy tankard of ale, Pepperrell and I jabbered about the twists of events in the Provinces and the scuttlebutt of the impending exodus of Appledore fishermen to Go's Port where they sought safety.

"I have little intention of going or staying for that matter," Pepperrell confessed. "This manse be but a hovel compared to the mansion I hope to build myself on Kittery Point, and the hermaphrodite brig be least in a fleet bound to make me wealthier than that impostor we call Governor of the Provinces."

"Mister Cutt?"

Pepperrell swigged down his brew. "I hope ye don't consider him a friend."

I hedged. "Not exactly."

"Good. Fer I'd rather give Maine my allegiance than serve that senile fusspot. Yew'll see. He'll annex the Shoals to Great Island to keep the Royal English Charter. But it won't amount to a hill of beans. There be considerable less trouble and more reward on the Maine side of the Piscataqua River—mark my words."

Content to listen where politics were concerned, I weighed the balance of my allegiances which since I'd been at Dover had shifted to Pepperrell's way of thinking. His ambitions ran high, but at least he made no secret of them. In fact, he disclosed his plans to marry a Kittery lass whose prominent family estate and fortune would fall to him in no small measure.

"Your appearance be well-timed, Thom." he told me. "I need someone to oversee my fishing stage on Appledore seeing as how that damnable Governor Cutt and his Boston cronies have filled the Shoalers' heads with tales of terror and Indian slaughter."

"It's not a lie, Mister Pepperrell. I saw it with my own eyes," I countered.

Pepperrell confided in me brother-like. "Aye, Thom, I can tell ye don't close the Indian shutters and tremble in the dark like others. But now we be at peace, and I aim to look to the future. What would ye say if I offered ye charge of this dwelling and the brig. Half and half on the brig—though ye must maintain the wormy wreck."

I thought back on his grand promises of a dory that turned out to be a rotten tub. But something told me he spoke square. I 'd lost too much to rejoice, yet was still young enough for dreams. I'd hold my cards close and play them one at a time.

"Be this contractual?"

Pepperrell smiled. "Ain't every blasted thing these days? Yew can't piss in a pot without a piece of parchment. But I leave ye to draw it up, Thom, for I have my marriage to attend to. Which reminds me, ye'll be keeping my Shoals accounts in exchange fer these lodgings. Done deal?"

I extended my hand to seal our pact and he poured me a tankard of beer. "Say, I meant to ask, 'ave ye no sweet-heart? It be damned lonesome on Hog—uh, Appledore—especially now that they be desertin' in droves to Go's Port fer The Main."

"Will Babb is lost in battle," I said, not really sure why.

He clanked his tankard on the table. "I'm sorry, though it does clear the coast fer yew and that green-eyed Barbadoes wench. By all means have a mistress, Thom. Just between us, I've had a few marmalade madams to keep the home fires burning, if ye get my drift."

The handsome rogue gave me a conspiratorial wink. To my surprise I winked back, and for the first time in my life I actually enjoyed the bawdry of his innuendo.

This time the partnership hinged on my wits and not those of the Cutt brothers or Will Babb, who more than likely moldered at Black Point with an arrow through his chest.

Now that I was master of my own fate, I decided to take Pepperrell's advice and ask Pru to move in. I'd wait until the very last moment when her heart ached at leaving Appledore. Like the others, she'd packed her belongings for the exodus to Go's Port. Proud of my new fishing stage and the brig, I promised to carry Shoalers and their wares across the channel in trade for the cumbersome barrels of dunfish they left behind. And though the crossing was short, the first immigration in September turned out agreeably profitable.

I was hopeful when Pru lingered on, and one glorious fall morning I took her aside, proposing we post our wedding banns at Church Island. Maybe I hadn't thought it through too well and I'm not sure what I expected, but she dropped the bowl she was holding, clotting my moccasins with oily clumps of cheese curd

"Whatever do you mean, Thom? You know I'm already spoken for."

I bit my tongue. Had some Shoals rake a hold on her?

"It's Will!" she cried.

Frustrated by her blind hope, I persisted.

"But Pru, won't you at least stay with me? I'll be moving into Master Pepperrell's manor to keep an eye on it and—."

I was ten years old when I first set eyes on Prudence Monforte. Maybe then I was too young, but I'd just turned nineteen and, God Almighty, how I wanted her!

"I can't, Thomas. I've arranged to live with Master Ford and his family. It would be intolerably lonesome without the others."

"But Pru, I'm here."

She looked down.

"I'd take care of you."

"While you're off in your brig?"

"You could sail with me. I've heard of women on board vessels."

She smiled. "Aye, with murderous pirates. Oh, Thomas, you've always been kind and generous, but I'm expecting Will any day now."

Saddened to my heels, I busied myself carting Pru's belongings to Pepperrell's Landing and stowing them on the deck with Master and Joan Ford's humble chattel.

All winter I was lonely to distraction. Unlike the Dover Minister, Pepperrell owned but one book, an account ledger. During January thaw I sailed over to Church Island to see Minister Belcher. His periwig was more moth-eaten than ever, but he did let me borrow a quarto of poems by the daughter of Simon Bradstreet who was the newly appointed Provisional Governor of Massachusetts. The title, *Several Poems With Great Wit of Variety and Learning Full of Delight by a Gentlewoman,* was so tedious it took me a week to venture a look inside. But once I did, to my great pleasure Ann Bradstreet's poems were more than companionable. One of the verses especially brought Sarah Walderne to mind.

> *Such despite they cast on female wit*
> *that what I do prove well, it won't advance;*
> *they'll say it's stol'n or else it was by chance.*

What I wouldn't give for one of Sarah's kisses, and the chance to advance it!

22

*I*n May I prepared to sail to Hampton to have my brig caulked at the shipyard. Pru asked me to call on the Babb clan, no doubt as a pretext for news about Will.

My commission was eased when by coincidence I ran into Skitters at Moorings' Turn. Although a few inches taller, he hadn't outgrown his stutter and I strung the bits and pieces together. Samson and Peter were fine. They'd both moved in with John and Rebecca Hussey who had a daughter, Bathsheba, just Peter's age, a comely girl sure to steal someone's heart. I teased Skitters about his weakness for pretty girls starting with Ann Smith who had been at Goody Cole's trial. Buoyed by memories, I told him how Will and I fled the notorious Simon at Pemaquid, and because his brother was good as dead, I added what a hero Will had been at Black Point. Everyone said so.

Skitters shrugged. "That be be behind us now, Thom."

I thought this a bit odd, recalling how long it had taken for me to get over the death of my older brother.

"Yew be fam fam ily and I'm invite inviting yew—tomorrow."

Skitters' stutter compounded by the noise from Taylor's River Stage stole the sense of what he was saying, but over the ruckus I agreed to meet him the following morning.

My brig waited to be careened among the carpentered skeletons of barques and fat hulls. I slept on her deck but awoke at dawn with visions of Goody Cole.

Wondering what had become of the ancient soul, I crept through the mist along the river path to her wattle and daub hovel and crossed the threshold calling her name. A party of vermin rustling in the gloom projected me through the rank river vegetation to meet Skitters.

I was about to pass a pair of fog-shrouded silhouettes when I recognized the unbearable woman and her daughter Debora from the Shoals. Not being in a mood for them, I ducked off the path and behind a shag hickory tree. The girl was decked out in flounces and stopped to adjust a bow on her bonnet.

"Come along, Debora. We shall be late to the nuptials," her mother barked.

Once they had passed, I clambered back onto the tote path, reproaching myself for my stand-off behavior. After all, Hampton was a common destination and they had as much right to be there as I.

Skitters and his brothers seemed to be going to the same wedding I'd heard about on the path. I shook hands with Samson Babb, who had grown tall and grave in my absence, and hugged little Peter.

Skitters must have known the groom because he was in charge of half a dozen Narraganset pacers which were there for a horse race to the wedding. I was glad Skitters thought to invite me to the festivity and fell in with Mister Gove, one of the Hampton revelers. He proved such a good listener that I found myself vetting my pent-up rage at the injustice of the Indian skirmishes. The north was in arrears financially and had lost too many lives.

Gove added several grievances of his own "Yew should be

voicin' yer opinions against this Randolph, Mister Taylor. He has Hampton and Portsmouth on their knees fer the King, ye know. If we don't watch out he'll sell us all down the river and tax us to Kingdom Come. We plan to take action and could use educated men like yerself."

Skitters sauntered up with a pair of horses. "Goodman Gove, here's yer stee steed. Thom, yew can ride the bay. I pre prefer shanks' mare."

A cloud of sand loomed like a spectre on the beach and a solitary rider churned like a windmill from the direction of Boar's Head.

"Here be the groom his his self!" Skitters cried. "If ye be wantin' a pri pri prized bottle to quench yer thirst—get goin'!"

I leapt on the bay, and digging in my heels, overtook Gove and the rest. I was too engrossed to see anything but a bent figure galloping neck and neck beside me. He raced by. A wide brim pilgrim hat hid his face as he beat the flank of his horse with a crutch and passed like a devil spout on the strand.

By the time I reined in at the cottage on Rye beach, the mysterious rider had jumped off, seized the bottle of Madeira tied by a ribbon to the spar of a dory, and uncorked it with his teeth.

I slid from my foamy mount with a pester of questions. Was he the groom? Where had the Shoals mother got to? Was her wanton daughter the bride?

A high pitched squeal answered all of them. I whipped around to see Debora naked as Lady Godiva at the cottage door. Poking her small head and large bosom through the swinging top of the Dutch transom, she screamed, "Will—Will—Give us a kiss!"

The bejeweled hand of the mother grabbed her from behind and slammed the door shut.

The groom staggered off with his bottle. I ran after him. The pits and pocks of the strangely familiar face startled me to silence.

"Aye, Thom, it's Will Babb in the flesh—what's left of it. The savage Indians at Black Point were crumpets and tea compared to the King's bastards. I begged to return to the Shoals but they sailed us straight into the Boston plague. I near died." Will took a swig of the Madeira and waved his crutch in my face. "My only fortune be Debora. God bless her!"

I gulped back the bile in my throat. All this time Pru was pining after Will, he'd been rutting this stupid wench.

Gove and the others rode up, jumped off, and with rowdy whoops carried off Will. I must have stood there a long time because when I looked up, they'd gone in. The door had been left open and I shoved into the crowded room.

Will and the Babb brothers stared at a crack in the door of a top-heavy armoire through which dangled a plump naked arm. A high-pitched cackle from within left no doubt that Debora was attached to its milky flesh. A minister in a fall collar handed his Book of Prayer to her mother, and, uttering a few unintelligible homilies, he placed Will's hand in the bride's. "Do you happen to have a ring on you?" he asked, squinting in the half light of the stone dwelling.

Will fumbled in his clothing, produced a gold band, tried to slip it onto the pudgy finger and, failing, squeezed it into Debora's palm. The disembodied hand undulated like the head of a swan as the minister intoned his ceremony.

"Be this a usual Hampton marriage?" I whispered to Skitters.

He cupped his fingers around my ear. "This way the cred cred creditors will not collect Deb Debora's deb debts."

It made no sense to me. But then, nothing about Will ever did.

Cupping my ear again, Skitters stuttered a moist addendum. "Will ass ass ass—."

He's got that right, I thought.

"Assures me she be deb debtless. But her ki ki kin has em to the hil hil hilt. Being naked symbolizes she bee ee ee free and . . ."

A resounding knock and bustle from within the monstrous furniture would have toppled it had Skitters and I not lunged forward and put our backs to it. The arm withdrew as we continued to shore up the rocking wardrobe. The minister licked his thick lips with a long narrow tongue and eyed the punch bowl. "You may come out now."

Despite our efforts, the armoire sighed and rattled on its spindly legs.

Will banged the door with his crutch, his pocked face red with drink and impatience. "Damn ye, Debora, come out'n that closet before I drags ye out fer all t'see."

The door popped open, revealing the bride still fussing with her wedding frock which she'd put on hind part before.

"The wretched thing be all wrong," she cried, tottering on red sateen shoes, her bosoms puffing like a pair of bellows. Hearing the gales of laughter that greeted her, she burst into tears.

Will threw down his crutch and grabbed her. "Don't matter a whit, Debora. I'll jest be takin' it off again."

The voyage home I caught a fearsome grip and lazed about on Appledore before crossing the channel to see Pru. Her cool demeanor at once made me wish I'd sent someone to tell her I'd been ill. Weak with fever, I disgorged my tattle. "Will is alive," I blurted. "I saw him in Hampton. He had the plague and has gruesome death tokens all over his face."

Too late I realized Pru wasn't alone. A figure crouched in the corner with light glinting off a gun. Pru looked outside, motioned me in, and closed the door.

Will Babb emerged from the shadows and wrapped his arm around Pru's waist. "I been lyin low."

"You mean you're a low liar." I accused with chattering teeth. "Did you tell Pru about Debora?"

Pru squirmed from Will's embrace and confronted me the way she was wont to do of late. "He told me all about Debora—and how he'd have died had she not brought him from the very jaws of the plague."

"And nothing else?" My voice wheezed in bronchial turmoil.

Will shoved Pru aside. "I told her how Goodman Gove and me

be wanted by Edward Cranston."

"Edward Cranston?"

"Aye, George Mason's puppet has been sent here to throw us poor bastards off our rightful land. Gove be in chains and bound on a ship fer the Tower of London. But yew wouldn't be privy to that, living out here wi' yer head in a kettle o' fish."

My fist shot out and I heard a crack. Unfortunately, my knuckles and not Will's head.

"Get out!" Pru cried, shoving me out the door. "I've had enough of your jealous meddling."

I backed into the drizzle and groped my way along the gloomy shore to the Go's Port Tavern, where I planned to numb my misery. But Divine Intervention would have it otherwise. The first person I met was William Phips.

"Thomas Taylor, I been lookin' high and low fer yew."

I shook his hand and sat atop a barrel.

"Has some calamity befallen ye, man? Ye look like ye just lost yer best friend."

Little and less would he know of my affairs. "I've caught a bad grippe," I told him, hiding my face in my muckinder.

"Sorry to see yew so down, but maybe this'll cheer ye up. The King has granted me a commission to dredge for gold in the West Indies."

Couldn't everyone just leave me alone?

"I be lookin' fer a quartermaster and asked around. First, I asked Mister Shapleigh, and who do ye think he recommended?"

I spat phlegm into my muckinder and shook my head.

"Why yew, of course." Phips' eyes glittered with ambition. "Then I went to Mister Pepperrell, and who do ye think came to his mind right off?"

My head was pounding. When would he give up?

"Thomas Taylor be a man of character and a fine sailor," says he. "Not only did he direct me to yer place on Appledore Island, but he give me this letter temporarily releasin' yew of yer obligation to the brig. Within this very hour I sent a gaffer across the channel to fetch yew."

My eyes blurred and three Phips appeared badgering me to death.

"What say ye, man? I be sailin' fer Bermuda day after the morrow. I drawed up papers to make it official. See?"

The words on the scroll swam and in an effort to get away I slid into an oblivion where his plots and schemes melted away.

When I came to, I was laid out on my bed at Appledore. I propped myself on an elbow and looked around. A blossomy aroma emanated from the kitchen and a bowl floated before me. I grabbed the burnished wrist holding the bowl and spilled hot liquid all over me.

"Shhh, Thom. Lie still." In what seemed a dream, Pru bent over me, her green eyes limpid as a calm cove. "Rest now or you'll have pneumonia."

Certain I was already asleep, this was no problem. But when I thought I was awake, there she was again. Pru smiled so sweetly I could not help smiling back. She bent over and kissed me on the forehead. "Ah Thom, at last you're better. I blame myself for sending you into the rain. I wonder if you'll forgive me?"

Her speech wore me out, but I nodded and eased into her lilting Barbadoes voice.

"After you left, Will admitted that he'd gone and married that Debora floozy." She laughed nervously. "I threw a basket of mackerel at him."

Her soft lips quivered. "He told me he never loved me and I could go to the devil for all he cared. "

I raised myself up to pull her near. "I ran to the tavern to apologize and found Mister Phips bending over you," she continued. "He told me he'd asked you to sail with him to Bermuda and you fainted dead away. His men got you onto a boat and across the channel. Mister Phips offered to pay me to look after you, but I told him I owed you my life!"

Tears welled in her eyes—and mine.

Our spell broke with a coughing fit that felt like a chest full of Indian arrows. Pru hurried to the kitchen, returning with a plaster of castor oil and a tonic of such soporific properties I soon was snoring like a swaddled babe.

After my noon bowl of bouillon, I propped myself on a bolster and was looking out the quarrel at the dreary sheets of late October rain when there was a sudden pounding at the door. Pru flung it open and there stood Will Babb dripping onto the planks. His fur hat was drenched and a black wool cloak clung to his long figure.

Pru grabbed my musket and pointed it at the sorry sight. "Get out!" she yelled.

I threw off the bed quilt and wobbled to my weak legs. My arm shook with the weight of the rifle as I took it from her and held it on Will. "You heard her."

Will fished under his cloak for a flask and swigged a great draught.

Someone else pounded at the door and when Pru moved to answer it Will grabbed her. Startled by the robust appearance of Captain Phips, he let her go.

Phips burst out laughing. "Here be a pregnant entanglement."

Will slung his sodden cloak onto a stool.

Phips' cannonball constitution and forthright greeting put me immediately at ease. "I'm glad to see ye lookin' hale, Thom Taylor," he said. "I can wait no longer on the Shoals. Be ye hardy enough to sail? "

Will hung onto every word. "Sail? Devil take me. Where be ye headed, Mister Phips?"

The Captain from Maine had a knack at getting to the point. "Bound fer the Bermudas, William, on a trade expedition. Thom has but to afix his signature as quartermaster and we hoist the yards. There be room below decks—though I daresay it mightn't suit yer nature."

Will's eyes were aglitter with the thought of a commission which by default might turn out to be his. He stepped forward. "I'd be greatly obliged for any position, Capt'n Phips."

Phips pretended to warm his hands by the hearth fire in order to approach Pru. "What do you say, lass? I reckon ye could help resolve this tricornered affair."

Ignoring both of us, she addressed the lucky son of a gunsmith from Maine. "Well, Sir, Master Taylor is well enough to sail, and he is the worthiest man I know to serve on your ship. You are exceeding kind to offer passage to Will. But with all due respect, Sir, within this very hour Will has promised to look after me, and for better or worse, we share a bed at Star Island.

Will lurched at her with his hand raised. Phips adroitly intercepted it, twisting it backward until Will grinced in pain. "The word of the fairer sex always holds our respect, William Babb. This be a lesson yew could learn." He thrust an inked quill into my hand. "Thom, it looks like ye must drown yer grief in an ocean voyage."

I signed the agreement without reading a word of it because Will, annoyed by Phips' upbraiding, had taken Pru aside and threatened she'd have hell to pay.

Hearing his threat, Phips jerked Will by the arm. "Step outside!"

Will fled into the driving rain followed by the brawny Mainer. I was wondering how Will would survive fisticuffs with such an adversary when Mister Phips stuck his head back inside. "In case yer wonderin', I plan to get the rogue stinkin' drunk and clap him in the stocks." With a look of fatherly concern, he added, "Make the most of leave-takin', Thom. "We sail at dawn."

PART FIVE

Bahama Gold

23

Master Phips quartered me aft. I'd barely stowed my duffel in the helmsman's cabin when an insolent looking officer in English uniform blocked my regress. He wore a wig and sucked a Seville orange. My stuffed nostrils hadn't smelled much of anything for weeks and the luxurious odor of the fruit deliciously wakened my senses.

"Who are you and what be your duty aboard this vessel?" he demanded in a flinty voice.

"Thomas Taylor, quartermaster, appointed by Captain Phips." Before I could think once, he grabbed my sore throat and spit half a dozen orange pips in my face.

"You lily-livered fibbing bastard. I should tear your heart out and feed it to your mother for lying to the Admiralty like that."

Fortunately, a second officer appeared in the doorway adjoining the Captain's cabin. The irascible officer eased his stranglehold, leaving me croaking for air.

"I say, Lieutenant Knepp. What can be the meaning of this?" the second man asked in clipped speech.

"Why, Admiral Solomon, I was just welcoming the new quartermaster to the *Rose Algiers*," he answered, procuring a smidgen of chocolate from a slit in his waistcoat and nibbling at it. "I informed Mister Taylor here that until the King's Quartermaster is relieved his services will not be required."

"Nor will yours if you persist, Lieutenant," the man called Salmon replied.

Stuffing the rest of the chocolate into his mouth, the obnoxious man fled, leaving the Admiral to apologize for his compatriot's strange behavior. The apology sailed into a fleet of complaints. Lieutenant Knepp was an ass. The crew (and now apparently the officers) were at each other's necks. Provisions were dangerously low. There had been severe storms the entire crossing and the ship had sprung a leak in the powder magazine. The Admiral ducked back through the doorway. "But do not bother yourself, Mister Taylor, everything will be ship-shape as soon as we reach Clark's Shipyard in Boston."

Exhausted by the ups and downs of a voyage that hadn't yet begun, I went to my cabin and flung myself on a hammock. I awoke from a dream about Pru at the sudden clangor of a bell. How oddly the room rocked back and forth. I thought I must still be in bed on Appledore until my hand poked through the rope hammock of the cramped cabin.

A round-faced man with dark unpowdered hair cupped his hand around a lighted candle as he moved slowly and gently through the room.

"Oh, I beg thy pardon, Mister Taylor. I was trying not to disturb thee. I am Francis Rodgers, Second Mate and Navigator of the *Rose Algiers*." He sank onto a nearby hammock and soon breathed as slowly as he had spoken.

Shouts and trampling that could have raised the dead brought me to my feet, yet the weary helmsman slept where he'd fallen. Anxious with the clamor, at first light I stumbled onto the quarter-deck.

Captain Phips, the surly Lieutenant Knepp, and Admiral Solomon stood on the steps of the forecastle before the crew which was in a callithump to get off the ship. Guards posted amidships plied their pikes to keep the fourscore sailors at attention, if not exactly in order.

"I'm lettin' yew English tars loose on Boston." Phips dark eyes flashed dramatically skyward. "May God preserve this fair city!"

They were the bloodiest bunch of cutthroats I'd ever laid eyes on—which was no small matter coming from a Shoaler.

Captain Phips struck a pose to bring his message home. "Any infringement on the hospitality of Massachusetts Bay will see yew in leg irons and headed for the nearest plantation. Do I make myself clear?"

"Aw, save yer fine speeches fer yer wife,"a dare-devil shouted back. "As for us, we plans to find us a Boston Kate in short order, don't we, mates?"

A cheer went up from the scruffy rattailed sailors.

"Devil cares if we ever set eyes on this leaky hull again," another ventured, despite a jab from a guard's pike. "We be sick to the death of yer weevilly biscuits and salt water. "

Captain Phips was all decked out in incredible London finery which, judging from appearances, might be the only drawing card left in his bid for their attention. Half-hidden by the breadth of Phips' powdered periwig, Lieutenant Knepp lobbed green grapes into his mouth.

Admiral Solomon climbed the forecastle steps to catch his gold braided tricorner hat from a gust of wind. Then, with a curt gesture he signaled the gunner to fire a salvo. "Company, dismissed!" he shouted over the cheers of the mob.

Within moments every last one of them had cleared the deck.

Captain Phips turned to me. "I believe Helmsman Francis Rodgers may still be in his quarters. Mister Taylor. Look in your cabin, will you? The *Rose* must be careened for repairs within a few hours."

I aroused Mister Rodgers and we waited while the Captain talked to the ship's carpenter. Seeing us, he broke off. "Ah, Navigator Rodgers, sorry to disturb you. Thomas Taylor here will see that ye get a proper lie-down at The Blue Anchor."

I'd never set foot in Boston and lacked the courage to say it. Once we were on dry land, I asked Rodgers if he might direct us to the The Blue Anchor.

He blinked and pointed down the cobbled street along the wharves. Tavern-crowded Ship Street gave out and I turned at the sign of Mackerel Lane. My sleep-walking companion assured me the sign we saw in the distance was The Blue Anchor. The sign was a Bunch of Grapes. Rodgers shook his head and shrugged his shoulders. I concluded he probably was a decent navigator on high seas but as good as lost on *terra firma*.

So much sewage puddled the street that I found myself wishing I had a pair of paten sandals on iron rings like the ones I'd seen New Hampshire women wear in their muddy gardens. I swerved around a man in regimental uniform strolling toward us down King Street. It must have been obvious we were from the boon docks because he stopped to ask if he might direct us. When I told him we were looking for The Blue Anchor he seemed delighted.

"But what a coincidence," he said. "I'm going there myself." He held out a roomy hand. "Mister Samuel Sewall at your service. You don't hail from Boston. Are you from the provinces?"

Fortunately, Francis Rodgers had not entirely lost his bearings and awakened long enough to be civil. "I navigate the King's ship, *Rose Algiers*, which we have left at Clark's Shipyard for repair. This is Quartermaster Thomas Taylor, who hails from the Isles of Shoals."

I was thrilling to the sound of being called quartermaster, when it dawned on me that I was talking to the most respected deputy of the Massachusetts Court. Samuel Sewall owned vast Maine properties and his marriage to the Boston Mint Master's daughter was legendary. Northerners never tired telling how Master Hull had placed his daughter on the scales, weighed her, and paid Samuel Sewall her weight in pine tree shillings as a dowry. The Shoalers version had the girl naked as a jay bird—so that her father needn't pay a shilling more than asked.

The portly Sewall talked as we walked.

"I've passed the Shoals on my way to Portsmouth to survey my holdings on the Sagamore River. I often dealt with Mister Shapleigh. Did you know him?"

Thankfully, before I could turn morose thinking of my dear friend who had been struck mortal by a falling timber at Diamond's Shipyard, we halted at the sign of The Blue Anchor. And with a flourish, Mister Sewall ushered us beneath a ditty.

> *With sorrows I am compassed round.*
> *Pray lend a hand—my ship's aground.*

Inside the cheery low-ceilinged ingle we were greeted by the tavernkeep Mister Monck. After praising the beaming man's turkey roasts and famous salmon suppers, Sewall introduced us. "They're new arrivals off the *Rose Algiers* and want lodging. Have you a room, dear fellow?"

While the busy taverner brought Sewall a pint, the serving maid accompanied us to a back chamber called The Court which gave onto a pleasant evergreen yard. Climbing under the bed covers, Francis Rodgers yawned an apology for not going to dinner with me and fell asleep.

In the taproom Mister Sewall beckoned me with a tankard of port. "George Monck, bring this Shoals lad your finest turkey drumstick and corn dressing. He has the look of a ravenous sailor about him."

He turned to me. "Now then, Mister Taylor, who is the captain of *Rose Algiers*?"

"Mister William Phips, Sir."

He scowled. "So—that persuasive Mainer who talked Boston into financing a vessel for hauling wood has enlisted still another vessel. From whom?"

Not wishing to disparage my congenial Boston host or Phips, I remained bolted. But being of a courtroom nature, Sewall would not condone my silence.

"I have a right to know," he argued, "having spent considerable capital in Phips last venture with little gain."

"King Charles, Sir." I told him. "But it was the Duke of Albemarle who interceded on Mister Phips behalf for an audience at London Court."

Sewall bit into his drumstick, smacked his lips and smiled. "Well, I must say you provincials don't give up easily."

I smiled back. "No, Mister Sewall, we be equal to the task."

He waved his drumstick in the air. "I dare say by hook or crook everyone is on equal footing in the New World. Matter of fact, this very week I wrote the first draft of a petition urging Massachusetts to emancipate Negro slaves. It 'll be a blotch on us for all futurity if we continue to treat men like chattel. But colonists' petitions are stacked on my desk at the printing press—and I doubt mine will see the light anytime soon.

He paused, then chucked. "I told my Negro servant Joseph he could have his freedom and signed over his indenture. But the dear man refuses to leave. I 'm extremely fond of the ancient fellow and have promised him a regimental funeral with a carriage and team of six. He has no kin of his own and I aim to lay him beside my family at Granary Burial Ground."

What he told me seemed daringly wondrous, and thinking of Winni and her son, I asked whether Indian boys and women in bondage as soldiers and servants might be emancipated as well.

Sewall gnawed thoughtfully on his drum-stick. "All slavery is a sad affair. But, of course, this is strictly between you and me, Mister Taylor, until my petition is printed and distributed."

He offered me his large greasy hand and I shook it. "Between you and me," I repeated, flushed with pleasure to think such a celebrated man was entrusting his private thoughts to my confidence.

Taverner Monck bustled up to our table holding out a pie. "Apples fresh from New Hampshire?"

Mister Sewall pushed aside the messy board. "Set it down, good fellow." He took up a knife and divided the pie round as his flushed face into two equal parts. "Bring us some English cheddar to accompany this pie and some coffee, will you, Publican Monck?"

I had never drunk coffee and nearly choked on the bitter brew. With a high sign from Sewall, Monck once more was at his service. "George, fetch Mister Taylor a pitcher of cream with maple syrup. I don't think the poor fellow is used to our strong Boston coffee."

He could easily have made light of my provincial ignorance, and I warmed to his kindness.

Sewall lit his pipe and leaned comfortably against the wainscoting. "Are you related to my roommate Edward Taylor who graduated with the Harvard class of 1671? I'm afraid I don't remember his English provenance. In any case, Edward has been posted to a wilderness ministry at Westfield, and with his latest letter he included a poem. The serious fellow is writing a spiritual verse every few months to accompany his ministration of the Lord's Supper. Well, that's neither here nor there, although it occurred to me you might be related."

The possibility of a family connection, no matter how far removed, seemed too good to be true and I told him I did have an uncle who came to the colonies, although I remembered he was studying to be a physician.

The colony printer puffed exuberant smoke rings into the air. "Dear fellow, Edward Taylor not only is a minister, but a physician as well! This divine occurrence cannot go unacted upon. You must write Edward a letter and I'll make sure he gets it. "

My heart could not keep up with common occurrences, let alone divine ones. Sewall signaled the taverner.

"Put us both on my billet, George. "

"But Sir," I objected.

He disregarded me. "You outdid yourself with that pie, Good Monck."

Flushed with pleasure, the tavernkeep bowed.

"Now then, Thomas Taylor, I must collect my girls at the Dame School or my wife will have my head on a platter. Will you be in Boston come Sunday? Cotton Mather is preaching at South Church and you're invited to accompany me in the Hull Family pew."

I was dumbfounded by his generosity. "Mister Sewall, you are consummately kind but, you see, I—."

He prodded his fingers into his gloves. "I understand, Thomas. It depends on the weather and the shipyard. Don't forget to write that letter, though. Leave it with George Monck and he'll give it to me." Once more he held out his roomy hand. "God speed, Mister Taylor. It was a delight talking with you." And taking up his regimental pike, Samuel Sewall emptied the room.

24

*T*he following day I wandered far and wide taking in the sights of Boston.

I'd heard the town's inhabitants equaled in number those of Portsmouth, Strawbery Banke, and the Shoals. But how differently the towns seemed in design and purpose.

Whereas every stage, wharf, and isle of Portsmouth was covered in cod, in Boston the wharves were busy with a panoply of carriages and vessels. Giant carracks, coastal merchant traders, and English brigs dwarfed mid-sized sloops and lighters. The smaller tenders, ketches, jollies, and long boats squeezed into every available space like barnacles. Off-loaded rolling barrels of Barbadoes rum and molasses were carted by stevedores along the great lengths of wharves stretching from both sides of Dock Square. Cinnamon and exotic fruits from the West Indies, billowy bales of cotton from southern plantations, and English fabrics crowded hundreds of docks from Scarlet Wharf in the North End to the South Battery Fort on the Shawmut Peninsula. Fish criers and butchers barked in my ears, and an aproned shopkeeper who had stabbed a slice of pineapple with his knife literally ran with it under my nose until I gave in and bought it.

Leaving the filthy squalor of The Dog and Bowl, Horse and Hound, and other shipjack digs, brothels and cooperages, I entered Milk Street and, passing the sign of The Blue Ball, bought a candle from the shopkeeper, Josiah Franklin. At the intersection of Milk and Cornhill Streets I stopped to admire a handsome fire-protected brick house with four dormers and an octagonal cupola topped by the weathervane of a Shawmut Indian.

By then I'd had enough of the pedestrian, and returned to The Blue Anchor taproom.

Just inside the door Lieutenant Knepp was engaged in a less than friendly conversation. He ignored my salutary nod, and I settled into a far corner with some parchment and an ink pot I'd purchased on my walk.

Truth be known, the content of Sewall's proposed letter to Edward Taylor had slowed my steps all morning. It's not easy to write someone you know let alone someone you've never met. Nothing beats the human voice, gesture, and mood to clarify one's meaning, and words set to paper can be taken as an affront where none is intended.

Nonetheless, Edward Taylor might be New World kin—kin I dearly longed for, though I must not seem too eager. My station as quartermaster of a King's Ship sounded grand and wouldn't hurt. Hoping to appeal to his spirit and learning, I larded the letter with Latinate phrases. Way too many of them. Still, I accomplished the letter and was affixing The Blue Anchor emblem to the melted sealing wax when unmistakable shots drove me into the street.

Lieutenant Knepp lay flat on the cobblestones with blood seeping through his buttoned officer's coat and death skulls engraven on his eyes. I hadn't been much disposed toward the man, but when the assembled company were reluctant to approach him, I knelt and lidded his fleeting spirit.

The flustered Mister Monck hailed a constable from down street and they charged through the crowd.

"Whoever knows this man, speak up," the constable ordered, pushing us back with his pike.

I recognized two sailors from the *Rose Algiers* in the crowd—the boatswain and his mate Hal King. Neither of them offered up their wisdom.

My only idea of the constabulary had been Phillip Babb, and fearing Boston ways, I too kept mum, leaving Taverner Monck to fetch his entry ledger and read what all of us knew—that the man whose lifeblood ebbed onto the paving stones was Lieutenant Knepp of the English Admiralty.

"Thank you kindly, George Monck." the constable said. "Now which of you knows Lieutenant Knepp and witnessed the shooting?"

A second constable appeared and laid the body of the man Knepp had shot on a barrow cart. During the stir this caused, I sidled over to Monck and placed my letter in his hand, asking that he convey it to Mister Sewall. This done, I boldly stepped through the circle of onlookers.

At once the constable seized upon his good fortune. "You, Mister, did you witness this gentleman's duel?"

Knepp was no gentleman. To stall, I backtracked to the Latin phrase *In certum quo Fata ferant* which I'd written Edward Taylor in regard to my imminent voyage on the *Rose Algiers*. It occurred to me that "None can tell where Fate will bear me" might smack of blasphemy to a minister of Puritan persuasion. But it was too late. The letter was sealed and on its way.

The constable impatiently swung his baton, awaiting my testimony while two men swung the greying Knepp onto the cart beside the other bloody sod.

Trembling somewhat, I told the constable I recognized Lieutenant Knepp, though I did not know him well. He'd seemed hot under the collar in the taproom, but I hadn't seen him leave. I heard pistol shots and rushed outside. If the constable thought it necessary, I'd accompany him to the Town House to help clean up the Lieutenant's bloody legacy.

So it was that we marched down King's Street beyond where I'd been that morning and then to Market Square. On the way, I asked God to forgive me. For if anyone knew my fate, He did.

The Town House was a wooden construction on great wood timbers with an overhanging roof for market stalls. A flight of stairs led to an outside roofed gallery and inner court chamber. The constable swaggered into the court and I followed with increasing unease. The echo of voices from the black robed counselors in that enormous room had the effect of a Greek play in its more somber aspects.

I'd done no wrong, yet wavered in my conviction to deliver an account and be gone. Before I could act one way or another, Captain Phips strode toward me, his fancy shoes clacking on the planks of the great chamber. I moved toward him with Knepp's death pounding at the portal of my lips.

"Thomas Taylor, I be glad fer yer support in this grave matter," he boomed, then lowered his voice. "Knepp and me shared no love from the start and that be no secret. His death has damned near scuttled my voyage."

The judges cloistered at their table stopped talking as a decrepit man in a black skull cap and robe hobbled to his feet. He pointed a withered finger at us. "Mister William Phips, approach."

I grabbed Phip's elbow, squeezing it and pushing him toward his duty.

"Yea, Governor Bradstreet," Phips answered loud and clear as was his custom.

"Four of your sailors last evening were incarcerated for wanton behavior and inebriate misconduct. No sooner were they released on your word than Officer Knepp engaged in a duel in which he and another man were mortally shot. Good Mister Phips, you have taxed the Massachusetts' Court's patience and over-reached our hospitality. We wish to see your backside, and the sooner the better. When will your ship be ready to weigh anchor?"

Phips took a broad breath and shouted at the ancient man who cupped an ear. "On the morrow, Governor Bradstreet."

The Governor's declaration sounded like a prayer it was so feeble. "No later than noonday, Mister Phips."

The Captain and I quickly tripped down the gallery stairs and back into Market Square glanced by November sunlight. Flakes of snow fell like lacy omens, and I offered a thankful prayer for our reprieve.

Phips resilience in the face of adversity flagged. "I don't know about yew, Thomas," he said, "but I sure could use a bolster of rum at The Blue Anchor. And then, lad, it be work, work, and more work to assemble the ship's tars, load the diving apparatus, and trim our sails by noon tomorrow."

Hurrying back to the shipyard, I was relieved to find the English-appointed quartermaster. I explained that we must sail earlier than planned and, since we were the only ones in charge, we must see the gear was stowed.

"I take orders off none but the King," the sullen quartermaster said, leaning against a man-sized diving tub Phips had invented for our voyage.

Provoked by the difficulty of being half a quartermaster, I paced down the wharf. Light was fading fast and the diving apparatus was too valuable to be left on the wharf. Ideas came and went—then I hit on an inspiration.

Descending to stowage I found the boatswain, Hal King, in a similar shiftless disposition. Using tidings about Knepp to whet his appetite, I explained my business. He agreed to my plan with more enthusiasm than I'd expected, and together we ascended to the second quartermaster, who remained as I'd left him.

Mister King stepped up to him haughty as you please and pronounced: "Petty officer Taylor be in charge of steering, binnacle signals, and the sailors' watch. And yew be in charge of stowage. Now get some brave jacktars and load this diving gear immediately.

That be an order!" I swear Hal King grew three fingers taller in the delivery of his speech.

The English quartermaster lolled an arm behind his head. "I've told Mister Taylor here and I'm telling yew, too, that I takes orders off none but the King."

I pushed the boatswain toward him. "Tell this man your name."

"I be Hal King, Sir."

I smiled pleasantly at the quartermaster. "Thus have you been ordered by a King and no longer are wanting in that respect."

The quartermaster stood up, shook his large lice infested head, and laughed outright. "Mister Taylor, yew certainly know how to gull a man. But steer clear. I'm warning yew, I can turn nasty."

At last we were under way. For awhile I stood with Helmsman Francis Rodgers at the whipstaff on the deck below as he masterfully worked the lever that moved the tiller, which in turn worked the rudder on the stern. Captain Phips stood directly above me and shouted his orders through the hatch so as to navigate through the swarm of vessels in Boston Harbor.

The boatswain told me I was wanted by the Captain, and I gladly climbed topside. Admiral Solomon had ordered the sails trimmed and a stiff breeze carried us merrily along. I stood with Captain Phips between the stern and mizzenmast and for awhile neglected my duties, so awed was I by the the busy port.

Phips took the lens cap off his telescope and peered at a vessel some distance away. The removal of the wood scope left a black ring on his suddenly livid cheek. "Thom, order Helmsman Rodgers to redress our course and pull us starboard."

I did as told and rushed back.

Phips put the telescope to his other eye—as if somehow it would change what he saw. "Captain Warren of the ship *Good Intent* will pay dearly for this transgression!" he barked.

Not being privy to the telescopic view, I peered at the *Good Intent* to see if I could make out the object of the Captain's sudden rage.

Phips put the lens cap on and held the scope in the pit of his arm like a fife player. "Thomas, fetch the gunner. Order him to fire a round of shot through Captain Warren's rigging!"

I stood transfixed by his command.

"Now, damn it!" he exploded.

I rushed down the narrow stairs two at a time and found the gunner in his cabin. After I conveyed the order, he questioned my authority, as indeed did I. I urged him to position himself at the porthole where one of eighteen black saker cannons stood on a wheeled mounting, telling him I would ask the Captain to communicate to him directly through a trap in the deck.

We now were near enough to see the upper deck of the *Good Intent* through the gunport. Numerous diving tubs, ropes, dredges, claws, and drags littered its deck, obviously meant to cut us to the chase for sunken gold in the Bahamas.

I scrambled up the trap door to explain to the Captain that his order was far too serious for the gunner to take off me.

Phips hastened to the trap and stuck his head through the opening where the gunner had readied a pile of chainshot.

"Fire, man! And don't leave a ratline in place on that blasted ship."

The gunner fired the cannon, squarely hitting the rigging with a cannonade that shook both ships from bow to stern. Captains Warren and Phips glared at each other from their respective forecastles while a longboat of soldiers from the Boston Fort rowed fast as the devil toward us.

Admiral Solomon attempted to subdue the crew. Insults and chamber pots flew at the jeering sailors on the *Good Intent*. A few tars hung over the rails brandishing their swords, and the ugly mood of the shipjacks did not abate, despite Solomon's order to swab the decks.

The Fort soldiers strong-armed the rivaling Captains into the longboat and rowed toward the King Street Wharf. Having worked like a dog for the now aborted voyage, I crawled into a pile of gunny sacks that had been thrown into Phips diving tub and sank into a reverie. If both Captains had diving equipment, it could mean only one thing. Sunken gold was a real possibility. All we had to do was sail the Florida straits and. . . .

I must have dozed off because when I crawled out of the tub, Phips and Warren were back on the wharf saluting each other like long lost friends. Whatever their differences, it was clear the court had straightened them out.

Our men swarmed upon the Captain like bees stirred into a frenzy,, and with customary vigor Phips leapt onto the steps of the forecastle. "Listen up, yew rascal tars. I've paid for the repair of Captain Warren's ship."

They hooted and bawled something fierce.

"And I've given Governor Bradstreet my word that the *Rose Algiers* will countenance the company of the *Good Intent* in our combined search for treasure on Bahama Banke."

A cry of betrayal rose from the rowdy crew, and I admit my voice joined their vexation. To share the bounty of the expedition with England was one thing—she had, after all, supplied our vessel. But to divvy it with another ship would dwindle our take to a pittance. We might as well have signed on for a broken piss pot.

An emaciated pock-faced tar approached Captain Phips with a bucket and threw dingy water all over him. The drenched Captain removed a brace of pistols from his belt and cocking them, shouted, "I know yew be displeased with this arrangement, mates. But I promise, as God be my witness. . . ."

"The devil, ye mean," shouted the bilge-thrower.

Phips thumped one of the heavy pistols over his heart. "I'll personally forfeit my share of gold to pay fer yer efforts!"

Gun metal caught in the sunlight, glittering its promise for all to see. Stunned by his unexpected offer, they fell silent. For like Phips they reckoned once we were free and clear of Boston, any arrangement could be rearranged.

25

I leaned out the lead casement window that opened over the limpid Florida water. Waves reddened by the late sun sloshed peaceably below, blending with shouts from the men as our ship moved down the jutting backbone of a long coral reef.

The English tars had assumed a desultory look reminiscent of the pirates I'd met on Appledore Island, and rather than think of this unsettling sea change, I stayed below. Phips hoped to keep the Royal Silver Master busy stamping and weighing gold and silver. The first evening of our voyage he came to the officers' mess dripping profusely in his high ruffed collar. But since then I hadn't seen hide nor hair of him.

Captains Warren and Phips hired several pearl divers from the mud and thatch huts on a nearby island and, wearing cloth bands to plug their noses and scant else, the bronze lads searched Floridian coral shoals for our sunken fortunes.

When we had nothing to do, which was pretty much of the time, Helmsman Rodgers apprenticed me in the art of navigation. In England the Chief of the Navy, Samuel Pepys, had presented

Admiral Solomon with a newly designed quadrant. Having no inclination for science, he gave it to my cabin mate, Helmsman Rodgers. The sight on the quadrant was hooked to a plumb line, which made it utterly worthless on a windy day, for though the stars, like love in Shakespeare's sonnet, were "an ever fixéd mark," our ship was not.

At noon on the third week of instruction, I carried the new quadrant and another Royal invention on deck. Rodgers had taught me to calculate the sun's altitude through moving parallel pieces on a cross staff. Now he wanted to try the new back staff, which resembled an Abenaki bow held backward with the arch at the nose.

Moving cross pieces at the top and bottom formed the sighting triangle. I thanked my lucky stars that I was asked to stand with my back to the sun because my poor red face was peeling like a Bermuda onion.

Dutifully, I sighted the sun's reflection in a small mirror affixed to the curved bow-piece, wrote down my calculation and handed the instrument back to Rodgers. He repeated my observation and we compared results several times before retreating to the welcome shade of our cabin.

After working another hour with dividers and a compass, to my relief our figures matched those in Johannes Van Keulen's *ATLAS OF THE WATER WORLD*. According to the new backstaff, we stood 4° above the Celestial Circle of Cancer and 27 ° north of the Equator.

At sunset the sailors took off their breeches and dove from the ship stern into the tepid water to swim over to the Indian village. I swam across, too, but kept my shirt on so that the quartermaster took to calling me "Fair Thomas." Tired of his juvenile taunts, I struck up a friendship with one of the divers. Captain Phips' idea of language was a string of curses, and I scrawled some Spanish words I thought might be useful on the end pages of a book.

The women stayed inside their huts, but when one of them did come out the men lost no time plying her with scarves, shirt buttons, and other tokens that might win her admiration—and hopefully more.

The sailors roamed freely, feasting on apricots, hedgehog dates, pulpy bread-fruit, and wild boar roasted over boucane-charcoal fires. Each day they looked more like the *boucaniers* I was reading about. My friend Estefano invited me beneath the shady palms near his hut where his mother served us roasted fish on woven palm leaves. Insouciant days drifted into months on this paradise which was so far removed from the wintry Isles of Shoals.

I tried to forget Pru. Our last night together, kissing had thrown me into such a bronchial spasm she had to give me slippery elm and Diacodium. The tonics not only suppressed my cough but also my desire, and I wakened in Pru's arms wondering whether the damp sheets were from sweating bullets or pricking my pistol. At the sight of her auburn hair on the pillow, a verse had popped into my mind.

> *Kissing and bussing differ both in this.*
> *We buss our wantons, but our wives we kiss.*

Winni certainly had needed no navigational instruments to sail our bodies and I longed to share my discoveries with Pru. But by the time she awoke, late for Phips, I bussed her and fled.

A blast of thunder shook me from my dreams and onto the deck. The sailors had tarred a sail and I took cover from the afternoon downpour under the pitched tarp-awling. Helmsman Rodgers and I marveled at these afternoon showers that arrived like clockwork, lasted a few hours as if the heaven needed rewinding.

I opened a book I'd purchased in Boston: *BOUCANIERS D'AMERIQUE* by a Monsieur Esquemeling who was indentured in the French West India Company of Louis XIV in 1661, the year I was born. On one voyage Esquemeling apprenticed to a barber surgeon, learning enough medical skill to make himself useful. Dissatisfied with the foul treatment of the men, he jumped ship at Tortuga, whose harbor was a natural redoubt fortified by magnificent mountains. My French was miserable but I stuck with his adventures, hoping they might shed light on my own.

Our miscreant crew was growing increasingly belligerent and bold. They paid Admiral Solomon resentful respect, and Captain Phips even less. Their lips were parched and their bodies stank of mutton fat slathered on supposedly as a sun shield. They wound red scarves about their heads, wore pursers' slops, chewed tobacco until their teeth were black, and pickled themselves in rum from dawn to dusk. The seasonal rains were further eroding their humor, and as I read my book I could hear them grumble beneath their make-shift sailcloth rain hats.

My apprehension increased upon reading that the boucaneers'' strategy for pirating a vessel was to shoot the helmsman and his apprentice and swarm aboard with a raiding party.

"*Tomaso, Tomaso!*" my friend Estefano called from Phips' diving tub pulleyed onto the deck. His wet shoulders glistened in sunlight as he chattered excitedly in his mother tongue.

I put down my book and went over to help him out.

He held his sinewy arms wide apart like Shoalers when telling their fish tales. I was reaching for my word list when I distinctly heard him say, "*Cañon, Tomaso. Cañon!*"

I rushed to fetch the Captain and, with Phips looking on, Estefano once again was lowered to retrieve the cannon he'd found. When he reappeared, the boy was so winded he flopped into my arms. Secretly, I cursed Phips for dredging up the useless thing. Apparently, the ancient armament had fallen off a sinking galleon which then drifted down into a deep chasm. The best diver could not penetrate such depths and our leadsman pulled up his line in defeat.

With news that the Spanish ship was irretrievable, Phips ordered our departure.

As I said good-bye to Estefano, he gently clasped my hands in his wet fingers. Feeling a heavy object, I opened my palms on a coiled encrusted chain about a foot long.

"Discubri este collar con el cañon."

I accepted the barnacled chain he'd brought up with the cannon. Although he called it a necklace, it appeared to be tiny linked balls of cannon shot. Looking into his innocent face, I reflected on how sadly accustomed I'd grown to muskets, pikes, cannons, and the destructive weapons of white men. As a mutual friendship token, I gave him one of the tar-pawling rain hats he had admired. And with a blast of the boatswain's whistle, we prepared to sail.

After months and months of fruitless effort to find galleon gold, Captain Warren decided to bring the *Good Intent* about and sail back to Boston. A sailor standing with me at the rail shouted, "God speed, ye lucky devils!" I must confess I felt the same watching that billowy vessel until it was but a dot on the horizon.

Helmsman Rodgers and I were summoned to the chart room to plot the onward voyage of the *Rose Algiers*. We would sail her through a new channel north of Long Island and by some nameless kees to Caicos Banke.

The once potable water had turned green and had so many somersaulting creatures it looked like an underwater flea circus. Officers switched to jugs of tamarind bought off the Indians and the sailors consumed so much rum I wondered how they kept from falling into the sea.

No sooner had we anchored at West Caico Island to replenish our water supply from a charted well than a scurrilous trio of English tars appeared in the mess. With a swoop of his bare arm, the ring leader cleared the vittles from the table.

"Either ye promise us a fortnight at Port Royal," he cried, "or we jump ship."

Captain Phips leapt onto the table, pushed up his shirt sleeves, and glared at the ruffians.

"Jump then! Jump, yew intolerable entrails. A ship with barnacles be less fettered than yew pustulous carbuncles on my beshitted arse. I'll give yew a fortnight on Turk's Island where yew can sodomize each other till ye croak."

"Parbleu!" muttered Admiral Solomon, loosening the collar of his shirt.

Phips ducked to keep from knocking his head on a beam. "Yew salts didn't know I had spies aboard, did ye? Well, I be well apprised of yer irregulous acts, and the sooner I deposit yew rambeggars on the sandfly-infested Turk Isles the better off we'll be."

He grabbed a wine flask from the table and threw it at the leader's head. The man fell instantly. Phips shoved me out the cabin to fetch the quartermaster who, though an officer, always seemed to dine in the cook's galley.

I climbed down two ladders to the odoriferous orlop where the *Rose Algiers* quartermaster loitered in post-prandial stupor. The fumes of the cooking fire, combined with the mildewed hull and stench of Royal initialed chamber pots, brought up an unexpected taste of my supper. Not waiting for the sea slug's answer, I delivered Phips' message and bolted back up the ladders.

While I was gone the traitorous triumvirate had been gagged and hog-tied, and the quartermaster, who appeared in his own sweet time, was ordered to lock them in the hold.

"By God, holding be too lenient fer the likes of yew," Phips shouted after them. "May the rats consume yer bowels!"

26

*F*rench *flibustiers* cruised their shallow flyboats along the north-western coast of Hispanola. Within a day's sail of each other, the Spanish ports of Monte Christi, Isabela, and Puerto Plata were exposed to constant raids. Buccaneers such as Henry Morgan turned whichever way the wind blew—now plundering for the King of England, now for the King of Spain. No cove from Hispanola to the Barbadoes was safe from their plunder.

Because of the pervasiveness of these coastal robbers, when we docked at Puerto Plata every indentured man on board was sworn to secrecy about our expedition. Grabbing a sailor's hand Captain Phips pounded it down on a moldy leather Bible, which resulted in an exodus of crawly creatures numerous as the tribes of Israel. The buccaneers' butcheries paled beside the Captain's roll of tortures for anyone foolish enough to let his tongue wag.

Below the fort *alcazar* and mission church, lime-washed colonial mansions cascaded down the hillside to a squalor of thatched dwellings on the port. An emaciated dog slunk across the plaza and growled at naked children throwing water at him from a crumbling fountain. The three devils who had been imprisoned in our ship's hold lazed with the quartermaster at the fountain. The sun was blazing hot and I thought of breaching their motley gang for a drink but decided it wasn't worth it, and instead turned up a cool passage to the rampart above.

The *alcazar* tower on the fort was a mere façade behind which the village disappeared in a tangle of growth. A few Spaniards lived in the port, but most had deserted the crumbling colony when the silver mines gave out.

"The only silver in Puerto Plata lies in sunken ships on the sea bottom," Captain Phips told us one day. "As for the Hispanic coffers, they be near depleted, too. What Tortuga rogues like Seigneur de Grammont and Marquis de Maintenant haven't run off with has been looted by the Dutch. Only last year—or was it the year before that while I was here—the Dutch flyboaters plundered English slavers, paid the Santo Domingo authorities to keep quiet, dressed out their ships and sailed to Vera Cruz nice as you please. The Spanish Armada sat in the bay of that treasure-laden town without firing a single cannon while de Graff and van Horn sacked the Vice Royalty. I swear, Spain has the balls of a *castrato*, but them flying Dutchmen be another matter, by God. The rutty bullies trim a fleet sail and if we're to beat 'em at their game, we must keep our eyes peeled!"

Thinking of his warning I looked up surprised to find I'd walked some distance into the jungle and, distracted by a wondrous flock of red and blue parakeets overhead, I stopped to get my bearings.

When my gaze returned to the pathway, a swarthy man stood before me. He wore a filthy sack tied with cowhide and his feet were outfitted with sabots tied on with untanned strips of animal sinew. At once I took him for one of the French *flibustiers* I'd heard so much about and instantly was on my guard. He very well could be flanked by desperadoes from Petit Goave to the south or Santo Domingo which had grown thick with men and guns. He looked harmless enough. Maybe like New World pioneers he lived peaceably with his animal pelts and cooking vessels.

I smiled as much to temper my fears as quell his. That morning before leaving the ship, tired of picking infernal tropical insects from my bushy web, I'd clean-razed my face. Unfortunately, all I could see of the stranger's was one alert eye peering from a greasy mess of hair.

"Il a la peau blanche comme une femme," he said in a peculiar French accent.

I didn't let on that I knew what he'd said. Even the English tars remarked about my fair skin, though they had yet to compare me to a woman. Suddenly, with lightning speed he closed the distance between us and holding me tightly against his scratchy sack cloth, he cried, *"Que tu es belle! Donne moi un baiser."*

Un baiser? God help me, he wanted a kiss!

Before I could struggle loose he wrestled me to the ground, pulled my face close, and planting his grease-smeared flabby lips on mine, inserted his cow tongue into my mouth.

I kicked and punched him anywhere I could but it was no use. He had my head in an armlock. In a last-ditch effort to escape, I let him kiss me, and when he relaxed his hold, I rolled beneath a thorny bush.

It's said that God works in mysterious ways and surely that bush was one of them. By chance I rolled into a wild boar and, since the bush wasn't big enough for both of us, it charged the two-legged swine. Not waiting for the outcome, I flew swift as an arrow back to the ship.

The *Rose Algiers* dropped anchor at a rocky promontory. Like Babb's rock at Appledore, it was near enough to lay a plank across, and the cove was deep enough to keep us afloat yet expose the hull for repairs.

Tars set about off-loading our heavy culverin cannons across the plank bridge and onto the island beach head. Midway through off-loading the cannons, the quartermaster convinced Phips it would be more convenient to accommodate the men ashore in tarp-awling tents so they could hunt game and cook over wood fires as they had at Bahama Banke.

Captain Phips called a muster to issue muskets to a shore party of eighty men, leaving himself, Admiral Solomon, our gunner, Navigator Rodgers, Ben the boatswain, a few other officers and myself on board—oh yes, and the carpenter, whom I failed to mention since he already had begun work on the hull.

At seventeen hours we sat down for an early supper. Admiral Solomon brought out several bottles of excellent Madeira and we enjoyed the vacancy of the evening in the Captain's great cabin. After supper, Phips indulged my interest in his spyglass by asking me take his glass on deck to observe and report how the shore party was getting on.

Propping both elbows on the rail I sighted the lens on three shipjacks walking the beach—walking so quickly that a few steps more and they'd catch me spying.

Ducking behind the aft mast where I wouldn't be detected, I sighted them again. That was odd. The carpenter, who was supposed to be working, was flanked by two sailors, and the one in the rear seemed to be shoving him onto the plank bridge. The leader looked my way as if concerned someone might be watching.

They were now so close I could see alarm in the carpenter's face. I sheathed the spyglass in my belt and without forethought I showed myself, determined to rescue him if need be. He said the crew had asked him to tie up their hammocks and he'd come back for his tools.

I sensed he was lying. A carpenter doesn't forget his tools. Besides, at Bahama Banke the sailors put up their own hammocks.

But I let him pass. Sticking to him like leeches, the sailors procured the tools and were on their way back when suddenly the carpenter doubled up in pain.

I rushed to his side and bent over, looking into his twisted face.

"Good Sir, what is wrong?"

He brushed my ear with quivering lips. "Mutiny," he whispered. Then groaning in agony he cried, "The medicine chest! I must have a dram."

The rattail sailors accompanying him hesitate, then sent me to fetch the chest, which I did—but not before rushing pell mell into the officers' mess.

"Mutiny!" I gasped.

Captain Phips took a sip of his Madeira. Perhaps he hadn't heard.

"Mutiny!" I shouted.

No one stirred. Were they deaf? My face heated with excitement. "The carpenter is waiting for the medicine chest. He has pretended a fit of colic before they take him back to their tents. Hurry!"

Admiral Solomon rose and went off to fetch the medicine. The Captain offered me a chair. It wasn't like him to delay. Blood pulsed in my temples as the Admiral returned with the chest and placed it on the table.

Phips jumped up. "Thomas, find out how much time we've got."

"I will, Sir," I said, grabbing the chest.

The carpenter had feigned his fit so well that the tars seemed relieved to see me with the medicine chest. I opened the chest, took out a bottle, poured a dram and bent over the brave actor. "What time?" I whispered. He opened his mouth, pretending to swallow the liquid I dribbled into his beard. I looked up at the rogues.

"There, that ought to do it," I pronounced loudly.

The carpenter sputtered and sat upright. "By God, I feared the sand had all but run through my hourglass."

Once they were out of sight I high-tailed it back. The hubbub emanating from the great cabin silenced as I burst in.

"An hour. We have an hour!" I panted.

Phips stood. "Men, I've plotted a course of action to take the mutinous devils. But yew must vouch to stand by me."

"Save us from them rogues, Captain, and yew have my word," the gunner pledged in a barely audible voice. I reckoned the shooting of cannons was enough noise for the soft-spoken officer.

Captain Phips banged his cup so hard on the table it shattered. "We'll show them double-crossing, terrorizing bastards to mess with Willy Phips. As God be my witness, I'll have the mutinous rogues by the balls and cryin' fer their mothers by sundown!"

He said this with such vehemence that every man promptly leapt to his feet in a rousing cheer.

"Now, here be what yew must do. Mister Taylor, take my spyglass and ascertain the position of the culverins on the beach."

I started out the cabin.

"Hold on!" Phips ordered.

I turned back.

"More 'an likely the rogues have trained the murdering cannons on our ship. Take the gunner here and Bo'sun Ben and creep onto the beach head. Turn the culverins around so they're pointed at their tents. Can yew do that?"

The gunner and boatswain jumped up.

"Hold on!" Phips thundered. He pointed at the First and Second Lieutenants. "After they've repositioned the culverins, yew two must draw up the plank bridge." He pointed at me. "Now, Thom, go look through the glass and tell me the rogues' whereabouts—whether in their tents or in the woods signing their stinkin' Articles of Mutiny."

The weather in those parts was fickle as a trade merchant and when I reached the deck dark clouds were scudding in. I could scarcely make out the cannons on the beach let alone their tents. Risking Phips' anger, I leapt onto the bridge, raced its length to the shore and hid behind a palm. Leaves flapped and clattered in the rising wind. Fortunately, the same wind carried voices from the woods.

Captain Phips guarded the ship end of the plank bridge and jerked me onto the deck.

"Damn yew, Taylor! Can't yew obey orders?"

"Well, Sir, I couldn't see and—."

Phips paced away and back. "All right, Thomas, yew be absolved of yer youthful sins. I take it yew located the scoundrels."

"Aye, Sir, in the woods. And as you said, Captain, the culverins are pointed at the *Rose Algier*s."

"I thought as much. Why those two-timing mutinous shit-tabeds! By the God of our Fathers, they'll pay for their betrayal!" Phips clapped me on the back. "But there's no time to lose. Off wi' ye, Mister Taylor."

The gunner and Ben stalled at the plank bridge waiting for my lead. Invigorated by our heroic intent, I bound across to the deserted beach. The three of us worked like the devil to heave the cannons around on their mountings to face the tents, primed them to fire and waited.

The sailors' torches flared through the woods and the sun shot through a cleavage in the storm clouds enough to target the rebels making their way toward the cannons.

Alarmed, the mutinous quartermaster waved for the tars to stand back. "We're undone!" he cried.

Admiral Solomon stood on the *Rose Algiers* with a saker cannon trained on the mutineers. Caught like vermin, the wretches ran every which way shouting and scuttering toward our murderous culverins. Whether blinded by sun glare or in a hurry to blow up, they continued straight for us.

Fearing we must blast them to smithereens or lose our lives, I yelled at the gunner, whose attention was on the rocky beach head.

Captain Phips' figure blazed in a burst of golden rays.

"Stand off!" he thundered at the confused sailors. "Yew wretches have my warning. Stand off at yer peril!" His formidable fury coupled with the great saker aimed to fire a nine pound cannon ball sent them to their knees.

The quartermaster made an attempt to get away, but with the advantage of height, Phips vaulted from the rocks on top of the villainous traitor, and knocked him flat on the sand. Placing his heel on the quartermaster's thick neck, the Captain ordered the rats to put down their firearms and roll on their bellies.

We officers collected their muskets while Phips considered punishments.

"By God, I have a mind to maroon the lot of yew on this island, seeing as how yew dogs had in mind to do the same to us."

Having adequate reason to believe the Captain was a man of his word, a hue and cry issued from the abject men groveling on the sand.

"I'd choose to die with Captain Phips than with any other!" one poor blighter sobbed.

"Aye, mercy, Captain," pleaded another.

Phips took his time letting the impact of their foul deeds sink in. I couldn't fathom sailing without a crew but liked even less the thought of these wasters loose on the ship. The Admiral, Captain, and Lieutenants deliberated among themselves while the gunner and I held the cannon on them.

In the end, we locked up their muskets and swords, marched the mutinous rogues back across the plank, and sailed the entire night on the Windward Passage to Port Royal.

27

When I saw Mister Sewall coming toward me in *The Blue Anchor* taproom, the three years I'd been gone slipped away. Over pints of ale I told him about the mutinous scoundrels we'd ditched at Port Royal.

The mention of the Jamaican port sparked Sewall's mercantile disposition. "Tell me what it's like, Thomas. Do traders like me stand a chance? Is Port Royal free of pillaging pirates like that contemptible Morgan fellow we've been hearing about?"

"Imagine if you will, Mister Sewall, a gold city reaching from Harvard Yard to where we're sitting. Hundreds of four-story buildings glisten with gold tiles on a spit of sand stretching far into the sea. As for security, the Governor, Mister Lynch, has all but quelled piratical terror in the name of trade. No doubt you've heard his Dutch saying: 'Jesus Christ is good but, by God, trade is better.'"

"What blasphemy!"

"Still, Mister Sewall, you have to agree he's turned Port Royal into a thriving West Indies trade emporium wealthier than the Isles of Shoals and Portsmouth put together."

Sewall bent toward me all ears."You don't say!"

"Every day, except the Sabbath, of course, the market is open for West Indies and Spanish exports, and commodious warehouses have been built for the stowage and exchange of English, Dutch, and New World goods. I accompanied Captain Phips into a warehouse several stories high with windows large enough to hoist hogsheads, great chests, and sacks from the street by pulleys which were attached to gable bolts through roof dormers. Similar to Boston, each warehouse has a chamber where the accounts are kept, though I've been told Port Royal enjoys twice Boston's merchants and wealth.

Pressed to go on, I racked my memory for my impressions of the accounting houses.

"We were there on a Saturday when the counting house was being washed and scrubbed. The treasure of bars of gold, pigs of silver, pieces of eight, and bushels of undrilled pearls is locked in a great vault on the Sabbath. I've done accounts for Mister Pepperrell, but was truly awed by the market values at Port Royal. Liquid assets exceed those of London. Phips was seeing about a loan and we were told that for a 20% advance he'd pay 10% interest. If he invested in commodities, they'd be insured at 2% against loss at sea."

Thinking I'd satisfied Mister Sewall's mercantile curiosity, I took a long draught of ale. But if anything, his interest in the factors and merchants compounded.

To keep his appetite off my personal affair, I asked if he'd be interested in an accounting of the items most sought after by Jamaican planters.

He chuckled with pleasure. "I wouldn't mind sticking my nose in their business."

Sounding like a chapter from Moses' book of *Numbers*, I listed the goods Yankee traders (myself included) smuggled in and out of New England to Port Royal under various ruses to avoid the King's heavy trade taxes.

"The items they covet most, Mister Sewall, are New England fish, pork, beans, timber, and all sort of 'stuffs' such as woven and beaver hats, shoes, woolen socks and caps for Negro plantation slaves—because, truth be told, slave labor provides the most capital with the investment."

The joy drained from Sewall's face and he had such a sorry countenance that I quickly changed course. "But to proceed with the telling of my voyage—. After the mutiny, we signed on a new crew of men and sailed for *Abrojos*, a squalid village near Puerto Plata in the Silver Keys. Relying on the word of a one-eyed jack, Captain Phips was convinced a Silver Flotilla had sunk on its reef.

"Between you and me, Mister Sewall, if it weren't for my promise to see the expedition to the end, I'd have given a storehouse of silver to sail home to the Isles of Shoals. Will Babb, who grew up on the Shoals, always complained about them, but had he lived on that ship for three years, I wager he'd have changed his tune!

"Anyway, the *Rose Algiers* anchored at a barren key where the tide seethed like a bubbling cauldron, fuming and crashing against the coral reef. Not long after we arrived at 'The Boilers' than a mid-size vessel sailed merrily over the horizon. Quick as the devil we hid our diving tubs under tarp-awling and weighed anchor to give the appearance we were seabound. It turned out to be a false alarm. The ship belonged to Captain Adderly, whom Phips had invited to salvage and divide the spoils. Not only was the water boiling, we were steaming mad at the thought of having to weaken our shares.

"Even Navigator Rodgers, who usually kept his thoughts to himself, expressed serious reservations about our venture. 'Gentlemen, Abrojos is thick with pirates,' he told the officers. 'Mister Adderly's share is puny compared to what will happen if they get wind of treasure. We can requisition a small tender-boat so as to reef close and bring up treasure. But if buccaneers find us, we've only got one great cannon. Admiral Solomon informs me that at this very moment the London Ship Yard is outfitting a 200-ton vessel, the *James & Mary*, with twenty-two guns and a smaller vessel, the

Henry which also is well armed. I suggest we return to England and properly invest in this expedition. Better safe than sorry!'

"Captain Adderly, who had started the groundswell, protested. He had business to attend to and couldn't possibly entertain a three month voyage to England. Although I'd scarcely met the man, then and there I prevailed upon his good will to carry me with him as far as Rhode Island.

"But Phips wasn't listening. Jubilant with the vision of fulfilling his Sheepscot birthright and anxious to meet a second King, in his thoughts he already was sailing back to London."

Sewall held up a large hand to stop me. "What exactly do you mean, Thomas?"

"Oh, forgive me, Mister Sewall. I thought you knew about the Sheepscot legend. In the northern provinces it's believed that Phips will meet three British Kings. Oddly, he's already knelt before King Charles and King James.

"Anyway, when news of our departure finally sunk in, Phips stomped over to the chart desk, whipped out my indenture paper, and tore it up. Cursing a blue streak he kept his back turned while I trembled with indignation. The lieutenant excused himself to whisper with Phips. I'm not sure what he said in my behalf, but suddenly the Mainer grabbed both my shoulders and drew me to his barrel chest in an apologetic embrace."

Emotional with this memory, I changed course again.

"But what about you, Mister Sewall?"

"I've come up in the New World, Thom," he said with a smile and shrug. "I'm now a dyed-in-the-wool Council member under Governor Joseph Dudley. I hope to help Increase Mather take back the Massachusetts Charter. King James' revocation, as you know, has caused more than a stir in the Colonies." Sewall lowered his voice so that I had to keel over the table to hear him.

"The new King is another kettle of fish. He has opened the churches to Anglican services, limited town meetings to one a year, and imposed oppressive trade tariffs. Perhaps you haven't heard that Sir Edmund Andros has been appointed Governor of New York, Massachusetts, New Hampshire and alas, all of New England. He marched into the Hartford Council Chamber without so much as doffing his hat and declared their Royal Charter null and void. The Connecticut Council deliberated till candlelight while Andros and his regiment champed at the bit in the dew. Suddenly, the candles blew out and the Charter disappeared from the table."

"Good for them!" I cried somewhat louder than intended.

"Andros sits in the Governor's chair all right, but as the French wit says, he still only sits on his bottom." Sewall's round jowls unhinged and he laughed freely.

"Now then, Thomas, George Monck has informed me you've been lodged here a week and scarcely ventured from your chamber. Are you in need of a friendly ear?"

I had a strong desire to weep and quickly turned my face to the wall. Either Sewall was a prophet or I was transparent as glass. He hurried me from the crowded taproom and onto the street.

"When I'm in the doldrums I take a long walk about town. Breathe deeply, Thomas. Get a hold on."

I thought about the women I'd comforted with sympathizing and of how confused I was when they wept. Being the recipient of Sewall's kind attention, I feared I might do the same. Fortunately, our brisk strides and breathing so regulated my thoughts that when I did unburden them they weren't all a jumble.

Sewall spoke first. "Since we've dwelt on the topic of trade, I propose we enter an exchange—my perplexity for thine, Thomas, measure for measure."

Having endured Phips' volatile temper and rude oaths nigh onto three years, I basked in Sewall's equable manner and dealing. And although I was ill-disposed to parade my grief before such a solid soul, I agreed to his proposal.

"'Tis concerning my son, Sam," Sewall began. "My wife hath born six children in almost as many years and we've buried half of them. I tell you, Thom, sorrow breaks wave after wave. I solemnly offer Sam to God's will, for much as I try with the lad, he tries me. The boy has a weak constitution and my wife and his sisters, Betty in particular, dote on him far more than they ought."

While he talked we followed Corn Hill Street south, turning westward up Beacon Hill into a part of the town graced with gardens and courtly mansions. We passed a chapel recently constructed in the name of the King. "Would you look at that bare-faced squat!" Sewall hurried by the new edifice and into the Old Granary Yard, which had been converted to a burial ground.

I ambled behind him to a long brick crypt, where we fore-stalled.

"Perhaps when Sam is catechized, he'll reform," I thought aloud. "On the Shoals I catechized lads in the Lord's Commandments and marveled at the change in their hearts."

Sewall stepped into an excavation and sat on a bench in the coolness while I hovered ill-at-ease among the family coffers.

"You may be right, Thomas," he said, nodding absentmindedly and looking about. "Ah, how glad I am to find everything in order after those terrible squalls in July. The coffins of dear Father and Mother Hull remain dry, and of my own Father and Mother at the lower bench. I had the plot bricked and a roof put on. Couldn't bear thinking of my dear ones in a puddle."

The desolation of the place reduced me to silence and its shallowness to bowing my head.

"And now it's time for your side of our bargain, Thomas."

Sewall knew the affairs of his Boston neighbors because he could be trusted not to tattle. And although I suspected the Massachusetts Councilor had turned a domestic trifle into a grievous complaint for my sake, easing onto the bench beside him, I bled my wounds. My voice echoed in the vaulted chamber as I recounted every detail of the final meeting with Captain Adderly, who for the past week had filled my nights with terror and days with fear.

"Captain Adderly and I left the expedition and were returning on his ship the *Providence* so that he could launch his new trade ship in Rhode Island. On the final day of our voyage together he asked me if I'd take over the operation of the *Providence* while he sailed back to help Phips. I suspected my hermaphrodite brig had been appropriated by Mister Pepperrell and gladly accepted Captain Adderly's offer so I could continue my Shoals fish business. We signed the papers and agreed to split the profits when he returned."

Sewall cut in. "Aha, you've been holding out on me, Thomas. I see you've trade in your blood, too."

Though what he said was true, it came as a bit of a revelation to think I'd done well in fish trade.

The tomb was too dark for us to see much of each other, but I caught a glint in his eye.

"Do I understand that Adderly sold you the *Providence*?"

"No, Mister Sewall, he only deeded it until his return."

Sewall sucked in a large breath. "And has he returned?"

"That's exactly it, Mister Sewall. Two weeks ago, laden with Shoals cod salted and packed in the hold, I sailed to Rhode Island and went to Adderly's counting house as agreed upon. When I asked for Captain Adderly I was told he no longer kept an account there. And when I asked where he did business, the solicitor told me he'd taken up residence in Lucayo on Great Bahama Island.

"My first thought was that I'd been betrayed. But since I had his ship and fish, I abandoned this line of reasoning. After pacing the wharf for some time, I presented my predicament to my crew on the *Providence*. We were seven Shoalers and the decision was unanimous—to chase down Adderly at Lucayo and demand payment for our considerable trouble.

"I sailed due east from Florida to Lucayo. Once we were in port I gave them shore leave on condition that they exchange watch.

"The English Magister Factotum who lived in a Spanish palace overlooking the sea sent an African lad to help me search for the elusive Captain Adderly.

"At first I hardly recognized him because of his beard and

native dress. Had appearance been the only change I mightn't have
been so disturbed."

Sewall moved to the edge of the bench we were sitting on.
"What else was it, Thomas?"

"At first I thought he'd been among natives too long. And I
was thinking I had him pegged when he—."

I faltered for words. "You've read King Lear, Mister Sewall?"

"I have."

"Well, when Lear meets his daughter Cordelia and the Doctor,
he says: 'I am not in my perfect mind. Methinks I should know this
man. Yet I'm doubtful, for I'm ignorant what place this is, and of
the skill I have, or where I did lodge last night.' "

"Adderly was deranged, then."

"Aye, Mister Sewall. So deranged he wanted to give me his
ship outright. 'I have no use for a ship, Mister Taylor,' he told me.
'Here are some papers. Take what you will.' He shuffled through
parchments and threw them about until I rescued him from his
confusion. I seized the bill of lading for the fish and showed him
the deed to the ship. He grabbed my hand. 'Promise not to tell a
soul and I 'll give it to you,' he cried.

"Captain Adderly, I cannot take your ship,' I argued. 'But if
you wish, I'll continue as its Captain—.'

His beard trembled. His hands trembled. His head trembled
and he ran out the door shrieking 'Tell! Tell! Tell!' "

Sewall placed a comforting hand on my shoulder. "I deeply
regret you were forced to undergo this strange occurrence."

But like a perpetual motion machine I'd reached a momentum
and went on. "I grabbed the ship deed and left. I was so distraught
by Adderly's laconic mood that I bought a bottle of rum and, putting up at a Lucayo inn, consumed the entire bottle.

"Rising at daybreak, I had a premonition I mustn't delay a
second visit to Mister Adderly for his consent to fetch a doctor. The
closer I came the faster I walked until I was running the dirt path
past the behemoth molasses vats and into his white bungalow.

'Mister Adderly!' I cried, rushing through the curtained door.

"He laid face-down on the floor with a pistol in his hand pointed at his head. A ball had torn through his temple. Dried blood stained his beard and his crazed eyes looked straight up at me. I heard a gurgle from his chest. Elated that he might still be alive, I put my head there but—." The cash box of my exchange suddenly was empty.

"Wave after wave," Sewall muttered, leaning against the brick vault.

"Mister Sewall, I've known the waves of misery that come with death. But that he died of his own hand in the vigor of his life is a sorrow I can't seem to reconcile.

"I went back to the Governor's Palace."

Sewall's voice echoed in the dark. "Oh, Thomas! You didn't report the death, did you?"

"I was going to. Thankfully I reconsidered. The English would take me into custody and I'd heard investigations of this kind could drag on for months. The *Providence* lay at anchor with a valuable cargo of fish and sailors anxious to unladen and return to the Shoals. I couldn't put them through such an ordeal simply because I was in the wrong place at the wrong time."

"Well said, Mister Taylor. Well done."

"Mister Sewall, I confess to you and none other that I fled for my life—and theirs—though they didn't know it. I told them Captain Adderly had come down with a tropical fever and died, that I was Captain of my ship, and if they'd extend their adventure by a month to off-load at Port Royal they'd be handsomely rewarded. The men took a vote and there was only one abstention, a Shoaler who'd left his woman with child."

"And here you are, Thomas." Sewall rose slowly so as not to knock his head on the brick arch of the crypt.

Slightly hunched and squinting, I followed him into the sunlight. A quick summer shower had freshened the air.

"Breathe deeply, Thomas. You've survived the ordeal and

acted wisely in the bargain."

His few words of encouragement filled me with sudden hope, and after the somber crypt the world seemed to sparkle like renewal at Easter-tide.

Sewall smiled kindly. "Exchange of this nature works up an appetite. Shall I accompany you back to *The Blue Anchor*? My wife and children have gone to Quincy and I hate supping alone."

"Of course, Mister Sewall. I don't know what to say."

He chuckled. "Well, I do, Mister Taylor. I do."

The high mowing of the burial yard steamed in the sunlight. Tiny ephemera that in the tropics had so annoyed me buzzed and flew by on gilded wings like a heavenly host.

Sewall strode through the taproom and found the tavernkeep. "Be a good fellow and pour us a pint of ale on the spot. And bring us a cool jug from the cellar, will you? And have you a couple of your famous drum sticks in the cellar, too? Mister Taylor and I'll be junketing on the wharf where there's a breeze."

The amenable Monck wrapped a handful of purple plums, a few turkey drumsticks and corn cakes in a cloth, tying the corners. I picked up the frosty clay jug and we walked down to the Town Dock. Sitting in our shirt-sleeves, I companionably gnawed a drum-stick with this man of high station.

"You're fortunate to have known Sir Phips," Sewall said, lobbing a plum pit into the sea.

My story had been long-winded and it was only natural for Sewall to founder. "Captain Phips, Sir," I corrected, hoping he wouldn't take offense.

"That's what I've been wanting to tell you, Thomas. In June your Maine Captain was knighted by King William and Queen Mary at Saint George's Chapel at Windsor Castle in London."

I nearly fell off the dock with the shock of his news.

"Mister Phips was offered a commission in the Royal Navy and given his share of sunken treasure—which amounted to £16,000."

In my excitement I pressed him for details.

"From what I gather, Mister Rodgers navigated the *Henry* and Mister Phips, the *James & Mary*. They implemented the plan you mentioned of using a lighter boat—a *pirogue*, if memory serves me."

"Aye, the Caribees call them *piraguas*. They look like Penacook Indian dugouts. Buccaneers balance boards across the middle so they won't overturn and maneuver them through the mangroves remarkably well."

"Is that so?" Sewall loosened his collar, took off his hat and looked for all the world like no one in particular.

"Well, as I was saying, Captain Phips anchored the *James & Mary* at the Abrojos Port, ostensibly to trade goods. But the look of trade merely was a foil so the *Henry* could slip off to the Silver Keys. For a fortnight Phips agonized that Navigator Rodgers had found the treasure and made off with it—or worse, hadn't. From what you've told me, Thom, I venture Phips nearly went mad with worry himself. God's Mercy, forgive me. I didn't intend to dredge up the troubled Mister Adderly again."

"Spare no details!" I implored.

Sewall wiped turkey grease from his face with the cloth and handed it to me. "They say Phips welcomed Captain Adderly's help. Of course they all were sworn to secrecy."

I was happy for Phips, although his ambition had pushed a good many of us to the limits.

Sewall intercepted my thoughts. "Surely you can't fault Phips for putting a lid on. If word had gotten out every pirate and freebooter from Boston to Barbadoes would have overrun the place. But I haven't come to the best part, Thomas!"

Frazzled with his news I took the cloth and swiped my brow.

"Rodgers' men were exhausted and several of the West Indian divers had got the bends. The *Henry* captain was just about to tell Phips the search was off and weigh anchor when a sailor spied a sea plant he fancied and asked a diver to fetch it.

"Five minutes later the diver bobbed to the surface holding the plant in one hand and a silver ingot in the other. Marking the spot with a buoy, they high-tailed it back to Abrojos Harbor. When Phips boarded the *Henry* he was at his wits end. 'They be waitin' in the cuddy, Sir,' the watchman greeted. Phips confronted Adderly and Helmsman Rodgers, who had a somber, unsmiling countenance."

"He's actually quite pleasant, Mister Sewall," I said. "He only looks stern."

"Then they must have convinced Phips they'd found nothing."

"But I thought you said—."

Sewall sailed past my objections. "So vexed was Phips to hear they'd come up short that he leapt out of his chair and struck his foot on something under the table. Hopping mad, he fired an explosion of his famous oaths and ordered a sailor on his knees. When the sailor surfaced with the silver ingot Phips cried, 'Thanks be to God! We are made!'"

I shook my head in disbelief.

"I tried to break it to you gently, Thom. Surely, you're one of the few people in the New World unaware of Sir Phips knighthood." Sewall patted my knee in a fatherly fashion. "I believe Captain Adderly was promised a quarter of the treasure. The oath of secrecy while Phips sailed to London with the treasure I suspect is what pushed him over the edge."

Phips had labored hard to find his treasure and deserved it. Still, beneath my joy was a fleeting regret that my own destiny seemed fettered by dross and loss. Heavy-hearted and stifled by early September heat, I paced my room at *The Blue Anchor*.

In the small hours of night, I threw the contents of my duffel onto my bed. The encrusted cannon shot chain Estefano had given me clanked onto the coverlet. Why on earth had I saved it? I was about to pitch it into the hearth when I noticed strange photism. I held the trinket to the guttering candle. Solidified on one of the links was a smaller link of red gold from which dangled a gold

crescent about as wide as the moon of my thumbnail. It was devilish sharp and while wiping blood from my pricked finger, I discovered a miniature ruby.

What a fool I'd been to think myself superior when it was
Estefano who knew the chain's real worth and gave it to me in
friendship. With a pocket knife scraped certain places where the
encrustations bulged, but gave up for fear of damaging whatever
was embedded beneath.

I slept so late Goodman Monck came knocking at my door to
see if I was all right. I roused myself enough to respond and,
remembering the events of the previous night, jumped from bed.
Instilled with more vigor than I'd felt in a long time, I placed the
barnacley chain around my neck and hastened to Mint Master
Hull's exchange on Market Square.

Outside the Boston Town House and opposite the exchange
bank stood a magnificent carriage. I loitered near the coachman,
realizing that Sewall's in-law, Mister Hull and Hull's partner
Sanderson, dealt only with monied clients. Still, I hoped an apprentice,
perhaps Jeremie Dummer or Samuel Clark, might assay the chain
for its worth. If I was to continue merchandising Shoals fish, I needed
collateral, and the chain was my only asset.

I entered the bank foyer. The comptroller gave me the once
over and after a good quarter of an hour in his ignorance, I spoke
loudly to the arrogant pip-squeak.

"I have business with the goldsmith, Mister Dummer."

"He's occupied with an emissary of the King," he answered
with annoying moderation.

"Well, when can I see him?"

"You haven't an appointment and can't see him at all."

"I have something that will change your tune."

"That's what they all say."

"You give yourself airs that stink!" I shouted, at the end of my tether.

The squabble stalled with the startling entrance of Mister Phips
majestically outfitted in a fashionable periwig and plumes.

"Beelzebub's balls! If it isn't Thomas Taylor. I never would have guessed it was you having a go at this pompous arse!"

A vested man with a roundness to his aspect came from the back of the exchange. "Sir William, had I known this gentleman was of your acquaintance—."

Sir William curtseyed as if he were at a court ball and ushered me through the door of the chamber he'd just vacated. "Mister Taylor here and I have some important business to discuss," he told the satin-vested goldsmith.

The man was following us when Phips barred the door with his bear-body. "In private, Mister Dummer. In private."

Once we were sealed inside I couldn't help chuckling, and Phips did too.

"Taylor, you ruddy cock, you look changed!"

"And you, Sir."

"Hey-dey! Dispense with all that knightly hogwash. We voyaged together and parted friends—."

So awed was I by the sequence of events placing me in his presence that I failed to remind him of his promise to imburse me.

"Mister Adderly engaged yew to sail his ship, I understand."

"Aye, the *Providence* is in the Boston Ship Yard." My voice trailed with the worrisome cost of her repairs.

"And did the *Providence* Captain whisper a word about the treasure we found?"

"Not a word."

"Ah, so the man kept mum."

"To the death."

Phips wheeled around.

"What? Adderly dead?"

I did not say the death had been self-inflicted, realizing the blame belonged to neither of us.

"He died in the Bahamas at Lucayo."

Phips stared onto the street and back.

"He was good as yerself, Thom. I trust the English have confiscated his share of the treasure. By right it should be yers."

"Well, Sir, I do have a small token of gold."

His eyes lighted up as I recounted how I'd come by the chain and my discovery. I fumbled in my shirt and laid the encrustation on the table.

Mister Phips grasped it and made for the door.

"Mister Dummer, on the double!" He thrust the encrusted chain into the assayer's fingers.

The goldsmith part of Mister Dummer handled the tiny gold saber with glee while the banker part of him showed extreme caution.

"I must put it in a bath. The chain is not gold or it would not have encrusted. We shall see."

While Dummer was gone Phips opened the leaded casement window and called to the coachman outside. He lifted his wondrous curled wig off his sweaty head and loosed his shirt. "I be stopping in Boston briefly to straighten out my affairs. Mister Narborough and the Duke of Albemarle would not allow me to leave England without bringing them along, much to my annoyance. I'm obliged to accompany them back to the Silver Keys."

I borrowed Mister Sewall's warning. "But it'll be overrun!"

"Aye. Moreover, earthly treasure falters beside my belief in the riches of the New World, Mister Taylor. Unfortunately, the King refused my petition to have our rights restored. He told me he'd offer anything but the Colony Charter."

I found it difficult to believe Phips had embraced the Massachusetts Bay Colony when it had done nothing but deny him. "Then what did you request?" I asked.

"Why haven't you heard? I be High Sheriff of the land, by God. And as soon as my affairs are in order I intend to give Governor Andros a run for his money."

Looking like a house domestic in a bibbed apron and with a towel over his arm, Mister Dummer returned carrying a large bowl. He set the bowl on the gate-leg table and we gawked at the transformed necklace within. The sea encrustations had fallen away, revealing a burnished chain somewhat misshapen here and there, but obviously well-wrought. What held our attention more than the chain were three emeralds, each the size of my eye.

"Mister Taylor, I believe yer ship has come in!" Phips exclaimed.

I reached for the chain but Mister Dummer held my forearm.

"It's in a delicate condition from more than a century under water," he muttered with propriety.

"Assay and tally the necklace!" Phips commanded.

Dummer put a loupe to his eye and examined the emeralds.

"I could pay £150 for each smaragd. As for the tiny gold tooth-pick—. "

"Toothpick?" I interrupted.

Mister Dummer feigned politeness, although I'm sure I tried his patience.

"The Spaniards have gold toothpicks. We use porcupine quills. What more can I say, Mister Taylor?"

Phips fumed. "You might say yer wastin' our time, Mister Dummer. Now what do yew tally all told for this undersea treasure?"

The goldsmith stood on one foot then the other, his moon face untroubled by weather, his hands white as a gentlewoman's.

"I'll offer £150 for the gold toothpick too—bottoming at £ 600."

"In that case, Mister Taylor and I will take our bottoms down-street to Mister Hurd or Timothy Dwight," Phips announced.

Was he bluffing? With £ 600 I could careen my ship and have something left over to continue in trade.

The goldsmith insisted. "Surely, Sir William, this is a fair price. The chain itself is junk."

Phips planted his wig on his head in an unmistakable gesture of departure. "I do not jest, Mister Dummer, and if yew want my business in the future I urge yew to reconsider. I've seen emeralds, Mister Dummer, a cache of 'em a quarter the size and quality of Mister Taylor's. And by God, Mister Dummer, I was rewarded double yer wretchéd price. Tally again, or I swear we go else-where."

If Phips was bluffing he certainly had the gift. No doubt the rotund Dummer thought in similar channels as he stared at my necklace. "The smaragds are beauties," he capitulated. "I'll give you not a shilling more than £300 each."

With such a deal I could trade fish till doomsday. But the indomitable Phips hadn't finished. "And the gold toothpick?"

I laughed nervously. Damn Phips. How could he do this to me?

"In truth, Sir William, I have told you—." Dummer's cool gave way to a solitary wrinkle on his smooth curved pate. "The gold is piddlin' and the ruby too."

The knighted Mainer yanked my arm. "Come, Mister Taylor!"

Before I could grab the necklace, Dummer had my other arm.

"Let go!" I yelled, suddenly weary of the both of them.

At my call the impertinent foyer watchdog came running. Assured his employer hadn't been done in, he retreated, leaving us to stare at the emeralds sparkling in their bath.

Squaring his stalwart legs and broad shoulders Phips faced the goldsmith. "That chain be off a galleon of the famed Spanish Flotilla and damn it, I know whereof I speak. Them emeralds be from the prized Muzo mines in Colombia. And even if the gold weighs little, some curioso will find the toothpick interesting enough to fetch a pretty price. Why my wife herself would pay £300 for a trinket with a hundred year history. Yew can't hoodwink me and get away with it. Make the tally an even £1200, Mister Dummer, and draw another £800 from my account. I owe Mister Taylor back wages."

The thought of owning £2000 and being responsible to a broker the likes of Mister Dummer fit me like a pair of breeches binding in the crotch.

"But Mister Phips—I mean, Sir William, surely you are too generous!"

Phips smiled. "It be the least I can do fer yer part in our expedition, which in the long run brought success. Besides, my true treasure be this desired place. God bless New England and all her peculiar provocations!"

William Phips could be a conniving cuss, but the more I dealt with him the more I realized his generous nature somehow always came to the fore.

Phips turned and shook the goldsmith's hand.

"Yew drive a hard bargain, Mister Dummer. Now call in that damnable Actuary and proceed. I'm beginning to feel I've vested enough time in yer establishment to own it."

28

My fish trade suffered terribly because of the Indian Wars and by the summer of 1690 Appledore Island was nearly deserted. After I let off my last worker, John Moody, to go live with his sister Betty in Go's Port, to protect my only vessel I sailed past Champernown's Island on the Maine side of the Piscataqua River and into the little harbor at Great Island.

Captain Laighton had been made Master Mariner and his shipping office was packed with sea captains clamoring for the protection of their ships. But luck was on my side. Remembering me from ferrying me to Dover, like a white-bearded great uncle, Laighton waved me through. Not only did he sign and seal papers for harboring the *Providence*, but offered me lodging. I explained that John Moody was expecting me at Go's Port. His sister Betty was expecting a babe and I was the god-father. The busy Laighton wished me well.

Having secured my ship in safe harbor, I rowed my dory past the small isles and inlets of Portsmouth to Market Square. Small shops had sprouted up while I'd been away. I hardly recognized the town it had grown so. At a smithy's near the wharf I found a delightful Apostle's spoon for the Moody babe's christening, then strolled across the Square.

The sun was strong and I stopped to take off my jacket when I noticed a woman in the stocks slumping from the heat.

The iron straps of a scolding bridle criss-crossed the crown of her bowed damp head, and I walked over to the constable loafing in the shade of the Meeting House to complain about her treatment.

He spat in the dust. "Rum be the only succor she craves," he grumbled.

Disgusted by the lout, I walked over to the well, drew up a bucket, poured the icy water into an empty tamarind jug, and drenched the discouraged woman's head. She didn't budge. Alarmed, I ordered the constable to unlock her collar at once. He looked at me as if to say, it's on your shoulders, and threw the keys in the dust.

Getting the poor woman out of the contraption was easier said than done, but finally I managed to lift her bowed head. The swollen slats of her glanced up and I near dropped her. It was Pru! Dumbfounded at seeing her green eyes once more, an ache surged through my chest and I gasped for breath. How could Pru have fallen into such narrow straits and what could I do to get her freed?

I stood and handed the keys back to the constable. "How long have you left this wretched woman in the sun?"

The brute counted on his fingers. "Huh, two—nay that were Sabbath—huh, three days."

I reached into my shirt and flashed my newly signed ship papers at the lout, hoping he'd mistake them as documents for her released. '"Has she been fed? Just look at her!"

He scowled. "She warn't hungered none."

I placed the tamarind jug to Pru's puffy lips, but she scarcely could swallow.

"My God, constable, are you without mercy?"

I was surprised how softly I spoke, given the rage I felt. "Where's your Christian charity, man?"

He folded his arms. "I've none fer the likes of her. She be pickled as a herring. Now if someone would take her, I'd gladly get rid of the shittabed!"

My fist slammed into the wall near his head, breaking the clapboard and sending a pain up my arm. "I'll take her," I said.

A woman who idled beneath the chartreuse canopy of a maple near the well walked across the yard. "I'm Goody Walford." She stepped out of earshot of the constable. "I will lodge the poor soul until she's back on her fee."

I carried Pru to my dory and rowed her to the good Samaritan's cottage. A few hours later I returned to find Pru in a private chamber with her hair streaming over a fresh white shift.

I took the bowl of broth she was holding and set it down.

"Dear Good Pru, do you remember me?"

Her face clouded with doubt. Her voice was so feeble I had to lean over the bed.

"I'm Thomas Taylor."

She stared at my beard. "Thomas Taylor," she repeated.

"We were friends at the Isles of Shoals. You and me and—," I hesitated, "and Will."

Her face turned grave. "Willy's gone. He disappeared."

"Will Babb?" I asked, at sea with her strange ship-wrecked memory.

Pru's cheeks flushed. "Of course not. Willy Monforte."

"And who might that be? A cousin?" We were sinking to great depths clinging to this strange wavery conversation. She looked so upset I turned to fetch Goody Walford.

"My son!" Pru cried in a pitiful voice. "They took Willy!" She looked distractedly around the room. "They've kidnapped him from Pest Island, but I'll find him."

I knelt close beside her. "Blesséd Lord, Pru. You have a son?"

Tears floated in her green eyes, enlarging them to the size of the emeralds in their bath. Why hadn't I kept just one of those rare jewels for the woman I loved? Before I could think, I blurted out, "Is he my son? Or Will's?"

For one breathless moment I thought I was home. But then Pru closed her eyes and shut me out. "Willy is my son," she whispered. "Mine."

Willy and I were sitting on a crude bench he'd helped me pound together on two levels so his feet could touch the ground. Past the tidal flats in the mist we could see the Isles of Shoals. The boy tugged at my sleeve.

"Fa! Fa, look! Is Appledore Island floating?"

In the few months I'd known the boy, I learned that if I didn't hurry, his questions would accrue at an astonishing rate.

"Aye, Willy. The sunlight and mist rising from the water have created the illusion that the Isles of Shoals are floating."

My life seemed as much an apparition as Willy's floating islands. While the boy chattered, I mulled over the remarkable events that led to having a six year old, his mother, and a stone dwelling on Rye Beach.

As Pru recuperated at Goody Walford's, bit by bit she confided what had happened before I'd found her.

It seems that while I was dealing with mutinous sailors in the East Indies, New Englanders were fighting a far more insidious enemy. The small pox plague was filling burial yards from Boston to Port's Mouth with small children. Ignorant of news on the main land, Pru had taken Willy to visit a friend at Odiorne Point. She was standing on the wharf collecting her belongings when a New Hampshire officer asked for her papers. Like most Shoalers she had none, and even if she had, they were with the Go's Port records.

The officer made a show of chucking Willy's chin. Then, stepping closer, he asked in none too friendly a tone how she came by such a fair child when she obviously was from the West Indies.

With the candor of a Shoaler, Pru spoke her mind.

"Willy is born out of wedlock."

He raised an eyebrow.

"So what? Half the kids on the Shoals are bastards," she said with a smile.

The officer let go of her wrist. But as they passed, he had yanked Willy's hand from her's and walked away with him.

"Kidnapper!" she screamed, running up to a second officer who ran onto the dock.

To her surprise he clamped his hand over her mouth and wrestled her away. "The kid'll be all right. Portsmouth has small pox and you should be glad Governor Cutt is ridding us of it. The quarantine lasts forty days, then you can fetch your brat. So quit your infernal yawling, woman, and look on the bright side. Pest Island has fish flakes and when you next see him, yer kid'll have learned a trade!"

From the moment he let Pru go until sunset, she tried to hire someone to row her to Pest Island, but no one would go near the place. She lingered at her friend's until she was unwelcome. Besotted with liquor, she sold herself to the soldiers at New Castle. That's when the constable clamped her in the stocks—and three days later, thank God, I'd found her.

The following day, I'd ferried over to Pest Island, but it was completely deserted—Indian raids being the greater of two evils. Desperate to find Pru's lad, I looked up John Shapleigh, Junior, who was familiar with the Kittery side of the Piscataqua River..

Pru soon was strong enough to join me, and we'd searched nearly a week when we came upon a salt marsh farm with a dozen children running about. The moment I saw the tow-headed child weeding the garden I knew our search had ended. The boy who ran into Pru's arms was the spitting image of Will Babb. The Quaker couple that fostered Willy thought his parents had been massacred by Indians and were glad when we rowed away with him.

From then on the three of us stuck together like barnacles. Thus it was that the following Sunday I picked up my musket and filed out the Portsmouth Meeting House with other family men. We posted two sentinels to watch the women and children who sat in the shade of a great elm. The August sun blazed down and church-goers welcomed the industry of a local tavernkeep who had set up a punch bowl. I bought some for Willy who held my hand as if he'd never let go.

Governor Cutt happened to be standing nearby and I gave Willy over to his mother to greet him. Though doddered with age, Cutt couldn't keep his eyes off Pru, and when his rheumy gaze fell on me, it took but a moment for him to recall my name.

"Hey-day, Mister Taylor, is this fine woman Goody Taylor?"

"No, Sir, she's without husband."

"But not without child," he said dryly.

"Willy here was born on the Isles of Shoals," I said to remind him of their lawlessness when it came to marriage.

"Well, Mister Taylor, we're proper in Portsmouth," the Governor said, ignoring my hint at his own dubious Shoals origins. He walked up to Pru. "Give us your hand, my dear."

The Royal Provincial's ogling was one thing, but this was another, and I siddled closer.

"What's your name, my good woman?" Governor Cutt asked.

Willy looked at the withered hand holding his mother's with a suspicious frown.

"Prudence Monforte, Sir," she obliged.

Then, what I'd dreamed of for so many years happened there, surrounded by town folk. The tottering Provincial Governor grasped my hand, placed it upon Pru's, and asked, "Good Prudence Monforte, do you take this man, Thomas Taylor, to be your lawful husband?"

Pru looked down at Willy and then at me. "I believe I do."

"That be one 'Aye.'" Governor Cutt unfixed his bleary ancient eyes from her beauty. "And Thomas Taylor, do you take this Shoals woman to be your lawful—."

"Aye." I blurted out.

He smiled. "I fathom bachelorhood does not agree with you, Mister Taylor. Well then, with the power invested in me by the Province of New Hampshire, from this time forward you be husband and wife."

Willy squirmed from his mother."What about me?" he whined.

Governor Cutt tousled his thick yellow hair, which annoyed the boy to a great degree. "You now have a mother and a father," he said, and hobbled away to talk military matters with Captain Marsh of the Portsmouth Garrison.

During January thaw Pru told me her menstruals had ceased. She seemed gladdened by the prospect of a child and I was ecstatic, for this time there was no doubt that I was its father.

Willy had grown up thinking his father was dead, and Pru made me promise never to tell him otherwise. But by a strange twist of fate, a few days later I unexpectedly heard of Will Babb's death in Salem, Massachusetts. Any death is a blow, but Pru's sudden disappearance into her room for days on end sent us all into wintry doldrums.

Willy had lost most of his baby fat and grown a hand taller. He could write well and read too, and I already pictured him at Harvard. But the poor boy was having a hard time dealing with his mother's big belly and black mourning dress.

One warm April day I asked him to help me gather driftwood for the hearth fire, and after our chores were done we sat on our favorite bench overlooking the Shoals.

"Fa, why is mother so sad?" he asked.

"She grieves the death of a man who was close to her."

"If he was so close, how come I never met him?"

The simple truth of what the boy was saying struck home. How senseless my lingering jealousy of Will had become. When Will was alive all he ever thought of was himself, to the point of abandoning his very own son!

"You're absolutely right, Willy," I said, putting an arm around his shoulder. "We'll have to tell that to your mother."

Our personal griefs and losses were over-shadowed by a surprise Indian massacre at Cocheco and Salmon Falls killing two dozen men. In revenge on Major Walderne for the '76 Indian round-up, Pequoket Indians tied him to an heirloom chair and carved their initials in his chest.

By the time they cut him loose, the sword they offered him must have seemed like the Holy Grail. I spent sleepless nights wondering if I'd saved Metacommet's son so that he could wreak his revenge on Walderne a dozen years later.

Shortly after the massacres, Captain Edward Willey of the Great Island Garrison came with orders for me to accompany him to the Isles of Shoals. I was reluctant to leave Pru and Willy. Captain Willey insisted. My family would be safe in Portsmouth, but the Shoalers were completely defenseless. He must billet soldiers there and had sent requests to absentee Shoalers in Boston, but they refused to quarter the troops. Never had he met a more ornery lot of people in his life. And if not by the grace of God, then by the seal of Major Marsh in Portsmouth, I'd be obliged to carry out my duty. With this ultimatum he wheeled his horse and rode off down the bridle path.

I'd just accustomed myself to marriage, fatherhood, and living on the main, and now I was being asked to give it all up. My heart begged me to steer clear of any more soldiery. Yet there was truth in what Captain Willey had said. The Indians were compacting with the French and several hundred of them had set fire to York, Maine, and stormed the Wells Garrison, killing a dozen soldiers.

Scuttlebutt had it that Shoaler Andrew Diamond's son, John, had been tortured with hot brands that stuck to his skin like stoat flesh on a spit—then scalped alive. By God, it was fearsome to think on, and I did everything I could not to think on it.

PART SIX

Dispelling Witches
& Sentencing Pirates

29

Once back on Star Island I reported to Captains Willey and Kelley who were holed up with a dozen soldiers at the new-built Go's Port Church.

I tapped my toes while they vetted their disdain for Star Island's absent landlords, especially Andrew Diamond whose wealth was made off Shoalers' sinful lust for drink. It was Diamond's duty to damn well protect his property and workers. I thoroughly agreed with them. But when they condemned all Shoalers as selfish shittabeds, I entered the fray, reminding them that when King Philip was on the warpath Shoalers sent more ransom for Hatfield captives than any town in New England.

"Well, now this is King William's War," Captain Willey griped, pounding the pulpit he'd appropriated as his desk, "and Diamond and the others are unwilling to part with one measly pine tree shilling to protect their fish—not to mention you and me—from Indian massacre."

I had orders to write Diamond one more time. Trying my best to influence the outcome, I whetted our thrust with pointed polish, edging in words like "terror, attack, grave risk, loss of property, spoilage, and ruin." Inspired by the might of my quill, I added a postscript of condolence for the loss of his son. Surely, the man knew he owed his wealth to soldiers like John who died protecting coastal concerns. Within a week we read his answer.

Know that I'll not entertain any man for the cost you've writ me of, neither feeding of them or paying anything more or less towards your charge; for I judge there's no present need. And further, let any man on the place know they shall not be master of my estate.

In another letter, Andrew Diamond ordered John Perkins who was minding his fish stage not to billet any soldiers. A few days later, the absent landlord Nathan Baker wrote his Shoals overseer, John Muchmore, that any soldiers kept there would be at his expense. *His wife Mary sank her oar into a postscript.*

I want to know whose idea it was to put a cuppell of souldjors in our house? Them what put them in must expect to pay for their lodging and expenses. Your acts would serve you right if the Indians had come!

When I heard several Star Island families had taken in seven of our soldiers at the peril of losing their jobs, I was so rankled by the Boston landlords that I promised myself as soon as Shoals business was usual I'd do everything in my power to buy them out. Meanwhile, Captain Willey parted for the mainland to consult with Captain Marsh, leaving me to draft a letter to the Massachusetts Court. And I have to admit I took inordinate pleasure blotting my outrage.

We are not only wanting the free quarters expected, but I understand Andrew Diamond, Nathaniel Baker and Mister

*Wanewright intend speedily to send for all their fish and transport
it to their mainland habitations, whereby they may have naught
here to defray the charges of quarters or wages of the soldiers. I
hope Yr Honors will give me and the soldiers continuance to stop
them from carrying the winter fish off the Isles. For by removing
it, the thirdsmen's and boat crews' portion will also be carried
away. Here there are good warehouses where we can secure the
fish. With all Diligence and utmost Understanding, ready to
serve Yr Honors,*

> *Captain Edward Willey*

The first of June, soldiers who were staying at the Meeting
House roused themselves for the Sunday sermon. Shoals fishermen
and their families side-stepped their quilts and muskets to sit on
the benches. Minister Belcher took his place at the pulpit and we
were just singing "Oh God our hope for ages past" when Captain
Willey burst in shouting, "Indians! They're making for the Shoals!"

Belcher raised his arms and recited the Lord's Prayer in Latin.
Willey shoved aside the mothy whigged minister and addressed
the riotous mob of soldiers and Shoalers.

"Most of you Star Islanders be gathered here already for
Church, but Lieutenant Taylor and I'll make rounds of the
dwellings."

Before he could say more I shot out the door. John Moody had
gone out fishing that morning and left his sister Betty with her col-
icky newborn babe. I sped past one of the chasms in which Phillip
Babb had hunted for treasure, and figured I'd hide her there rather
than the Church, which was a sitting target.

" John?" Betty half questioned, half cried as I knocked over the
hearth stool.

The girl wasn't pretty like Pru but had a strapping strong body
and Shoals spunk. She never talked about the babe's absent father,
though I remarked that at supper she drank more than a little rum
and molasses. I'd heard of a preacher in Ipswich named Richard

Moody who drew large crowds and it crossed my mind they might be kin. I meant to ask her, but she was tight as a clam and I didn't pry. The weight of stowing her safely compressed my speech to spurts. "Waste no time, Betty. Indians are coming. Bring the babe. Hurry!"

The silent girl wrapped her wriggling babe in a shawl and tromped with me through the high sea grass to an opening in the rock. I waited while she secured the babe to her chest with the shawl so she could hold on as we climbed down the narrow crevice of the deep fissure.

We stood on the grotto floor with spray flying in our faces and I coaxed her to a dry back ledge above tideline. "If you hear voices hush the babe at once," I warned, "or the echo might give you away."

The glint of fear in Betty's eyes kindled my own. Had the Indians attacked the mainland? Who was helping Pru and Willy? I laid my hand on her restless babe, kissed its fuzzy little head and with a brief prayer for their protection climbed to the surface.

Once there, I hunkered and crawled, bobbing up behind a bush every once in awhile so I could see where I was going. At the Rhymes cottage, Samuel, who had grown taller than me, towered in the door looking in surprise at his employer bellying like a snake on the ground.

I gestured in case he couldn't hear. "Samuel, for God's sake, get down. Indians!"

He hit the dirt and we both shimmied up the eastern slope of Fort Star where I was to rendez-vous with Captain Kelley.

Fort was a grand name for the shored up fish house on the West end of the island. Its only fortification features were the natural granite flanks of the hillside, a view of the main, and a half-built stockade. We'd mounted two cannons but no one knew for sure whether the powder was dry. Ocean fog permeated everywhere, and because Star was sheer rock, we'd built the powder magazine above ground.

Holed up in the dilapidated fort, all night long I relived the terrors of fighting in the Provincial Regiment—the English trickery that led to the Pemaquid massacre from which I'd barely escaped alive, the betrayal of the Penacook Indians who were blasted to bits by English cannons, the only too recent deaths of Major Walderne and John Diamond who were tortured and mutilated to the death.

At dawn I jumped up to the cries of our sentinel. The enemy Indians had changed course and were paddling down east. When Captain Kelley ordered us to spread the word, I ran to rescue Betty from her fearsome vigil. In my haste to bring the good tidings, I strained my leg and limped cautiously toward the bottom of the steep rift.

"Betty, the coast is clear!" I called.

"Betty, the coast is clear!" my breathless voice answered.

Thinking she and the babe might have fallen asleep, I shouted again. "Betty, you can come out now!"

"Betty, you can come out now!" the echo taunted.

While favoring my strained leg, my foot struck something and I nearly fell off. Kneeling and groping like a blind man along the slippery ledge, to my relief I touched the fringe of her shawl and soft skin of the swaddled babe. Carefully lifting the sleepy treasure in my arms, I climbed back into sunlight. The baby's eyes stared wide and its cheeks were ashen. Saddened at the sight, I put my ear to its small chest yet heard nothing but a wave of grief.

Smoke wafted from Go's Port chimney pots and the cannons at the Fort fired a salute. The Church bell clanged merrily as I stumbled toward the Moody's cottage clutching the dead babe. Trying to piece together what had happened, I wondered if Betty had been so terrified she fled home. But finding the cottage vacant, queasy with apprehension I soaked an oil torch, lighted it, and rushed back to the cavern, sick with the thought that I'd hidden Betty there and told her to quiet the babe

Setting the bundled babe on the ledge, I was on my way down again when I heard the raucous cries of gulls. Looking back, I saw

THIS DESIRED PLACE

one of them land. Forgetting my bum leg, I leapt from that dark crevice onto the ocean ledge. Already, half a dozen black hooded gulls covered the babe, hopping and screeching.

"No!" I cried, waving my arms in anger or defeat—I knew not which—"Oh God, no!" One of them pecked my arm, drawing blood to get at the bundle. In a frenzy the scavenging gulls drew off the shawl, exposing the little face. Lashing with their talons, they thrust their necks forward in defiance, hitting me with menacing wings. Desperate to retrieve the body, I covered my head with my arms and running in their midst pulled the babe free. Screeching and bickering, they trailed after a ring-leader gull who dragged a piece of the bloody shawl in his beak.

"By God!" I yelled with tears on my cheeks.

In a heartbeat they lifted and soared squawking toward Londoners Island. Hugging the ripped bundle in one arm, I picked up the blazing torch and poked its smoky flame into every nook and cranny.

"Betty!" I called limping down the dank defile.

"Betty!" reverberated with the insouciant slap of the waves against the wall.

Worn with worry and exhaustion, I fell into a fitful sleep. Startled awake by the stiff babe, I let it roll from my arms, got up, and finding a stone, knotted it with the babe in the torn shawl and heaved them into the sea.

As the sun came up I roamed the deserted cove asking the Lord what mysterious Providence chose me to deliver two babes to this great dike on Star Island. Pru's Negro bastard and—oh, my God! What if Pru were to have another Negro babe? No, of course not. Willy was fair like his father and I was fair as they come. Still, if mothers disappeared so easily and babes were abandoned, I was beginning to think anything was possible.

I reported Betty's disappearance to Captain Willey and, having set it down in ink, reluctantly made my way back to the Moody cottage.

John stood in the door smoking his pipe. He and another fisherman had sailed out to Jeffrey's Banke that day and weren't aware of the danger until they returned. "Captain Willey tells me not one Indian set foot on Star," he remarked. "I believe Betty's out gathering gooseberries. She said she would this morning."

When I told him she'd disappeared he stomped on his pipe, picked up a lantern, and once more I was obliged to return to the cursed chasm. The tide was out and we took off our shoes to walk through the tidal pools and look into the dark recesses swept clean by the waves. Though my leg ached, I dragged from cove to cove all afternoon until both of us were dead tired. At sunset we called it a day, ate supper, and drank enough rum to spill our grief.

"John, I can't fathom what happened," I said, blinking back my tears. "All I know is that I left Betty safe and when I returned she was gone."

"She and the babe?" he verified for what seemed the hundredth time.

"Aye, she and the babe, John. Perhaps it died because she stifled its cries."

"By God, Thomas, be you telling me Betty suffocated her own babe?"

"The babe had the colic. Betty was frightened. Maybe—."

His head drooped into his hands. "She and the babe be washed away by the tide, Thom. The Lord giveth and taketh."

I let him believe Betty and the babe drowned together. It was a harmless lie to get both of us through the following few days.

The next week when John saw me off he gave me back the Apostle spoon Betty had been saving for the christening and a pine cradle filled with swaddling clothes. When I told him to keep them for a future day he smiled warily.

"No, Thom, they're yourn and Pru's. I can't bear to look on em."

Frankly, neither could I, and on my crossing to Portsmouth I threw the spoon and cradle overboard.

Pru welcomed me round with our child, Willy chattered nonstop, and the blossoming apple tree in Goody Walford's yard showered our threesome with fragrant petals.

I knew that if I didn't tell Pru about Betty and the babe, some gossip-monger might tell a tale neither of us could live with. So after a few days I came out with it. Thankfully, I didn't have to exaggerate our fright of attack or describe the chasm every Shoaler knew well. But coward that I was, I couldn't bring myself to tell Pru more than that they disappeared. She held me to her full breasts and bulging belly. "Ah, Thom. You can't blame yourself if they drowned."

I stayed a fortnight with them before breaking the news that I must sail to Boston to deliver the remainder of Andrew Diamond's Shoals fish to his Massachusetts warehouse. I told him he was lucky to find a ship in such desperate times and tripled my price. With our babe on the way I was determined to look after our welfare and to hell with the scoundrel.

Willy was so disappointed he wouldn't talk to me. The schools were closed in the Colonies and the lad was idle. I charged him to look after his mother and before sailing gave him an ancient musket, which brightened Willy considerably, but not his mother.

All ships except Provincial Regimental vessels required special permission to sail out the Piscataqua River. Shipmaster Laighton was so overwhelmed with unrelenting duty to protect the busy port that I feared he wouldn't see me. But friendly as always, when I told him my business in Boston, he set his seal on the document, tied a ribbon around it, and I was off.

30

At Star Island Diamond's workers loaded his fish on the *Providence* while I went to engage Samuel Rhymes and a stalwart friend of his to sail with me to Boston. The wind was with us, and well before noon we were anchored at Ipswich Harbor. I had two personal obligations in Ipswich—to see Sewall's son Sam who was apprenticed in trade, and find Minister Moody to tell him of Betty Moody's disappearance.

Judge Sewall had every right to worry about his son. Either the large boy lacked stamina or was wretched in his employment and I bought him a pint at the local tavern, hoping to figure out which.

"Are you well-treated by your master, Sam?"

"Aye."

"Do you have a message for your father?"

"Nay."

"Might I buy you another pint?"

"Nay."

Dreading another moment of the stalled interview, I excused myself for my second visit, which turned out to be even more vexing.

"Good Day, Minister Moody."

"Good Day," he said looking over his spectacles.

"I've come about someone I believe is a distant relation of yours."

"Ah? Who?"

"Betty Moody of the Isles of Shoals."

"The slut."

"What did you say?"

"Unwed and with a babe. I hear enemy Indians rowed away with them."

"Well, Sir, no one knows for certain." I could have told him the truth but he wouldn't have listened. "She's lost."

"Thou art telling me!"

I was getting nowhere and turned to leave.

He spoke to his papers. "Moodys are an uncommon big tribe and some are bound to be sinners. I can't abide falsehoods and am glad you stopped by so I could set you straight. I have it on the best authority that Betty Moody and her babe were carried north by Indians. What you Shoalers lack is the moral compass of an Anglican preacher."

I felt a sudden duty to defend the moth-eaten, tone-deaf Belcher. "Minister Belcher shepherds our Shoals flock."

"So they say," he mumbled with a glassy stare and dismissive nod of his set jaw.

Back on the *Providence* sailing for Boston I regretted the time I'd wasted in these self-imposed duties. If Sewall couldn't get through to his son, how could I? As for Moody, the poor man wouldn't recognize the truth if it hit him broadside. Real good came from a generous heart and not dutiful obligation, and from now on I'd mind my own damn business. A few honest men are better than numbers—and God snatch Cromwell from the devil for saying so.

At Long Wharf in Boston Harbor I charged the lads with off-loading Mister Diamond's salt-fish while I walked to his mansion.

The former Shoals taverner received me in a powdered

peruque and fancy yellow frock coat. I presented him the bill of lading, demanding immediate payment for my trouble. He pretended not to have it. With somewhat prideful confidence I told him I was laid over in Boston a few days to meet with Judge Sewall and Governor Phips. He could deposit the sum into my account at the exchequer office of Mint Master Hull.

"You've changed, Mister Taylor," Diamond said, taken aback.

"And you, Mister Diamond."

"Do you still oversee Pepperrell's fishing stage?" he pried, hoping to worm into the core of my Shoals' affairs.

"You, better than most, Sir, know Appledore is deserted."

"But after the Indian war, Mister Taylor? Do you plan to work the stage? I was thinking of buying it."

He picked up the tails of his frock coat and waved his hand for me to sit. I stood in the doorway.

"Perhaps after the war, Mister Diamond, if your price is right."

Happy to leave the double-crosser guessing, I walked across town to the North End, passing over a bridge that connected the south and north sides of the Shawmut Peninsula. I'd been warned the bridge was guarded because folk on both sides were territorial to a ridiculous degree. But I was waved across without a hitch and waited in the cobbled street before Sewall's narrow brick dwelling.

It was the first time I'd had the temerity to seek out my friend at his residence and a woman my age opened the door. She wore a lace cap and plain house smock, and when I introduced myself she smiled so sweetly I forgot the purpose of my visit.

"Oh, Mister Taylor, I've heard so much about you. I'm Betty."

"Betty—Betty—," I repeated at the sight of Betty Moody's ghostly shade evoked by the name.

"Mister Taylor, please don't stand in the hot sun. Come in."

I stepped into the cool foyer. In the parlor a straight-backed man was reading a book.

"Are you all right?" Sewall's daughter asked, looking worried.

"I knew a Betty at the Shoals, and—."

She patted my shoulder. "That's all right. You needn't explain. Would you rather call me Beth?"

I looked around for Sewall.

"Oh, I do apologize. You must be here for father. I'm sorry to say he'll be held up at court all day."

I edged past the rigid reader and back into the cramped street.

"I'm wondering—could you tell him I've seen Sam at Ipswich and the lad seems fine."

She smiled. "Father's taking part in the Harvard graduation tomorrow. You might catch up to him there. As for Sam, you're very kind, Mister Taylor. My brother hasn't been fine a day in his life, but I'll convey your message. "

I smiled at her quip and secretly hoped to 'catch' both of them.

Harvard Yard was a festive place with trestle picnic tables set out beneath wide-girthed shade trees. The ceremony started at the top of eleven o'clock. Justice Sewall in his black robe and starched hang collar presided along with the man I had seen in his parlor the previous day. Each of six graduates in tasseled mortar boards and red surplices paraded forward to the pomp of a trumpet fanfare. A stiff breeze carried away most of the speeches as milling spectators strolled about the Yard.

A broadside listing all of the names of Harvard graduates since the school's founding had been tacked to a great elm, and with pride I recognized many from Portsmouth who had helped their fathers deal in its growing commerce. I also noted that the 1690 graduates preferred law to the ministry. There was Benning Wentworth who dominated Little Harbor with his new-built mansion, and then there was Major Walderne's son Richard, and George Jeffrey who owned the meeting hall on Great Island. Reverend Reyner and General Plaisted joined the ranks of the scholarly deceased.

While I mused over whether my son Willy one day would be on the illustrious Harvard roll, Sewall came up and gave me a hearty handshake.

"Thomas, my Betty told me you'd be here. If this isn't Divine Providence I don't know what is!"

The man I'd seen the previous day looked like an unlikely companion for the affable Judge, but Sewall obviously was taken by the don in his reverential collar. "My dear friend and classmate, Dr. Edward Taylor, may I present another dear friend, Thomas Taylor of the Isles of Shoals. "

How long ago I'd written my letter from *The Blue Anchor*. Then, I'd staked my happiness on every word, hoping this man was an uncle or cousin. And now, strange as it seemed, I had a family of my own to love and protect. Pru and our unborn babe and our son Willy counted on me. I must take back something for Willy— maybe the hornbook I'd seen in a shop window. The irony was that all the time I yearned for my lost family, no lesser men than Judge Sewall, John Shapleigh and William Phips comforted and guided me through thick and thin.

Sewall placed his large hand on my shoulder. "Edward, you may remember Thom here inquired about whether you might be kin. I say, Edward, this young man is quite the adventurer." He waved across the field to the drill sergeant. "Now if you two Taylors will excuse me, I must get out of this robe and into my dress uniform. The drill band is on parade today and I am being awarded a silver pike. By God, it's good to be alive!"

Thus abandoned, the Puritan slid beside me. "My father, William Taylor, was a yeoman from the farm country and a Calvinist."

"Mine plied a ferry in London and was Anglican through and through," I said, sweating profusely in my starched collar.

"It is doubtful we are related," Edward Taylor ventured. After a short uncomfortable silence he pulled a small volume the size of a prayer book out of his pocket. "By the way, did you see this pamphlet which Mister Sewall printed at the Colony Press?"

I took the almanac and read the cover of the folio.

Years of

THE BOSTON ALMANAC	1692
THE WORLD	5641
SINCE THE FLOOD	3985
SINCE THE SUFFERING OF CHRIST	1659
SINCE THE PLANTING OF THE MASSACHUSETTS COLONY	64

With a bemused look at my delight Reverend Taylor sat on a bench near the picnic victuals and with over-rapt attention we watched Mister Sewall march by in the parade.

"Are you a physician?" I blurted, desperate to discover a topic that would set us at ease.

"Both of body and soul," he replied.

"I hear you have a penchant for versifying," I knew this was the key to the man; for I could almost feel a lock unspring in his stiff Puritan joints.

"As a matter of fact, I have written a spiritual verse every two months, starting about the time Mister Sewall gave me your letter posted from *The Blue Anchor*. One of my latest reminds me of this banquet before us.

> *Here is a feast indeed! In ev'ry dish*
> *a whole redeemer cooked up bravely good*
> *is served up in holy sauce that is*
>
> *a mess of delicates made of his blood.*
> *Adorn'd with grace's sippits, rich sweet-meats*
> *comfort, and comforts sweeten whom them eats.*

Piecemeal, I'd eaten pickled herring and shucked oysters, lemon tarts and cheeses, and washed them down with lemon beer being consumed in great quantity by the merry graduates. Overwhelmed by Edward Taylor's peculiar allusions to the Lord's Supper, now these victuals sat inert in my stomach. But the poet was all wound up and chimed on.

"Or what about this, which I call "The Heart a Fortress?" *March in rank and file, proved to make a battery, and the fort of life to take.* But I like this part the best:

> *When the sentinels did spy, the heart*
> *did beat alarm up in every part.*
> *The vital spirits apprehend thereby.*
> *Exposed to danger, great the suburbs lie.*

I thought his views painfully orthodox, though I had to admit his imagination was not. "I'm quite impressed, Reverend, huh, Doctor Taylor. You could be referring to the Indian wars." My lukewarm praise spurred him on, for in verse the man seemed unstoppable.

"I don't know what possessed me the day I wrote "The Flood,"" he mused. "There was a great thunderstorm that day, or perhaps I doctored too many Westfield settlers.

> *Are the Heavens sick? Must we their doctors be,*
> *to make them purge and vomit? See!*
> *We've grieved them by such physic that they shed*
> *their excrements upon our lofty heads.*

I believe I left out a line, but you get the gist of it."

I smiled in my beer, amused by his audacious images.

"My best meditation I've saved till last, but won't recite the whole of it because it's rather lengthy. Meditation 38, "Oh What A Thing Is Man?"

God's judge Himself, and Christ the attorney is.
The Holy Ghost, the Registrar is found;
Angels the Sergeants are. All creatures kiss
The Book, and do as evidence abound."

He was not John Donne. On the other hand, I'd never heard poetry quite like it, and I was asking if he intended to publish these Meditations when Sewall came up thirsty for libation.

The Judge set to the groaning board with gusto, talking between bites. "My colleague Cotton Mather was to give the invocation but he could not leave Mercy Short."

"Who is Mercy Short?" I asked.

He turned to Edward Taylor. "Who is Mercy Short? God have mercy, Edward, I hope you can set him straight."

"Mercy who?" the Puritan echoed.

Sewall laughed, picked up a herring in his rosy plump fingers, and starting with the head, swallowed it. "I say, dear fellows, both of you have been in the wilderness far too long. Haven't you heard of the witches at Salem? She is the one Mather has been observing in Boston."

Reverend Taylor animated. "A witch!"

"Aye, Reverend Mather has asked me to judge at the Salem witch trials in July. I'm somewhat reluctant, although I must admit the situation there is grave."

Edward Taylor grabbed the hand about to dispense another herring. "Why Samuel, you should be honored. The Lord has called upon you to fight the Devil. Were it in my power I'd jump at the chance. Indeed, I suggest we call on Reverend Mather this very afternoon."

Torn between the graduation conviviality and catering to his classmate's unexpected whim, Judge Sewall asked if I was up to it.

Remembering Goody Cole's Hampton witch hearings, I was not. On the other hand, I yearned to meet the celebrated Reverend

Mather, and agreed.

On our walk to the people who were keeping Mercy Short, Sewall explained how the girl had been orphaned and carried off to the north by Indians. The maroon servant who opened the door eyed us skeptically. "I take you twa spirit chamber ofa hebeje girl," she muttered, swishing her Indies skirts.

She unbolted a door off the narrow hall and with a dusky moan left us facing the man I presumed to be Cotton Mather. He placed the Bible he was reading on his lap, greeting us with clear wide eyes, upturned cherub lips, and a periwig curled fashionably to his shoulders.

A pretty girl in a night shift jumped from the covers of a narrow bed tossing a head of shorn black ringlets. I stared at her while Edward Taylor turned for introductions, watching in awe as she stuck her tongue out and made faces behind his back.

I wondered if she were doing the same to me as I bowed before Reverend Mather, telling him how I admired his pamphlets and publications. He nodded politely, but was more interested in his Puritan brother, Reverend Taylor.

"The other day," Mather told him, "I read Mark 9: 29. You must know the passage, Reverend Taylor. And do you know Mercy leapt out of bed and tore a page from my Bible?" He held up what remained of the ripped page. "You see, it all started when Sarah Good who awaited hanging asked Mercy for some tobacco. Mercy threw it in her face and Sarah flew into a raging fit. I granted Sarah a stay of execution—for I now believe Mercy bewitched her."

The girl on the bed hugged her knees to her chest and contorted backward until I thought her poor spine would break.

"Sodom buggers, the lot of you! A pox on yer lecherous scrotum!" Her voice dropped to a whisper "Are you God? No! Leave me in peace.

"YOU DEVIL!"

She screamed so loud that Sewall and I backed toward the door while Taylor and Mather huddled closer.

Mercy folded back the bedcover, crawled out and leaning forward resumed her whispering.

"Yea, Sarah, I'll be good. I promise."

I was thinking the cursing had come from the street when suddenly the angelic girl bounced upright, whirling her head and arms dangerously near the ceiling. This might have been the mere cavorting of a child, had she not cajoled in a deep male voice.

"Aw Sarah, yew pistol sucker. How we'd like to tiddle yer little bodices!"

Alarmed at the Devil hopping up and down in Mercy's flimsy shift, I reached out to grab the girl before she cracked her head on a timber. But the Falstaff spirit was too quick and bellowed his bawdy with ever greater zeal.

Reverend Mather and Doctor Taylor consulted on the end of the quilt, odd bedfellows who seemed more interested in the fine points of witchcraft than helping the poor girl regain her equilibrium.

Tripping on a tangled sheet she fell backward, landing flat on her back with her curly head between them.

"My moles be better'n Sarah's. See! Fat little Judas kiss ones."

Fascinated, I watched as she pulled the white shift over one shoulder and poked her rosebud breasts into their peering faces.

When Reverend Mather ordered her to cover herself with a sheet and lie still, I had little confidence she would do so. But like an obedient dog she crawled under the drape, laid her damp curly head on the bolster, folded her hands on her chest and closed her glowing eyes.

The soggy stench in the close chamber had grown unbearable and I walked over and swung open the gable window. Judge Sewall mopped his brow with a muckinder and leaned out for several gulps of sultry air. Grateful for the respite, I eavesdropped on the Harvard Divinities.

"Are you familiar with the process of the determination of a witch, Reverend Taylor?" Mather asked his newly-met colleague.

"I know that the witch must confess and witnesses come forward with their depositions."

Judge Sewall sat down on the window bench and I stood near the door desperate to sail, but curiously anchored.

"That is correct. And I must call in a doctor to examine Mercy Short for extra teats and witches' marks," Mather said, gazing at the girl's body shaped by the sheet.

The Westfield Puritan flushed with excitement. "Would you allow me to examine her?"

Mather shifted uncomfortably on his side of the bed. "Nay, Reverend Taylor, I did not mean a Doctor of Divinity."

"But Reverend Mather, by God's grace I am also a practicing physician."

Before we knew it, Edward Taylor had been closeted with the girl while Judge Sewall, Cotton Mather and I stood in the dark hall peculiarly ill at ease. A few minutes later a scream brought us pell mell back into the chamber.

The girl wriggled and writhed, holding her shift to the waist and exposing her private parts.

"Reverend Mather, secure her arms, I implore you!" the Westfield Doctor ordered. "Or I cannot complete my exam."

The famous New Englander grabbed Mercy Short's bare arms and pinned them down while Edward Taylor sat atop her legs rubbing his fingers across her naked white belly.

"Ye maggot boweled lechers! Get yer filthy hand out of my placket. Whoreson devils!"

While a part of me reasoned that Mather was intent on saving the Colonies from witchcraft, another part wondered if this wasn't a job for a midwife. Still, Cotton Mather was looked upon as the leading authority on witch markings and had even published a booklet of his findings.

As the esteemed preacher grasped Mercy's wrists, Doctor Taylor poked and prodded under the sheet. The girl was draped for decorum's sake, but from my vantage I could see a lot more than propriety allowed. And frankly, I couldn't take my eyes off that moist labyrinth between her white thighs. Her body quivered and the bedstead creaked as she pushed her knees open and flung a long leg out of the token sheet.

"Giddy-up giddy-up. Ride the rocky horse. Oh oh, that's it. Put your potato finger down there. Beget some little witchies."

Mather pinned down her arms and bending over her shivering torso intoned a scripture.

In the excitement of their inquiry, surely these men had forgotten themselves. I looked over at Sewall who was frowning, but like me seemed reluctant to leave.

"Put your pistol in my bung hole," the girl moaned. "You Devil! Sarah sucks carrots and leeks. I suck 'em, too. What a stew!"

She giggled and raised her buttocks off the bed. "Come on, you viper. That's it. In and out—in and OUAahh!"

I looked away, though my discretion was too late to stop an excited swelling in my codpiece.

Dripping sweat, Doctor Taylor stuck his head out of the sheet and wiped his hand. "I've discovered two tets on her privates. Take my word, the girl hath been hatched in the nest of the Devil under the Old Biddy Antichrist!"

Embarrassed by my growing tumescence, I ran down the hall past the startled Negress and behind the house to relieve myself. So horrified was I of their witch hunt that instead of going back I hastened to the harbor to sail on the high tide.

31

*A*t our Rye Beach cottage I found a message from Willy on his school slate.

MOTHER HURTS. I HAVE TAKEN HER TO GOODY W.

I sped to Odiorne's barn, borrowed a horse and galloped the cart path, dodging salt hay carts and jumping tidal ditches. When Goody Walford didn't come to the transom, I barged in and found another message on the torn end page of Willy's Latin book.

THE BABE IS DIED. COME TO MEET HOUS. WILLY.

With a leap I was back on my horse and riding breakneck to the Portsmouth Meeting House. Willy jumped up as I wheeled the horse to a standstill. Pru sat with her head bowed and locked in the loathsome iron headpiece.

I jumped off and was about to punch the Portsmouth Constable when Willy grabbed my hand and started bawling. What was I doing? If I didn't watch out I'd be keeping Pru company in gaol.

The Constable brushed off his arms and straightened his coat as if I'd assaulted him. "That woman in the scolding brank be a damnable witch, and that un, too." He nodded to a pillory at the other corner of the building where Goody Walford's head protruded through a yoke.

Willy put his skinny arms around my chest. "Mother was hurting bad Father," he sobbed.

I caressed his yellow locks. "It's not your fault, Willy." Choking back my anger, I had my foot in the stirrup when the surly Portsmouth Constable yanked me down and dragged me up the Meeting House steps. By Divine interference Governor Cutt, whom I'd been on my way to see, shuffled toward me.

"Mister ah Mister—ah—."

"Thomas Taylor, Your Honor."

"Well then, Taylor, what have you to say for your wife's bewitchments?"

"She lost our babe. If that's witchcraft, Your Honor, half the wives in the province should be in stocks."

The ancient Governor tottered and leaned against the Constable, "I thought you'd say as much. Perhaps you're unaware that your wife refused the Ordeal of Touch and filled the Church with oaths I'm loathe to repeat. We're proper here in Portsmouth, Mister Taylor. Moreover, the woman is possessed."

"For God's sake!" I cried. "We've lost our newborn babe!"

"Be that as it may, I'll not release her to your custody until she passes before the Provincial Council for the Ordeal of Touch."

I quelled the rage that boiled inside me—for it wouldn't do if Willy were the only one left to save us from this madness.

"Your Honor," I said in a loud, calibrated voice, "I can't persuade my wife if she's unable to talk."

The Governor sighed. "It be insufferable hot out here." He pointed a trembling finger at the Constable. "Release those women."

The Constable deposited the Governor on a bench in the shade and came with the key.

Thinking how strange it was that Pru and I once more were having a run-in at Market Square, I fetched some well water and revived her. Holding her in my arms, I entreated. "My love, you must do as the Governor wishes and go through this Ordeal of Touch."

She said nothing.

"I promise I won't leave you alone again, Pru." My scalp prickled with guilt at my dubious pursuits in Boston while she was in labor with our babe. "Please, Pru. Willy and I need you," I pleaded with all of my powers of persuasion. When I was about to give up she kissed me and wept so piteously I vowed to see her through the wretched ordeal—whatever it involved.

In the meantime, a pair of soldiers were sent to convene the members of the Provincial Council. Ordinarily, knowing the Governor would have been a boon. But as luck would have it, Cutt barely remembered his own name, let alone mine. Nor was I too sure of Pru who laughed one moment and wept the next. This meant I must depend on my connections in Portsmouth, which had dwindled to passing acquaintances like Walderne's son, Mister Jeffrey, and men newly arrived from London.

The Constable brought us into the Meeting House and the Councilmen took the bench. Governor Cutt hobbled over to a great chair and was swallowed by it quick as a skeleton in a coffin. A Portsmouth Councilor I'd never clapped eyes on officiated.

"Prudence Taylor, please rise and come forward."

I helped my enfeebled wife to the bench and waited at her side.

The Councilor walked over to a table and picked up a covered bundle. My hand gripped Pru's as he came toward us.

"Prudence Taylor, this is the babe you delivered early this day at the house of Good Woman Walford, the same who has been accused in deposition as a witch by Mister Walton and several others. If you are guilty of wrong-doing, the cloths that cover this babe will bleed. I ask you now to place your hand on the babe's head."

Pru shook from head to toe. Desperate to be done with the nightmare, I embraced her for all to see. "Please Pru," I whispered. "Touch the babe for Willy and me."

Goody Walford urged Pru, too, though she had ordeals of her own to face.

I held my breath, tense with what seemed years of waiting—only to come to this. When I thought I'd go mad with waiting, Pru's hand floated through the air and landed on the covering.

The Councilor peered down at the bundle. "It does not bleed!" he pronounced in a ceremonious tone.

Pru laughed.

"Silence!" Governor Cutt squawked from the depth of his chair. "It be no laughing matter."

"My wife is distraught, Your Honor. May I take her home now, Sir?"

The addled Governor seemed overly puzzled by my simple question. Annoyed, the Councilor held up his hand to shut off the lengthy pause. "Go in peace."

I helped Pru out the building and gave her to Willy waiting with the horse. "Walk your Mother home, Willy," I whispered. "Go gently with her. I must stay with Goody Walford."

Back in the Meeting House, the Councilor had picked up our poor swaddled babe a second time and was about to hold it out when Mistress Walford grabbed it and clasped the bundle to her breast. "This is the babe!" she cried out. "It came too soon and died. I grieve for the poor little soul and for Pru and Thomas Taylor whom I've grown to love like my own kin. As God is my Divine Maker, I'll bring suit against those who have called me a witch!"

The Councilor snatched back the bundle and walked over to the Governor's chair. What I feared would be the brave woman's death sentence turned into an audible series of snores. Knowing when he was beaten, the embarrassed Councilor again pronounced: "The babe does not bleed!"

"Of course not," Goody Walford retorted. "The poor soul be dead and departed for Heaven."

Aggrieved as I was, my heavy heart lightened at the thought.

32

Governor William Phips sat in the cabin of a brand new ship anchored at Go's Port on the Isles of Shoals. His capture of Port Royal and other exploits were heralded throughout New England. Now he was bound for Pemaquid Maine and wanted me to come along. The face of a devil scowled at us from the high-necked Rhineland Belarmine jug which we'd drunk nearly dry. He poured another tot of wine into our tumblers.

"What be eatin you, Red? You look down at the mouth."

"Nothing."

"Nothing, my kicky-wicky." Although Phips was Royal Governor of the New World he still had a feisty mouth.

"My wife has died," I said, startled by the stark reality. I hadn't spoken about Pru's death for months and my unstoppered grief spilled out. I told Phips about the Ordeal of Touch and how I'd left Pru with midwife Goody Walford. I relived the image of her waving to me at the dock in Portsmouth. I'd put off several commissions at the Shoals until Pru was back on her feet. That evening in high spirits with business dealings, I returned to discover my wife

dead from a sudden issue of blood. Goody Walford said it sometimes happened, but I wasn't comforted.

Phips poured me the last of the wine.

I ran on about the dire events related to Pru's death. John Cutt,
the proper but forgetful New Hampshire Governor, it seems, never
had recorded our marriage on paper. North Church refused my wife
an Anglican burial. Then, rumors circulated that Pru was a Barbadoes
witch and should have a stake driven through her heart. Goody
Walford, who had been exonerated by the Council, told me to pay
them no heed and even offered to bury Pru in her own back yard.

But the next day at dawn I sailed with my coffined wife to
Pepperrell's Cove. There wasn't a cloud in the sky to keep company
with my dark and heavy heart. Willy and I buried her on a knoll
looking southward to her cherished Barbadoes. Across the channel
at Go's Port Church I posted a broadside with an hourglass border
and an elegy Willy and I had composed:

> PRUDENCE MONFORTE TAYLOR
> IN MEMORIAM
> WILLY AND I CANNOT FORGET HOW
> WE LOVED YOU BEFORE
> AND DAILY REMEMBER HOW
> WE LOVE YOU YET, MORE.

Phips swiped wine off his mouth with his galloon-edged sleeve
and pounded the table. "It be a sorrowful lot, Thomas. But if you
come with me to Pemaquid it'll do you a world of good. There's
nothing like a voyage to ease the heart. I be on my way to build
Fort William & Mary, and I'll put you in charge. I've confidence in
you, Boomer."

Coming from Phips, the nickname I'd once abhorred sounded
strangely like a benediction. Here he was, the twenty-first son of a poor
Sheepscot yeoman, recently knighted and on top of the New World.
Now was the chance to throw off my sorrow, gird my loins, and work

like a red squirrel to safe-guard the coast from pirates, French, and Indians. All I had to do was heft stones and order men about.

The New England Governor unscrolled a parchment on the table before us. "This be the stone compound a hundred paces each side. The walls will be higher than this cabin and six paces wide. I'm building the Pemaquid Fort over that leviathan rock where King Philip's Indian savages hid in the massacre of '89. By God, they won't be achievin' that again anytime soon! I'm carrying six 18-pounder cannons on this very ship." Phips finger ran along a watergate passage from Pemaquid Harbor to the channel. "Now see this? It gives us safe access seaward."

During his long speech about defense and war I kept seeing Pru lifeless in her coffin. No. Though racing off with Sir Phips was tempting I would not go with him. My beliefs had turned idle, maybe even Quaker. I used Willy as an excuse to decline his offer.

"Damn the whoreson!" He rolled up his prize draftings and beribboned them. An officer entered the cabin, but Phips was so intent on winning me over he didn't acknowledge the man. "Bloody hell, Thomas, bring whoever this Willy be along."

"Willy's my son and I've entered him at the Appledore Academy where I'm Latin Master."

For the first time since I'd entered Phips' cabin, he was speechless. "You've double reefed me, Thomas. I had no idea you had a son—or that an Academy had been planted on Appledore. The Massachusetts Court has been debating a law for a school in every town. But deep as I fathom, it capsized. How old be yer boy?"

"Twelve."

Phips whistled through a hole in his front teeth which probably had been put there by a miscreant fist, for Phips' wealth and ambition inflamed his enemies to the point of fisticuffs.

"Do the boy a favor and stop mollycoddlin' the lad, Thomas! When we was twelve we were sawyerin' planks and workin' the fish flakes. Thank God I learnt to write. But it were sawyerin' and sailin' that taught me most."

"And death," I said, despite an inner conviction to rally.

With a loud belch Phips beached the conversation. "You be otherwise employed. So be it." He drank a dram, crashed the tumbler on the table, slapped me on the back, and waved for the officer to escort me ashore.

Although the Boston merchants liked to think of their Appledore Academy as a New World Seminary of Arts and Sciences, it lacked considerably in that direction. The boarding school had been launched by Commonwealth round heads who could not stand their slothful progeny. By isolating their sons on an isle the way coastal farmers did their hogs, they hoped to fatten their boys heads with learning and keep them from dance, drink, dice, and deflowering.

I agreed to be the Master, hoping to cram my own son's head with so much Cicero, Plato, and Prospero that both of us would forget Pru's absence. Work was the solution, according to Phips, and I set myself to teaching with renewed zeal.

The wealthy Bostoners had built a less than satisfactory school smaller than a ship's cabin with two small windows and a chimney. On three sides of the room an elevated wide plank served as a common desk. My table faced opposite the door at the hearth. I thought this an advantage until soot sifted on my coat and scorched my breeches. A dozen boys boarded in the deserted fishermen's cottages. Though a goodly sum kept them in quills, ink, paper, candles and firewood, my salary was far less. The gentlemen at the helm preferred a Veritas candidate, but until a Harvard graduate applied, the position was mine.

They all aspired to send their sons to Harvard and to that end I labored the poor dunces like plow horses. I quickly discovered that unless Harvard stooped to a doctorate in trade, they'd never get in. Even Willy who had the most inquiring, albeit restless, mind was not up to the mark. The stinking rich lads were numbskulls. The only thing they really understood was the translation of pinetree shillings into treats by marmalade madams at Strawbery Banke. I detested caning them and took to marooning the younger boys, including my son Willy and his friend Andrew Pepperrell, on Babb's Rock. When the older boys acted out I took them to my fish stage and had them slice off cod heads. I figured it couldn't hurt my business and might even turn the over-indulged brats into men.

I was just about to pack it in when an outbreak of coastal Indian raids from Maine brought a slew of correspondence from concerned fathers. The weaklings high-tailed it back to their Boston mansions—which was just as well. They were a clinchpoop lot, and frankly, I'd had it with higher education.

Shortly after I closed down the school, Willy and I sailed to Kittery Point to ask if his friend Andrew Pepperrell could spend the summer at my fishing stage.

I found the ambitious Pepperrell dandling a new babe on his knee. "Give Andrew all manner of consignments, Thomas," he prompted. "And keep him for the winter, too. From what you tell me the lads don't take to book learning. But damn my hide if the Shoals won't anoint them for trade. Right, son?"

Andrew stood straight and stuck out his lower lip. "Aye, Fa."

Willy looked as if he'd been struck on the head with a heavy object. He ogled the furnishings of Pepperrell's great mansion crowded with trade goods from London, Lisbon and Barbadoes. Silver plate and Royal china glittered in corner cupboards and the gateleg table was spread with a rich damask cloth. The walls had been plastered with clay, and large open casement windows over-looked the water. Willy's wide blue eyes took it all in, and I took in how awed he was by the fancy trappings.

"Be this your son?" Pepperrell asked. "Tar and feather me if he don't look the spittin' image of that waster Will Babb you used to hang about with."

I could've hauled off and shut his big Devon mouth for his con-founded prying.

Willy shot off like a loose cannon. "Are you saying my grandfather was the same scoundrel who indentured my mother? What the Devil! Phillip Babb wasn't wedlocked and neither was my father! I 'm destined to a lineage of bastards!"

Before I could think what to do, my son's blond hair flashed through the open window as he ran by.

Pepperrell shook his head. "Thom, I'm sorry. I just—. Well, I thought surely someone had mentioned his resemblance to Babb before this."

Although I wanted to go after Willy, I felt I owed Pepperrell an explanation. "Pru wanted the lad's father a secret."

"So, Thom, you finally bedded that saucy Barbadoes wench."

I let his teasing slide like water off a duck. "Governor Cutt came along one meeting day and married us on the spot."

"And you actually obliged the old windbag?"

"I wanted a family!" I said with more passion than intended.

To my surprise he put an arm over my shoulder. "I be family of sorts, Thomas. Put our sons on the flakes and you'll see—Willy'll forget all about it."

Once we were back on Appledore I sat Willy down and told him about his father, emphasizing the better points of Will Babb's nature.

But Willy wasn't about to be white-washed. "Did you like him?'

I confessed I'd been jealous because of his affair with Pru and cut our converse short.

Soon I realized that turning Will's pisspot actions into the Jordan was doing him more harm than good. A lad likes to oppose his father, and when I gave Willy an untarnished image his rebellion grew insufferable. One day he slugged my foreman so hard the poor man had a goose egg. This was bad enough, but then Willy made off with my dory.

Several nights later I awoke in my loft bed to a terrible row. I stumbled down the ladder to find Willy shuckie-shoeing around the room totally pickled. Hearing a woman's voice, I walked out the door and nearly stepped on a trollop spread-eagle on the granite step. I'd seen the Strawbery tart once or twice with soldiers. Her flimsy rain-sogged bodice revealed every detail of its pendulous containment.

She was no mere slip of a girl and when I hauled her to her feet she listed and slobbered in my ear.

"Willy rowed me to this curséd place. He promised to pay. I feel—. I feel—."

Before she could puke on me I shoved her head into a bush and she heaved, moaning and weeping.

"He's piked me day and night and hasn't paid his purse. Be you his brother?"

The strumpet knew damned well we were both the same age, though, thank heaven, not of the same disposition. I led her inside and wrapped her sodden bosom in a quilt. Willy had crashed to the floor and I near slipped on the spilled contents of his gin bottle. I helped the woman to a chair, instructing her to wait but I could have saved my breath, for it was apparent she was going nowhere fast.

In the loft I pulled on my breeches, counted some shillings into my purse and hurried back. It took all my strength to drag and coax the inebriate madam to my dory. The sea was calm as auk oil and I was forced to row the distance with her bottoms up in the boat.

Strawbery Banke had yet to stir when I slipped into a berth at Puddledock. Having no smelly salts, I picked up a putrid fish lying nearby and held it under the stupefied woman's nose. In the dawn light her face had aged a good ten years.

"Wha' the Devil!" She sat up, bursting out of her bodice piece with the sudden movement.

Why man craves a naked woman I don't know, but for an instant I thirsted on the desert of temptation. Then, ogling my fill, I tugged out my purse to pay Willy's seedy marmalade.

"You be too kind, Sir," she simpered. "Would you like me to stand you a treat, too?"

She hove her breasts from their lodging and would have

caught my jumping codpiece with her fumbling fingers if I had not squeezed coins into her hand instead. Grabbing the hawser, I hopped back into the dory and rowed a hasty retreat around to a newly opened Portsmouth coffee house.

I picked up a *Boston Almanac* left behind on the table and stopped short at a passage about my friend Sir William Phips. Apparently, he had been sent to London for having caned Captain Short of the *Nonesuch* in a back alley of Boston. While clearing his name of the trumped up charges, it seems the new Governor Dudley sued Phips for £20,000. In London, meanwhile, a good chap bailed Phips out of pauper's prison. But his charity came too late, and one of the wealthiest and worthiest New Englanders died penniless far from home.

I choked back my tears of grief and indignation. Last I'd seen Phips he'd been buoyant with responsibilities for the Massachusetts Commonwealth—and just look how they'd treated him! I wouldn't put it past Cotton Mather to have been involved in the affair, remembering how the Puritan minister similarly pulled Judge Sewall under his murky influence.

Just as I was thinking of Sewall, his name popped up in the *Almanac*. At a Fast Day for the nineteen Salem souls condemned to death, my dear friend Sewall publicly confessed before the congregation at Old South Church.

> *Samuel Sewall, being sensible to the Guilt contracted upon the Commission at Salem (to which the order for this Fast Day relates) is more concerned than any he knows of—desires to take the blame and shame of it, asking pardon of men, and specially desiring prayers that God—who has Unlimited Authority—would pardon that sin and all other of his sins.*

Cotton Mather and a dozen other Justices had been involved in the witch hangings, but only Mister Sewall was man enough to stand and admit his guilt.

Weary of Boston tattle I was about to ditch the dog-eared rag when I saw an item closer to home. The Royal British Navy had launched the *Falkland* at Kittery ShipYard and was building other navy ships as well. Hauling northern masts down the Piscataqua River and to England made little sense when the King's men could outfit their ships right here. Pepperrell and several other wealthy merchants were supplying the Yard with men and lumber. Halfway through my second coffee it dawned on me that Willy might board with his friend Andrew Pepperrell and work at the Naval Ship Yard.

Soon after I left the coffee house, I set my idea in motion. I had no more time to waste over Willy's fate. He was twice the age I'd been when I started working for his grandfather Phillip Babb on the Isles of Shoals, and it was high time he found a trade.

Pepperrell agreed to lodge Willy and a few short days later I let my son off with at Kittery Point. "Beware of loose women, Willy," I warned in a jesting tone so he wouldn't dismiss it as none of my business. "He who focks gets the pox."

Willy laughed. "I learned my lesson, Fa. No more marmalade madams for me."

The boy had grown strong as a cedar and I had no reason to worry, but that was easier said than done. He looked down at the new hobnail boots I'd bought him and we shook hands like strangers. All at once his gangly arms flew round my neck.

"Oh Fa, thank you. I'll work hard."

Braving unexpected emotions, I jumped in the dory and rowed like the devil, though the tide could have swept me back to the Shoals without rowing at all.

I made a concerted effort to fish from my own wharf and not interfere with Willy. During the French and Indian wars Boston merchants traded stuff with Virginia and Maryland plantations. Meanwhile, holding their fish deeds, I filled the deserted stages with able-bodied mainland men tired of building burnt houses up from cellar holes. I prospered as never before.

One evening as I strolled up the hill to stare at the stars I saw bon fires on Rye beach—big ones. A breeze blew the smoke and funked me into a morose reverie of the Guy Fawkes dance so long ago at Babb's tavern. When I went inside to tally the day's dealings in my wastebook, I noticed Guy Fawkes was long past; we were nearly at Plimouth Thanksgiving.

Grabbing my spy glass, I hastened back up the hill. Seeing Rye houses on fire, I hurried to warn the few men and their families who still lived on Appledore, promising to keep watch until first light. Then, I rushed back to point my musket out the loft window.

Indians moved in silence. On the ocean they plied the quietest barques in the New World and their birch canoes could sneak uncanny close without one murmur of an oarlock or wave hitting the bow.

Quaker silence, on the other hand, had a palpable presence. The intolerance that had sent Skitters and his Quaker in-laws to New Jersey was no longer a threat. In fact I'd been to a Hampton Quaker meeting where one of the Elders gave me a copy of William Penn's *Fruits of Solitude*. To blot out my fear of Indian attack I propped my musket in one hand and the Quaker book in the other.

"To do evil that good may come of it is for bunglers in politics as well as morals," wrote Penn. Certainly we were subject to the Puritans' bungled morals. Judge Sewall more than any had learned what came of their bungling at Salem.

I'd nearly read through two candles when dawn crept over the Isles and woke the others to keep watch. I awoke with visions of Pepperrell's great house charred and smoldering with Willy nowhere in sight. Unable to shake free of this vision, I sailed to Kittery Point. To my relief Willy ran from the great house with news that the Kittery Navy Yard had closed and was under guard. Portsmouth soldiers also had been posted at strategic points from Odiorne, New Hampshire, to York Harbor, Maine.

Mistress Pepperrell greeted me at the door, giving toddler

William over to her daughter Mary.

"He's a fine fellow. My, how he's grown!" I greeted, remembering women liked to hear this sort of thing.

But Mistress Pepperrell had much more on her mind. "How grateful I am Willy and Andrew were here last night, Mister Taylor. Indeed, they've kept turns at the look-out two nights running. My husband's at the York Court this morning for the construction of a Kittery Point Fort."

In the corner of the commodious common room, three girls played with china dolls in the cradle vacated by baby William. Having enough quiet at my Appledore house, I welcomed their sweet chattering and musical laughter.

Mistress Pepperrell took me over to them. "Have you met my girls, Mister Taylor?" She tapped each on the head as she introduced them. "Margery is ten and Joanna, seven."

The third little girl shawled her head with the cradle blanket and could be seen only from the waist down. The Pepperrell sisters giggled and their mother smiled. "The poor child is still terribly shy." She drew me aside and lowered her voice, "Like our Mary she's adopted. Her foster father was tortured and scalped in a field near their cottage. Alas, her mother Goody Porter has six mouths to feed and seems to have neglected the poor child."

I bent to address the girl hiding beneath the cloth.

"Won't you tell me your name?"

She pulled back the ends of the blanket, her face lingering in the shadow. "Thankful," she said so low I had to hunker closer.

"Thankful—. That's a special name."

"Yea."

"And how did you come by such a pretty name?"

Joanna tugged on my coat sleeve. "Mister Taylor, let me tell you. I can tell you."

"Mister Taylor asked Thankful, not you," her mother scolded. "Now come along, Joanna. You too, Margaret. It's time to unmold the candles." She turned to her eldest daughter. "Mary, please look after Mister Taylor, will you?"

The moment they left the room the orphan girl revealed a wondrous head of strawberry-colored ringlets.

"Why Thankful, you shouldn't keep such pretty hair covered. Can't you see we're alike?"

This remark caused her to look at me for the first time, and so startled was I by the intensity and color of her eyes that I stood upright. She was piebald, with one green eye and one blue. To hide my amazement I repeated my question.

"How do you come by the name Thankful?"

Like a wild animal wary of human encounter she kept her distance. "I heard Goody Porter tell Mistress Pepperrell that my true mother bore me a week after a still babe and was so glad she called me Thankful."

I laughed. "You must have misunderstood. A proper babe is created in nine months."

The child nearly dissolved in tears. "She said a week."

Not wishing to distress her further, I held out my muckinder so that she could dry her eyes and went over to Willy standing ill at ease beside the winsome Mary. I'd promised myself not to interfere in my son's life, but could not stand by while Willy pined for the girl.

"Since the Kittery Yard has shut down, Willy, I've arranged to have you at the Shoals through January thaw."

Hearing this, Willy paled, Mary ran from the room, and Thankful hid beneath her blanket.

33

*T*he tail end of the century brought a glimpse of hope to the Northern Province. The previous year a thousand outlyers trooped into Boston to keep the King's man, Earl of Bellomont, from taking the fort. Our success against the Royal stooge who had the gall to think he could trot in and take Boston reinforced our trust in Governor Dudley of Massachusetts, and for the first time in a decade we enjoyed relative peace and prosperity.

New World astrologers and versifiers were delighted we were entering a fortunate century blessed by the number seven. Puritan preachers filled our heads with acrostics on the seven days God made the world, seven virtues, and as Shakespeare put it, "seven hundred pounds and possibilities."

Willy wouldn't be seventeen for a few years, but I remembered how at his age I'd struck out on my own. He was useless at the Shoals, mooning like a weaned calf over Mary Pepperrell. The kid badly needed a change.

I wrote *The Blue Anchor* to secure rooms for the January Fair when Boston was overrun with tucknucking provincials. With the same dispatch I wrote Sewall that we'd be in town and sent word to my Boston accountant.

The day before we sailed, Willy told me why he was in such a funk. While he was staying on Kittery Point, Pepperrell yelled at Andrew for not getting into Harvard and threatened he'd better make something of himself. Then, turning to Mary he warned, 'And I expect my daughters to marry well.' When she asked what her father meant by well, Pepperrell said, position and property.

Willy's shoulders slumped. "I've neither."

"Willy, you're barely sixteen," I objected

"Didn't you say you proposed to mother when you were my age?"

"And she turned me down. That's when I discovered other women and a far wider world."

But Willy wasn't listening.

I'd purchased a mid-size pinkie for coastal trade and let him navigate us to Boston. Meanwhile, hoping he'd join the living, I plied him with scuttlebutt.

"Say, Willy, have you heard the latest? The Trade and Plantations Council has confiscated Privateer Kidd's treasure from Gardiner's Island in New York. Mister Pepperrell told me that Christmas pardons were granted the crew but denied Captain Kidd and Long John Avery."

"Mister Pepperrell! Mister Pepperrell!" Willy shouted.

The pinkie careened dangerously and I took the helm afraid he'd scuttle my boat. Thank goodness, once we'd docked in Boston Harbor and were settled at *The Blue Anchor*, Willy rallied. The boy had never been outside the Northern Province, and seeing through his wide blue eyes expanded my own horizon.

Our first stop was the tailor. I outfitted him like a new ship and sailed him in full regalia through the mercantile houses and mansions of Boston tradesmen. Willy listened attentively while my exchequer droned over endless accounts. I owned quarter share of a 300-ton ship built by Daniel Bacon in Salem Shipyard—quarter of which had been sold to Londoners for £3612—which profited me £1000 in addition to the fish I sold off her. All tolled, I dithered over end-of-voyage accounts for six ships, two of which I owned in full.

As we left the conference of lading accounts and tallies that had given me a pounding headache, Willy exclaimed, "Lord's Mercy! Your trade is awesome!"

Bolstered by his praise, I breathed in a chestful of the earthy air released by milling hawkers and buyers crowding Market Square for January thaw, which this year dawdled into February.

We took a bite and draught of beer at the *Two Palaverers* and trudged through slush over Middle Street to Hull House in the North End where I hoped to find Mister Sewall, my intent being to have some of his good influence rub off on my impressionable son.

Mistress Betty, in a morning shift and house cap, embraced me like a long lost relation. "Pray, did you bring a valentine card, Mister Taylor?"

Flustered by her remark, I hemmed and hawed.

"Oh Mister Taylor, I do love jesting with you."

The humor of her father's disposition clearly played at the corners of her eyes. Just the sort of girl for Willy.

Emboldened by her familiarity, Willy stepped forward, introduced himself and bowed proud as a peacock in his new-bought apparel.

She curtseyed and like a true Bostoner began talking politic. "Isn't it exciting about Captain Kidd? They have him locked in Stone Prison."

Betty glanced at Willy with inclination. Unfortunately, her interest was wasted, for he remained dumb as a halibut hidden in sand.

"I hear Mister Kidd has trailed treasure from Hispanola to Block Island," I remarked from the cobbled street.

High and dry on the granite step, she conversed down upon us.

"Father's at Lieutenant Governor Povey's this very morning counting the treasure. If you wish to see him, Mister Taylor, go there. Until Kidd's loot is safely stowed aboard the *Adventure Galley* and on its way to London none of us will have a moment of peace."

I thanked her and turned to leave when with an unexpected flourish Willy extended his front clod-hopper forward and sank it in a puddle. I could have kissed Betty who made a production of giving us directions to disperse his embarrassment.

Povey himself answered the door, but when I asked for Judge Sewall he ordered us to wait and bolted it. Upset by his rudeness I was about to leave when Sewall thrust open the door.

"Why Thomas Taylor, I'm glad to see you. And who is this?"

At the sight of him, my misgivings melted like the ice underfoot. "This is Willy, my son."

"Of course. I remember your talk of him. Welcome, Willy. Do come in." He made a swoop of his arm, encompassing us around and into the parlor.

Two large tables had been brought together and on them in the glow of oil lamps was spread the treasure of the notorious Captain Kidd of New York. Willy took a step toward the tables with the same wonder I'd observed at Pepperrell's bountiful mansion. A natural attraction, I assured myself, remembering my own wonder at the Counting House in Port Royal.

Rubies and diamonds glittered in small piles on their velvet pouches. Glistening gold and silver bars tumbled like dominoes on the table carpet and a pile of gold dust swung in the balance dish to be weighed. A silver box set with emeralds the size of my Bahama smaragds and diamonds and rubies by the dozen glinted in the light, splotting their color on the plastered ceiling.

In his rush to look closer at the loot, Willy stumbled and fell on a mound of linen bales stacked before the tables.

Povey scowled and grumbled. "Now I've lost my count and must start over."

They were so intent on getting the treasure tallied they put Willy to work counting the bales. "Forty-one bales of East India linen and silk," he announced some time later, thrilled for his part in the famous affair.

I was asked to weed out silver plate and stack it in a sack which would be returned to Lady Sarah Kidd, for it seems while ransacking her husband's lodgings, that they appropriated her possessions by mistake.

Sewall good-naturedly answered Willy's non-stop questions about Kidd's arrest. The Earl of Bellomont had been Kidd's partner from the start. With the backing of a private syndicate in New York they outfitted the 287-ton *Adventure Galley* with 34 guns and a 100 men in order to chase after privateers of dubious intent and seize the bounty.

For three years the New York merchant sailed from Johanna, Africa, to Malabar, India, where he seized the *Quedah Merchant* and an official pass from the ship's captain for the confiscated stuff. But the Board of Trade got wind that Kidd was a turncoat and called him in. Kidd hid the *Quedah* and its cargo at St. Thomas and high-tailed it to New York in a borrowed sloop. Meanwhile, the Earl of Bellomont sent us an appeal. If Kidd gave the King's bounty to the Boston Council, he'd be exonerated. Picking up his wife Sarah at their Wall Street mansion in New York, Kidd stopped in Rhode Island to see Thomas Pain (who unfortunately had gone to the other side). Then, dropping the bales of dry goods at Mister Gardiner's Island, he sailed into Boston Harbor.

A fellow Scot, Duncan Campbell, offered him lodging while the alleged pirate met with the Boston Council which demanded a written report of his activities. But that night, aroused by officers, Kidd escaped to Bellomont's for the protection he'd been promised.

"Do be quiet!" barked Povey, counting a pile of gold fingerlings.

To our consternation Sewall cut his tale short to stow the gold Povey handed him in an iron chest. My job was to secure the bales with new bale seals while Willy and a soldier hefted the bales on their shoulders to the ship. After what seemed like a dozen trips he returned hot under the collar.

"Mister Sewall, Sir," he yawped.

Sewall looked up and mopped his brow.

"They won't give me a receipt until the bales are in the hold."

"That's all right, Willy. Let's have some refreshment?" Sewall proposed. "You deserve it."

My woolly under drawers had been prickling me to a scratchy madness and, leaving the somber Povey in charge, we hurried into the fresh air for a cool limey beer.

In the taproom Sewall slapped Willy on the back. "I don't know what I'd have done, Thomas, if this able-bodied son of yours hadn't come along to help carry the bales down to the shipping office. Great God! I'm glad Povey and I agreed in our tally and the store house hasn't been raided or caught fire!"

Willy tossed off his beer. "Did it all come from Duncan Campbell's house, Mister Sewall?"

"We took the bales from Gardiner's Island where Kidd left a proper receipt. I believe he intended to hand them over as he said. But our Boston Court can no longer try witches or pirates because of what happened in Salem. And Captain Kidd must go to London to be tried which, if you ask me, is a Royal pain in the arsenal." Sewall looked around. "My hands are tied judicially, and Kidd's, alas, literally."

"Then he did no wrong?" Willy asked with wide-eyed innocence.

Until now he'd shown little endeavor, and his sudden interest pleased yet confounded me. If I had ordered the boy to lug 41 hogsheads of fish, he'd have found every excuse not to, but today he'd carried bale after bale.

"We've no proof Captain Kidd was in the wrong, Willy,"Sewall told him.

"But surely the silver and gold are proof enough," I objected.

Sewall drank a long draught of beer. "Kidd swears he brought the treasure to Boston to hand over to the Earl of Bellomont. The Boston Councilor swears the Earl is a cunning Jacobite. None of us likes him meddling in our affairs. King William the Third may have appointed him Governor of New England, but the sooner we see his Royal backside, the better. Kidd was arrested without the Council's consent, mind you. We asked Bellomont point blank the reason for the arrest. He claimed Kidd wanted their partnership papers and when refused, Kidd threatened to take what he wished. 'It was such a great impertinence, I arrested him,' Bellomont told the Council. 'Besides, the man looked guilty.' Lord's Mercy! You and I know that if we arrested every man-jack for being impertinent and looking guilty, we'd have a prison from here to Quincy! Kidd insisted the valuables in his rooms were gifts. The same day Bellomont clapped Kidd in irons, he gave Lady Bellomont a jeweled necklace valued at £1000 pounds."

Willy whistled. "Whew, this stinks like day-old fish!"

"Willy, watch your tongue!"

Sewall laughed. "I agree with Willy, and truth be told I welcome your company. Mister Povey's a stickler to be holed up with. We've kept the whereabouts of the treasure secret so far, but I sure could use a guard to protect the loot and ensure Kidd's safe passage to London. Earl Bellomont has every jack-tar in Boston looking for treasure from here to the Shoals. God's Mercy, the man tries my patience!"

"I could go." Willy chimed in.

"You wish to go now?" Sewall fished in his purse and put down a pine tree shilling for our small beer.

"I mean, I could go with the treasure to England." Willy eyed me with bold defiance.

Outside the tavern a wave of pedestrians engulfed me. Distracted by my anger at Willy, I stepped into a pothole of slush up to my calves. The frigid water oozed into my shoes.

Sewall retreated to rescue me.

"Hurry durry!" I exclaimed in a temper. "Whatever does my son hope to accomplish by such an outlandish proposal?"

Sewall pulled me onto the comparatively dry wide step of a shop. "Come now, Thomas. We do need a sentinel—and Willy is thrilled with the idea of being one."

I crossed my arms in a huff. "Would you send your son Sam on a dangerous mission to the other side of the world?"

"Samuel is so weak that the ferry from here to Lynn tires him. But Thomas, tell me, have you ever seen Willy so keen?"

We stood in a dank doorwell waiting for an opening in the crowd. If I let the lad to go to London he might not return, but if I made him stay he might bear me an irreconcilable grudge.

Willy had retraced his steps to look for us when I grabbed him from the rushing throng. Taken unawares, he punched me so hard he knocked the wind out of my sails.

"Fa!" Willy shouted, helping me up from the cobbles steaming horse piss. "I didn't see—are you—?"

The busy pedestrians shoved us toward King's Wharf where the treasure was to be hoisted with the ship crane. Dim sun poked through the haze and water sloshed gently against the pilings. Willy stood a good head above me, his blond hair in a neat pigtail with a bow. How grand-grown he looked in his new duds.

I gripped him by both shoulders. "For God's sake, Willy, learn to look before you leap! And when you get to London send me a letter by advice ship."

"Then you're letting me go, Fa?"

"That's exactly right, Willy. I'm letting you go."

34

*T*he next few months laid me low with a feverish ague I thought I'd die from, and lie-abed proneness wracked me with such sciatic rheumatism I could barely tolerate the weight of my own body. I mixed onions, rum and neat's foot oil into a plaster recipe I'd seen Pru slather on stiff fishermen. It didn't do much for my sore hip but cleared my nose remarkably well.

Though springtide brought physical relief, my mind was adrift on Willy who'd been gone half a year.'

After work one day I sailed a brisk westerly wind straight to Pepperrell's Point in Maine to see if Will had posted a letter to Mary. The fair rosy-cheeked girl showed me familiar deference despite a palpable reticence to talk about my son. No, she hadn't heard from Willy and wasn't aware he'd sailed to London.

It was a sticky mistake and I turned to leave when Mistress Pepperrell intercepted me. "I say, Mister Taylor, since it's so late, I was wondering if you could row Thankful to her dwelling down river?"

The child I'd seen on my last visit hung in the shadow behind her. To cover up my gaff with Mary I agreed, though I was hard pressed to secure my own lodgings in Portsmouth before nightfall.

Low sunlight burnished the girl's dark red hair and I found myself staring at her as we walked down to my dory. "You don't look happy to be going home," I observed from the stern.

She trailed a small hand in the water. "Goody Porter will be vexed with me as usual."

Her sad face dredged up memories of how I'd coveted Mary Babb's love when I'd first arrived at the Shoals. "I've heard Mistress Porter lost her husband. Think of the great burden she suffers and perhaps it will ease yours."

The girl wordlessly pointed out a dock down river and when we arrived I held out my hand, peering into her stoic little face. "Come, lovely Scarlet."

A tear rolled down her fair freckled cheek."Oh, Mister Taylor, couldn't I live with you? I could cook and clean yer dwelling and be in yer indenture. Would you not have me?"

Her impassioned trembling voice turned my heart to jellyfish. "We'll see," I acquiesced to get her out of the boat. Hidden by bushes, I watched as she trudged through the muck toward a woman standing near a wretchéd hovel.

"Yew brat!" the woman yelled. "Where 'ave you been? You was suppose to fix supper for the young-uns and hoe the sallet greens in the garden. Merciful Heaven, I dread the day I—."

A gaggle of wild kids bound from around back. "Cane her, Ma! Cane her!" the largest taunted wielding a birch whip.

When I stepped from behind a bush, the woman I presumed to be Goody Porter backed to the door of her rude wattle dwelling and picked up a musket.

"I brought Thankful home from the Pepperrell's," I shouted over the din—holding both hands in the air to show I meant no harm.

She dropped the heavy musket butt in the dirt and caught one of the rowdy boys running past her.

Thankful took my hand.

"This be Mister Taylor of the Eyen of Shoals."

I smiled to think of the Shoals as eyes in the sea and gripped her small hand in mine.

The boy with the birch stick was dragged inside.

I followed uninvited. "Could I speak to you?"

The woman grunted and waited. She might have been listening, but I doubted the lad was, so mangled and red was his ear when she let go.

"Could we converse in private?" I persisted.

She laughed scornfully. "The only privacy ye'll find here be in the privy." Nevertheless, she herded the kids like sheep into the hovel and bolted the door, leaving us in the peeper-filled spring twilight.

A deafening caterwaul rose behind the door and I stepped a few paces into the open.

"It's about Thankful."

A light came into her eyes. "She be yourn at the right price."

It so rankled me that I jumped into a transaction which until that very moment I hadn't considered. "How much?"

"Three hundred pound."

I held out my hand to clench the dark agreement.

"Per anus," she added, dropping my hand as if it were a hot turnip.

I smiled at the absurdity of her Latin and she sniggered with pride.

I didn't overlove the woman, but aware of the pandemonium behind the door, I well understood her husbandless plight. "On one condition—you must tell me about the girl."

"What's to tell?"

"Does Thankful know about printing off?

She squinted at me in the gathering dark. "I beg pardon?"

"Stamping and engendering babes, Goody Porter. I'm ill disposed to keep a girl on the Shoals who does not own this knowledge."

"Lord a Mercy, my eldest be scrambling atop the girl every

chance he gets and she brung my own last babe into this world nice as you please."

These proofs did not ease my mind a great deal. "Thankful told me she was born a week after a stillbirth. You and I know that's impossible," I coaxed with the complicity she relished.

Her overworn face floated in the light of the rising planter's moon.

"Thankful may be the laziest kid on God's earth but she don't fib. The midwife what brought me Thankful told me her Ma had a male babe what died in an issue of blood a week afore Thankful arrived. It were plain the girl were a twin."

Goody Porter's thin blue lips continued to move in the moonlight, but for all I heard I could have been deaf. Had my own babe lived he would be Thankful's age. Surely it was a casual coincidence yet I was compelled to ask: "The midwife you speak of, was she Goodwoman Walford of Portsmouth?"

She clutched my arm and eyed me with a peculiar off-kilter tilt of her bulwark. "Be yew the devil? Not even the child be knowin' this affair."

Like an actor who wishes to let his audience in on a secret, I leaned closer and showed my purse.

She picked distractedly at a mole on her chin. "Aye, t'were Goody Walford. She must o' had property fer she paid regular fer our takin' the brat. The Ordeal o' Touch were one thing, but when she were accused of witchery, Goodman Porter and I thought it spedient to flee to this side o' the river. God A'mighty, then my husband were carried away by savages and a few days later Goody Walford followed him. I suspicion she were a witch like they said, and Thankful, too, fer all the trouble she's caused me."

I eased the moanful woman's complaints with several shillings and the promise to pay in full when I returned for the girl.

Back at the Shoals, I transacted with myself. First, I wouldn't tell Thankful that I was her father, thinking she'd rather have no father at all than one who had deserted her to Goody Porter. Second, I'd indenture her until she was thirteen when I hoped we'd be familiar enough to reveal my true identity.

This resolve was drowned in a flood of doubts about loosing Thankful on the Isles of Shoals. The fishermen were a crude lot and there were only two other women on Appledore Island. What would the girl do when I must sail to Boston and the Indies on business? Worries pestered me like blackflies on the Mainland, itching and biting my conscience to such a degree that I sailed to Mistress Pepperrell for advice. Learning of the imminent indenture of the girl to my household, she said she'd be delighted to board Thankful when I was gone. Furthermore, she loaded my boat with bundles of dresses, muffs, ribbons, pitchers, quilts, and a quandary of stuff for the child.

I'd accustomed myself to manly habits, and having Thankful at my beck and call plummeted me into a such a dump I might have destroyed everything—had it not been for her cooking. From porridge to potage she performed miracles almost as surprising as the fact that she was my lovely, grateful child.

One day she would serve up a delicacy of sea urchins and spring dandelion salad gathered all over Appledore Island. The next day I convived on fried sunchokes and a goose that landed in our cabbage yard, all bubbled in port with dried beach plums.

I felt vital, working less and accomplishing more. Better yet, with the green and ease of summer Thankful's sorrowful aspect faded. By the first frost I'd managed to convince her that reading was part and parcel of her indenture and we set about elementary Latin and arithmetic. When she fussed that surely it took too much of my time, I told her that if I fell ill she must keep my correspondence and accounts. Encouraged by her facility for learning, I added navigation and charting to the curriculum.

One sunny day the following spring, I ventured setting down the first stone in the foundation of her true birthright. "Have you heard of Barbadoes?" I asked.

"They be—huh, it is a distant island south of the Bahamas

filled with pirates and brigands."

Since Kidd's arrest, strange ships were harboring at the Shoals and jack-tars had been seen scrambling through the caves like water rats looking for hidden treasure. Those of us who lived there bolted our doors at night.

"Pirates are everywhere these days, Thankful. We mustn't let fear lock our hearts to the beauty around us. But I wanted to tell you somewhat about my wife who was a Barbadoes woman firm as the cedars of her native island and sweet as vanilla blossoms. Her father owned a French plantation on which her mother was a Negro slave."

Thankful covered her full lips with a white freckled hand.

"Pru—my wife—lived in the plantation house and was raised as kith and kin."

"As Goody Porter raised me?" she asked doubtfully.

"I dare say kinder. But then, the buccaneers burnt her home and she was carried here on a slave ship. Her father named her Désirée but when I met her she was called Prudence."

Thankful's hands fluttered like moths in the light. "I often talk to her, Mister Taylor. Isn't she laid on the south hillside beneath a pile of banded stones?"

"Yes, Thankful, you're right and I must confess, I talk to her too." Afraid I might blurt out the truth before she was ready, I launched into an elaborate tale of a feast I'd once attended at the palace of a merchant in Port Royal.

"We began with veal dressed with oranges, lemons and limes. Then came turkeys, capons, hens baked with eggs, ducklings, turtle doves, hare, and cold sliced roast beef.

"This was followed by bacon, fish roe, and pickled oysters accompanied by a special Barbadoes condiment of anchovies and olives.

"After that, the Barbadoes merchant served custard desserts, pastry cream with plantain and guava preserves, puffs made with English flour, and cassava cooked into bread—.

Thankful's fair cheeks flushed with excitement. "Cassava?"

"It's a fruit they eat like bread."

Her eyes danced with the lust of Tantalus tempted by a repast of the gods. I stretched my memory and imagination as we rested in the shade of a leafy apple tree. Decidedly, the Isles of Shoals agreed with the girl. Freedom from the tyranny of the Porter brats had done wonders, and I reveled in her quick spirit and loving nature.

"On Barbadoes they make froizes, which are thin eggy pancakes," I resumed. "Ah, what a wonder they were."

She clapped. "Oh, shall I make them for you, Mister Taylor?"

"I dearly would like to taste them again, Thankful. But you have no custard-apples or bananas or guavas with which to fill them. And it's all washed down with a—."

One of my workers appeared and handed me a sealed letter from a London advice ship in the harbor. I had Thankful fetch the fellow a shilling for his trouble, and in my zeal nearly tore apart the confounded thing. I hadn't mentioned the business with Willy to anyone for fear something might happen to him. It was a Shoals superstition, and much as I thought it absurd, I thanked the Almighty for sealing my lips.

London May 23, 1701

Dear Fa,

I have delayed writing, being disposed in my duty as guard to Captain Kidd until he was hanged along with Darby Mullins at Wapping Gallows. Perhaps you heard that the British Court did not hang him for piracy but disloyalty to England. In his final hours I solaced the man best I could. The crowd on Hangman's Holiday shared their spirits with him along the way. At the tail end when the hangman closed the noose I was near enough to hear his declaration. "My Lord, this is a hard sentence," he cried, "for my part I am innocent—sworn against by perjured persons." The rope broke and he disappeared unstrung through the trap to the mud flats below. You can imagine how the crowd

cheered. For nigh unto a year he avowed his innocency and I, like
them, thought surely this was a sign of Divine Intervention. But
the King's men would have nothing of the uncommon occurrence
and forced the poor drunken soul to ascend the steps a second and
last time.

You were right, Fa. I had much to learn of the world. Mary
Pepperrell be long forgot. You are not.

> *Yr Loving son*
> *William Monforte Taylor*
> *Willy*

I looked up, startled by Thankful's hand on my arm.

"Won't you read it aloud to me?"

Her previous gay mood lapsed into pensiveness as I read her Willy's letter. It's amazing how words fulfill their import when spoken. Suddenly, I saw how grown Willy had become, and when I'd finished I couldn't help saying I was right proud of the lad.

Thankful disdained me in a peculiar manner. "How old's your son, Mister Taylor?"

He'd been gone so long. "Nineteen, I believe."

"Then he's hardly a lad."

Dispirited by this thought, I was stuffing Willy's letter into my belt when I saw some writing at the fold:

PS I shall sail on the next ship and with fair weather I hope to
reach the Isles of Shoals by mid July.

From then on 'When Willy comes' larded our conversation and hope sizzled like meat drippings on the hearth.

One noontide I returned from my fishing stage to find Thankful weeping. She'd been berrying barefoot and an itchy rash rose from her delicate fingers up her limbs. I took one look at her and with my back turned, ordered her to disrobe and lie still beneath the coverlet.

She stared at me ruefully. "What if Willy comes?"

"Thankful, you've walked straight into a bed of poison ivy. You must lie still," I ordered.

She whimpered. "I only wanted strawberries to fill the froizes for Willy."

I poured her a tumbler of water. "Willy this and Willy that! One would think you were preparing for the Second Coming."

"Oh, Mister Taylor. What blasphemy!" She put a swollen hand to her mouth.

I pushed it away. "Keep your hands from your face or the toxin will creep there, too. Believe me, I've had the misfortunate ivy rash and know whereof I speak."

"Aye," a deep voice cut in, "and I never heard the end of it, either."

I turned to a bronze blue-eyed sailor towering in the doorway. "Have you a message?"

"God have mercy!" he shouted leaping into the room. "Don't you recognize your own son?"

I choked back my joy and staggered in Willy's fond embrace.

My daughter squirmed beneath her blanket.

"Poor Thankful! We must make up a salve, Willy, and give her a mithridate at once for her poison rash.

Willy threw down his duffel and stared at her scarlet hair. "Thankful?"

"The girl has been in my indenture for over a year now," I explained.

"I daresay you'll be in hers til the rash stops pussing. Doesn't she know any better?"

His reprimand hardly eased her pain. What's more, no sooner had he dropped his duds than he went off in my dory to Hampton. As he shoved off I implored him to bring back a mess of touch-me-not for Thankful's itchy blotches. Several hours later he threw a bunch of the wilted orange and red flowers on the table, which by now Thankful usually had laid with supper.

"We'll have to cross over to Star tavern for our victuals," I said in a testy tone. "The poor girl's fit to be tied with her malady."

"She certainly has you on the run," Willy said purposely loud.

A wail rose from the trundle bed at the cold hearth.

"Now see what you've done! After all, the girl clambered through the ivy for you."

"Pish-pash," he scoffed.

"She was going to make you strawberry pancakes with *créme fraiche*!" I flared. How had we gotten off to such a bad start? I'd longed for a proper family and now that I had one we were at each other's throats.

I mulled over this dilemma while polishing off half a dozen fried smelts at Go's Port. As prodigal son, naturally Willy assumed superior standing, relegating Thankful the dubious distinction of household servant. And why shouldn't he, since she herself thought as much?

The sea looked like someone had poured auk oil to the horizon, and midway across I lifted the oars and drifted on its calm red and gold surface. "The girl I've taken in—."

Willy lazed back, his face bronze and fine. "She's pitiful scrawny."

"But what I wanted to—."

"Her color's strangely identical to yours. Folk might mistake her for your daughter."

I dabbled my fingers in the water. "She is my daughter, Willy."

"I understand you think of her as your daughter, Fa. That's precisely the trouble."

"Willy, will you let me finish? The girl is my flesh and blood and yours as well. Your infant brother died. His twin sister did not."

"What the—?" Willy knelt in the ribs of the boat, leaned back, and stared hard at the first stars shining like gold doubloons in the sky. All at once he threw up his brave muscular arms. "By God in Heaven! I have a little sister!"

I feathered the oars and looked out at the oil-smooth waves. "I haven't told her."

His mouth tightened.

"Don't you see? The poor girl was so abused when I found her, I thought she'd never forgive me. I thought—."

In his hurry to communicate, Willy near rocked us into the deep. "The Lord who brought us together can't wrench us apart! We must tell her at once!"

We rushed to our Appledore house and through the transom only to be accosted by woeful cries. Thankful's eyes had swollen shut and she was half out of her mind.

I suggested we brew calamint herbs and soak her in a tub of them mixed with cooling well water. Making a chair of our arms, Willy and I carried the delirious child out to a large tub at the well. When we'd placed Thankful in the herbs, I knelt beside the tub and Willy dropped beside me.

"Dear Lord," I prayed, "save my daughter Thankful from this affliction and forgive me for being absent when my wife gave birth to her. In your mysterious way you hid my daughter as a candle under a bushel. Oh Lord, please save her from death." My shoulders shook and I fell in a heap in the sythed grass.

Willy's firm hands raised me up and I crouched at the tub. A black clump of leaves stuck to my child's forehead and red hair strands straggled on her frail cheeks. Her teeth chattered fearful in the cold spring water and suddenly her head slipped under. Splashing water every which direction, Willy and I hauled her onto a sail-cloth we'd placed on the grass, rolled her up, and carried her back to bed. I was dull with anguish at her stillness.

Willy placed his head to her chest. "She breathes, Fa!" he cried. "She breathes!"

We watched and waited in the candlelight. When the silence was too much, we reached for a Belarmine jug and let the wine loosen our grief-stricken tongues.

Willy unstoppered his regret for Captain Kidd's death. "He paid harsh for his iniquity, Fa. It's just as Mister Sewall said, the

Earl of Bellomont had the poor Captain's head on a pole. I'm not saying Kidd was guiltless, but—."

"It's a dangerous time for sea traders," I whispered. "One might as well eat pease porridge in a fog than reckon the distinction between privateering and pirateering."

Excitement mounted in my son's voice. "Aye, Fa. And that's why I aim to trade fish for my keep—if you'll have me. Pirates and privateers care little for cod."

I rejoiced at his change of heart and we were about to toast our new partnership when Thankful stirred.

"I had such a strange dream, Mister Taylor," she said, sitting up and staring at us as though we were ghosts." I dreamt that I was drowning in the sea and heard you pray 'Dear Lord, save my daughter. Do not let her die.' And Willy was there too and he said he was my brother."

I smoothed her feverish brow. "It was no dream, Thankful. I am your father and the Barbadoes woman I told you about is your and Willy's mother."

Unburdened of this long-kept confession, I embraced my ivy-blotched daughter in one arm and grown son in the other. All said and done, not a dry eye was left in that warm wildernest.

35

*O*ne ominous day in May, Willy made to depart in the driving rain. I'd given him the *Providence* to set up his fishing trade on Star Island where he had his eye, and probably more, on a tavern wench.

"God's Mercy, Willy! It's a wicked nor'easter. Can't it wait?" I shouted over a blast of thunder. He slammed the door in reply, leaving me to light my pipe and sink onto the settle near the hearth beside Thankful, who resembled Pru in figure and beauty more each day. She handed me a bowl of chowder steamy with fresh clams in their broth, thick cream, a few kernels of hominy and new spring mushrooms.

I held up my spoon. "What's this pungent herb? Rampions?" She savored my guesses much as I did her cooking. "Yes, I believe you found some rampions."

"You're close, Fa. They're—." All of a sudden she clutched her belly, doubling up in pain.

It was so unexpected that I spilled the chowder. Fearing the girl had eaten a poison toadhat, I was running for a vial of Cortex to purge her when she grabbed my leg.

"Fa, I'm bleeding to death. Oh, Father!" She sidled across the bricks to show me a horrid pool of blood.

I sopped up the blood with a shirt Willy had left in a heap and lifted her onto the settle. With a trembling hand I measured the purgative into a spoon.

She pushed it away. "I'm not poisoned. It's my time."

Visions of the grim reaper holding up his hourglass rushed through my brain.

"I never thought it would be so painful," she moaned, clutching her stomach.

"Take the purgative, Thankful!" I prodded. "You've eaten a poison toadhat."

Wan as a ghost, she smiled. "No, Father. I'm having my first mense." She sucked her knuckles to stopper a scream. "Can you get me some Diacodiom?"

I ran to the shelf in the herbal shed. Like her mother, Thankful collected herbs, made tonics, ground powders, and distilled potions. Wouldn't you know it! The Diacodium vial was empty and I'd have to sail to Star to get some from Moll Pulsey. The thought of leaving Thankful alone troubled me beyond reason, but I boiled up a brew of chamomile, and leaving her with a clean cloth to sop the issue blood, I leapt into my small pinkie and tacked gusty winds across the channel.

Go's Port Harbor teemed with fishing vessels and several stranger ships waiting for the squall to blow over. I purchased enough Diacodium off Goody Pulsey to knock out a horse and waited out the sudden storm at Whitcomb's Ale House. I was standing at the transom coddling a mug when I saw Willy deep in converse with an uncommonly merry stranger about my age. The kid had told me he'd be fishing and I was so peeved I stood myself another mug. Mellowed by drink, I blamed the foul weather for my son's aimless ways and was about to leave when I noticed the tavern-keep staring into his palm with a face near merry as the stranger's.

Waiting until they were gone, I intercepted Richard Whitcomb. "Do you want my money or not? I've waited inordinate long to pay."

Distracted by my belligerence, the tavernkeep opened his fingers, revealing a gold nugget the size of my back molar. I dropped my pence into his palm and raced back to my sailboat. Were it not for Thankful, I swear I'd have chased Willy to the ends of the earth. Damn the kid. When would he ever learn?

A tail wind flew me across the channel and I was just about to luff into the Appledore wharf when I turned to stare straight into the puss of a long scruffy jack-tar. With a twist of my arm he brought me to my knees, hog-tied my ankles and wrists with yard rope, and kicked me into the pitchy hold. I lay on the hull dazed by a boister of worries. How had he sneaked up without my knowing it? Where in the hell was he sailing? And what would happen to Thankful without the Diacodium in my purse?

The pinkie hold was token shelter from the elements with nothing remotely possible to free me from my bondage. A scuttering, which I took to be a rat in the ribs of the makeshift cabin, increased my terror. With a rocking motion of my body I managed to lodge my chest onto a pile of stowage. The snot rag plugging my throat near choked me, and my wrists ached from the cutting of the hemp.

Like most Shoalers I had a keen ear for the rote of the waves about the Isles. I recognized the sound of clam shells scrubbing Devil's Dance Floor, then a shout and stampede as if a regiment drilled on the deck above. I was straining to make out their purpose when a sudden light blazed in the hold and the piratical Viking plummeted down the hatch and slipped something into my purse. Before he could get away, a regimental soldier appeared and pinned him to the stair railing. Spotting me, he shouted.

"Major, come look!"

The Major cut my bonds with his rapier and shoved me into daylight beside the devil that had kidnapped me. I unwadded the muckinder from my raw mouth and drank large gulps of moist spring air. The blackguard whistled free as a bird, and fearing he might jump ship, I grabbed the officer's sleeve.

"Major, this rogue pirated my pinkie and threw me down the hold!"

The Major bent the point of his rapier into my chest. "I'll do the talking. What's your name and provenance."

"Thomas Randolph Taylor of Appledore Island. I was bringing a sorely needed remedy to my daughter from Go's Port when this cur jumped me from the hold of my ship.

The officer looked doubtful. I tried again.

"Lord's Mercy, Major! Just look in my purse. I have the Diacodiom I fetched for my sickly daughter." The thought of Thankful's long-suffering caused me to bolt. But before I could find the vial, a soldier did it for me. To my surprise, with the vial he held up a small blue velvet pouch.

"What have we here?" the Major asked, grabbing the pouch and untying the drawstring. A stream of gold dust sifted into his palm.

"The rogue must have planted it on me!"

"What say you, Swede?" he asked the villain smirking at my side.

"I say he turn tail for his own goot. He board my sailing boot uninvited. Thank Gott I belt the man broadside—and he confess he bist John Pitman of *Larrimore Galley.*"

A lieutenant stepped forward. "One of them's lying, Major Sewall. We've captured John Pitman already."

"Major Sewall!" I was beside myself with my good fortune. "Are you the brother of Judge Samuel Sewall?"

Being a military animal from head to foot, the Major gave me no quarter. "I am, though I don't see what bearing it has on the outcome of this matter."

"Your brother's a good friend of mine." My heart sank as I perceived how unlike the Major was from his easy-going brother. "I'm confident the Judge would uphold my honor in this affair." Trapped in a whither-whatie confusion, to further prove my innocence I added, "Of course I can produce the deed to this vessel."

My promise of proof brought the Major's order to release me and I secured my strongbox from beneath a loose plank down in the hatch.

Seeing his goose was cooked, the rogue Swede made a last-ditch effort. "Yup, them be my papers where I hided 'em."

The Major waved them in his face. "Then tell me from whom you purchased this vessel and what month and year."

The Swede mumbled and coughed, spat and leered. "I purchase her, why were it not? Nay, that un were a brig. Umm—. It were near September. Because I be Swede I buy this here sail boot by proxy—from uh, from uh Providence."

Major Sewall waved the papers beneath my nose. "And you?"

"I bought this pinkie off the Salem Syndicate. Is this June 1704? "While he answered I hastily reviewed the titles to my half dozen brigs, pinkies, and dories purchased within the past few years.

The Major and his lieutenant waited.

"Well then, I purchased this pinkie exactly two years ago in June, 1702—as I said, in Salem, Massachusetts."

Major Sewall returned the papers to the strongbox and made a high sign for the lieutenant to take the Swede into custody. "I owe you an apology, Captain Taylor. It seems I've caused you more trouble than you deserve. I'm required by writ to apprehend the pirates of the *Larrimore Galley*, and it hasn't been easy. But I can proudly say not one gun has been fired or life squandered thus far."

As if on cue, the *Larrimore Galley* floated broadside. Being windward, its captain, a Mister Abott, backed his mainsail.

The Major waved to Abott and ordered me about. "Back your foreyards for gamming, Captain Taylor, and we'll take this scoundrel off your hands."

His lieutenant marched the pirate past me and down a gang-plank to a smaller coastal vessel.

"You puke shit sailor!" the Swede growled as he passed.

Justice Hinckes, whom I knew from Star Island, waved at the

Major and me from his boat the *Fort Pinnace*. "Hey-dey, we got the three King brothers!" he shouted. "They ain't from the Orient but they come bearing treasure gifts."

Major Sewall laughed, I supposed from relief that he was done with the mess.

I waylaid him as he passed."Begging your pardon, Sir. Could I see the pirates you caught?" The memory of seeing Willy with the stranger filled me with foreboding.

The Major pointed at the deck of the *Fort Pinnace*. "There they be, Captain Taylor. My brother is off chasing several other pirates in hiding on the Main. These seven were taken at the Shoals."

The Major boarded his vessel *The Trial* which had joined the flotilla and as he sailed by I pulled out my spyglass for a better look at the men in chains. Thank God my son wasn't among them—nor the stranger. I should have been satisfied, but somehow I couldn't shake the feeling that for better or worse, Willy was gone.

Home at last, I rushed to Thankful. My run-in with the pirate had me looking distractedly into corners.

"Are you all right?"

She smiled. "In truth I was so weary I wouldn't have waked if a ship of buccaneers had sailed straight through my chamber."

When she said this, despite my best intentions, I started to rattle on about the pirates who invaded the Shoals—but the opiate took hold before I could tell much of the bum-gut escapade, and she drifted to sleep.

Gazing on my daughter, I thought how in an instant one's life can undergo such a dire change nothing is ever the same. Here was Thankful grown into a woman overnight. And there was Willy asserting his independence and gallivanting about God knows where. For the past two years we'd lived in such harmony that in my ignorant bliss I thought nothing could tear us asunder. I expected us to grow like coral affixed to one another—and in truth we were delicate as coral, breaking away at the least provocation.

Thankful turned the heads of every hobby-horse on the Shoals,

and though I didn't like the thought, I knew she'd soon start a family of her own. And despite Willy's brave desire to fish, I could see how he craved adventure, alas, was over his head in it.

My daughter waked the following afternoon with color in her cheeks. Over a bowl of warm milk and griddlecakes lumpy with my culinary ignorance, I gave in to her pestering and told her about Willy and the stranger.

"Oh Fa, what can we do?"

"I'll sail to Boston and speak with Judge Sewall—if he has time to see me."

A look of determination flushed her cheeks. "Merciful Heaven. You don't propose leaving me here wondering what's happened to Willy?"

I knew I couldn't leave her behind with pirates giving chase and promised to take her with me. Just as I sat down to write the Judge, a courier arrived with an Express from Sewall himself, asking if I could deliver one of the accused pirates from the Salem gaol to Stone Fort in Boston.

Thomas Taylor
Appledore Island, The Shoals

Dear Thom,
Governor Dudley presses us to proceed with the pirate hear-
ings. Commander Quelch of the Charles pleads his innocence,
claiming that when he took the Portuguese vessel and her treas-
ure and fled Brazil, he had no inkle of the new-made treaty
betwixt her Majesty of Britain and the King of Portugal. Jack
Quelch consistently asks for Council and it is thought Mister
Meinzes will be appointed. My evidence has been recorded by
John Valentine for the Admiralty Court and I am writing up
the Marblehead escape and subsequent capture of several pirates
at a lone-house near Salem for the Boston Almanac. My brother,
Major Sewall, informs me you witnessed the Shoals seizure and

I look forward to an exchange which I will not entrust to this hasty Express. The prisoner must be relayed to the gaol no later than Thursday next. Oh, by-the-by, you are expected at our town dwelling, for I fear every room in Boston will be occupied for the pirate hangings.

Godspeed,
Yrs, Samuel Sewall

Willy had sailed over the horizon in the *Providence* and I was forced to launch my new brigantine. No sooner did I announce my departure at Thursday God'sip than I was saddled with a score of passengers. One of them was the mother of John Templeton. Her son had been hoodwinked by pirates to keep a look-out on the *Larrimore Galley* while they ditched their gold. Will Whiting also had been deceived, and his kinfolk clamored to board the *Thankful* on her maiden voyage.

As we sailed out of Go's port I thought back on Captain Phips and his crowded Sheepscot ship crowded with fleeing villager, the difference being that he saved his people from enemy Indians, whereas I was transporting Shoalers to a hangman's holiday. A few sailed with mournful countenance for the condemned—Thankful and I numbering among them for reasons we dared not disclose.

At Salem a guard delivered the prisoner Sewall had mentioned to my ship. No sooner was he hauled aboard than the sorry man was hounded by a mob.

"Where did ye hide yer treasure?" a jolly fisherman prodded.

"Aye, ye might as well spill the beans fer ye'll soon be blithe-meat fer the vultures."

An ancient Shoaler I knew from bygone days hobbled over and splashed rum at the poor fellow's mouth. "There, that'll loosen yer tongue."

They pestered him so, I took mercy and closeted him in my cabin.

"Thank ye, Sir. I be John Lambert, a ship-wright from Salem,"

the prisoner told me with trembling lips. "My fa and his fa afore them were honest fisherfolk. I be innocent, but none will listen. Ye see, I fell ill in the gun room of the *Charles* and when I rallied, the vessel already sped past Halfway Rock at Marblehead. Captain Plowman was sicker 'an a dog, too. I was on my way to his cabin when Jack Quelch grabbed me and told me Daniel Plowman had plowed his-self a grave and he and Scudamore had dumped him in the deep. Fearing mutiny, I begged to be let off. But he pointed his pistol to my head and threatened to blast my brains if I didn't sail South. Yew do believe me, Sir?"

The soft-spoken balding man looked as much a pirate as a mackerel.

"I got kids, Sir—six of 'em, and a wife in Salem what I love wi' all my heart. Will they condemn me for being at the wrong place at the wrong time? By God, they near strung up my daughter at the witch trial, and now they be after me. I swear I be innocent."

He broke into such sobs I ran out of the cabin for fear I'd loosen the man's shackles on the spot.

Sam Rhymes who had been with my fish trade for quite awhile, steered the ship, and several of his Shoals chums tended the yards in return for a seaside view of the hangman's gallows at Scarlet Wharf.

I discovered Thankful in the cook's galley stirring a pot of chowder. "My dear Scarlet."

"Oh Fa, don't call me that!" She gave me a doleful look. "For all we know Willy could soon be hanging from Scarlet Wharf."

I took the spoon from her and handed it back to my galley cook, Squinty Scruggs. "Get topside at once, Daughter, and that's an order. I intend to lodge you at Mister Sewall's and will not present my daughter to that distinguished Boston family all covered with splots and splats."

The breeze tossed her red ringlets and caught at the hem of her skirt as she hung over the rail watching the porpoises. Samuel Rhymes near fell off the poop deck for a better look at her.

"Reef in the sail, Sammy," I barked at the befuddled lad, "and your desires while you're at it."

The schooner to starboard was standing us a race to Pulling Point and I wagered a communal bowl of my daughter's chowder we'd beat them fair and square. As we neared Boston a hundred boats of all sizes crowded the coast, and I proudly overtook them in my new brig.

Leaving Thankful and my crew riding anchor at the South Battery below Fort Hill, I lugged the reluctant prisoner onto the wharf and shuffled him under the scrutinous eye of the Stone Fort Sentinel.

We were halfway to the gate when the Templeton woman hurled herself at my feet.

"Please Capt'n, take me wi' ye. I must see my son. Lord o' Mercy, please!"

John Lambert joined his soft-spoke tenor voice to her's. "I be innocent, God in Heaven, I be innocent!"

The Fort Sentinel thrust his pike across my face. "Why this confernal rumpus and what be yer business?"

"I have an Express from Mister Sewall to deliver this prisoner, John Lambert, from Salem to join the other alleged pirates."

"Indeed. Major Richard Sewall?"

He'd have lowered his pike had I not erred on the side of honesty. "No, Judge Samuel Sewall who is acting Chief Justice of the Superior Court."

The Fort Sentinel cast aside my arm and the proferred letter. "I'll take the rogue. Be she kin?"

The woman's anguished cries augmented. "My son! Please. Please!"

"Her son John is within. If you might permit her—."

The Sentinel's bushy brows poked through his barred helmet. "I've orders to let none into the gaol til the Boston Court sits on June 16. None, that is, but the Honorable Cotton Mather."

"Her so, John Templeton is only fourteen. Surely—." The Shoals woman crumpled in a weepy heap at my feet.

The Fort Sentinel shoved the prisoner so hard he toppled in his chains.

Lambert grabbed my coat tail. "Captain Taylor, don't let them take me. I be innocent!"

The armored guard kicked, pushed, and maneuvered his reluctant prisoner up the tote path to the gaol. With considerable effort I unclenched Goody Templeton's stronghold on my legs and rowed the poor soul back to the brig.

Although every wharf berth was taken vessels continued looming over the horizon from all points of the compass. I dropped anchor off Clark's Ship Yard and Sam Rhymes rowed Thankful and me ashore in the dory.

I clutched my daughter fast as we made our way to Judge Sewall's town house in the North End. Several folk gathered around a constable tacking a broadside on the wall of a fish warehouse and we stopped to read it.

"What do it say?" asked a woman carrying a basket of cackling hens on her head.

I cleared my throat dry from worry over Willy, Lambert, and the whole miserable affair.

"It says: 'Faithful warnings to prevent fearful judgements uttered in a brief discourse occasioned by a tragical spectacle—.'"

"In plain Anglish!" the woman complained.

My daughter stepped forward unruffled by the rabble.

"It advertises a publication sold by Timothy Greene in the North End on June 22, 1704, telling the last words of some of those under sentence of death for piracy."

Thankful judiciously paraphrased the broadside. It was one thing for girls to display their reading skill on a sampler and quite another to do it in public.

"By gory!" shouted a cooper, setting down his barrel and swiping his brow. "If that don't boil my blood. They 'aven't e'n tried 'em and a'ready they 'ave em swingin' from the gibbet. That Governor

Dudley be a connivin' lot. In it fer the treasure, I wager."

Before there was a full-blown row I whisked Thankful away.

Betty Sewall had been apprised we were coming and greeted us with her infectious smile. She was about to show me to an upper chamber when I waylaid her, explaining I'd a good many matters in town and had reserved my room at *The Blue Anchor*. I'd be most grateful, however, if she could lodge my daughter.

I hadn't bothered to inform Thankful of my plans and she cried out in hurt indignation.

Betty put a sisterly arm about her. "Don't fret, fair Thankful. We can do without Mister Taylor. Perhaps we'll go to my seamstress Mistress Levoir to fit you for a new dress." She turned to me. "Say, where's your son Willy? I would have thought he—."

Thankful plunked down on a dainty parlor chair, removed her bonnet, and looked up with a gaze few could ignore. "Ah, Mistress Sewall—."

"If we're to be friends you must call me Betty."

"Well then, Betty, could I trouble you overmuch for refreshment? It's so terribly hot and I'm unaccustomed to Boston and all the commotion."

Glad for Thankful's quick thinking, I excused myself and hastened away. I would trust no one with the secret of Willy— none, that is, except Samuel Sewall.

36

*O*ver the boisterous crowd in the Town Square, regimental pikes gleamed and glinted in the sun. Two pikes criss-crossed at the stair to the upper Court. I waved Sewall's Express, but it might as well have been a snotty muckinder for all the attention the sentinels gave it. All I managed to wrench from the stentorious pair is that Jack Quelch was testifying

Thwarted in my mission to locate Willy, I bought a sweetmeat off a stall, crammed it into my mouth, and myself into the crowd.

After nearly an hour the pike barricade lifted for Major Sewall's regress, and in an instant I was in his face with the Express from his brother. He read it on the spot and arranged a post prandial meeting. A hubbub spread through the rabble as he elbowed through.

"Here be Jack Quelch," a wiseacre cried, tossing a dummy in a noose from an upper window. When a piece of straw stuffing hit me me in the face I had a mind to decamp. Had the Major asked me to wait because of Willy? The hanging mob churned my stomach with such worry that when the Major finally did show up I near tripped him in my anxiety.

He waved off the sentinels' pikes, hurried me up the stairs, and abandoned me in the foyer to the Admiralty Court. Left in the lurch, I stuck my head out the gabled casement window.

"What news of Jack Quelch?" a lad yelled from the Square.

A regimental soldier jabbed me so hard in the backside with his pike that I nearly fell into the crowd.

The soldier made a show of straightening his shoulder braid. "Be you Thomas Taylor?"

Queasy with the thought of finding Willy inside the chamber, I was thinking of making a dash for it when the soldier poked me a second time. "Get along, then," he prodded. "Nobody keeps Governor Dudley waiting. They be ready to pass sentence on the scoundrels."

I walked dignified as I could into the large room I'd navigated so long ago when Bradford was Governor. Since then, the Boston chamber had been white washed and aggrandized with a handsome chandelier and polished cherrywood rail.

As soon as I entered I was summoned before Governor Dudley wearing a monstrous black curled wig. I glanced discreetly to either side at the brocade waistcoats, big wigs, voluminous robes, and eyes—all of them trained on me.

Major Richard Sewall wasn't the friendliest man on earth and his slight nod did little to shore up my courage. My impression of Dudley was of a lackluster fish that better be attended—or it would haunt you later. He fixed me with a pewter glare. Lieutenant Governor Povey sat to his right with no apparent sign that he'd spent the good portion of a day in my presence tallying Captain Kidd's treasure.

After interminable mumbling and consulting with the Governor, Povey waved for me to sit down.

I pulled up my breeches and sat embroiled in thought. It took a cough and the palm of a hand on my shoulder for me to realize I wasn't alone on the front bench. Samuel Sewall slid over so as not to call attention to his effort.

"What a grave countenance, Thomas," he observed.

I let out a large sigh. "This is a serious affair, Mister Sewall. Innocent Shoalers could be condemned to hang."

He lowered his voice to a whisper. "The Admiralty has asked for arraignment on nine Articles of Piracy and they've proceeded with utmost caution, Thomas. Though to my mind Mister Dudley is over-zealous. When I refused to testify against the rogues and then wear my judges robe to condemn them, he had one of his fits. Fortunately, Mister Povey took my place. Now, tell me, has my wife set you up?"

"Mister Sewall, I—."

Before I could confess the real nature of my presence in the courtroom, Registrar John Valentine paraded in bearing The Silver Oar. Banging it three times on the floor, he pronounced the Court in session.

The Provost Prison Marshall growled, "Matthew Pymer, John Clifford and James Parrot, stand forward."

Three men who'd squashed behind Dudley's high-backed chair appeared and Povey presiding as court defense took over.

"Having been accused and pleaded guilty to robbery, murder, and other Articles of Piracy drawn against Jack Quelch, as his accomplices you are herewith sworn witnesses for Her Majesty, Queen Anne of England."

I swallowed hard. How could condemned pirates bear witness to their own vile deeds? I was about to complain to Sewall when he beat me to it. "By God, were I presiding they would not be witnesses. Those three are cunning as the day is long. Their testimony is good as useless."

The Prison Marshall consulted with Registrar Valentine and barked, "Caesar-Pompey, Charles, and Mingo stand forward."

A chained trio of Negroes that had been with Quelch shuffled and clanked to the rail.

Dudley and Povey mumbled and consulted so long it set the frightened blackamoors to eerie moanings.

"Silence!" the Provost-Marshall ordered, agitating his pike.

Governor Dudley addressed the Admiralty in a high nasal twang. "I would point out that these prisoners are of a different complexion. It's well known that the first and foremost pirates in the world were of their color."

A short gentleman in tight gold breeches and a crimson waist-coat rushed to the rail.

"Mister Meinzes?" Valentine called, fastidiously routing papers every which way.

The advocate for the defense leaned over the rail.

"Your Honors, we have here Mister Hobbey's slaves. These Negroes were convinced by a blade held at their throats to board the *Charles* for Brazil. You make them out to be crafty as Shylock when their duties simply were to cook and sound the trumpet. Hardly an offense for hanging."

"Unless you et their food," someone jibed.

Povey motioned for the Provost Marshall to return the Negroes. Making no effort to hide his rage, Meinzes stalked out.

Major Sewall's order to bring in the crew of the *Larrimore Galley* gave us a chance to loosen our collars in the airless upper room. June days were long and it was a good thing. Because, when asked to tell his part in the capture of the pirates at the Shoals, the Major launched into a waste-book of detail.

Judge Sewall leaned over to whisper in my ear. "My brother has many fine qualities—brevity isn't one of them."

The Major's long-winded account came to a sudden halt at the mention of my name.

Lieutenant Governor Povey waved the Major to his seat and called me forward. Not knowing what to expect, I waited in the lee of the accused men who were looking decidedly worse since I'd last seen them.

"Do you recognize these sailors?" Povey asked.

"Yes, Sir. They're the ones I saw from my pinkie on June tenth off Appledore Island. That long fellow is the Swede, Erasmus Peterson, who stowed on my boat and jumped me. I still have rope marks to prove it." I shoved up my sleeves and displayed my black and blue arms, which caused quite a hubbub. "Peterson threw me into the hold and when he saw the *Fort Pinnace* closing in he hid his gold dust in my purse. Fortunately, Major Sewall saw through his deceit."

The red-faced Swede raised his tied fists. "I break that man's scruffy neck. He lie damn goot. Queen mudder of Angland knows I be no pirate! Let me at that bastard. I punch him goot!"

The Fort Marshall silenced the Swede with a cuff on the jaw.

"And the others?" Dudley asked me with frigid reserve.

"I would not have them on my conscience, Your Honor."

"Speak plainly, Mister Taylor," a Judge I knew as Nathaniel Byfield advised.

I'd spoken plainly as I could, but it was obvious the Admiralty wanted more than I had to give them.

"I saw these men on the *Larrimore Galley*, Your Honor, after they'd already been taken into custo—."

The Governor gave Valentine a high sign to intervene. "You may sit down, Mister Taylor. We have recorded your testimony."

Reeling with the travesty of the trial, I took my seat and prayed to God Willy was far from Boston.

Major Richard Sewall returned to the rail. Each time he mentioned one of the King brothers they bickered and blamed each other. Francis, the eldest, was so spat upon by Charles and John that the bailiff had to fetch a muckinder and mop his face so he could see.

They reminded me of gulls I'd once seen feeding on their own progeny, and the pangs I'd been feeling ebbed to a dull ache. I'd had quite a revelation about how Admiralty law reeked of private interest and nepotism. No wonder rumors were circulating that Joseph Dudley and his son Paul had their hands in the pirate pot.

At about twenty hours, Judge Sewall and I escaped to *The Blue Anchor* and prevailed upon George Monck to a tuckanuck of turkey drumsticks which, for old times sake, we ate on the quay.

Oil lanterns swinging from the masts of the ships twinkled like stars in the darkling harbor. I'd waited all day to tell Samuel Sewall about Willy's flight, but now that we were alone I had a hard time coming clean.

"We've been friends too long not to be forthright," he said, perching on a wharf piling.

We'd drunk a good deal of limey beer and were punch-drunk with our freedom from the stifling Court. Safe, at last in his confidence, I unburdened. "It's about Willy."

He laughed. "When is it not?"

We'd drunk a good deal of limey beer and were punch-drunk with our freedom from the stifling Court.

"My son has disappeared."

Sewell threw the remains of his drumstick off the pier. With a loud squawk, a patient gull that had been strutting the rotten planks plunged in and retrieved the greasy flotsam.

"Your son's full of spit and vinegar, Thomas. He's off seeing the wide world and you should thank God Almighty."

"But—."

"Now take my Sammy. If he makes it through the summer, we'll consider it a blessing."

I was so startled by this news I couldn't speak.

"Sammy never was strong, Thomas. Each day has been a gift to the poor boy. But Willy's a fine strapping lad. Can't you let him go?"

I pitched my drumstick into the garbage awash on the tide. "He disappeared in my ship the *Providence* on the very same morning pirates landed at the Shoals. I can let him go. But I'm not sure the Royal Admiralty would, especially after today."

A brawl of revelers sang at the top of their lungs.

> *Ye pirates who 'gainst God's Law did fight*
> *have all been taken, which is all right.*

Despite the oppressive heat a shiver shot down my spine at the thought of Willy hanging from a noose.

Sewall engulfed my shoulder in his commodious arm. "What can I do for you, Thomas?"

In all the years I'd known him I'd tried not to impose on Sewall's reputation and accommodating nature. Now, in desperation I told him I couldn't rest until I'd seen whether Willy was with the newly captured pirates in Stone Fort Gaol.

Sewall stood and dusted off his breeches. "I was there when they brought them in and Willy wasn't among them. A few have been caught since then, and eighteen managed to get away with that sly devil, Anthony Holding."

I loosed my collar. "I'd be most grateful if you or your brother would let me see them for myself. I hardly recognized Willy when he returned from London. For all I know this man Holding might have given Willy the slip and left him to swing!"

A rowdy soloist nearly tripped over us.

> *Some of 'em were old and others young*
> *And on the flats of Bostown they were hung.*

Drowned out by their merry-making, Sewall and I retreated down the wharf where, unnerved by the sea shanty, I brooded in silence.

Sewall stopped in the lamplight. "Tell you what, Thom. Cotton Mather has declared the condemned must be catechized. To my way of thinking, his preaching atonement suits his own finical character more than theirs. But it does give me an idea. I seem to remember you once catechized some Shoals lads. What say I take you with me to Stone Fort Prison tomorrow morning. I'll put you to work and you can look for Willy in the bargain.

37

*T*he clatter of wheels on the paving stones outside *The Blue Anchor* brought me to a rude awakening. Having slept in my clothes, I sloshed my face, pissed in the pot, and dashed into the driving rain. In the dark interior of the hackney I greeted Judge Sewall dressed in his train-band uniform. We dozed and nodded as the horses slipped on the cobbles and careened onto a dubious old wharf road near the South Battery.

Although the gaol was new, the stench of the place was ancient. Shackled men curled like bugbears in the filth, moaning as we passed through to a locked cell.

Reverend Mather sat in the fumes of a sooty oil lamp reading Psalter to a torpid man in soiled officer's attire. Mather sighed and waved a hand at the prisoner. "I present you Jack Quelch, a stubborn sinner. He knows his catechism backward and forward but will not repent."

"Why should I? I did not know about her Majesty's treaty with the Portuguese when I took that vessel and am innocent." The officer's tone was strangely dispassionate without a smidgen of malice toward the zealous preacher.

His quiet demeanor came as a surprise, since scuttlebutt had it that the ring-leaders were cutthroats.

The Fort Sergeant-at-arms saluted Judge Sewall, whom I suspected wore military duds so that he could call the shots in our little subterfuge.

"This gaol funks like a reasty sty," Sewall told the Sergeant. "Have the guards see to it on the double or I'll have the provost marshall after you."

With considerable effort Jack Quelch got to his feet.

Annoyed by the interruption, Mather snapped shut his *Book of Common Prayer*.

Quelch held his stomach in a most peculiar manner as he addressed Sewall. "The men have dysentery. Captain Plowman, as you know, died of it. William Whiting couldn't appear at Admiralty Court because he's so enfeebled. But whatever I say falls on deaf ears."

A poke of sun shot through an upper oriel window and lighted a patch of straw.

"Rouse the prisoners at once and march them into the yard," Judge Sewall ordered the Sergeant.

"We cannot catechize them outdoors!" Mather objected with obvious animosity at Sewall's pulling rank.

"It served the Good Shepherd well enough," Sewall rebuked, and went off to help the sergeant.

When the last man had filed out and Willy wasn't among them, I whooped for joy.

Reverend Mather raised an eyebrow. "What are Mister Taylor's qualifications for catechizing these men?" he asked, waylaying the adversary who had the gall to publicly confess repentance for the Salem witch hangings.

Sewall broke off his instructions to the guard. "Thom was Latin Master at the prestigious Appledore Academy and assisted Minister Belcher at the Isles of Shoals."

"The Shoals!" Mather scoffed. "Well, Mister Taylor, you'll be right at home among these sinners."

Had I not been delirious with Willy's escape I'd have hauled off and torqued the cheeky round-head in the jaw.

Jumping puddles, Sewall came up and shook my hand. "You're out of the wood, Thomas, and I'm glad for you. But now I must get over to the Admiralty Court. Fifteen of these men are to be tried this afternoon and I have to consult with Lieutenant-Governor Povey. You'd be doing me a favor if you could come tomorrow to catechize the Shoalers."

While we were in the yard I'd found the boy Johnny whose mother was on my ship, and as Sewall and I rode back in the hackney I put in a word for him. "He's just a lad, Samuel, and terribly afraid. Isn't there anything we can do?"

I'd never called him by his given name before, but somehow the urgency of my petition seemed like a ripe time to begin.

"Don't worry, Thom," he reassured me as he leapt from the hack in his hurry to court. "The Admiralty will commute the sentences of most of the men except the principals."

The next few days we made our rounds of the prisoners, catechizing and hearing their confessions. Seven had been isolated, including the eldest King brother and Erasmus Peterson who had stowed aboard my ship. It was good riddance as far as I was concerned. In chains or out they meant nothing but trouble.

Tuesday, June 20th, Sewall brought the joyous news that William Whiting and his bonded fourteen-year-old apprentice, Johnny Templeton, had been acquitted and were free to leave. When they still hadn't been released by day's end I went to the Stone Fort Sergeant-at-arms.

Like everything connected with Her Majesty's Service, he wanted imbursement. "They owe the Admiralty prison fees," he complained.

"They were brought here with the shirts on their backs. How do you expect them to pay?"

He remained moot.

"Look here. I'll pay for Whiting and Templeton."

"Go see the burser then," he ordered, buckling his sword and heading for the door.

When I blocked his exit, the Fort Sergeant sat back down to consult a ledger. "That'll be three pounds all tolled."

I boiled over. "Now listen to me, Sergeant, I've heard you've extorted sums from several of the prisoners so they could walk in the yard. If you dare ask more than a pound a piece for keeping Mister Whiting and his apprentice in this miserable hell-hole, I swear Governor Dudley will hear of it."

He smirked. "Governor Dudley, that's a good one."

Realizing the blackmail I spoke of was endemic, I counted out three pounds and hurried to release the lad and his ailing master. Sewall and I carried the sickly Whiting on a pallet to the Fort long-boat that would ferry him to my ship in Boston Harbor.

John Templeton shook my hand in gratitude. "If you want to thank me, see that you and your mother look after Mister Whiting." I boxed his ears playful-like.

"Ma! Be she aboard?"

"Aye Johnny, I transported her from the Shoals," I told him, glad for the outcome.

As we climbed back up the ramp to the Fort, Judge Sewall stopped and waved at the exuberant kid in the longboat. "I'm aware you paid their fees, Thom. And when I'm reimbursed I'll make certain—."

"I only hope someone does the same for Willy."

Grabbing my shoulders, he stared straight in my eyes. "The difference between that kid and Willy is that Willy's full-grown and responsible for his actions."

"Thankful told me as much," I admitted.

"Then she's a bright girl and you should listen to her. You can't protect Willy from his destiny any more than I can keep my Sammy alive."

Ordinarily, I'd have welcomed his advice, but I didn't like what he was saying and listened in moody silence.

Two days later our ministrations took on nightmare aspects when seven of the fifteen men were sentenced to death. Several times I thought of quitting. After all, I owed them nothing and they paid me nothing. Yet, I prevailed.

"Say the 'Our Father,' Goodman Lambert." I struggled to keep my voice from wavering. "It'll ease your tribulations."

"'Our Father who art—.' But I be innocent! I transgressed nobody. I got six kids who count on daily bread and a wife. She—."

He broke into such sobs I went out into the sun and sank on my knees to pray for strength.

Sewall came up and laid a comforting hand on my shoulder.

"Dare I impinge on your good judgment again, Samuel?"

"Impinge away," he said.

"John Lambert has never let up that he is innocent."

"True, Thomas. All but he and Quelch pleaded guilty and threw themselves at the mercy of the court."

"But there's been no evidence presented against Lambert," I argued.

"He is recalcitrant, Thomas. And Mssrs. Dudley and Mather want these men on their knees."

"It's on my conscience and—well—I heard Reverend Mather has the power to free one of the condemned at the last minute. I had in mind to ask him to let Goodman Lambert go."

Sewall strolled me out of earshot. "You'd just be tightening the noose around Lambert's neck. Unfortunately, Thom, you pay the price of being my friend. As you may have observed, Mister Mather and I have less tolerance for one another. But don't burn your bridges yet. While you've been talking I've hatched a scheme that might bring Mather around. Go ask him to let off Lambert while I engage a few soldiers to help us."

With the execution less than twenty-four hours away, more soldiers milled into the yard and I could hear the drill band shouting formation commands on Fort Hill.

Francis King blubbered and groveled before Mather in the

grassy yard. "Forgive my sins, Divine Lord. Lead me from mine iniquities," he parroted.

Dressed in a shimmery black robe and new platinum wig parted into billows, Mather looked on with a satisfied smile—until I came on the scene. "Mister Taylor, these poor souls have little time in this world. Would you snatch it from their repentant hearts?"

"I've catechized John Lambert and he consistently claims his innocence."

"Which only means he's a very good liar, Mister Taylor."

"Couldn't you stay his execution, Reverend?"

The man's face rouged as though he were being strangled, and I must say I enjoyed this effect.

"Reprieve is my decision and mine alone! How dare you interfere?"

"Isn't it a matter of Divine Intervention, Reverend Mather?" I inveighed, intent on saving the poor ship-wright. Not bothering to answer, he turned back to his blubbering charge.

Sad with the vagaries of men, I walked a few paces away and slouched in the cover of a bush.

The soldiers I'd seen Sewall talking to strode by and halted near the famous minister.

One of them spoke uncommonly loud.

"Seven poor wretches. I wonder which man they'll let go."

"Quelch and Scudamore be good as dead," another belted, looking straight in Mather's direction.

"They ain't got a snitch of evidence on poor Lambert. I'll stand ye a pint of ale Reverend Mather'll grant him the reprieve. And if he don't, by God A'mighty, he ain't got an ounce of justice in him."

The final day of June 1704 I rowed out to the *Thankful*. Sammy Rhymes offered a welcoming hand. He hoped I didn't mind but he'd given the ailing William Whiting my bed in the captain's cabin. The Shoals lad, Johnny, and his ma were looking after him. I told Sammy I couldn't have done better myself and momentarily was cheered by his prideful smile.

Preferring to gaze on the pirate spectacle from the tideline of the Charles River, Samuel Sewall came too. The crew saluted as the Massachusetts Judge climbed aboard, though they'd never been regimental in their lives. Sewall produced a fine basket of straw-berries, passing it among them, and soon they spoke freely with the celebrated man in his brass and braid. I myself wore a newly pur-chased coat of light linen with wide lapels and ample girth for the cookery accumulation at my waist.

The ratatat of the drum corps marked the turn of the military escort from Town Square down to the wharves. A cheer swept over the water from spectators on ships as the silver oar, carried by the Stone Fort Provost Marshall flashed in the sun. Behind him a pro-cession of two score musketeers, ten to a rank, boxed in the seven condemned men.

Contrary to my objective of keeping our distance, we sat nearly on top of the gallows built on a smirch of tidal rocks called Nix's Mate. Throngs of by-standers streamed onto every vantage point, along the wharves from Hudson Point to Broughton's Warehouse, straining and yelling at the sight of the scaffold on the kelpy reef.

Reverend Mather accompanied the prisoners to the waiting longboat and stood on the bow where he could deliver excerpts of last Sunday's sermon to the crowd. This was followed by a prayer which, despite his loud declamatory, was drowned out by the excited hubbub emanating from every boat, wharf, and spit of land.

I took advantage of the interlude to stir my gams and scold Johnny Templeton, who had crept on deck to watch the wretchéd ordeal.

"Aren't you ashamed, lad? There but for the grace of God go you! Now go hide your face in your ma's bosom and deliver thanks to the Almighty on your knees."

Meek as a mouse, he disappeared.

Entry the Last
Appledore Accounts, June 10 — July 4, 1704

My new ship proved sea worthy on her maiden voyage to Boston. I've recently appointed Sammy Rhymes as her Captain and offered him a percentage of trade with a promise of partner-ship if—

T hankful and I sat in the shade of our favorite tree. I looked up as she chatted and wove daisies into a chain.

"What I liked best, Fa, was the dinner at Mister Sewall's. Have you ever seen dishes so blue? And I wore my new dress. And— Oh, I was relieved about Willy!"

She kissed me on the cheek. "But we must forget him now," she said in a small grown-up voice.

I put aside the ledger which was in a frightful muddle from having been abandoned so long. "I agree, Thankful."

I let her pull me to my feet and lead me along the path to Broad Cove on the windward side of the Island. I hadn't told her the extent of the impression she made at the dinner Mistress Sewall gave. My week at the prison had seemed like a year, and seeing my daughter so transformed at that distinguished table completely blotted out my woes and worries.

Still, it was here that I saw her true spirit. The moment we arrived she'd changed to a simple lawn frock and the skirt flowed gracefully as she hopped over a clump of poison ivy in the path.

She knelt to pick some huckleberries, loosing her bonnet to let her reckless red curls tumble down her back.

The cove glistened so white I shaded my eyes.

She offered me a handful of berries.

I smiled at her gift and savored them one by one, thinking surely God smiled down on me. "This is where I washed ashore. I was not even ten years old."

"Yes, Fa, you told me."

I lay back, thinking of Origen's strong arms about me and Pru at the door of Babb's Ordinary. I tickled Thankful's bare arm with a blade of grass. "So, you liked Boston?"

It was a sounding. I wanted her to be happy. If she coveted a brick house and Delft china, they were no longer beyond my means.

She picked up a clam shell and let it drop into a tidal pool. "Oh, Fa, don't think me ungrateful, but I could scarcely wait to sail back to the Shoals."

ACKNOWLEDGMENTS

My appreciation to persons past and present who helped locate research material: Elaine Peverly, Kittery History & Naval Museum, ME; Bill Teschiek, Assistant Director, Hampton Public Library, NH; Carolyn Eastman, Special Collections Librarian, Portsmouth Athenaeum, NH; Hope Neilson, Librarian, Rice Public Library, Kittery, ME; Ann Ames, Librarian, Rare Book Collection, Keene State College, NH; Dennis Brown, Manager, Pemaquid Maine State Park; Essex Institute and Peabody Museum, Salem, MA. I am grateful to the curators for a special tour of the Damm Garrison (1675) at the Dover NH Woodman Institute. Special thanks to archeologists Neill De Paoli for his observations of pre-colonial Pemaquid communities, and Faith Harrington for her field work at the Isles of Shoals. Their research and articles have greatly enhanced the understanding of the provincial colonies of Maine and New Hampshire. Thanks to my dear friend Zoe Montana for the early map of New England, to Fleur Weymouth for the rare illustrated Boston booklet, *Indian Events of New England* (State Street Trust, Boston, 1941), and to Judy and Arthur Ginsburg for the Shoals photo and safe harbor. Heartfelt thanks to writer Steve Sherman for wielding his mighty pen on my mutinous prose. I treasure his partner-ship.

RESOURCES

The bibliography for this book could be a book in itself. The following acknowledgments are of primary source material either excerpted and/or quoted from original books and documents: *Fisherman Calling Indenture Paper*, Peabody Museum, Salem, Massachusetts (Chapter 1); Sir Philip Sidney, *The Witts Recreations* from *ARCADIA* (p 25 Chapter 1); Edited account of Dr. Greenland from the *Massachusetts Maritime Records* Volume 1 p 282 (pp 52-53 Chapter 4); Anonymous, seventeenth century verse from *ANTHOLOGY OF NEW ENGLAND POETRY*, Untermeyer, ed. Random House, NY (p 56 Chapter 4); Pastiche of a stanza from *The Day of Doom* by Michael Wigglesworth, 1662, (p 69 Chapter 5); Estate Inventory

Babb Family Records, Portsmouth Athenaeum, NH (p 79 Chapter 6); Legend of Wm Mase in Celia Thaxter, *AMONG THE ISLES OF SHOALS* 1873 (p 87 Chapter 7); Anonymous, Drinking Song, 15th century, *EARLY AMERICAN POETS* (p 95 Chapter 7); John Donne, (d 1631) *Go And Catch A Falling Star, THE VIKING BOOK OF POETRY OF THE ENGLISH SPEAKING WORLD*, NY (p 97 Chapter 7); Richard Walderne warrant: *Dover Town Records* Portsmouth Athenaeum (p 100 Chapter 8); John Heywood (d.1580) *Be Merry Friends* from *BARTLETT'S QUOTATIONS* (p 125 Chapter 10); Anonymous, Maypole Song (p 137 Chapter 11); Sayings by Cobbler of Aggawan, *THE WIT & HUMOR OF COLONIAL DAYS* by Carl Holliday, Corner House Books, Williamstown, MA 1975 (p 153 Chapter 13); Information about Ordinances, Arms, Train Bands from *Laws Concerning Colonial Militia*, London 1709, and Leo Bonfanti, *NEW ENGLAND INDIANS* Volume V, *Indian War 1675-1677*, New England Historical Series, Wakefield, MA 1976 (pp 176-177 Chapter 15); Josselyn: *New England Rarities* published in London by John Josselyn, (reprint in Bonfanti); (pp 182-183 Chapter 15); John Bunyan, *PILGRIM'S PROGRESS* from *Apology*, 1678 (p 183 Chapter 15); Hopehood: "Medicine Song" adapted from versions transcribed by Mary Austin from *THE AMERICAN RHYTHM*, Houghton Mifflin, 1930 (p 203-205 Chapter 15); Town Meeting: *Dover Town Records 1675-1677*, Portsmouth Athenaeum (p 214-215 Chapter 17);*ANNE HUTCHINSON: AN AMERICAN JEZEBEL* (pp 219-220 Chapter 17); Indian Treaty: Leo Bonfanti, *NEW ENGLAND INDIANS* (See above, pp 231-232 Chapter 18); George Herbert (d 1633) *The Collar* from Richard Aldington, Ed., *THE VIKING BOOK OF POETRY OF THE ENGLISH SPEAKING WORLD* (pp 274-275, Chapter 20); French wit: paraphrased quote from Montaigne's *Essays, Book III 1595* (p 333 Chapter 27); Shoals letters: Massachusetts Archives *V 37* and J. S. Jenness *ISLES OF SHOALS* Houghton Mifflin, 1884 (pp 358-359, Chapter 30); *THE POEMS OF EDWARD TAYLOR, DIARY OF EDWARD TAYLOR* Francis Murphy, Ed., Connecticut Valley Historical Museum (pp 370-372. Chapter 30); *Boston Almanac 1692*, Massachusetts Archives (p 370 Chapter 30); Judge Samuel Sewall's Confession: *SALEM IN THE SEVENTEENTH*

CENTURY (p 388 Chapter 32); Barbadoes Menu: *No Peace: English in the Caribbean 1624-1690* Bridenbaugh, Oxford, 1972 (pp 406-407 Chapter 34); "Execution Song:" Anonymous, seventeenth century verse from *EARLY AMERICAN POETS* (OP) (p 431 Chapter 36); Declarations by Captain Kidd, Jack Quelch, John Lambert, and Cotton Mather: Dow & Edmonds *PIRATES OF THE NEW ENGLAND COAST 1630-1730*, Marine Research Society, Salem, 1923; Also: *The Boston Newsletter* and *THE DIARIES OF SAMUEL SEWALL (1704)*, Ayer Research Library of Colonial Americana, Reprint, 1972 (p 439 Chapter 37).

Glossary

(Spellings change from century to century)

aftmast	behind the mast	*bottoming*	deep line fishing
aide de camp	assistant officer	*boucaniers*	charcoal fire builders
ancient	elder	*brace*	a pair of pistols
Apostle spoon	Christening spoon	*brank*	iron headpiece
arrack	distilled rum	*Brantle*	a dance
ash cake	baked on the hearth	*brig*	square-rigged ship,
assize	court hearing		a jail
auk	diving NE seabird	*brigands*	lawless bandits
Aunt Sally	privy	*broadside*	guns on one side,
bale seal	official wax stamp		a news poster
ballycater	ice on hull of a ship	*bullet glass*	thick blown glass
bandolier	colorful military sash	*bursar*	treasurer
bangue	hemp, marijuana	*buss*	kiss
banns	official postings	*butt stock*	rear-breech of gun
bawdry	ribald, innuendo	*cached*	hidden
beaker	drinking glass	*cachier the-*	torture device, ride
Bezoar	medication	*strapadoe*	or hang from rope
bight	a small cove	*calumet*	ritual Indian pipe
billet	soldiers' lodging	*cannonade*	salvo of cannons
binnacle	contains compass	*cans*	cylindrical cups
blackstrap	dark molasses	*capuchine*	monk-like cloak
blade	knife	*careened*	ship on its side, in
blighter	good-for-nothing		dry dock for repair
blithemeat	festive food	*carrack*	square rig 3-master
blunderbuss	muzzle, firearm	*chamber*	room, hall
boatswain	equipment officer	*chart*	map
boomer	red squirrel	*chipmunk*	rodent, ambush
boon	favor	*clinchpoop*	one who holds onto
Boston Kate	common for a girl		the poop deck

clout	cloth
codpiece	male breech-flap
Congo	African Negro
cooperage	barrel making
corn cake	Indian bread
cote	cottage
counting house	bank
crane berries	native cranberries
creuset	beaker dish
cross piece	navigational bow-shaped instrument
crow's nest	platform on top mast
cruisey	oil lamp
cuckold	has adulterous wife
cuddy	boat pantry, galley
culverin	murdering cannons
cunctatious	one who delays
Day of Intervention	NE fast day
death tokens	small pox
Diacodium	opiate of poppy
dike	stone waterway
disorderly marriage	unlawful
Divine Intervention	God given
dry sack	Fr. sec/dry, Spanish sherry
duffel	coarse cloth
dugout	tree trunk canoe
dunfish	cured, air-dried fish
dunnage	stowed cargo
ell	measure of forearm
emporium	market/trade place
esker	glacial ledges
Express	speedy letter
faggots	bundles of twigs
fall band	neck collar
fathom	ocean sound line
flagon	globular bottle
flake	table for air-curing fish
flanart	fort lookout
Flanderkin	Flemish
flibustiers	swift ships
flip	hot beer and sweet liqueur
forecastle	raised bow-deck
free-booter	pirate
French pox	syphilis
Friend	Quaker
frigate	swift war ship
funk	state of slow burn
gaffer	grapple spear
galley	ship kitchen
galloon-edged	braid
gambrels	horse manure
gams	jambs, legs
gaol	jail
garrison	fortified dwelling
Godsip	gossip
great coat	overcoat
Great Migration	in 1640-41
green sward	grassy common
grimp	climb
groaning beer	birth-labor brew
gundelow	NE river barge
gunny	hemp sack
gunwhale	top edge of vessel
gurry	refuse fish bait
hackney	stable horse coach
hangman's holiday	execution day
hardship	toiling, misery
hasty pudding	Indian meal/water
hawser	mooring cable

hemp	cannabis, fibrous plant	*Marmalade-Madame*	prostitute
hermaphrodite	combo schooner-brig	*Maroon*	W Indies fugitive, dark slave,
hobnail boots	soled w. big-head nails		
hogshead	large cask		
hot shot	skill in musketry	*Maypole*	May Day dance pole
impost	impost tax, duty	*Micmacs*	Maine Indian tribe
indenture	apprentice contract	*midden*	clam shell piles
inglenook	chimney corner	*mint master*	in charge of coining
jackboots	riding boots	*mithidrate*	antidote, mustard
jack-knife	large pocket knife	*mizzen sail*	foresail
jacktar	young sailor	*mollycoddle*	mommy's boy
Jacob's ladder	long boarding ropes	*Monmouth*	cape
jerkin	wool vest	*muckinder*	handkerchief
jigging	handline for fishing	*mum*	keep quiet, secret
jolly boat	ship row boat	*muster*	roll call, take stock
junketing	partying	*muzzle-loader*	barrel-loading gun
keeping-room	waiting room	*nanny plum*	goat droppings
ketch	small vessel	*Narragansets*	R.I. Indian tribe, NE pace horses
kicky-wicky	"My old lady!"		
kill-devil	West Indies rum	*neat's foot oil*	oxfoot oil
killick	anchor stone	*nippers*	woolen mitts
lanyard	sailors' hold-ropes	*od's pittikins*	oath, God have pity
Lecture Day	Thursday meeting	*ogive*	arch
leech	barrel-made lye soap	*ordinary*	public house, tavern
lighter	flatboat for unloading	*outlyers*	out of towners,
lignum vitae	waterproof wood	*over a barrel*	punishment
linsey-woolsey	wool and flax	*oxbow*	river turn
long	tall	*Oyer & Terminer*	King's Court
longboat	ship shore row boat		
longhouse	communal native Indian dwelling	*palisade*	stockade fence
		pansy	effeminate male
lot	parcel of land	*papoose*	native babe
Lubberland	wilderness	*parbleu*	oath, "By God!"
luff	windward heading	*parchment*	writing paper
main	mainland	*parley*	discuss, confer
manse	large house	*partnership*	vessel co-owners

paten	leather shoe	*quarrel*	small window
pawpaw	New World game	*quiddits*	quibbles
pea shot	small scatter shot	*quintal*	measure of fish
peage	toll	*rambeggars*	sodomites
peltry	fur skins	*rampions*	pungent bulbs
Penacooks	NH Indian tribe	*ratline*	step-ropes on sails
Pequoket	NY-Conn. Indian tribe	*rattail*	sailor's hair braid
periwig	round full wig	*reasty*	rancid
pewter	tin-lead alloy	*receipts*	recipes
pickpack	piggy-back	*redoubt*	protected fort
piebald	two-colored		enclosure
pieces of eight	Spanish currency	*redskin*	settlers' name
pig	block of silver, metal		for native
pike	military spear, pole	*reefed*	reduce sail
Pilgrim	New World Puritan	*ropewalk*	bldg to make rope
pillory	public wooden stocks	*round head*	wig-wearing Puritan
pinkie	Atlantic fishing boat	*Sachem*	native clan chief
pinner	woman's hair pieces	*saker*	small ship cannon
piragua/pirogue	dugout canoe	*sallet*	salad greens
Piscataquas	Indian tribe	*samp*	hominy corn
planked	cooked, served on board	*sawyering*	lumbering
plantation	colony	*schooner*	swift NE vessel
plaster	cloth with medical herbs	*sconce*	fire screen,
Pokanoket	Indian tribe		run up a bill
pompions	pumpkins	*scuppenong*	wild grape wine
poop	ship stern	*sedan chair*	wheelless vehicle
popinjay	conceited, parrot figure	*seine*	fish net
poppet	witches' doll	*Selectman*	NE town officer
post	horse riding technique	*sennight*	seven nights
potage	soup	*settle*	high-backed bench
praying Indian	Christian native	*shallop*	small light boat
print off	have children, reproduce	*shanty, chanty*	Fr. chant, sing
privateer	merchants turned pirates	*shilly-shally*	indecisive
Provincial	northern New Englander	*shingle*	plank for serving
provost	military jail officer		fish and meat
pung	sleigh	*shittabed*	lazy oaf

shuckie-shoeing	do a dance	tet	teat-like witch mark
shuttlecock	feathered ball game	thole pin	fulcrum for boat oars
silvered glass	mirror	thornback	ancient woman
silver master	weighs silver/gold	tidings	news
silver oar	MA Court icon	tie and ride	horse livery service
skelete	skeleton	tiffany	silk hood
slawbank	wall bed	tote	road
sloop	one-masted vessel	trainband	drilling citizen
smaragd	emerald		soldiers
snaphaunce	flintlock musket	trencher	wood or bread platter
snit	snuff out a candle	trundle	low roll-away bed
Sokokis	ME Indian tribe	tucknuck	eat heartily, inn food
spar	ship mast, boom	turncoat	change coat, affiliation
squaw	native woman	vittles	(slang) victuals, food
stockade	palisade	wampum	native shell/ bead
stocks	public wooden		trade-necklace, early
	punishing frame		NE currency
stomacher	laced corset	wastebook	account book
stuff	cloth	wattle & daub	branch/mud huts
swale	lowland	weigh anchor	under weigh, to sail
swamp hog	beaver	wherry	row boat
tail	back of cart	whipstaff	rudder steering handle
tamarind	West Indies tree,	whittie-whattie	mutter, mumble
	fruit drink	wigam	native dwelling
tankard	one-handled mug	Yanqee	Dutch nickname for
tarpauling	tar-coated sail-canvas		New Englanders
tattle	chat, gossip	yards	ship ropes, lines
tender	shore boat, loan,	yeoman	New World settler,
	kindling		landowner

from Cotton Mather's
Magnalia Christi Americana, 1702
Courtesy of Sturbridge Village, MA

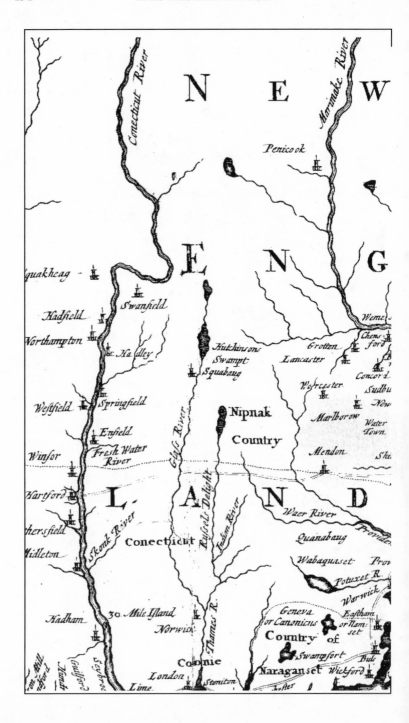

Map

455

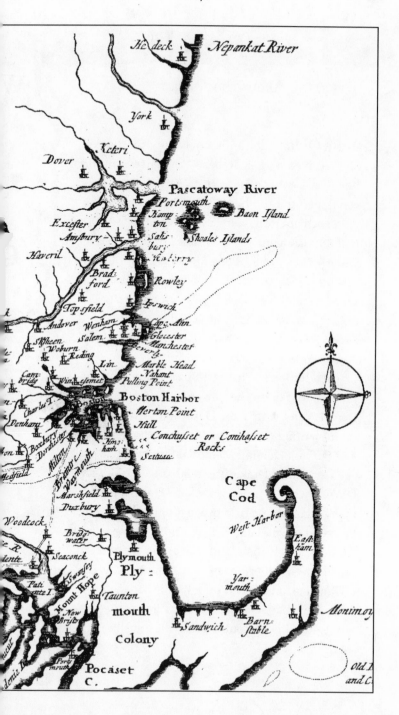

About the Author

Julia Older is the author of twenty-five books. She received a Mary Roberts Rinehart Grant for her first book *APPALACHIAN ODYSSEY*, a personal account of her 2000-mile walk on the Appalachian Trail. Her first novel *THE ISLAND QUEEN* was featured in *Paz Reading Group Choices*. Older's story translations *BLUES FOR A BLACK CAT* by French author Boris Vian have editions in the States and New Delhi, India. Her own stories, poetry and essays have appeared in *Best of Furious Fiction Online, The New Yorker, Entelechy International, Poets & Writers,* and other publications.

In addition to Pushcart Prize nominations in prose and poetry, her awards include a First Daniel Varoujan Prize, Hopwood Award, and recent writing grants from the Puffin Foundation and Barbara Deming Memorial Fund.

Her father Drake was related to the British Drakes whose famous son Sir Francis looted many a galleon on his voyage around the world. Before she was land-locked, Older crossed the Atlantic on British and Yugoslav freighters, sailed the Mediterranean from Piraeus, Greece, to Tangiers, and fished off a Pacific banana boat from Mazatlán, Mexico, to San Francisco. She writes full time in southern New Hampshire.